NB

Ark[illegible]
Aith[illegible]
what
learn
[illegible]
words

[illegible]
[illegible]

FIRST Time
seen it spelled
out

P 283
[illegible] HAS —
GUTS

Hanson [illegible]
P516

note sign Bach
have [illegible]

DARK BLUES

To Jerry—
And the things
we have in common

DARK BLUES

By

Peter Georgas

Cover design by Pedro Rodriguez

ISBN:1483900053
ISBN-13:978-1483900056
LCCN: 2013921236

Acknowledgments

I believed Dark Blues was consigned to oblivion, buried as it was inside two floppy discs from the Fourth Dynasty of the computer age, until Jan Ebbert, a coffee-mate (not the non-dairy creamer kind), told me about Saving Tape, a media conversion firm located in a small house on 36th Street in South Minneapolis. As careful as archaeologists sifting sand, Thor Anderson and Kyle Sobczak uncovered my novel from its magnetic tomb and converted it to MS Word, a format that enabled me, finally, to publish my story.

Zoe Johnson, assuming the role of objective editor rather than daughter went over the author's proof line by line, not only to correct typos but also to tone down her dad's occasionally flowery metaphors. And, speaking of family, I am also indebted to my wife, Peggy, whose patience and moral support provided the atmosphere writers need in which to write. She also deserves a lot of credit living with a Greek.

Early on, when the novel was twice as long as it is now, Marc Burgett and Carol Purcell (yes they are married), read the raw manuscript, offering critical but encouraging commentary as well as advice which included, believe it or not, eliminating a chapter. I always thought murder your darlings meant cutting a sentence or phrase, but an entire chapter? They were right, of course.

Earlier than that, going back several decades as a matter of fact, are the men and officers I served with on the USS Floyd B Parks whose bow number, 884, matches that of my fictional destroyer. They were great sailors, greater than I, who made the ship hum and fight. The Parks herself deserves honorable mention as one of the finest in the US Navy's destroyer fleet. I look back with pride serving on her for two years, but at the time I was less complimentary. I was 22 then.

Last, I owe a great debt of gratitude to Nini Frangis of Atlanta with whom I corresponded during those two years. She saved the documents and the almost daily letters I mailed her detailing life aboard a tin can during the Korean War. Without them I could not have recreated the immediacy of that long-ago time.

For
Peggy, Zoe, Scott, Emily and Ruby

CHAPTERS

THE HERO

Someone had covered his shoulders with a navy blanket but he still shivered. His hair was matted and sticky from the oily water. There were bruises on his face and blood oozed from abrasions on his knuckles. He stared numbly at the activity on the water illuminated by arc lights redirected from the Sprague's repair work. Behind him, sailors and officers stood in silent groups. It was eerie. The harbormaster had dispatched a boat to search for the body. Rescuers using grappling hooks came up with only detritus: a pair of dungarees, a barrel, even a hubcap. Everyone wondered where the hell that came from. Finally the Exec radioed the USS Wisconsin for help. It took a half hour for the battlewagon's launch to show up with a diver, a big burly sailor who wore a t-shirt and standard navy swim trunks. The boat engineer helped him wrestle on a tank with two flex hoses connected to his face mask. He strapped a waterproof flashlight on his wrist and fell backwards into the water, making an untidy splash that rolled the launch. The coxswain followed the ghostly underwater light and the diver's trail of bubbles.

Ten minutes went by and the diver broke the surface holding Clayton under the armpits, his eyes rigid, his lips puffy, his skin white, his dark blues sodden. The boat engineer took the lifeless body from the diver, dragged it over the gunwale and plopped it into the boat. Then he helped the diver aboard. The diver pulled off his dripping gear and rubbed his body down with a towel. The boat engineer poured coffee into a mug that was stained with finger smudges and handed it to the diver. He drained it in two swallows.

The coxswain rang his boat bell and moved the launch to the caisson wall, slimy with algae. He bumped the launch against the ladder and nimbly held it there while hands from above lifted Clayton and placed him on a stretcher and covered him. A gray-painted ambulance sat nearby with rear doors open, engine idling, rack lights blinking. Two sentries with web belts and carbines stood on either side, staring straight ahead as Clayton was put inside.

The ambulance pulled away and the shivering sailor watched until he could no longer see the blinking lights. Oddly, his only thought at the moment was that he had to type up a Page 14: Record of Discharge, Release from Active Duty, or Death.

He felt a light touch on his shoulder. It was Malone, the Sprague's medical corpsman, wearing a red cross armband. "You better get aboard and clean up, Poulos."

He stood but was wobbly on his feet. The shock of adrenaline that had sustained him till now was wearing off and he finally became aware of the men standing behind him. They were in a subdued mood. A shipmate had died. He spotted Ltjg Radinger, rocking on the balls of his feet, his perennial clipboard at his side. Rauenzahn, the Exec, was standing next to him. The Captain was on the base for a meeting with the Commodore and Rauenzahn was in command. Ensign Porteous was there, so were Lts. Anderson and Kuder. Poulos looked for Lt. Gildenhall hoping for a sign of support. He was standing behind the other officers as though he didn't want to be noticed. Poulos searched for his buddies, Witter, Scotty and AJ, but the men were starting to disperse, turning their backs on him. Poulos felt alone and friendless. There was no reason to think otherwise.

Malone took the blanket off his shoulders and led him up the gangway, through the midship's passageway, to sickbay. The last time Poulos was in here the Doc saw him, but now that the Sprague was in drydock he had been transferred to the Orleck, at sea with the two other Destroyers of DESDIV 1, the Sumner and the Craig.

"After you shower I'll patch those cuts," Malone said. "I'll give you some bacterial soap to ward off infection." He rummaged through the storage cabinet.

Radinger stuck his head in. His moustache was quivering. "I want to talk to you, Poulos," he said ominously.

Malone turned. "Not now, Lieutenant, he's still in shock."

"He'll be in more shock when I get through with him." Radinger disappeared.

Poulos went below to his compartment and stripped off his clothes, clammy and stinking. He tied a towel around his middle and showered in the forecastle head. Afterward he smelled of disinfectant.

He returned to sickbay and Malone put mercurochrome on his cuts.

"Those bruises on your face will have to heal by themselves."

He spent the night in sickbay on a real mattress. Malone wanted to give him a sleeping pill but he turned it down. The ship was strangely quiet, as though in mourning.

Reveille woke him. He dressed and carefully rinsed his face in the metal washbowl. In the mirror he saw his right eye red and puffy, the purple bruise on his left cheek was yellow at the edges. He didn't try to shave. He sat on the bed and waited. Fifteen minutes later Malone came in with a tray of Malt-O-Meal, banana, milk and coffee. “I thought it might be easier if you ate something soft."

When he was through eating, Malone said, "The Captain wants to see you. He said to report to his cabin whenever you're ready.”

“Whenever *I'm* ready?"

“That's what he said.”

Poulos looked at the red mercurochrome stains on his knuckles. “I've never been to his cabin. Where the hell is it?”

“Forward of the wardroom.”

Poulos followed the fore and aft passageway to the officers' wardroom and looked through the window. He was relieved to see it empty. He entered, walked around what to him was the equivalent of a banquet table compared to tables in the mess room where he ate, and stepped through the doorway on the opposite bulkhead and into a narrow passageway. He found a door marked Captain. He tapped it with his fingertips; his knuckles were still sore.

“Come in.”

Poulos opened the door. The Captain was sitting at his desk, a tiny shelf that folded down. He was looking through a file. His braided hat was lying on his bunk bed. Poulos couldn't remember seeing him before with his hat off. He had a round bald spot on the back of his head like a tonsure.

The cabin was tight and efficiently laid out. Along the bulkhead were bookshelves with a metal bar to keep the volumes from falling out. There was a reading light above the Captain's desk and another above his pillow. A stainless steel washbasin with a mirror was tucked into the corner between the door and the bunk.

“Sit down, sailor.”

Poulos sat in the chair by the desk. It had a green leatherette cushion and a metal frame.

Captain Blessing looked at his bruises. “How are you feeling?” His expression was kindly. Whenever Poulos saw him on the bridge his demeanor was that of an attack dog.

“Ok, sir.”

“You got some licks.”

“Not bad, sir.”

"Haven't lost a man since the typhoon of forty-four. It's one thing for a man to fall overboard at sea; it's quite another when his ship is in fucking drydock. We're the laughing stock of WESPAC. But we're going to do something about it." Blessing tapped the file folder on his desk. "I have Lieutenant Radinger's report here."

This is it, Poulos thought, Blessing is going to throw the book at me.

"I'm not in the habit of countermanding my officers but in this case I'm going to."

"Sir?"

"I'm dropping the charges Lieutenant Radinger placed against you." The Captain opened the file folder and turned it so Poulos could look at the topmost sheet, Seven-Eighteen D. "Your record has been cleared."

Poulos didn't know how to react. Should he thank the Captain? Shake his hand? Get on his knees?

"I have other plans for you."

Poulos stared questioningly.

"We have to restore the Sprague's reputation. She was once the pride of WESPAC, highest scorer in rounds expended from the thirty-eighth parallel to the Siberian border before she ran aground."

"I wasn't aware of that, sir."

"She fought fifteen engagements with enemy shore batteries, accounting for 6,540 casualties, 40 gun positions, 19 vehicles and 35 bunkers. She fired more than 8500 rounds, half as many as she had fired in all of her World War II engagements."

Poulos was impressed that the Captain could recite these statistics from memory.

"If I've learned one thing in my seventeen years in this man's navy it's this: inaction breeds sloth. The Sprague will have her day again but in the meantime we must recapture the morale we lost when we had to set her on stilts. Right now morale is lower than her keel."

Poulos nodded in full agreement.

"If we allow Clayton's drowning to be another setback, another reason for the crew to lose its fighting edge, we're sunk, metaphorically speaking. I didn't sleep last night thinking about it. Then it came to me. I talked to the Commodore this morning on the radio and he approves of my decision. We're going to turn our lousy luck around. The Sprague needs a hero and you're it."

Poulos was confused. "Me, sir? A hero?"

"You put your life at risk trying to save another. In my book, that makes you a hero. I'm recommending you for the Silver Star."

"The Silver Star?" Poulos repeated, incredulous. "It was my fault that Clayton went into the water. If you want to give a medal to someone, give it to him."

"He's dead, for Christ's sake. The Commodore wants to hang the Silver Star on you, not some fucking corpse. This is big time, a full ceremony with all hands in dress blues. I'm inviting Admiral Hollowell, fleet commander. We'll take pictures for newspapers back home. We'll have reporters do stories for All Hands and Stars and Stripes. The publicity will make the Sprague's reputation as shiny as that fucking star." He smiled proudly at his metaphor. Then he looked critically at Poulos "How's your head?"

"My head?"

"Your bruises."

"A little sore, that's all."

"Good, I need to send a letter to Clayton's family. I want you to write a sympathetic piece of bullshit for me to sign."

"I'm the last person who should write a letter to his parents."

"Don't feel bad. They collect ten thousand dollars insurance money. Think you can get a draft done this afternoon?"

"Yes, sir." Poulos answered. His voice lacked the enthusiasm of the Captain's.

"Go with Lieutenant Radinger to clean out Clayton's locker. Dig through his private stuff to help you write something personal. Dismissed."

Poulos stood and saluted. His middle finger grazed the swelling around his eye. "Ouch!" he yelled involuntarily.

The Captain was concerned. "Watch it," he said, "I don't want any more damage to my hero."

Poulos entered the wardroom. Rauenzahn and Porteous were sitting at the table drinking coffee. They looked up and Poulos had the sense that they now held him in high esteem. He stepped onto the main deck and headed toward the midship's passageway. Sailors stopped what they were doing to stare at his bruised face. Last night no one talked to him because he was a Prisoner at Large; now no one talked to him because he was a hero.

Radinger was waiting in the Ship's Office holding a pair of wire cutters. He was seething; the fat in his body seemed to be boiling. "You are one lucky son-of-a-bitch," he snarled. "You jumped ship and dumped Clayton into the drink because he was trying to stop you. And now you're getting the fucking Silver Star?"

He led the way to the aft sleeping compartment where Clayton had his rack. Most of the snipes and greasers slept here. Clayton probably felt more at home in engineering than administration. Radinger and Poulos climbed down a ladder into a twilight zone of fartsacks, lockers and stale body odor. A scuttlebutt was at the foot of the ladder where Poulos often stopped for a cold drink of water. While the compartment was over the screws and vibrated a lot, it was directly accessible from the maindeck and had three layers of racks rather than four. It was mostly above the water line while Poulos' forward compartment was two levels down and fit only for troglodytes. If the Sprague ever sank, sailors in Clayton's compartment had a far better chance of saving themselves than those in the forward compartment Poulos called home.

Radinger flicked on a pocket flashlight whose beam guided them to a lower rack in the corner where they found Clayton's name written on a piece of tape stuck to a foot locker. Radinger had Poulos hold the flashlight while he cut through the combination lock. He grunted and squeezed the handles until there was a loud snap. He stopped to catch his breath. "Heavy fucking work."

He opened the locker and bent over to look at Clayton's belongings. Clayton was neat as a pin. Extra dungarees, shirts and socks were neatly folded. His white dress uniform was wrapped in tissue paper. Tucked under his clothes were two bundles of letters held together by crisscrossing rubber bands, and several books. Radinger didn't give a shit about the books but Poulos studied the titles: The Power of Positive Thinking by Norman Vincent Peale, How to Win Friends and Influence People by Dale Carnegie, The Great Philosophies of the World by Will Durant, a collection of short stories by William Faulkner. All of these were familiar to Poulos except one: The Mind of the South by WJ Cash.

Poulos picked up the packets of letters and the unfamiliar book on the South.

"When you finish with that shit, put everything in Clayton's seabag and we'll ship it home."

Poulos returned to the Ship's Office feeling like a voyeur. He undid the rubber bands from the smaller of the two stacks of letters, five in all, addressed to RB Clayton, YN2, Bldg. 23, Yokosuka Naval Base Hospital, c/o Fleet Post Office, San Francisco, California. The other stack was thicker and addressed to Clayton before he was transferred off the Sprague. The return address was a post office box in Mills Gap, West Virginia. The letters were sorted according to postmark, the one on top being the most recent. Poulos withdrew lined stationary, the kind you buy in a drug store, and unfolded it. The handwriting was curvilinear, a product of the Palmer method. Dear son, it read,

Your father and I pray things are going better since you went to the hospital. Remember, God is by your side. We knew how difficult it was for you when that new sailor came on board. It's hard to work with someone who doesn't appreciate what you do, but keep praying that he will see The Light. And do try to forgive him. He probably doesn't realize that a person has to be little to belittle. Father sends his love and Missie wants to write something too.

Love, Mother

Hi Bro how ya doin? I might get on the Honor Roll, but I have to do better in English. I wish you were here to help me. If I go to college, I'll be the first one in the family! How about that???? Don't let that sailor give you any more you know what.

Your Sis, Miss

Poulos put the letter down and opened an earlier one from Clayton's father which was filled with advice on how to cope with the new yeoman in the Ship's Office. Pray for his soul, hold positive thought towards him, compliment him. It was evident that Clayton expressed frustration that nothing worked in his relationship with Poulos because his father insisted that his son try even harder. "Keep turning the other cheek" was the phrase he used.

Poulos couldn't read any more. It was too painful. He picked up The Mind of the South and opened it to the verso of the title page. The copyright date was 1941. He skimmed the contents. It looked fascinating. He fanned the pages with his thumb. Every now and then he saw a marginal note in Clayton's cramped hand, and sentences underlined with a pencil. He set it down and spun a sheet of paper into the Underwood and began typing:

Dear Mr. and Mrs. Clayton:

It is with great sadness that I must write this letter to you. By now you have heard from the Navy Department that your son, RB, drowned in the waters of Tokyo Bay. I want to add my own condolences to those of the Department of the Navy for which RB so ably served. He was a dedicated sailor and a genuine human being who met with an unfortunate and untimely death. As parents, we expect our children to outlive us, but this is not always the case.

Tragedy is the visitor we cannot lock our door against. While your son was robbed of old age, he departed this life with much to be proud of. Even though he had lost his rating, he was diligent enough to be able to earn back his stripes and, I'm sure, had he lived out his career in the

Navy as he wished, he would have retired a non-commissioned officer.

I would also like to note that your son had a great deal of intellectual curiosity. He was a reader of fine literature as evidenced by the books he left behind. These and his other belongings will be shipped to you in due course.

The officers and men under my command join me in expressing my sincere sympathy in the loss of your son.

Kenneth B. Blessing
Commander, USN

Poulos showed the draft to the Captain. "Ok, as far as it goes," he said. "Put in some of the hero stuff about how you tried to rescue Clayton."

"I can't do that, Captain."

"Why not?"

"I'm too close to the situation."

"That's why you're writing it in the first place, because you *are* close to the situation."

Poulos retreated to the Ship's Office and struggled through another paragraph:

A valiant effort was made to save your son. One of our sailors dove in after him and they nearly made it to a life buoy, but both men were fully clothed and the waters were cold. The rescue failed but not for lack of effort.

Poulos rested his fingers on the typewriter keys, lining them up on the center row as he was taught in typing class. Clayton was a hunt-and-peck typist. Like the rest of his knowledge, typing was something he taught himself. What would Clayton have become if he had the same opportunity for a college education as Poulos? His wandering thoughts hit on something Voltaire once wrote, something he read in a humanities course and stowed away in his memory. To the living we owe respect. To the dead we owe the truth.

Poulos did not respect Clayton as he should have when he was alive. Now that he was dead, Clayton was owed the truth. Poulos's fingers began striking the keys in rapid order.

You have a right to ask about the circumstances surrounding your son's death. RB was trying to prevent a fellow sailor from going AWOL. If it wasn't for that, your son would be alive. He tried to help this sailor from doing something foolhardy but the sailor wouldn't listen to reason. There was an argument on the caisson and your son fell into the water. When the sailor realized RB couldn't swim, he dived in to save him. Unfortunately he failed. It is a failure the sailor will suffer the rest of his life.

Poulos stopped typing and read what he had put down. He also wanted to tell Mrs. Clayton who the sailor was but he knew the Captain would not permit it. Maybe he will approve this much but Poulos was wrong. After Blessing read the addition, he took a pencil and scratched it out.

"Won't you use even some of it, sir?"

The Captain stared at Poulos. "Clayton had a record of mental instability. He spent a month in the psycho ward at the Base Hospital. They gave him shock treatments. He was suicidal. He jumped into the water and you tried to save him. That's the story."

"It's not the truth…"

The Captain's face became mottled with angry blood. *"Truth?* How the fuck do you know what the truth is? Were you inside Clayton's head? Type the goddamn letter on my personal stationary and make plenty of carbons. I want it bcc'd to COMCRUSDESPAC, CINCPAC, the Commodore, and the Captains of DESDIV 1. I want everything to go out with the afternoon pickup."

Poulos remained where he was hoping he could still reason with the Captain.

"Did you understand everything I told you?"

"Yes, sir."

"Then what are you standing there for?"

Poulos tried to squeeze back the pain throbbing behind his eyes. "I'm not a hero."

Blessing stood up. He was tall and rawboned. He might have been a cattle drover in another life and another time. He glared at Poulos. "Then act like one!"

Poulos went back to the Ship's Office. There was only one thing left for him to do. He would write his own letter to Clayton's parents and tell them the truth. Fuck the Navy. But first he had to do its dirty work. He pulled out a sheet from a file folder containing the Captain's personal stationary and five tissues with carbon paper between them. He had to type it letter perfect because he couldn't correct that many carbons without smudging. His mind was not on his work and he kept making mistakes. It took him nearly two hours to turn out a letter without errors in it. The waste paper basket was full of his balled-up rejects. Poulos delivered the finished product in a fresh file folder. The Captain was in the wardroom drinking coffee. He was not alone. The Exec, Commander Rauenzahn, and Radinger were also there. Radinger had a look of extreme discomfort as though his stomach was churning.

"Did you proofread it?" the Captain asked, opening the folder.

"Yes, sir."

"No mistakes, if you know what I mean?"

"No mistakes, sir."

The Captain read with concentration. The room was silent. Blessing removed his gold Parker Pen from his shirt pocket, unscrewed the cap and signed the letter.

Poulos looked for a private place where he could read Clayton's book without being interrupted. He climbed into the gun tub of the portside three-inch-fifty and sat on the metal seat. Shaped like the seat on a John Deere tractor, it was tolerably comfortable. When dark fell he went to the Ship's Office, turned on the lights and shut the double doors.

The Mind of the South was densely written and deeply analytical, every paragraph loaded with content and meaning. Poulos discovered very quickly that this was a book not easily paraphrased. After a particularly cogent thought, he looked up and tried to reconstruct it in his mind but found it nearly impossible. As he read, concentrating on the lines Clayton underscored, Poulos came to see a far more complex individual than the Clayton he knew; as complex as the South that unfolded in Cash's long essay. It was evident from the paragraphs highlighted that Clayton was interested in the heritage of those Southerners known as "white trash," whose ancestors were a collection of convicts and slum dwellers, peasants and laborers that emigrated from Europe in the eighteenth century. These were Clayton's "kin," a physically, culturally and intellectually inferior type, according to Cash, not the proud ruling class, the plantation owners with many acres of cotton, many horses and so many slaves they couldn't count them.

Or were they?

Poulos read that the development of the South, as romanticized in Gone With the Wind, had been accomplished in a mere seventy years, "the lifetime of a single man," according to Cash. How could an aristocracy be established in so short a time? It couldn't, obviously. They had simply invented themselves. Those proud plantation owners who claimed they were descendants of European royalty were mostly uneducated horse traders who, with the advent of the cotton gin, got rich and built huge estates on forest land they had burned and cleared in their youth. Once they achieved wealth, they wanted class.

On the other hand, there was no such affectation among the white trash who, like as not, were "kindred" with the wealthy planters—related by the "the ties of family." These white trash cousins "plowed a little, hunted a little, fished a little, and passed their time on their backsides in the shade of tree with a jug of 'bust-head.'" What was startling to Poulos was the physical description Cash gave them: "striking lankiness of frame, a boniness and peculiar sallow swartness and a not-less sallow faded-out, colorlessness of skin and hair." My god, Poulos thought, a perfect description of Clayton.

The more he read, the more he felt he finally understood Clayton. He was a man who agonized over his ancestry, wanting to dispel the notion that he was "white trash." And to discover that he was as legitimately tied to the aristocracy of the Old South as the squire who rode a stallion, fought a duel, danced at the cotillion and lived in a mansion "preferably white with columns and Greek entablature." That's how Clayton wanted to be seen. If Poulos had recognized that, Clayton might still be around. Oh, how Poulos wished he had come across this book in college. It was a masterpiece.

It was after ten when he finished. He went to his compartment and placed the book inside his locker. Poulos had made a decision. He was not going to write a letter to Clayton's family; he was going to deliver the book personally, talk to Clayton's mother and father and sister face to face, look them in the eye and tell them what really happened. As Voltaire had written, Poulos owed Clayton the truth.

He labored over Page 14, the official record of Clayton's death. He had to attach the coroner's report which listed the cause of death as water ingestion, not drowning. The Navy was averse to factual language; the emphasis was on the euphemism. Water was found in Clayton's lungs and stomach. His organs were sound, he had a healthy heart. Prospects for a long life were good. Unless of course too much water was ingested. Clayton's body was embalmed and shipped home in a cold storage locker.

There was a memorial service for Clayton on the fantail. The base chaplain visited the Sprague, Lieutenant Commander Swift, tall, bald and bespectacled, a Nazarene from Missouri. He conducted the service from a small stand set up in front of the ship's ensign. Sailors crowded between the depth charge rack, on the O1 deck, and up either side of the main deck. Shipyard noise nearly drowned out the Chaplain's words. He shouted from his Bible, quoting John Chapter 5: "Truly I say unto you, whoever hears my words, and believes in Him who sent me, has eternal life. He will not be judged but has already passed from death to life."

He closed his Bible and gave a short sermon: "St. John of Damascus is credited with authoring most of the Christian funeral service which comes to us relatively unchanged from that time. The main themes deal with pain and grief which are surmounted by resurrection and hope. However, there is a sub-theme that I think serves well our memory of RB Clayton, and I paraphrase: I look into the grave and behold naked bones. To whom do these belong, king or soldier, rich or poor, righteous or sinner?

"Death," the Chaplain concluded, "is the Great Equalizer."

The men dispersed after a closing prayer.

The Captain called a meeting in the wardroom with Division Officers to plan the award ceremony. Poulos was ordered to attend. He came in last, feeling awkward and hoping that the Captain didn't need him after all and dismiss him. He removed his cap, rolled it up and slipped it into the hip pocket of his dungarees.

Finally Blessing looked at him. "Don't just stand there, Poulos, come in." The Captain was sitting at the head of the table with Commander Rauenzahn, and officers on either side: Hendershot, Engineering; Morrell, Supply; McNeil, Gunnery; Hysong, Navigation; Porteous, Deck; Gildenhall, Operations--and Radinger, Communications, at the foot of the table, nearest the door, his eyes as round and hard as steelies. The green-felt table was crowded with hats, cups and saucers, and note pads.

Poulos slid behind Radinger's chair to the back corner of the wardroom and squeezed himself against the sideboard.

The Captain convened the meeting. He had a checklist in front of him. "You all know why we're here," he began. "The award ceremony is a major event for the Sprague, as major as any since her commission, and I want everything to go like clockwork."

The officers nodded except for Radinger who could not eliminate the scowl on his face.

"There's the matter of timing I want to discuss. We've got another four weeks in drydock and I was hoping to delay the ceremony until after our shakedown cruise. For me, it's far more impressive to have the Sprague afloat than in drydock. On the other hand we risk losing the impact of the moment if we wait till we get back to sea."

There was somber reflection over this potentiality.

"It might be more difficult to get the base commander," Rauenzahn offered. He was taking notes of the meeting.

"Good point. If we have the ceremony here, he'd be driven right to the pier in his staff car. Otherwise we'd have to transport him in a launch. Lieutenant Gildenhall, what information do you have on our anchorage after we leave drydock?"

"Not confirmed, sir, but my guess is it will be one of the outer buoys. It would be a long trip in a launch."

The Captain checked off an item on his list. "That settles it, we'll have the ceremony in drydock. Now, what about the date?"

A discussion followed. It was decided to present the Silver star to Poulos on Tuesday, October 14, at 1430, and the Captain checked off another item. "I want the men positioned so they add a nice backdrop. Can we get them all on the starboard side of the O1 deck?"

Ensign Porteous unfolded a large mimeographed schematic of the Sprague. He studied it a moment and shook his head. "Not very likely, sir. Too crowded."

"Split them between O1 and main. Will that work?"

"I think so, Captain, but we have to be sure there is enough room for the dignitaries on the main deck."

"Good point. The ceremony will take place in front of the midship's passageway." Blessing glanced at Poulos. "Make it close to the Ship's Office where Poulos and Clayton worked together. I like the symbolism of that." He returned his attention to Porteous. "Get some men forward and aft of that position on the main deck. Line them up in two ranks against the bulkheads. Leave room for the brass. You can stack the rest of the men on the O1 deck. And get some men on top of the turrets. That always looks impressive. Lay out a plan for each division."

"Yes, sir."

"I want every man to have his uniform cleaned and pressed. Shoes spit-shined. Clean white hats. And regulation neckerchiefs, rolled not flat. Every man has to get a haircut at least three days before the ceremony, and I want beards neatly trimmed. Each division will have an inspection at 1330 on the fourteenth. If anyone looks bad he goes below decks and stays there until the brass leaves. I don't want any shit-eaters out there, you got that?"

"Yes, sir."

"And don't forget to fly the pennants, including the Commodore's."

"No, sir."

"I want this event well-covered," Blessing said to Radinger, who was in charge of publicity and gave a report on coverage including photographing the event. His manner was of someone tasting vinegar.

"What about air photos?"

"Sir?"

"Get a helicopter to take some pictures from above."

The officers exchanged glances. “Pretty noisy, Captain.”

“Not to mention the downdraft of the rotors.”

"I want the whole ship photographed. How do we do that?”

“How about using a crane? We’re in a shipyard after all,” said a voice. It belonged to Poulos. Everyone turned to look at him. Radinger’s eyes were on fire.

“What was that, sailor?” the Captain asked.

Poulos had his elbow on the sideboard. He straightened. “It occurred to me, sir, that you don’t need a helicopter with all those cranes around.” He was right, of course, and it was so logical, so apparent, that none of the officers thought of it.

“What do you suggest?”

“Get a photographer up on a crane and he can shoot those long shots you would like to have…sir.”

Blessing looked at Radinger as if to say why the hell didn’t you think of that? “Make a note of that, Lieutenant, and see if you can get clearance to use one of those cranes. You may need Jap approval.”

“Yes, sir,” Radinger said flatly.

“Now, the presentation itself. I will introduce the Commodore who will do the actual presenting. We will need a PA system to be heard over shipyard noise.”

Who was in charge of public address? The officers looked down the line to Radinger.

The Captain didn’t need a consensus to determine who should be nailed with that assignment. “Lieutenant Radinger, see to that as well,” he ordered.

Radinger stiffened. “Sir, I don’t think that’s my bailiwick.”

“You run communications on this ship, don’t you?”

“With all due respect, Captain, a PA system doesn’t communicate, it amplifies.”

The Captain was losing patience. “How the fuck do you communicate if you can’t be heard?”

“We don’t have any portable unit on the ship. I don’t know where to begin looking for one.”

“Use your ingenuity, Lieutenant. Get Baker to rig up something off the ship’s PA system. If that doesn’t work, there’s gotta be a dance hall on the base where you can borrow one; or find a store in Yokosuka where you can buy one. The fucking Japanese must have something they make that we can use. I’ll sign a disbursement voucher if you need it.”

Radinger slunk in his chair and stewed. Poulos could feel the anger radiate from his blubber, clearly directed toward him. He debated whether to help out the Lieutenant by telling him about the night he and his buddies dated nurses at the base hospital. The nurses had purloined a juke box for their off-duty lounge. With that kind of resourcefulness, they could surely get their hands on a PA system.

The meeting proceeded. The Captain was thorough, he ordered Hendershot to use his navigation skills to chart deck positions for the Sprague's officers, the visiting dignitaries, Poulos and the Commodore. He was also concerned about the sun hitting them in the eyes until he was reminded that the starboard side of the ship faced east and the sun would be over their shoulders by that time. "What about the Commodore? He'll be facing west awarding the medal, won't he?"

There was a discussion about reversing positions or placing Poulos and the Commodore in the shadow of the number one stack, but that might interfere with good lighting for photographs.

Finally Hendershot suggested, "We can have them facing each other fore and aft."

"Good point."

Then came the final item on the Captain's agenda. "Who's going to write my introduction and the Commodore's presentation of the medal?"

The officers looked at each other and shrugged their shoulders. Poulos began to get nervous because he could feel the shift of attention toward him.

"How about Poulos?" the Captain asked of no one in particular.

"Captain, I can't write my own ceremony."

"It is a bit irregular, but no one else puts words together like you do." Blessing scanned the group. "Anyone ever get a medal around here?"

"I believe there is a manual on presentation of awards, Captain," Lieutenant Gildenhall volunteered. "I'd be happy to get the proper wording for the Silver Star."

"Good." The Captain was relieved. "That leaves my opening remarks. You can handle that, Poulos. Just paraphrase the letter you wrote Clayton's family." He closed his folder. "I guess that covers everything. When each of you has completed his assignment report to Commander Rauenzahn." He stood. It was now all right for the other officers to stand. Rauenzahn worked his way over to Poulos and gave him his notes of the meeting. "Type these up and distribute eyes-only copies to the officers present."

"Yes, sir," Poulos said wearily. More work to do. He placed his hat on his head and left the wardroom.

Everything was out of hand.

Tuesday, October 14, dawned clear and cool. It was going to be a perfect day as far as the weather was concerned. The ship was in a state of frenzy akin to that of general quarters, as though the crew was preparing to engage in combat. During the week prior to the ceremony, the deck hands were busy scraping and painting rusted corners. The decks were hosed down the day before and the ship's brass bell and brass fittings were shined to a dazzling mirror finish.

Everything was in readiness. Poulos had spent the evening in the charthouse where Browning and Witter showed him how to spit-polish his black shoes. If one listened carefully, one could hear spitting throughout the ship. Browning laid out several towels on the chart desk so they could press their blues. They also pressed their neckerchiefs, a square yard of black silk, and rolled them up and stored them in map tubes until it was time to dress.

Radinger stopped talking to Poulos after the wardroom meeting. If he had an order he wrote it down and left it on the desk in the Ship's Office. So Poulos penned a note to Radinger informing him that the nurses at the base hospital might know where to locate a public address system. It wasn't until he came up from breakfast the morning of the ceremony and saw Radinger hooking up a microphone on the main deck with the help of Baker that he suspected the Lieutenant had taken his advice. A wire ran from the mike to a speaker box. Another wire was hooked up to an electric outlet that had been screwed into one of the sockets on the system of lights used to illuminate the ship. Poulos went to the Ship's Office and kept hearing "testing-one-two-three-four" until it was about to drive him crazy.

He had dutifully written an opening script for the Captain which, after several edits, was finally approved. Gildenhall had taken the wording for the presentation of the medal from a manual he had dug up at the base library. The Captain sent out invitations to a cocktail reception for the brass at the Officers' Club following the ceremony and so, at least for a couple of hours, there would be relative peace on the ship. In the meantime, there was a dress inspection by division at 1330, and at 1400 the men lined up in their respective positions. A few sailors shot Poulos dirty looks because it meant standing in one place for at least an hour. He had never seen so many perfectly turned-out sailors.

Like the crew, the Sprague was spick and span. She virtually sparkled. A slight breeze unfurled the flags hoisted up the mast by the signalman moments earlier: the American flag topmost, below which fluttered the Commodore's white and blue pennant and a series of communications flags to add variety in case anyone had color film in his camera.

About 1415 the visiting brass turned up in two navy staff vehicles, black Chevrolet sedans with tiny flags fluttering from their front fenders, one the American flag and the other a navy ensign designating the status of the occupant. The cars stopped at the gangway and the drivers, first class bos'ns, jumped out, opened the doors and saluted smartly. It turned out to be impossible to free up Hollowell, the fleet admiral, but there was still an impressive array of top navy brass: a rear admiral and two vice admirals, as well as the Commodore himself who emerged from one of the shiny black cars.

Captain Blessing and his officers made a phalanx of smart black uniforms with crisp white shirts, black ties, service ribbons and brass buttons, and hats with glossy black bills. They stood in two ranks facing each other on either side of the gangway to greet the dignitaries. The bos'n piped them aboard and the saluting was very impressive. Poulos stood behind the junior officers. He was first in the front line of enlisted men forward of the midship's passageway, all of whom stood at rigid attention, eyes looking straight ahead, fingers pointing straight down, and hearts pounding.

When the saluting was over the introductions and handshaking began. The Rear Admiral whispered in the Captain's ear and the Captain nodded his head toward Poulos. The Admiral, a white-haired man who looked like he had been sent over from central casting, gave Poulos a fatherly smile.

Everything was in readiness. A photographer was sitting in the monkey seat of a crane that had been moved into position on rails. Another photographer was free to wander about for the best ground angles. He carried a boxy Speed Graphic camera with a flash attachment as big as a saucer. He was standing in the middle of the gangway waiting for the ceremony to begin.

Chairs from the wardroom were lined up behind the mike. The Captain ushered the Admirals and the Commodore to their respective seats and the officers of the Sprague positioned themselves behind their chairs. The Captain stood at the mike and the Exec stood next to him holding a black velvet case like the kind jewelry comes in.

Captain Blessing tapped the screened head of the microphone and loud popping noises made everyone jump. Radinger leaned forward and whispered, "It's on."

The Captain cleared his throat and the freeing of phlegm was heard for yards around. He removed a folded typewritten sheet of paper from an inside pocket which contained the remarks Poulos had composed. Here and there phrases were lined out and others written in.

"Admiral Jensen, Admiral Karstairs, Admiral Hanley, Commodore Katz, officers and men of the Robert B. Sprague." The Captain's voice boomed. Apparently the microphone had only one volume setting. Loud. "We are gathered on this glorious day with mixed emotions. On the one hand, we are here to acknowledge an act of gallantry by one of our own, Seaman Alexandros Poulos, but on the other hand remember with sadness the unfortunate passing of another of our own, Yeoman Second Class RB Clayton."

Poulos gritted his teeth. The Captain had slaughtered his copy leaving bloody entrails where clear exposition had once lived.

"It is ironic that Seaman Poulos's act of heroism occurred when our proud fighting ship was landlocked because of damage to her hull. But bravery, like tragedy, visits us when we least expect it. No one starts out being a hero but sometimes circumstances, no matter how unpredictable, can bring out the best in us. I feel that any of my men under similar conditions would have done the same thing, but today we single out one individual to represent the brave spirit of the Robert B. Sprague, the spirit that makes us all heroes."

Poulos's mind began to wander. He'd gone over those sentences too many times to pay attention to them now that they were being delivered. He thought about the conversation he had had the night before when he, Browning and Witter were shining their shoes. Poulos admitted how troubled he was about accepting the Silver Star.

"Don't rock the boat," was Browning's advice. "If the Navy Department approved it, you deserve it."

But the Silver Star was meant to honor servicemen for gallantry in action. Where was the gallantry? Where was the action? He thought about the words he put in the Captain's speech: that anyone would have done the same thing, that Poulos was representing all the men on the ship, not just himself. He desperately needed to believe that.

The Captain ended his remarks by saying, "and now it gives me a great pleasure to present the distinguished leader of Destroyer Division One, Commodore Bernard W. Katz."

If this were a meeting of the Kiwanis or Rotary there would have been a warm round of applause, and the ensuing silence seemed like a gap in the proceedings, as though the program committee had left something out.

The Commodore got to his feet and Poulos, as rehearsed, stepped forward. They faced each other fore and aft, and the photographer on the gangway moved in for his shots. Poulos had not seen the Commodore since he transferred his flag to the Yarnall after running the Sprague aground. He looked different. He did not have a cigar wedged into the corner of his mouth, and his usual apoplectic expression was gone. His beady eyes were actually twinkling.

He cupped his hands over the mike so he could speak privately to the young seaman. "What's the matter, sailor, you look tense."

"It's because I am, sir."

"Only stage fright. Don't let those four stripers scare you." He studied Poulos a moment. "Say, aren't you the smart sailor that helped me get rid of the dumb sailor with the squeaky shoes?"

Poulos recalled the Commodore's angry reaction to Browning's Hong Kong purchase. "I'm afraid so, sir."

"I didn't recognize you at first. It's hard to tell the enlisted men apart."

"Must be the uniform, sir."

"Those were loud shoes and I'm not talking about their style," he said, winking broadly at his turn of phrase.

"You know how it is with Hong Kong leather sir."

"He better oil them or I'll give him twenty hours extra duty."

"I'll be sure to tell him, sir."

"I like the way you came to my rescue that night, like the way you dove in to rescue that psycho in the water."

The word psycho made Poulos flinch. Clayton was no psycho. If anyone on the Sprague was a psycho it was this pompous old man grinning like a jack-in-the-box. Poulos glanced down at Captain Blessing who had returned to his seat. He felt sorry for him. This was the moment he was waiting for, the moment designed to redeem the ship's misfortunes, but Poulos could not be a part of this charade. He didn't want to betray the Captain but he didn't want to betray Clayton either. It was time to take matters into his own hands, fuck the navy.

Poulos straightened his back and inhaled. "That's not the way it happened," he said to the Commodore.

The Commodore took his hands off the microphone and pointed to the script he was holding. "Sure it is, it says so right here." His words boomed out of the loudspeaker.

"Clayton deserves the medal, not me."

Perplexed, the Commodore turned to Captain Blessing. "What the hell is going on here?"

The brass began to stir uncomfortably in their chairs. The enlisted men began looking up and down the ranks at each other.

Captain Blessing motioned angrily to Rauenzahn. "Hand him the medal before everything is completely fucked up!" he snarled under his breath.

The Exec opened the box and withdrew the Silver Star with nervous fingers. It hung from a red, white and blue neckband. Below the neckband was a square pad of blue satin with small white stars embroidered on it, and below that was the medal itself, a small bronze star set on a silver star about the size of a silver dollar.

The Exec gave the medal to the Commodore and got out of the way. The Commodore lifted the ribbon expecting Poulos to bow his head so that he could slip the ribbon around his neck and let the medal hang on his chest.

Poulos stepped back.

The Commodore moved forward and tried again.

Poulos retreated another step.

Frustrated, the Commodore dangled the medal in front of the seaman's face. "Goddamnit, sailor!" he exclaimed, "Do you want this fucking medal or don't you?"

BOOK ONE

THE SHIP

The rising sun cast long shadows on the deck of the tanker, brightening the sky and rousing Poulos out of his fitful sleep. The undulating horizon was making him seasick. He sat up from his cot and looked down, concentrating on the wood strips bleached white by salty air. The fresh morning breeze slowly cleared his head, and when he was confident his gorge had finally settled he pushed his blanket out of the way and stood. His crotch itched and, when he scratched it, felt wool and remembered he had slept in his dark blues. He knuckled sleep from his eyes and listened to the sea sweep by the tanker's steep sides. He knew without having to look, at this hour of the morning, that the water was still more black than blue.

He squinted through the sun's rays at the tanker's forward superstructure, the bridge and cabins, the booms and cables, the ladders and railings. The single gray stack, relieved by a ring of black around the top, was hissing at him, expelling shimmers of heat that streamed up and aft, high over his head. The ship not only sliced the water, it also cut the air when heading into the wind, creating two wakes, one seen and one felt. He preferred heading into the wind, the fast-moving air tingling his cheeks and billowing his jumper. When the ship sailed with the wind, it was as if he were becalmed, suspended in time, going nowhere.

The huge, wood-slatted deck spread unbroken from port to starboard, and extended fore and aft half the length of a football field. It was damp from the mist thrown up by the sea. He stared at the portholes on the upper deck—officers country no doubt—and wondered if anyone was curious enough to look out at the transit sailor, his gray seabag at his side.

He tucked his loosened t-shirt back under his jumper, and retied his neckerchief. He rolled up his blanket and stuffed it into his seabag, and wondered why he hadn't heard the bo'sn blow reveille when suddenly the loud speaker crackled and the sound of the pipe broke the stillness. Keening and high-pitched, it wailed the crew awake. Then the voice of the bo'sn announced, "Reveille, reveille, reveille, heave to and trice up." And again the shrill notes pierced the air, only to fall away like air escaping from a bagpipe.

"What does a Scotsman wear under his kilts?" Poulos sang under his breath, "A-whang, a-whang…"

He walked forward, compensating for the roll of the ship, and stepped over the high sill of an open door. He had to duck to keep from rapping his skull on the top rim. He was in a gangway lighted by red bulbs enclosed in metal cages. A black rubber runner covered the steel-plated deck. Sleepy men emerged from compartments with their dittie bags and rubber sandals. Poulos followed them to the midship's head and looked in. A bare-assed sailor nudged him aside. A tattoo of a chain disappeared down the crease of his buttocks. Blue lettering on his left cheek read, "If you want more chain holler down the hole." He sat on a crapper. The rush of sea water running along the trough drowned out the hissing of urine pouring from his full bladder.

Another sailor shaving over a metal sink looked at Poulos through the mirror, staring at the seaman's stripes sewn on his sleeve. Poulos finally realized he was in the wrong section. This was the chiefs' head. The enlisted men's head was probably another deck down, somewhere in the tanker's bowels. He had to piss real bad. As a sailor in transit he knew better than to walk in without permission, especially the preserve of petty officers.

"Mind if I take a leak?" he asked, standing on one foot and then the other.

The sailor shaving sympathized with his need. "Go ahead."

Poulos unbuttoned seven of his thirteen buttons as he walked to a stainless steel urinal and peed in extended relief. He shook himself off and buttoned up. He glanced at himself in the mirror. His eyes reflected weariness from a month-long trip that began on a train traveling from Minneapolis to Seattle, a flight on a cargo plane to Treasure Island in San Francisco, before boarding a troopship packed with a mixed assortment of military bound for Tent City in Yokosuka, Japan, where he awaited assignment to the Chemung, the tanker he was on, for final transfer to his new home, the USS Robert B. Sprague, DD884.

He looked at his black hair, sticking out in odd directions. He'd had one haircut, a Pier 91 Special in Seattle, and the barber might as well have used a bayonet. Without longer hair he no longer could soften what he perceived as a head shaped like an inverted pyramid.

A tough-featured sailor stood next to him shaving. He had squint lines and skin leathered to a betel-nut brown from years on open decks. Despite beer gut, Poulos envied his looks, wishing he too had as hardened an appearance. “You headed for DESDIV 1?” the sailor asked.

“Yes, sir, he replied, erring on the side of caution.

"We're petty officers," he smiled. "You don't have to sir us."

"Sorry."

"Don't they teach you anything at boot camp?"

"I didn't go to boot camp."

The tattooed sailor sitting on the latrine screwed up his face and a turd splashed into the sea water rushing beneath him. "So you ain't regular?"

"No, naval reserve."

"Which one we're high-lining you to?"

"The Sprague."

The chief at the mirror asked generally, "Isn't she the flag for Krazy Katz?"

"Yeah," the one on the crapper said. "Hey," he cautioned Poulos, "see if you can get a transfer to one of the other cans. I heard the Yarnall ain't bad."

"What's wrong with the Sprague?"

"Commodore Katz, that's why," the chief who was shaving said.

"What about him?"

"Nothing but bad luck follows him around. They say the Sprague is jinxed because of him."

That’s comforting, Poulos thought.

Another chief came in with his shaving kit and picked up on the conversation. "He's a pathological schizophrenic."

The other chiefs laughed. "Where the fuck did you learn that?"

"I took a correspondence course once."

The chief at the latrine was now wiping up. "Hey," he said to Poulos, "what you do when the engineering officer orders you to grease the relative bearings?"

Poulos shrugged. "Follow orders, I suppose. What are relative bearings?"

Howls of laughter filled the head.

He was puzzled at first and then got it. Relative bearings were used in navigation, not machinery. "What if he orders me to get a squeegee sharpener, do I do that, too?" This evoked another round of laughter. Poulos didn't elaborate, but he learned this one through bitter experience when he had KP at Pier 91 and a bos'n sent him to the supply depot for a squeegee sharpener. He was the butt of the joke that day, but his embarrassment was somewhat tempered when he was told this was an initiation rite, the same as being ordered to grease the relative bearings. Poulos had joined the club like everybody else, along with the chiefs, probably, when they were young recruits.

"Hey," the persistent sailor called out to Poulos, "you are one unlucky sonovabitch to be assigned to a destroyer."

"I wasn't assigned, I asked for it."

The chiefs exchanged glances confirming their suspicion that Poulos was truly a raw sailor. "You asked for it all right. Why do you suppose they call them tin cans?"

Poulos returned to the main deck and retrieved his seabag. He dragged it over to the port railing and sat on it. In the distance he saw four gray destroyers, one behind the other, bouncing like bobbers as their sharp outlines cut into the waves. He watched with fascination as the lead destroyer, not his according to her bow number, drew alongside. For a moment it seemed that the tanker and destroyer were standing still while the water between them moved at a fifteen-knot clip, churning and roiling as deckhands in life jackets stood by. Using a modified M14 rifle, the tanker's deck crew launched a shotline across the water. At the sound of the rifle being fired, Poulos looked up quickly and saw a weighted line make a nearly straight trajectory toward the destroyer. The weight bounced off the rear gunmount and landed on the deck. A deckhand grabbed it and, with the help of his shipmates, hauled it in, coiling it up until they got to a heavier line attached to the shotline, which they secured to a winch on the O1 deck, becoming an umbilical cord connecting the two ships across twenty yards of water. Black hoses were strung and fuel was transferred. Mail pouches and film canisters came next. Poulos wondered why the men working on the wet, pitching deck were not swept overboard.

The third ship in the squadron was the Sprague, her identification number 884 painted on the bow in large white numerals outlined in a black drop-shade. As she came alongside, Poulos scrutinized the men scurrying on the deck, the officers on the flying wing of the bridge, signalmen hoisting a refueling pennant--these would be his fellow shipmates.

"The smoking lamp is out," echoed across the channel from the destroyer's loudspeaker.

The Sprague, Poulos had read up on, was a Gearing class destroyer, the smallest combat ship in the navy at 2250 tons and 390 feet long. She carried six 5-inch/38 caliber guns on three mounts, four anti-aircraft batteries, as well as torpedoes and depth charges—a floating arsenal with a complement of 335 enlisted men and 20 officers. She was built in a Galveston shipyard in 1944 and named for a navy pilot who was killed in the Battle of Midway.

A bo'sn came up to him and shook his shoulder. "Your turn, sailor."

Toting his seabag, Poulos followed the bo'sn to the main deck forward where a wood chair was being hitched to the tensioned high-line stretched across the sea like a clothesline. The chair had a canvas seat with a back and sides and a lap safety belt.

"Put on a life jacket." The bo'sn held out a well-worn orange kapok vest. "You might get dunked."

Poulos slipped it around his shoulders and tied the straps together. He sat in the chair and the bo'sn secured the life belt. "Thanks for the ride," he called out as he was swung over the churning water. He was alternately yanked, then suspended motionless, then yanked again as the deckhands on the destroyer pulled him across hand-over-hand. Below him the waves seemed to want to reach up and drown him. Nearing the destroyer, he looked back at the tanker and saw it whole for the first time. She was immense compared to the destroyer, like a semi-trailer alongside a Nash. Finally he was over the deck of the destroyer where rough hands grabbed him and loosened the safety belt around his waist. He slid off the canvas seat and hit the deck. The sound of waves sliding past the hull five feet below him was immediate, intense. The sea was virtually at his feet. He was exhilarated by the intensity of the activity around him, the nearness of the ocean and the sense that, at any time, this narrow, top-heavy vessel which was now his home could hit a big wave and flip over. The words of the chiefs echoed in his head, why do you suppose they call them tin cans?

He was pushed out of the way against the rear gun mount and watched as his life jacket, strapped to the empty bo'sn's chair, returned to the tanker on the highline. Without weight the chair swung wildly back and forth. His seabag came on the next delivery. It fell with a thud on the deck. As he picked it up, a voice of authority shouted at him. He turned, shifting his weight from one leg to the other to maintain balance on the heaving ship. A slender officer dressed in khaki approached him from the aft door to the midship's passageway.

"Lt. Gildenhall, Operations Officer. Give me your transfer orders." The officer was delicately handsome, the skin covering his cheekbones was fair, almost translucent, like that of someone who burns easily in the sun. But behind the fragility was a reserve that reminded Poulos of a finely sculpted statue that said look but don't touch. He undid the knot on his seabag and pulled out the manila envelope containing his orders.

Gildenhall opened the envelope and referred to the typewritten entries. Under Name was POULOS, ALEXANDROS N. Under Branch USNR. Under Rating GM STRIKER. Under Transferring Ship USS CHEMUNG (AD 31). Under Authority BUPERS MANUAL Art G-10107. Under Ultimate Destination, USS ROBERT B. SPRAGUE (DD884).

He looked up. "Naval Reserve, huh?"

"Yes, sir."

"Weekend warrior?"

"No sir, Monday night warrior for more than four years."

"What did you do?"

"Looked at films, listened to lectures, shot baskets."

"Jesus." Gildenhall made a face of disapproval. "What did you learn about gunnery?"

"I can field strip a forty-five."

"Don't be a smart-ass the first five minutes you're aboard, Poulos."

"Sorry, sir, but that was about it."

Gildenhall leafed through the pages. "You go to college?"

He nodded.

"Where?"

"University of Minnesota."

There was a glint of recognition in Gildenhall's light blue eyes but he did not reveal what was going through his mind. "What did you study?"

"I split my major, Humanities and English."

If Gildenhall was impressed he did not show it. "Graduate School?"

"Three credits shy of a Masters."

Gildenhall was far from impressed. "Can you type?"

"Thirty words a minute."

The officer scratched out GM Striker on Poulos's orders and wrote in Yeoman. "Report to the Ship's Office." He turned and shouted "Baker!" and jumped as he realized Baker was standing right behind him, looking over his shoulder at the change in Poulos's orders.

He wore a Jerry Colonna moustache whose tips were as curled as the rim of his white cap. "Good," he said, "we got enough gunner's mates that can't tell a barrel from their ass."

"Show Poulos where to report." Gildenhall began to walk forward, an arm extended for balance, when he stopped. "Come over here," he shouted as Poulos was bending over to hoist his seabag to his shoulder. Poulos dropped the seabag and went to stand by the Operations Officer.

"First time at sea?"

"Except for a two-week training cruise to Bermuda."

"I mean for two months at a crack in hostile waters."

"I guess not."

"I guess not, *sir*!"

Poulos drew back from the unexpected harshness in his voice.

"Let me give you a piece of advice, Poulos. The Sprague is not a cruise ship and she is not going to some goddamn resort in the Bahamas. Nobody gives a shit who you were or what you did before you came aboard. And because you have a college degree, don't get the idea that you are better than an officer. Got that?"

Gildenhall saluted swiftly. By the time Poulos saluted back the Lieutenant had already run up a ladder to the O1 deck.

Poulos followed Baker forward, his seabag providing ballast as he walked on the pitching deck. Overhead a fat oil hose pulsated fuel into storage tanks below. Baker pointed to a wide opening that bisected the middle of the destroyer. "This here is the midship's passageway. Ship's Office is on the port side. Follow me and I'll show you your compartment."

Poulos followed the bos'n down a steep ladder. There was barely room for him and his seabag. An overpowering odor accosted his nostrils and made his stomach turn. There was not one smell but a myriad of them—frying oil, body sweat, garbage, Lysol. They entered a narrow aisle with a steam table. "This here's the galley."

They stepped through a doorway into the mess room. Benches and tables were folded out of the way and a young sailor was mopping the steel deck in a desultory manner. It was greasy underfoot and Poulos nearly slipped. In the center was a hatch with high rim around it, and a second ladder that led down to sleeping quarters.

"Pick a rack that hasn't got anyone using it."

Poulos could barely see. As his eyes dilated, low wattage lamps revealed a depressing collection of pipe-framed bunks with flat springs and thin mattresses. There appeared to be 25 or 30 of them lined up fore and aft four deep. They were triced up to permit a few more inches in the narrow aisles. Below each tier of bunks were metal lockers side by side. He dropped his seabag. The air was foul.

"How do you know which ones are empty?"

"The ones that don't have fartsacks on them."

Poulos watched Baker's legs go up the ladder, the only way out the compartment. He heard the sea whooshing by the slanted hull. He was below the waterline. It occurred to him that in the event of flooding the watertight hatch above would be slammed shut, and any poor saps left in the compartment would be sealed off, doomed. Pleasant thought. The top rack next to the ladder was unused and Poulos selected it even though ketchup, mustard and coffee stains covered the mattress like an abstract painting. At least he could get out of here in a hurry. The lefthand locker was empty and surprisingly clean, even in the corners. He changed into his new dungarees and chambray shirt with his name stenciled on the back, clothes he was given at Pier 91, and packed in his seabag till now. Crisply folded and brand new, he looked very much the raw sailor that he felt inside. He stowed his dress uniform in the locker and secured it with his combination lock. Lastly he made up his bunk with fresh mattress and pillow covers and his blanket, everything stenciled with his last name. He was ready to report for duty.

"What time is it?" someone said.

The voice startled Poulos. He stared into the gloom and spotted a pair of stockinged feet protruding from a rack next to the ship's hull.

Poulos looked at his watch. "Nearly nine, I mean nearly 0900."

There was a movement of stretching. Poulos wondered how anyone could get by sleeping this late in the morning. "Are you feeling ok?"

"I always snore like that."

"I mean I thought you were sick."

"You can sleep in if you have the midwatch." The stockinged feet shifted into the aisle and a well-built sailor stood up. He was so tall his head nearly grazed the overhead. Large biceps and thick pectorals strained the cotton of his t-shirt. His belly was so tight his boxer shorts hung perilously low. He got under the light to dress and Poulos saw a roughly handsome face. A scar on his cheek pulled his left eye at a slight downward angle.

"Name is Witter."

"Poulos."

"You come with the mail and movies?"

"And the fuel."

"You transferred from another ship?"

"From the states. A week on Pier 91, two at Treasure Island, ten days on a troop ship, three weeks in Tent City, and a day and a half on the Chemung."

Witter hitched his belt. Poulos noticed he used the second to the last hole. What a waistline. "What did you do all that time?"

"Read, watered flowers, watched training films."

"Where you working?"

"Ship's Office."

"Met Clayton yet?"

"No. Who's he?"

"Lead yeoman."

'What do you do?"

"I'm a signalman."

"Sounds interesting."

"Come up to the bridge sometime and I'll show you around."

The Sprague freed herself from the tanker's high-line and picked up speed as Poulos and Witter came out on the main deck. They were turning in a wide arc away from the tanker and the deck quickly slanted by several degrees. Poulos hung on the railing for dear life while Witter rode the ship like a broncobuster.

He climbed a steel ladder to the O1 deck and another to the bridge, taking the steel rungs three at a time. Poulos watched his litheness with an admiring eye and then worked his way to the midship's passageway. He stepped over a sill which kept seawater from sloshing in and found himself in an area like a small waiting room. Several sailors were shielding themselves from the mist-laden wind. They didn't seem to be doing anything, just hanging around. A rubber mat covered the deck plates. On the forward side of the passageway was the laundry. Big dryer drums turned slowly and a Filipino man folded fresh cloths into wire baskets with Division numbers stenciled on them. On the aft side was the Ship's Office. A dutch door with the top half standing open revealed a space as confining as a broom closet. Two metal desks with typewriters and chairs were squeezed side by side against the outer bulkhead. The opposite wall was filled with filing cabinets and shelves, and a mimeograph machine. There didn't seem to be a square inch of space that wasn't appropriated for something. The bulkheads were painted a bilious green. The single porthole was lugged shut. Under it a streak of dry salt ran down riveted steel. Poulos tried to shake the sense of dread that a new inmate feels upon seeing his prison cell for the first time.

Pecking at one of the typewriters was an anemic-looking sailor with hazel eyes. He was bony with a thin neck and wrists, and sandy hair yellowed at the tips. He was concentrating so hard he didn't notice Poulos standing at the door.

One of the sailors lounging in the passageway came over. Acne scars covered his cheeks and his hat was tilted back to make room for a pompadour of curly brown hair.

"Hey, Clayton," he said, "you got a customer."

The sailor looked up from his typewriter.

"I was told to report to the Ship's Office," Poulos said.

The yeoman gave him an I-know-that look. “I’m finishing up your record of arrival. I still have to put you on the roster.” He spoke with a Southern drawl.

“What’s he supposed to do, Clayton? Wait out here till you’re done?”

“Keep him company.”

The sailor extended his hand. “My name is Scott Karl but call me Scotty because everybody else does, even the Captain."

“Alex Poulos.”

“You going to be the new yeoman?”

“That’s what Lt. Gildenhall said.”

“Fuck Gildenhall. Lieutenant Radinger is the one you have to look out for. He’s in charge of the Ship’s Office.”

“I haven’t met him yet.”

Scotty looked around to make sure there were no officers walking by. “He’s a lard-ass with a birthmark on his neck that acts like a flare. You’re in trouble if it gets red.”

Clayton’s own face was getting red. “Lay off, Scotty, he’s not your division officer.”

“I don’t kiss the asses of junior grade lieutenants. They gotta have a higher rank.”

Poulos was getting uncomfortable. “What do you do?” he asked Scotty.

“As little as I can. But since you ask, I operate the main battery director.”

“Where’s that?”

“The highest occupied space on the ship, right over the pilot house. I tell the gunners in the five-inch mounts where to point their guns. High school.”

“What?”

“The fucking navy recruited me right out of high school.”

“Oh, I see.”

Clayton put some papers in a folder and opened the door. “I have to deliver these to the Exec.” Clayton walked away, leaving Poulos to his own devices.

“What am I supposed to do now?”

Scotty shrugged. “You can always write a letter home.”

The last thing Poulos felt like doing. He opened the door and stepped into the office, slightly less crowded with Clayton gone, and began a closer inspection, opening drawers, sifting through papers in a wire basket, figuring out how the mimeograph machine worked. He spotted a name plate in a slot under a sign that read Duty Yeoman: RB Clayton.

"What does RB stand for?" he asked of no one in particular.

"Southern dicks use initials because they can't spell." Scotty said, looking in.

"I have a feeling you don't like him very much."

"He reads the Bible."

"That's bad?"

"He quotes from it like he's judging your moral character."

"That's bad."

Scotty surveyed Poulos's face. "Are you religious?"

"Me? Religious? God would have hysterics."

"You better be careful what you say around him, then."

"I haven't noticed any restraint from you."

"Have you heard me say Jesus H. Christ or Goddamnit?"

"But how can Clayton stand being in the navy? That's all you hear."

"He winces a lot."

The intercom system suddenly crackled and a metallic voice broke into their conversation. "Karl report to gunnery control, on the double."

"That's me," Scotty said, and disappeared up the fore and aft passageway.

Poulos sat in front of the typewriter Clayton wasn't using. The chair had a metal-ribbed back and a well-worn, dark-green linoleum seat. The legs were solid metal to keep the chair from sliding around in heavy seas. He noticed that the clearance between the chair back and the filing cabinet behind him was not much more than a couple of inches. The office was more claustrophobic than he expected. He played with the keys of the Underwood. So this is the navy, he thought.

Clayton returned and sat down. Their elbows nearly touched.

Poulos stole glances at his new partner's profile. His forehead stood out almost as far as his nose, and his lips were tight lines. "Is there any mail for me?" Poulos asked, not really expecting any, but he needed to say something to break the silence.

Clayton pointed to the wire basket between the typewriters. It contained a stack of mail, probably what just came across from the Chemung.

"I already looked at it." Poulos began to fidget. The hard seat was uncomfortable. He was going to need a pillow of some kind. "Isn't there something I should be doing?"

Clayton gave him a thick file. "You can type the deck logs."

Poulos went through the stack till he came across handwritten entries with the heading Deck Log Remarks Sheet. “Is it ok to read what’s on here?”

“Why not?”

“It says Restricted.”

“You’re in the navy, aren’t you?”

“Unfortunately.”

Clayton returned to his typing, shaking his head.

“What am I supposed to do this on?”

Clayton opened a deep desk drawer between them and removed a manila folder titled Deck Log Forms. “Make three copies.”

“Three? Plus the original?”

Clayton nodded. “There’s a box of carbon paper on the shelf behind you.”

Poulos helped himself to three carbon sheets and interspersed them between the forms, smudging his fingers in the process. He began typing:

Steaming independently patrolling the east coast of the People’s Republic of Korea on boilers #2 and #3 with the engineering plant split on course 325 (T), 323, pge, 332 pstge, speed 9½ knots (082 rpm)

Without warning, Clayton said, “What did Scotty say about me?” The question jarred his concentration and he typed rmp instead of rpm.

“Jesus.” Poulos said, without thinking. Sure enough Clayton winced.

THE BARTENDER

The March sun was heating up classroom 117 in Temporary South of Folwell, one of four World War II wood-frame buildings the University of Minnesota used for overflow classes which, despite their names, were destined to live on forever. They lacked amenities, principally insulation. To compensate, the University's Building Services had installed commercial radiators under the windows. The combination of shimmering heat rising from gurgling, clanking radiators and the sun streaming through the windows had turned the classroom into a sauna, forcing the professor finally to open the windows an inch or two. Relief spread among the students, especially Alex who was sitting next to a radiator not by choice but because this was where he found the only left-handed desk chair in the room. The right-handed kind, found in superabundance, were hard if not impossible for lefties like him to write on because you either had to twist your body into a corkscrew or hang your left cheek off the seat. Regardless, after a two-hour final, you end up with a bad back if not a bad grade.

Staring into space, formulating his answer to an essay question before writing it down, his wandering eye spotted a coed several rows away bending over her work, her back an arc, and her head so close to her paper that it was out of view. He recalled a month earlier when the professor sprung what he diabolically called a quizzie fifteen minutes before the bell. The question was memorable: Define Illusion as it pertains to Western Concepts such as Dream, Image or Myth (pick one). When the bell rang the exasperated coed threw her paper on the professor's desk and remarked for all to hear, "If this one of your quizzies, I'd hate to see one of your testies."

He nearly laughed out loud at the vivid memory but it did little to lighten his concern that he was not doing well, quizzie or testie. He had not responded to 17th century philosophy as he had hoped when he registered for the class way back in December, a lifetime ago it seemed to him now. Descartes looked interesting then, when he signed up for the course, but in the intervening months his life had become so unpredictably difficult that "I think therefore I am" had become "I am not thinking therefore I am not." He flipped to a fresh page in his blue book and wrote bullshit across the top, a word meant to define not only Descarte's philosophy but also the circumstances of his life. Realizing what he had done--he couldn't turn in his book like this!--he erased the word, but it remained permanently impressed in the soft paper and so he began to blacken it in, working the flat of his pencil point back and forth rapidly.

"Mr. Poulos."

He looked up like a dog having pulled a lamb chop off the dinner table.

Professor Moffatt was staring at him. "Are you having trouble with your pencil?"

"I'm just putting a point on it."

"There *is* a pencil sharpener on the wall," he said.

"It's ok now," Alex said, not wanting to parade to the front of the room, vulnerable to irritated glances, as he made grinding noises sharpening his pencil.

Presently the bell sounded, putting an end to his misery. He made quick work of a summing-up sentence, added his book to the growing stack on the professor's desk, and joined the other students quietly shuffling out of the room and into the hall. He slid on his reserve-issue peacoat as he exited Folwell Hall and walked next door to Nicholson, a two-tone brown, fin-de-siècle building that formed the University's original mall together with Folwell, Pillsbury, Eddy and Wesbrook. They all could use some sand blasting. He made his way to the basement bookstore of Nicholson to a pay phone next to a rack of Classic Pocket Books. He dropped in a dime and dialed the number of the Star and Tribune, not the central switchboard, but the operator on the third floor where the executives had their offices, a number he knew by heart.

"Mary Lou Stachich," he said and looked at the book titles as he waited to be put through: Tristram Shandy, Main Street, Bleak House...

"Mr. Rand's office."

"Hi."

"Alex," Mary Lou said happily, her voice tinkling like fine crystal. "How did your final go?" Before he could give her his measured response, she answered for him: "I bet you did well, you're so smart," adding extra o's to so. She liked to bring out the best in people by complimenting them whether they deserved it or not.

"Are you free for lunch?"

"I had a feeling you'd call so I didn't make any plans. Would you like to eat here at the cafeteria?"

"I was thinking of Richard's."

She wasn't crazy about the place, a watering hole near the newspaper plant frequented by reporters, pressmen and ad salesmen, those she was not likely to associate with since her boss was assistant publisher and Mary Lou was status-conscious. "I don't have much time," she said by way of an excuse.

But Alex persisted, "If I leave now and hold a table we can beat the rush."

"I suppose so," she said reluctantly. "Eleven-thirty?"

"Eleven-thirty," he said, ready to ring off.

"Three little words."

"Three little words," he repeated, their secret way of signing off.

Alex nursed a beer waiting for Mary Lou to arrive. The waitress, not pleased to have a table for four monopolized by one person, inquired if he was ready to order lunch. He put her off by asking for another beer, which he really didn't want. She went to the bar and placed the order. The bartender made a big show of holding the mug aloft for Alex's approval, suds dripping down his fingers.

Alex made an expansive smile and waved.

The waitress delivered the beer. "You know the bartender?"

"Off and on," Alex replied, wishing it was mostly off. "One of my Greek associates." He refused to use the word friend.

"You Greek, too?"

"A hundred per cent."

"Is Tony a hundred per cent?"

"A hundred ten per cent." Tony's mother had married a Greek twice her age and became a widow before she was thirty, forcing Tony into the role of the devoted son which required him to be more Greek than his immigrant father. "How come he's doing lunch? I thought he worked nights."

"Filling in."

Too bad, Alex thought. He didn't expect to run into Tony who was the king of gossip in the Greek community. He wished now he had agreed to eat in the newspaper's cafeteria. He knew that as soon as Tony had the chance, he would be on the phone to his mother. Alex could easily predict the conversation: "Hi Mom, guess who I saw today with an

Americanetha, a red-head at that. Alex Poulos!" And his mother, no doubt crossing herself in the process, replying. "Panagia mou!" My God!

Each time the entrance door opened, cold air spread across the tile floor like an unwelcome visitor, and people queuing at the entrance coveted the table Alex was occupying all by himself. Unwilling to make eye contact, he played with his coaster, pretending not to notice the impatient stares.

"Alex!"

He jumped. Mary Lou was standing over him, pulling off black leather gloves and snapping them over her matching handbag. "Didn't you see me come in?" Her voice was thin with exasperation. "I waved and waved."

"I was waiting so long, I forgot why I was here."

"You're here because you didn't want to eat in the cafeteria."

He rose from his chair and helped Mary Lou slip off her gray wool coat. He was going to hang it on the bentwood rack near the wall but she took it from him and draped it over the back of her chair, arranging the folds to provide a cushion for the hard, wood seat—a reflection of her distress at being dragged to a bar she didn't like in order to sit on a chair that wasn't comfortable. She removed a gray knit tam and shook her head until her well-trained waves of amber curls fell into place. Today she was wearing a high-necked powder blue satin blouse and a darker skirt with shiny buttons down the side.

"Why are you late?" he asked, sitting back down.

"I had to take some last-minute dictation. Unfortunately, Mr. Rand doesn't plan his day around me."

"Maybe we should have cancelled lunch."

"And how could I have reached you?" She was obviously wondering how a brilliant brain like Alex's couldn't figure that out.

"You could have called Richard's. The bartender knows me."

She looked over her shoulder. The bartender noticed and smiled at her. "And how was I supposed to know that? The way my morning went, I didn't have time to go to the bathroom, let alone wait on the telephone for you to be paged." She sighed in frustration. "It would have been so much simpler meeting in the cafeteria."

"All I had in mind," Alex said, measuring his words with every heartbeat, "was to celebrate the end of finals in a place with a little ambience."

"What's wrong with the Star and Tribune cafeteria?"

"Jello on Melmac?"

"At least it's safe to eat. I'd hate to look in the kitchen of this place." Mary Lou finally zeroed in on the reason for her distress.

“The food here is just fine.”

“Oh really?” she said, looking askance at a napkin dispenser whose shine was lost long ago to finger smudges. A menu leaned against it. She took the menu and held it gingerly with red-lacquered fingernails. “Tuna on whole wheat.” She laid the menu on the edge of the table as if hoping it would fall to the floor where it would be more at home.

“Is that all?”

“Tea."

Alex tried to get the waitress’s attention, which proved harder now that he really wanted it.

"Tell me about your philosophy exam,” Mary Lou asked, more to break the tension than to express interest because Alex tended to use phrases she didn't understand, like dialectical materialism and existentialism, even when he tried to explain them to her.

“It was tough."

His response was not what she wanted to hear. Positive thinking according to Norman Vincent Peale was her philosophy of life. "I'm sure you got an A." She parted her lips in a smile of reconciliation, exposing a small overbite that Alex found very appealing.

He pushed his beer mug toward her. "Sip?"

She accepted the mug, not that she liked beer but rather the act of sharing. Under the table she moved her foot forward, found his ankle and rubbed it with her instep, making up.

That's all it took for Alex to become putty in her hands or, in this case, her foot. He looked longingly into her gray-green eyes even though she used an eyelash curler that gave her an almost Ella Cinders appearance. But it matched her ethos, friendly and freckled, like the girl next door. That was probably why he was attracted to her: she was so unGreek looking. Hair so fair and fine it was like flax spun from a wheel, not heavy and peat-black like so many Greek girls he knew, invariably reminding him of Elsa Lanchester in the Bride of Frankenstein.

He hoped his attraction was not entirely physical but it would be hard to deny it if he were truly honest with himself. She didn’t like abstract art. She didn’t like Pete Seeger. She didn’t like experimental films. What she did like was Normal Rockwell paintings and Frank Yerby novels. He recalled the first time they met, a casual encounter in men's sportswear at Dayton’s three weeks before Christmas. Mary Lou was buying a sweater for her brother-in-law. Alex was merely browsing because he didn't have money to buy what he really liked when he spotted her from behind, holding up a brown cable-knit, examining it for size. With her arms raised, her skirt had hiked up an inch or two and he was admiring the turn of her calves. As she lowered her arms, her coat settled on her hips and he wanted to go over and pull it down for her, following the line of her body with his hands. She sensed his stare, perhaps even his prurient thoughts, and turned suddenly. He felt his cheeks flush and wanted to head over to socks and underwear but there was that smile, captivating, ingenuous, sincere, welcoming him to stay put. How many times had he been in a position to talk to a girl whose skin, like the Camay woman, he would have loved to touch but who was so formidable in her femininity that he was afraid to speak to her? It was happening again. He was voiceless, his armpits getting moist, and his heart beating like a bongo drum. She seemed to take pity on him. "You look about Larry's size," she said. "He's my brother-in-law, not as heavy but as tall. I think your shoulders are nearly as wide, but your waist is certainly smaller." He was caught off guard that this pretty woman, a complete stranger in a department store during Christmas season, would not only smile at him but also begin a conversation. All he could do was stare. "Turn around and let me put this sweater across your back for a measure…mind taking off your jacket?"

Mary Lou's real, not her imagined, voice interrupted his thought process. "Can't we get some service? You said they knew you around here."

Jolted back to the present Alex renewed his effort to hail the waitress, this time standing up and waving at her. She came over, a bit nettled.

"The lady doesn't have much time," he said.

"Neither do I."

Mary Lou's stare told the waitress she had some nerve treating customers like this.

Alex ordered for Mary Lou and then for himself, a California burger, hold the onion, and coffee. The waitress scratched it down on her pad and sped away.

"I don't want to belabor the point, Alex, but next time let's go to another place."

"I'm getting bored with Richard's anyway," he replied, checking the bar where he caught Tony looking their way whenever he had the chance. "It's lost a lot of charm ever since they hired that bartender."

Mary Lou looked over her shoulder. Tony nodded at the recognition he was getting.

"Ignore him."

"Well, he's not ignoring us. Who is he?"

"A guy I know."

"Is he Greek?"

Alex nodded. "His last name is Pappathos. You can't get any more

Greek than that."

"He seems nice."

"How do you know? You haven't even met him."

"He smiles all the time. Look at the way he treats his customers."

"People who sit at a bar and drink their lunches are lushes. They're easy to please. All you have to do is keep their glasses full."

"My, you certainly are touchy."

"Sorry."

"You are not sorry, you are defensive. What's wrong with him?"

"He's Greek," he said as if that explained everything.

"Aren't you?"

"I try to ignore it."

"Why do you have such a hard time being Greek?"

"I don't have a hard time, it's easy."

Mary Lou shook her head in frustration. "Every time I try to get serious you get flippant." She gave him a hard stare. "Alex, when am I going to meet your parents? Any other man would have introduced me by now. It's been three months already."

"No it hasn't."

"What do you call two months, twenty eight days, and…" Mary Lou consulted her wrist watch "… twelve hours and fourteen minutes?"

"Your watch keeps better time than mine."

"Alex stop clowning. Can't you see how wrong this is?"

Of course he knew how wrong it was. But how could he explain to her that she was an Americanetha, a Catholic Americanetha at that, who was older than he was, several years older. Any one of these, taken singly, was a kiss of death. He ticked off her positives: pretty, optimistic, practical, but none could overcome the single most damaging disqualifier of all: she wasn't Greek.

He could hear her toe tapping on the tile. "You haven't said a word to them about me, have you?"

"Not yet."

"When?"

"Soon, after I finish school. I'll get a job, I'll move out of the house, I'll be independent."

"You're afraid of them aren't you?"

"No I'm not!" he said strenuously enough to turn heads at a close-by table. He leaned forward, "Look, Mary Lou, give me a chance to get my degree. The pressure will be off and everything will be better, I promise."

"When will that be?"

"After I finish my thesis."

"That paper about the man whose name sounds like a negro's?"

"Erasmus."

"You've been working on that ever since I met you."

"There's a lot of research to do. And my advisor has to approve everything. He's going to Europe this summer but he promised to take it along with him."

Mary Lou let out a long breath of frustration. "You know what you really are, Alex? A professional student, that's what. You really don't want to graduate because that means you will have to take charge of your life—having responsibility, a job, a family."

The subject of family was creeping into Mary Lou's conversation more often, like a footnote attributed to her main goal in life: procreation. On the night they began to discover one another's bodies, she whispered in his burning ear that they would produce beautiful children.

"There's no need to rush into anything," he said.

"Rush?" Mary Lou shot back. "I'll be twenty-nine in October."

"It's not as if you're an old maid."

"Really? At my tenth reunion at Hibbing High I was so embarrassed I wish I hadn't gone. My friends were showing off pictures of their kids. Irene Cassidy was pregnant with her fourth."

"My God, that's practically every other year."

Mary Lou said, "Two are twins."

"That explains it."

Mary Lou leaned forward, ignoring his innuendo. "You don't seem to understand, Alex, or maybe you really don't care, but time is running out for me. I can't wait much longer to have children."

Alex said a little too dismissively, "There's more to life than just reproducing it."

"What can be more precious than a baby coming into the world?"

"I want to plan their arrival, not just have them pop out all over the place." This was a touchy subject for Mary Lou, one on which Alex usually trod lightly but right now he was too frustrated to be considerate of her strict belief that contraception was sinful.

In a slight voice, Mary Lou said, "My mother used to say that a tear can be forgotten but a hurt stays in the heart." She withdrew from him in injured silence.

Fortunately the waitress came with their orders. She placed the check face down next to Alex's plate. There were greasy fingertips on it like evidence of a crime scene. He concentrated on opening his bun and squeezing circles of ketchup as though practicing the Palmer method. Out of his peripheral vision he noticed Mary Lou lift her sandwich and examine the tuna that appeared to be forty per cent mayonnaise. She took a small bite of crust and set the sandwich back down on her plate, and it occurred to him just then that she was demonstrating a saintliness befitting a clergyman's wife, except that in her religion she could never be one.

The sounds of the restaurant came into focus as they sat without speaking to each other, people talking and laughing, dishes and glasses being set down, cash registers ringing. Mary Lou finished her sandwich, as much as she was going to eat of it, and sipped her tea. She looked at him over her cup like a soldier peeking out of his foxhole. "I think I understand why you have so much trouble with things I feel strongly about. It's because you don't have any strong feelings of your own. You don't stand for anything Alex. If you did you would have more understanding of mine."

Alex finished his hamburger and wiped his fingers. He had the sneaking suspicion that those were not her words, that she was phrasing someone else's comments, perhaps criticism of him from someone in her family, like her sister Patty who never liked Alex in the first place. "Has Patty been lecturing you about me?"

Mary Lou set down her cup, meeting him head on. "No, Patty has not been lecturing me about you. And why do you think I can't have a thought of my own?"

"It just doesn't sound like you, it sounds more like a lecture."

"Really, Alex."

"It does."

“Does it matter? That's how I feel.”

“Well somebody’s been filling your ear.”

“Yes,” Mary Lou finally admitted. “Father Bassagni."

“Who?”

“My priest.”

Alex pushed his plate aside. He couldn't believe it. Was nothing sacred anymore? “You’ve been talking to your priest?”

She dropped her hands into her lap and looked down at them. “I went to confession.” She hesitated a moment. “I told him about the night you took me to the Segovia concert.”

Mary Lou was on the edge of her seat that incredible night listening intently as the graying master commanded the attention of a full house at Northrop Auditorium with only a chair, a footstool and a guitar. That's all she talked about in the car on the way home, to Patty and Larry's house where she had a room. Parked in front, she rhapsodized about the passionate music she heard, a vulnerability Alex was more than eager to plumb. Before long his hands were between her legs in spite of her protestations. We mustn’t, not here, not in the front seat of a car that isn’t even yours. So the car belongs to my father, so what? It’s like he’s watching. But we have to do something. I can't stand it. Give me your hanky.

What remained permanently ingrained in his groin was not so much his own heavenly discharge as her reaction to it. Desire was so close to the surface of her own being that if they hadn't been in his father's car Mary Lou could easily have slipped into the abyss with him.

"Did he get excited when you told him?"

"Father Bassagni?" Her cheeks glowed with embarrassment. "How should I know? He was on the other side of a screen."

"Couldn't you even tell if he was breathing hard?"

She threw her napkin down on the table. "This is getting out of hand…" When she said that her face got even redder. "I have to go back to work."

"You haven't finished your sandwich."

"I lost my appetite." She reached for her tam and, from long practice, fitted it neatly on her head, tilting the border just so over her right eyebrow. "You probably think this is silly, but it's true, confession is good for the soul. You should try it sometime."

Watching her put on her tam, he was overcome with a sense of loss, as though Mary Lou were leaving and never coming back. He was thinking only that he will never feel her grip on him again, never experience the soft line of her inner thigh, never…

Suddenly something, somebody, interrupted the train of amorous thoughts that was carrying him on an express ride—a white knight in a crisp white shirt and folded white apron. Alex jumped to his feet, his chair skidding behind him on the tiled floor. It was Tony the bartender, unctuous and smiling, lifting Mary Lou's coat, shaking out the wrinkles and holding it open so that Mary Lou could slip into it.

To Alex it was the same as watching a slow-motion film. Mary Lou fastened her belt and turned her face up to give Tony a warm smile, her voice filtering through an echo chamber as she made a totally gratuitous comment: "The bartender here, like everything else, is very special."

Special? Alex wondered in disbelief. Was Mary Lou's memory that short? What about the impatient waitress, the greasy menu, the mayonnaise sandwich?

Tony was looking at Alex now. "Aren't you going to introduce me to the lady?"

Lady, of all things! "Ah…sure," Alex stammered. "I'd like you to meet Mary Lou." First names were as far as he wanted to go.

"Just Mary Lou?"

"Stachich," Mary Lou broke in, giving Alex a sidelong glance asking where the hell are your manners?

"Is that with an S-h or a C-h?"

"C-h."

"Czech?"

"Croatian."

This apparently was beyond Tony's geographical grasp.

"Croatia is part of Yugoslavia."

"Oh, I see. So you are Orthodox?" he asked.

"I beg your pardon?"

"Aren't people from Croatia Orthodox?"

"Mostly Catholic, Serbians are mostly Orthodox."

This was beginning to beg the question. Alex had to interrupt. "Tony, aren't you needed back at the bar?"

"I'm on break," he said without taking his eyes off Mary Lou. "I take it, Miss Stachich, you are not an Orthodox Christian?"

Alex held his breath, knowing the answer would land like a time bomb that would explode when Tony called his mother.

"I'm Roman Catholic."

Tony's eyebrows closed in on his hairline. "I must profess that I know very little about the Catholic faith."

"Come to mass sometime," Mary Lou said, more to goad Alex than to invite Tony.

If there was a vomitorium handy, Alex would have used it. "Mary Lou has to get back to work," he said, taking her by the arm. They were almost out the door when he suddenly realized, because of his agitated state, that he had forgotten to pay the check. He turned to see Tony waving it in the air.

"Never mind," Tony called out, "lunch is on me."

Alex dropped Mary Lou's arm and marched back, so annoyed he accidentally bumped a table and nearly tipped over a customer's beer glass. He excused himself to the man with the glare, only to recognize him as a columnist for the newspaper, then he turned to Tony and said, "Stop playing the big hero, and give me that check."

Tony held it behind him like a kid in a schoolyard. "I can afford it."

"What makes you think I can't?"

"You don't have a job."

"You know I work for my old man."

"I mean a job like I have, one that pays a wage, not an allowance."

Alex struggled to keep his voice down, causing his words to quiver. "It doesn't matter what you call it, Tony, it's still money."

"I know how hard your father works to provide you with a college education. I never had that kind of good fortune."

"If you don't give me that goddamn check, you'll need good fortune just to eat your dinner."

Tony measured the boiling point in Alex's eyes. "Ok, I'll give it to you, but I want to tell you something first."

Alex glanced over his shoulder. Mary Lou was standing at the door tapping her fingers on her handbag. "Ok," he said, "make it fast."

"Think of your mother."

"I think of her all the time."

Tony touched Alex's arm, his eyes like those of a funeral director. "Don't disappoint her." He surveyed Alex's face for a grain of understanding but not finding any he shook his head. "I wish I had your looks. Every Greek girl I know is waiting for you to make a move. All you have to do is take your pick. I hope you come to your senses before it's too late." He handed over the check.

Alex took the check without looking at it. His eyes were so blinded with anger he couldn't read it anyway. He reached in his pocket for the ten dollar bill his father had given him yesterday—his weekly allowance. It grated on him that Tony was gainfully employed while he was on the dole. The waitress walked by and Alex pressed the sawbuck into her hand. "Keep the change," he said.

He watched the waitress almost skipping with glee to the cash register.

Tony was horrified. "The bill is only four-twenty-five. You're tipping her almost six dollars."

"What the hell," Alex said with fake bravado, "it's only money."

THE MANUALS

The smell of denatured alcohol nearly overpowered Poulos as he checked in at sickbay, a narrow space next to the laundry in the midship's passageway. Bottles of drugs, and packages of bandages and syringes stood in neat rows inside a locked glass case stenciled with a red cross. The Doc, whose glasses settled at the tip of his nose, perched on a stool next to his writing desk. He wore a white jacket over his summer khakis. "Name, rank and serial number."

"Poulos, seaman, 249-36-15."

The Doc wrote down the information on Form 218, Record of Injury, Illness or Complaint. "State your condition."

"Constipation."

The Doc tore up Form 218 and dropped the pieces in his wastebasket. "If you came in for gonorrhea, body lice or a stab wound I could help you. All you need is a good shit."

"But, Doc, that's the point." Poulos poked at his belly. "My stomach is like a rock. I need a laxative."

"First sign of irregularity and you come to me crying for a laxative?" He shook his head at Poulos's lack of toughness. "Once you start taking laxatives it's a slippery slope to dependency."

"I'd be willing to take that chance."

"Not in my navy. Clear your mind and you'll clear your bowels."

Poulos went back to the Ship's Office grumbling to himself.

"What's the matter?" Clayton asked.

"The Doc won't give me a laxative."

Clayton shrugged. "He's the doctor."

"He's not a doctor he's a sadist."

"Honor a physician with the honor due unto him."

"What?"

"Ecclesiastes."

"Ecclesiastes this!" Poulos showed Clayton his finger and stormed out of the office. He went below to the forward head and sat over a trough of seawater, cursing both the Doc and Clayton for his misery. He was ready to throw in the Secretary of the Navy when all of a sudden relief came. Anger was his diuretic.

He was pulling up his dungarees when Scotty came in to piss. "What's up?" he asked over his shoulder, clattering water against the metal urinal

"I just had the shit of my life."

"Congratulations. Did you take Ex-Lax?"

"No, Ecclesiastes."

In the month since Poulos got his bowels moving, his relationship with Clayton was also going down the toilet. They barely communicated and work inevitably suffered. There were daily logs to type, orders to process, ID and liberty cards to file, mail to distribute--and there was always someone at the door wanting something ASAP.

Lt. Radinger called a meeting. Poulos didn't think it was possible for three men to fit in the Ship's Office, especially if one of them was a lardball, and he was mostly right. Radinger's butt stuck out of the doorway.

"Men," he began, "we're seriously falling behind and we have to do something about it. Let's review where we're at." He consulted a checklist locked on his clipboard. "Quarterly roster of the crew." When neither of the men answered, he glanced up. "Well, who's working on it?"

Poulos looked at Clayton "I thought you were."

"The roster is in your basket."

"My basket?" Poulos was perplexed. "I didn't know I had one."

"Well, you got one now," Radinger said, his birthmark heating up at the edges. "What about last week's smooth logs?"

"Here, sir." Clayton held up a file.

"At least half of this office is on the ball." Radinger checked smooth logs off his list. "How about BuPers and BuShips notices? Where are they?"

Clayton glanced at Poulos.

"Are those in my basket too?"

"Jesus H. Christ, don't you two ever talk to each other?" Radinger snapped, and then looked apologetically at Clayton. "No offense," he said. "I know how you feel about the Lord's name and all that, but I got a right to be upset. The Captain is going to kick ass and I don't want to be the first in line, you know what I mean?"

Clayton nodded in silent agreement.

"Your partner is pulling his weight, Poulos, how come you aren't keeping up?"

"I'm dancing as fast as I can, Lieutenant."

"And what is that supposed to mean?"

"Just a joke."

"Humor me."

"A sailor is trying to make out with a girl at the USO Club and, while they're dancing, he whispers in her ear that he only has a weekend pass. And she says I'm dancing as fast as I can."

Radinger's face was without expression. "That's it?" He shook his head. "I'll never know what Gildenhall saw in you."

"Me, sir?"

"When he assigned you to this office."

"He knew I could type."

"You can also scrape paint, can't you?"

"I suppose so."

"Then why aren't you on the deck gang?"

"If it were up to you, I would be, right?"

Radinger glared. "Fucking-A, Poulos, and you know why?"

"Why?" Poulos glared back.

"Because your attitude is up your ass, sailor."

"At least my brain isn't," Poulos fired back. The words just tumbled out, born of a recklessness particularly well-suited to him.

The air in the Ship's Office suddenly went flat as though the oxygen had been sucked out of it. Not that it mattered, nobody was breathing anyway. The inference that the lieutenant's brain was somewhere other than in his skull was not lost on Radinger. Watching his birthmark change from hot pink to livid red, Poulos knew he did not skirt disaster, he hit it head on.

When the Lieutenant finally managed to speak, his words were as measured as if he were using a yardstick. "Get me a report chit, Clayton."

Clayton was relieved to have something to do. He opened a file drawer and pulled out the form. He handed it to the Lieutenant with a shaking hand.

"It was a just joke," Poulos pleaded.

"Like I'm only dancing as fast as I can?" Radinger replied sneeringly. "Well, this one isn't any funnier and neither is your timing. You were insubordinate to an officer in the presence of another enlisted man. You think I can let that pass?" He laid the form on top of the filing cabinet, unloosed the cap of his fountain pan and began writing. Under Details of Offense he wrote:

> During a briefing in the Ship's Office with Yeoman 2nd Class Clayton, Seaman Poulos and the Division Officer in charge of said office, Seaman Poulos made a remark disparaging of the Division Officer which, by extension, also disparages the Naval Service, to which, as a member of said Service, Seaman Poulos has sworn to honor.

> Under Comment by Division Officer, Radinger added:
> Seaman Poulos has the capacity to be industrious if he applies his college-educated mind to it.

"Sign it." Radinger handed Poulos his fountain pen.

Poulos took the pen, contorted his left hand with his fingers pointing down instead of up and signed on a line that read PAL Acknowledgment. The pen skipped and scratched across the paper.

"What the fuck are you doing to my pen?"

"That always happens, Lieutenant. I'm left handed."

"Can't you do anything right?"

Easy swells lifted the Sprague and gently set her down again, her narrow wake an aqueous umbilical cord connecting her to her sister ships steaming behind in single file: the Meredith, the Yarnall, and the Orleck. At sea the destroyers were known by their voice calls: the Sprague was CanCan; the others in order were HickUp, BarnDoor and MooseJaw. Having been relieved of picket duty with the USS Forrestal off the coast of North Korea--a bleak landscape of craggy hills and dirty clouds--DESDIV 1 steamed south for more hospitable activity, including ASW training with a British task force in Formosan waters and an eagerly anticipated liberty in Hong Kong, the jewel of the Orient.

It was Sunday, a day off except for duty watches. After breakfast Poulos went to the Ship's Office knowing he would have the place to himself for a while because Clayton attended religious services on the fantail. He sat at the typewriter and tried composing a letter to Mary Lou for the umpteenth time. When Clayton returned with his Bible and a beatific expression, Poulos retreated to the signal deck with a writing pad and a frown on his face.

The signal deck was located on the aft part of the bridge, wedged between the Captain's sea cabin and the mainmast. Poulos liked being up there in the open air, especially when flags were hoisted and the silk colors hummed against the rigging, as soothing to the ear as a lullaby. Most of the space was taken up by a pair of flagbags, not bags in the literal sense but large metal trunks holding dozens of signal pennants. The flagbags were covered with protective canvas because no messages needed to be sent aloft while the squadron cruised south in single file, making it a convenient if not entirely comfortable place to sit and contemplate the ocean. Besides, the bridge was quiet, the only activity coming from inside the pilot house where the conn officer, navigator and helmsman directed the ship.

As the afternoon sun crept inexorably toward the horizon so did his resolve to finish a letter to Mary Lou. Everything he tried was worthless; the bottom of the slop bucket at his feet was covered with his balled-up drafts. He couldn't even settle on a salutation: Dear Mary Lou, Dearest Mary Lou, or simply Mary Lou. He finally chose Mary Lou. It was better to be formal, he decided, because what he had done could not be explained in any personal way or even in a way that begged forgiveness. Perhaps a third-person approach was the way to go, the way a film director shoots a movie--a horror movie.

I hope you don't tear this up and throw it away before reading it, he wrote, but if you do I will understand. There is no excuse for my behavior but there may be an explanation. If you're willing to hear me out, then maybe ...

"Writing the Great American novel?"

Startled, Poulos looked up from his writing pad. He had not noticed Witter standing in front of him, his weightlifter's biceps firm under his chambray shirt.

"The Greek-American novel," Poulos said.

Witter smiled. "I read somewhere that writers throw away more words than they keep."

"So far I haven't kept any." Poulos ripped the sheet off his pad, balled it up and dropped it in the slop bucket.

Witter looked down at the balls of paper in the slop bucket. "Are you really working on a novel?"

The question prompted Poulos to look at his letter-writing efforts in a way he hadn't thought about before. He was making one vain attempt after another trying to make sense of the events that had brought him to this moment, aboard a ship of characters plowing through an Asian sea. Why not a novel? Isn't it, after all, a long letter--words structured from real-life experiences? Maybe that's what he should do, write a novel.

"You know," he said, "that sounds like a good idea."

Witter turned his broad back to the late afternoon sun and leaned against the azimuth. "I stopped by the Ship's Office looking for you but you weren't around."

"I came up for air. Did you know I got put on report?"

Witter nodded. "I heard."

"It's a fucking joke. I'm restricted to the ship. So what? Where else is there to go?"

"You can't even hide."

That was painfully true. Poulos thought about the brilliant novel Mr. Roberts which he read in college, taking classes in the same building as the author Tom Heggen had only six years earlier, and he took heart in how Ensign Pulver managed to keep out of sight of his deranged skipper. If only he could do the same with Clayton. But Pulver was on a supply ship with many compartments, quarters, holds, and lockers to disappear in, while Poulos was on a ship no wider than three parked cars. All he could do was find reasons to run errands.

My typewriter needs a new ribbon, he would say to Clayton. Even though supply was right around the corner, he would walk to the fantail, around the depth charge racks, and return via the O1 deck, past the torpedo tubes, up the ladder to the charthouse for a cup of coffee, stop by the radio shack for nonexistent messages, and finally head down to supply for the ribbon he didn't need anyway because there was a box of them in his desk drawer. If he was in luck, when he finally got back, Clayton was out running errands of his own.

"You could spend more time with Clayton. He thinks you're avoiding him."

"For once he's right."

"Why can't you get along with him?"

It was as if Witter had turned on a spigot. Words began to pour out of Poulos's mouth--if only they would pour out as easily on a piece of paper. "Clayton is so pious his hands bleed on Good Friday. Radinger acts like he's in church whenever he comes into the office, which gives Clayton the notion that he can get away with anything. He took himself off the duty roster so he won't have to stand watches. What else do you want? Oh, I almost forgot. Clayton keeps quoting the Bible. If you say fuck he tells you to keep your tongue from evil. And don't dare complain about anything or he'll tell you that the Lord should be your rock and your fortress. Here's another one: a soft answer turns away wrath. It's enough to make you puke."

"Maybe that's his way of defending himself."

"Defending himself? From what?"

"You."

"Me?" Poulos asked incredulously.

"You don't see it but Clayton is defending himself against your superiority by using the only weapon he's got, the Bible."

"Superiority my ass. He's lead yeoman."

"You act like you are. You graduated from college. Clayton didn't."

"I never bring that up."

"You don't have to, it oozes from your pores."

"I sweat like everybody else."

"Yours smells of intelligence. His just smells."

Poulos could not bring himself to have empathy for Clayton. "Tell him to take a shower."

The sun was finding its way to the horizon. If the day is cloudless and the ocean smooth, the yellow of the sun blends with the blue of the sea and in a split second combine to make a green streak on the water's surface. Poulos had seen the green flash only once. It required concentration, patience and an ability to keep checking the setting sun without going blind. He wasn't looking for it now as he stared at the ocean, he was looking for a way out of his dilemma, as difficult as trying to spot the green flash. "Six-hundred-seventy to go," he mused aloud.

"Six-hundred-seventy what?"

"Days."

"You're counting the days?" Witter asked in amazement.

"I scratch them off my desk calendar. Today I scratched off number sixty."

"How can you go from normal to paranoid in only two months?"

"Two months and three days."

Witter shook his head. "You should see a doctor."

"I did. He wouldn't even give me a laxative."

"Not our Doc. A shrink at the base hospital. You could get a temporary transfer."

Poulos felt offended. If anyone needed a shrink it was Clayton.

Directly off the port beam, a dozen gray dolphins were playing tag with the ship. Their backs glistened as they leaped out of the water and their black eyes shone with an uncanny awareness. They were known to rescue sailors washed overboard by pushing them with their snouts toward shore.

Poulos stared at the animals who were probably as bright as humans. "I'm not nuts."

Witter struck the contrapposto pose of a classical sculpture with his weight on one leg, making Poulos wish well-built men weren't always so fucking sure of themselves. "But you're driving everyone else nuts. Why don't you make up with Clayton?"

Poulos was ready to listen. "Where do I start?"

"We're going on liberty in Hong Kong. Hit a bar and get drunk."

"With Clayton?"

"Believe in miracles. He does."

Witter stood on the ladder ready to go below. "By the way," he said, "AJ has a new Errol Garner album. He's playing it in the chart house after chow." He disappeared out of sight.

Poulos understood that this was more an announcement than an invitation, letting him know he was welcome but that he was also on probation. If he didn't change his ways, no more invites to the chart house, the hottest ticket on the ship.

A. John Browning had a nonpareil record collection--not only Errol Garner but also Gene Ammons, Earl Bostic, Ike Carpenter, Stan Kenton - a new album every time mail was high-lined over. He was the coolest cat on the ship, thin, not reedy like Clayton, but willowy with a gently curving spine and rounded buttocks. He wore tortoise-shell glasses on a pug nose. His dream was to be a drummer in a jazz quartet and he walked around listening to endless riffs in his head while his hands made corresponding jitter-moves in the air. Poulos couldn't wait to join him and Witter but in the meantime he had to make peace with Clayton.

He was feeling better. He stood and stretched, determined to believe in the miracle Witter was talking about. Buoyed by a sense of purpose he hadn't felt in a long time, Poulos rode the ladders down on their handrails and hit the main deck in full stride. He even felt better about Mary Lou. He began to sing her favorite song, further lifting his spirits: "When you walk through a storm keep your chin up high..."

Unfortunately his chin was up so high he didn't notice a pool of sudsy water that had collected on the deck in front of the Ship's Office. He skidded and grabbed the door frame to keep from falling. He looked in. The chairs were turned upside down on the desks. The typewriters had their covers on. The rubber mat was rolled up on top of the filing cabinet. Clayton was swabbing the steel-plated deck. A line of sweat ran down the back of his shirt.

"What's going on?"

Clayton dipped his swab into a bucket and slopped more water onto the deck. "Getting ready for inspection."

"What inspection?"

He stopped mopping.

"Lieutenant Radinger called for an inspection."

"That's Monday. Today is Sunday."

"So?"

"The Lord's day off."

"Not the navy's."

This was absurd. There was plenty of time to clean the place in the morning. Poulos was going to make this point when he checked himself, Witter's words echoing in his head: make up with Clayton. Challenging his martyr complex was not the way to do it. Cooperation was, a friendly attitude was, rolling up the sleeves and helping was. He stepped inside. "I'll give you a hand."

Clayton tightened his grip on the swab, his bony knuckles as pointed as shark's teeth. He swung it in a wide arc as a warning not to come any closer. Dirty water flicked onto Poulos's shoes.

"Look out Clayton!" Poulos shouted, jumping back. He wiped the tips off one at a time on the back of his dungarees and forced a laugh. "No harm done." He looked around for something to do and locked his sights on the gunmetal gray bookshelf above the mimeograph machine. It was packed with manuals no one ever looked at and a collection of pocketbooks--shitkickers in navy parlance--contributed over the years by transferred yeomen.

"The manuals need dusting."

"Go back to the bridge. I don't need any help."

"Don't you want me around?"

"You don't want to be around."

"That's what I'd like to talk to you about, Clayton," Poulos said, looking for an opening to make amends.

"Why don't you call me by my first name?"

"You don't have one."

"It's RB."

"Those are just initials."

"That's what my Daddy named me. Does it bother you?"

"It's different."

"Not where I come from."

"Where do you come from?"

"West Virginia."

Hillbilly country, Poulos thought. "RB," he said as if trying out Clayton's first name to see how it played on his tongue. "RB" he repeated. "What does RB stand for?"

"Just RB."

Rather quaint to Poulos but he never wished he was in Dixie and consequently did not understand the mores of the South, a place as distant as a Martian plain. Rather than try to reignite a conversation that appeared to have come to a dead end, he decided to make himself busy by taking the volumes down from the shelf and dusting them. His mother was a compulsive housekeeper which always annoyed him but now, as the Old Dutch Cleanser urge began to take hold, he could appreciate the rush cleaning must have given her. He wanted to convey his newfound enthusiasm to RB who held his mop handle like a flagbearer and watched Poulos with wary eyes.

"You know the old saying, Cleanliness is next to Godliness," Poulos said, almost humming a gay tune.

"John Wesley."

"Who?"

"John Wesley, founder of the Methodist church."

"I know he founded the Methodist church."

"He was the one who said it."

'Said what?"

"Cleanliness is next to Godliness."

"Oh really?" Poulos said as if he really gave a good Goddamn, forgetting in his growing frustration that his real mission was to make friends with Clayton, not further alienate him. He proceeded to pull the manuals down half a dozen at a time and stack them on the desk. Next to come off were the paperbacks with titles like Ride My Saddle, Hot Tamale and Rodeo Romance. He piled them on top of the manuals, making a disorderly mess.

Clayton stared at Poulos with concern. "You're getting them mixed up."

"Which ones, the manuals or the shitkickers?"

Clayton leaned his swab against the aft bulkhead and started rearranging them. "They should be in alphabetical order."

"I can do that when I put them back on the shelf."

"It's easier to keep them in order in the first place."

"Well, then, how about the shitkickers? You want them arranged by title or tit size?"

Clayton stiffened and tried to maintain his dignity. He gathered up the paperbacks, tamped them to line them up, and set them back on the shelf.

"Don't put those away yet. I haven't dusted the shelf." Poulos ran his finger along it and wagged the dirty digit in Clayton's face. "You want Radinger's white glove to look like this?"

"Lieutenant Radinger does not wear white gloves."

"It doesn't matter. You can't leave the shelf dusty."

"I'll do it."

Poulos's eyebrows raised. "That's what it's all about isn't it? You don't think I'll do a good job, right?"

Clayton didn't waver. "You're the one who got put on report." He began to put the manuals back on the shelf.

His frustration turning to anger, Poulos grabbed the manuals out of

Clayton's arms and clutched them to his chest as if he were protecting the Holy Grail.

"Give them to me!" Clayton demanded and tried to wrest the books from Poulos's grip but Poulos hung on.

The two men slithered and slid on the wet deck, grunting from effort, neither willing to be the first to let go. Their struggle began to attract attention. Sailors walking through the midship's passageway stopped and looked in, wondering what the hell was going on.

"Looks like they're doing some kind of weird dance."

"No, it's a fight!"

"Fight!" someone repeated and the incendiary word spread quickly. Poulos and Clayton were finally having at it. Many wondered why it had taken so long. In no time the doorway to the Ship's Office was crowded with sailors who were yelling encouragement to continue the struggle until bets could be laid down.

Poulos and Clayton were now locked in an epic struggle that quickly grew out of all proportion to the circumstances, and came to be known as the Battle of the Manuals, which would enter the annals of the history of the Sprague as long as she sailed the seas, becoming part of her lore along with her battles, her mishaps, her victories; and the sailors who witnessed it would brag about being there and would be remembered with envy by those who only heard of it second-hand, and these eyewitness accounts would be passed on to future crews, embellished in the repeated telling until the protagonists, had they heard them, would no longer recognize themselves.

Baker, the chief bos'n, yelled over the crowd. "Whatever the fuck you two are doing in there quit it now!"

"Let 'em alone, Baker, we're making book."

A sailor called out, "Eight to five Clayton wins!"

"Screw those odds," another sailor shouted, "Clayton is much lighter."

"Look at his face. Is that someone ready to give up?"

"Ok, you're on!"

The two yeoman struggled like elk whose horns were locked in a life and death duel.

"Poulos's got a half-Nelson on Clayton!"

"Looks like a full Jeanette MacDonald to me!"

Guffaws filled the passageway.

Sweat poured down their faces as they twisted and turned, oblivious to the cheering audience. Clayton, twenty pounds lighter, was lifted off the deck as Poulos spun in an effort to loosen Clayton's grip but the cords in the yeoman's arms had the strength of cable. Minutes passed and it looked as if the two would collapse to the deck in exhaustion when Clayton said into Poulos's ear: "You are going to dust."

"What was that?" Poulos gasped.

"You are going to dust."

"Good!" Poulos was relieved that Clayton was finally listening to reason. He let the manuals go expecting Clayton to put them back on the desk so that Poulos could start dusting them, but instead Clayton clutched them to his heaving bosom, grinning in victory.

"Wait a minute, you said I was going to dust."

Clayton's eyes burned like those of a zealot. "That's right. You *are* going to dust, because dust thou art and unto dust thou shalt return."

"What?"

"Deuteronomy."

Poulos screamed like a gored matador. "I don't care if it's Leviticus!" How could Clayton do something so unChristian? This Bible-quoting hillbilly from West Virginia had outwitted Poulos not by superior strength but by a cleverer mind.

Sailors shouting "Clayton won, Clayton won!" assailed his ears, and money began to change hands.

Poulos looked around in bewilderment--right, left, up, down--his impotent gaze sweeping the small confines of the office looking for an answer to the eternal question: how could this have happened to me?

His eyes were drawn again upward to something he had seen many times before but never separating it from all the other things packed into the small confines of the office: a bag attached to the ventilator grate above their heads. The sack was used as a filter, and as far as Poulos knew it had never been cleaned. He had a sudden flash of inspiration borne on the wings of desperation and spurred by a need for vengeance.

"You think you're the only one who knows the Old Testament?" Poulos raged. "Well, I took eight credits of it!" He made a fist and punched the sack. A cloud of putrid, filthy dust burst over them. Poulos knew what was coming and ducked out of the way but Clayton had no time to react and, as he instinctively looked up, ancient soot fell over his face like a shroud.

"Dust thou shall eat all the days of thy life!" Poulos shouted triumphantly. "Psalms!"

Except for his eyes, which were as wide and white as saucers, Clayton's face was the color of lampblack. He dropped the manuals and stumbled against the file cabinet gagging, coughing and spewing.

"While you're at it," Poulos taunted, "why don't you sing Mammy?"

The sailors betting in the passageway were thrown into a state of confusion. Some yelled that Clayton had still won while others claimed that Poulos was the victor even though he was accused of playing dirty.

Clayton suddenly put his hands to his mouth.

"Look out! He's going to heave!"

Everybody jumped back as Clayton pushed his way through the knot of sailors and ran to the railing, but he didn't make it. He threw up all over the deck.

THE FATHER

Alex's cheeks burned with humiliation as he walked from Richard's toward Hennepin Avenue. He was thinking about the money he had just thrown away. And for what? To show up Tony? If so, Tony won that round. All Alex had in his pocket were four streetcar tokens and for all his seething anger he might just as well have given the waitress these too so his punishment would be complete, a four-mile hike home, plenty of time to think about what he'd done.

What troubled him more was how he was going to explain this to his old man, that the ten from yesterday was gone today, and convince him to turn over an advance on next week's allowance. He laughed, an advance on next week as if he was good for it. He was good for nothing and he could read it in Mary Lou's eyes after they left Richard's. Steam from their breaths co-mingled in the cold air as they stood facing each other on the sidewalk.

"Who were you trying to impress," Mary Lou asked, "Tony or the waitress? Because you sure weren't impressing me." An aura of resignation enveloped her figure. "I feel sorry for you, Alex. You never think things through, you don't foresee the consequences of your actions. You just threw away a lot of money to show off, pretending that you were John D. Rockefeller. Come to think of it, Rockefeller stopped to pick a dime off the sidewalk didn't he? And he had oil fields. You don't even have a job, you just have an allowance."

Her words struck him like hard snowballs. "It's not an allowance," he replied through gritted teeth. "I earn it."

"You better get busy then." Mary Lou walked away.

The streetcar ride gave him the opportunity to get over his burning embarrassment, at least most of it, and formulate a strategy as the car creaked and rattled past the Basilica of St. Mary, its copper dome patinaed to a muted green, the rose garden covered with hay, Walker Art Gallery and its Lipschitz bronze, Prometheus Strangling the Vulture, dominating the entry, the statue of streetcar magnate Thomas Lowry for which Lowry Hill was named, and the stately Kenwood mansions dating back to the gilded age still disdainful of the traffic rumbling by.

As he took in the familiar landmarks, Alex began dreaming up excuses--no not excuses, explanations--for having been parted with the ten-dollar-bill his father had given him only yesterday. He played around with opening lines:

1. A bum on Washington Avenue picked me clean
2. It fell out of my pocket while I was taking a crap in the Folwell Hall toilet
3. I gave it to the Greek-American Relief Association

He sighed outwardly. The problem was not so much that he tipped the waitress too much money. The problem was that he wasn't in charge of his own finances. If he had a job what he did with his money would be his own business and he wouldn't have to live like a beggar. The time had come to turn an error of judgment into a plan of action. He was going to stop sponging off his dad and get a job. He dreamed about being a reporter for the Star and Tribune, not because he would be close to Mary Lou but because the fourth estate was an honorable profession. Newsmen didn't have a union, they had a guild. He liked that. He could earn a decent salary, maybe sixty a week. He'd have plenty of money to rent a bachelor pad somewhere, buy a car, come and go as he pleased. And Mary Lou would have every reason to be proud of him.

Independence. That sounded really good and took the sting out of his earlier mortification. He settled back on the streetcar's wicker seat, feeling better. He was confident he could handle his father, his mother was another case, but his father of all people would appreciate the need for a son to break away. Why, his dad was only fifteen when he left home, not just home but country as well. This was a remarkable journey Alex heard about as a little boy. His mother got up early to open the restaurant, giving Alex the opportunity to sneak into bed with his father before school and ask him about the strangely exotic place he came from, real-life stories that became an indelible part of his psyche, torn as he was between the alien culture of his parents and his own boyhood, as American as Penrod's.

His father, Theodore, was born in 1890 in the remote mountain village of Haraka where the ancient Spartans once ruled. At fifteen he was sent to Istanbul to work in his uncle's loukoumi factory. The village's only link to the Aegean, the seaport of Kiparisi, was down a steep trail hacked out of a mountain slope centuries before--a precipitous collection of switchbacks and narrow, rock-strewn steps so risky, before descending, travelers prayed and blessed themselves before a large metal cross imbedded in the rock. The Haraka Trail had claimed its share of victims, including Theodore's brother Gregory whose donkey slipped and fell into the gorge with him on it. For Theodore, the cross was where he parted with his parents whom he would never see again.

Three days later he stood at the Golden Horn, awed to be in this cosmopolitan city with its throngs of men who wore black business suits and maroon fezes, the Turks' national headdress. They chain-smoked thin cigarettes and drank thick coffee. Theodore heard they beat their wives. By 1910 political unrest was shaking the foundations of the Ottoman Dynasty, and the young candy maker, dodging bodies hanging from lampposts on his way to work, decided it was time to emigrate to America.

(Periodically Alex would interrupt his father for clarification. Why, for example, did he refer to Turkey's capital as Istanbul when in the World Book Encyclopedia it was named Constantinople after the Roman Emperor Constantine I? His father explained that Istanbul was a Turkish corruption of the Greek phrase Steen Poli, The City. It was simpler for Greeks, who dominated Istanbul's foreign population for centuries, to say they were going to The City rather than using the polysyllabic name given it by the Romans.)

In New York, Theodore had new wonders to absorb and a new language to learn. He worked in the Olympia, an ice cream shop on Delancey Street on the Lower East Side. One Sunday in July, he told Alex, they were so busy he was convinced all of New York's entire population of four million came in to buy an ice cream cone. A year of that and he headed west to make his mark, first in Escanaba, Michigan, then Baraboo, Wisconsin, settling finally in Minneapolis, joining a growing community of recent immigrants. Driven to be independent businessmen but not in competition with each other, the Young Greeks fanned out around the state and opened restaurants, candy kitchens and ice cream parlors in separate small towns. Theodore chose Waseca in southern Minnesota, divided between Irish Catholics and German Lutherans, and opened the Crystal Cafe. It was in this town of 4,500 that Alex began life on Saturday, February 1, 1930. (As Saturday's child he was supposed to work hard for a living but he still had not lived up to that expectation.) His young life took an unexpected turn when the Crystal Cafe burned down along with several other businesses on

Waseca's main street on a frigid day in January 1942. Theodore collected the insurance money, more cash than he had ever seen, and moved the family to Minneapolis.

The streetcar screeched to a stop at Lake Street where Alex got off to catch the Glen Lake bus that served the western suburbs. He stood in the cold for ten minutes till the bus turned the corner and picked him up along with half a dozen other shivering passengers. The green and tan bus skirted Lake Calhoun, its shoreline already showing signs of spring with a glittering formation of splintered ice. The bus passed barren North Beach, its aging stucco bath house with fake turrets and crenelated walls rising up like an over-ambitious sand castle. Heading toward the afternoon sun the bus rumbled over the cobblestoned road bisecting the Minikahda Golf course, the front nine on one side the back nine on the other. Beyond the cyclone fence Alex could see fairways, verdant green in summer but now, in March, brown and laced with bands of dirty snow.

The bus drew up to the Lilac Lanes Shopping Center, airbrakes snorting, to drop him off. He hop-scotched across the slushy parking lot to his father's candy store tucked between Walbom's Apparel and Red Goose Shoes, the display window featuring milk chocolate bunnies and Easter baskets in assorted flavors wrapped with cellophane. He pushed open the glass-paneled door and stepped inside, the hydraulic closer whisking the door shut behind him. The all-too-familiar, thickly sweet smell of chocolate nearly clogged his air passages, like an asthmatic attack, forcing him to ask himself every time he walked in if this was psychosomatically induced. Chocolate ruled his life and that of his parents, the common denominator that bonded them as a family and separated them from other families. The gooey confection permeated clothing, skin, fingernails, defining them the way grease defines a mechanic.

At the sound of the door whispering shut, his mother came out from behind the latticed partition to see if it was a customer. She was dressed in an American Linen uniform, white and so stiffly starched it hid every body contour. A tremor in her right arm was the only thing she could not control. When she saw who it was she turned and went back behind the partition without speaking. She was upset with him for being late and expressed her anger not with words but with silence, eternal maddening silence, more deafening than the loudest air hammer he could imagine. All he heard was the rip-snap of the Scotch tape dispenser and the rustle of paper behind the screen. He looked around as if searching for an escape but everywhere he looked there were overpowering symbols of his entrapment: stacks of candy boxes and displays of Easter baskets, trays of hand-dipped chocolates, nougats and caramels, nut clusters and turtles, squares of divinity and fudge, peanut brittle and English toffee, rows of mints. Candy candy everywhere and all the nasal passages did shrink.

"Hi ma," he called from out front, "I'm back," stating the obvious, an art form he had years to perfect. Behind the partition the sound of cellophane crinkling and tape dispensing became more pronounced, her way of letting him know she knew he was back so why bother even acknowledging it. He had told her before he left for his final that she could expect him right after his test to help pack orders and so she was expecting him around noon and it was now past two. He needed an excuse, let's see…

1. The professor ran out of blue books and had to run to another building to get more.
2. I hung around to post-mortem the test with other students.
3. The bus broke down.

Alex stopped himself. On the streetcar he was thinking up lame excuses for throwing away his allowance and now he was thinking up lame excuses for being late. When was he going to start acting like a man? he asked himself. Not now. Another time maybe. He inhaled deeply to calm his nerves and walked behind the counter to join his mother in the stockroom. She stood with her back to him at the wrapping table, covering chocolate eggs and bunnies in yellow cellophane and tying them with blue ribbon. Stooped shoulders de-emphasized her height. A small, regular tremor worked its way across her right shoulder, down her arm and out her fingertips. Her wispy gray hair was held in place by a black-net snood, exposing neck tendons so taut he expected them to snap at any moment.

He found it difficult if not impossible to reconcile this gaunt presence with the image of the young mother she once was. Chiseled in his memory like a marble sculpture was the recollection of her drawing a bath while he, a toddler, sat on his enameled potty in the bathroom, his mother a towering figure of white skin except for a v-shaped darkness where her legs came together and burgundy-colored nipples. She didn't seem to mind that he was staring. In fact she seemed to take pleasure in the rapt attention she was getting.

"Dad in the basement?" he asked, another pointless question, but everything about his life was pointless anyway.

Her answer was to turn and give him a hurtful stare.

What he saw filled him with consternation. "Ma!" he exclaimed. "Did you have another nosebleed?"

A wad of cotton encrusted with dried blood was stuffed in her nostril, puffing out the right side of her nose and tilting her bifocals upward. A glint of satisfaction played in her eyes. She was finally getting attention even if she had to lead him the way a shrewd lawyer leads a witness. "What you care?"

"Look at you, thin as a rail. You don't eat anything but aspirin."

"Aspirin stop the headaches."

"You get headaches because you don't eat."

It was a vicious cycle that had grown along with her palsy. He should make an effort to get to the doctor, he knew, but the last time was such an unmitigated disaster that he shrank from even thinking about it. Her tremor had developed over time and as it became more pronounced so did his guilt that he should do something, and so he checked at the University Hospital information service about what caused such shaking and learned the symptoms pointed to Parkinson's disease. He was urged to make an appointment for his mother to see a neurologist. It took a lot of coaxing but he got her there, at least as far as the lobby where she saw painted letters on a glass partition: Department of Neurology and Psychiatry. The latter word threw her into sudden fury and she walked out of the hospital and down the sidewalk. When Alex caught up to her, she shouted, "Crazy? Is that why you take me here because you think I'm crazy?" The sidewalk was busy with students and many turned their heads at the spectacle of a young man trying to deal with his mother, raw research for a term paper in Psych 101.

"You have to see a doctor."

She tensed warily. "Doctor?"

"Not that kind, ma, a doctor to see about why you have nosebleeds all the time. If I make an appointment will you go?"

"You, I need to make an appointment with, not a doctor."

She had expertly turned the conversation to where she wanted it to go. "Ma, so I'm a little late. I got here didn't I?" It was futile to argue with her any longer. He made a move toward the basement door to join his father.

The scissors in her hand waved threateningly. "Pou eisanai?" Where were you? She had finally dug to the core of what was troubling her--the reason behind his tardiness.

"I stopped off for lunch," he admitted.

"Mono sou?" Were you alone?

The metaphoric ground under him began to cave in as he came to realize that his mother had got a phone call after all. She was much too suspicious, part of her nature in any case, but her question was more sharply honed as though she was trying to get him to admit to it before she told him what she already knew.

Go ahead, his seedy alter-ego was telling him, tell her you had lunch with a Roman Catholic seven years your senior, a woman you are so hot for you could have done it on the floor right there in the restaurant just to impress Tony Pappathos what a great cocksman you are. Ought to be worth another nosebleed, right, ma? A real gusher this time.

Embarrassment coursed through his veins. Why can't I just tell ma I had lunch with the girl I love. I'd like to have you meet her. She's really nice. Why can't I just say that? "So I wasn't alone. I had lunch with a gal from class. We were talking about the final." The last part was true enough.

"Pseftis!" Liar!

"What?"

"You hear me," she said in English to make sure she was understood. "I know who you have lunch with."

"Mrs. Pappathos called you?" he asked, pretending innocence, and continued the charade by fidgeting with stock boxes lined up on the shelf over the wrapping table. Each was labeled with a creme filling and chocolate coating, D for Dark, M for Milk: D Orange, M Cherry, D Lemon, M Strawberry, M Vanilla, D Chocolate. "Maybe I should pack some one-pound assortments. They look low."

"Pay attention to me! You think I don't know what you do behind my back? She say Tony see you have lunch with a Katholiki." She spat out that awful word as if it were something caught between her teeth. "I am ashame of you. I am ashame to go to church." Her arm began to shake more severely and the scissors she was holding turned in the air like propeller blades.

"I only had lunch with her, I didn't sleep with her!" The defensive statement came out in a flood of hurtful words, unthinking, even uncaring, as though he intended to shock his mother, and he certainly did. The mere suggestion of sleeping with a Katholiki and what it might foretell was a distinct possibility and it frightened her that Alex might act upon it. Words uttered aloud stayed in the air like evil omens.

Her face was an expression of ineffable sadness. "Poulaki mou," she said. My little bird. He could not remember her calling him that since he was a child.

"Grieah!" Old woman! It was his father calling from the basement, his voice echoing up the stairwell behind the closed door. Alex opened it. A bare bulb hanging by an electric cord from the sloped ceiling cast a ghostly light upon his father standing at the bottom of the stairs, a shadowy figure wearing a white apron and white pants.

"Oh it's you," he said when he saw his son. "I was wondering if you show up."

He wore a paper cap on his head soiled by chocolate finger smudges. He worked without a shirt, the wide straps of his one-piece underwear fitting over his bare shoulders like the chest armor of a centurion. His right hand, which he held up in the air, was covered up to the wrist with melted chocolate. "Where in the name of Greece you been?"

"Talking to ma."

"All day?"

"I was going to pack some one pounders."

"Let her do that. Come down and separate turtles. I have to finish dipping."

"Are you working your way through the Minneapolis Club order?"

"No, I'm working my way through college." He disappeared around the corner.

The wisecrack only pointed out the curious dichotomy between his old man and himself. On the one hand he wanted Alex to go to school (what Greek immigrant didn't want to see his son get an education?) but on the other he resented the time it took Alex to attend classes and study when he was needed to separate turtles. Maybe it was his major, not Civil Engineering or Law or Medicine, each a profession with a title, but English of all things. Spend four years at the University to study, what, a subject everyone else used? His father taught himself English, not elegant but well enough to be understood. Alex even wondered if his major made his father feel resentful, as if Alex had chosen English in contempt of his father's limited ability to speak it.

He sighed with frustration. Maybe he was reading too much into things, always analyzing and second-guessing, hoping if he dug a little deeper he might finally find the truth. He looked at his mother, pathetic but persevering, wrapping chocolate bunnies again, her back to him.

"Ma," he said, "I'm going to help dad." Without waiting for a response which he knew would not come, he went downstairs and rounded the corner into a narrow, troglodytic basement that was his father's workplace.

When the family moved to Minneapolis after the Big Fire, Theodore bought the candy store from another Greek who was retiring. It had been a retail outlet. The candy was made in a small factory downtown and so Alex's father converted the basement into a candy kitchen, lining the cement-block walls with sheets of gray masonite, and making shelves and a counter out of structural two-by-fours and half-inch plywood which he painted gloss-white. Three fluorescent light fixtures, hung in a row from the ceiling, buzzed slightly because his dad did the wiring himself. The concrete floor painted shiny gray was mopped with trisodium phosphate after three holidays: Valentine's Day, Easter and Christmas. A four-by-six-foot marble slab sat in the middle supported by a pair of heavy duty sawhorses also built by his father. Next to it against the wall was a ring stove, a circle of steel set over a burner which held a large copper kettle with a rounded belly. Spoons, ladles, spatulas, knives and a wood paddle big enough to propel a canoe hung on nails pounded into studding behind the masonite wall.

His father was sitting at the dipping table which, like the candy, was handmade. He had cut a round hole in the table top to accommodate a hot plate elevated off the floor by a crate. On it a double boiler was warming milk chocolate. A trail of brown lines led from the double boiler to a square piece of marble on which he did his dipping. On his left was a stack of masonite pallets lined with wax paper to hold freshly dipped turtles. Behind him on a shelf, crisscrossed stacks of pans contained dollops of caramel and pecans waiting to be dipped. He dropped dollop after dollop onto a mound of melted chocolate on the marble slab using his clean left hand and dipped it with his chocolate-laden right hand. He moved in a regular cadence and filled a pallet in less than a minute.

As usual a Lucky Strike dangled from his father's mouth. The smoke moved along the white paper cylinder and curled up his nose to his left eye, forcing him to squint and hold his head at an angle. The developing ash came perilously close to dropping into the chocolate but he always managed to turn at the last moment and flick the ash with his little finger into an old nut can sitting on the floor.

Well into his sixties, his father kept strong by the physical effort it took to make candy. Alex watched quietly as his father dipped turtles in a rhythmic motion an efficiency expert would admire. There was never a wasted movement in his labors, he worked tirelessly and without complaint producing prodigious amounts of candy. Preparing for major holidays like Easter he worked sixteen-hour days, eating sandwiches between tasks, daylight an elusive memory. Alex admired his father's big wrists, and well-developed forearms and biceps that effortlessly stirred thick caramel of cream, sugar and butter. Alex wondered how he endured the repetitive acts, the endless solitary hours, the heat of boiling simple syrup, the overpowering smell of sweet chocolate. Maybe it was better than having to be with his wife, she upstairs he down, coming together only at the end of the day to drive home tired, spent, silent and indifferent.

"Separate some turtles, I'm running out," his father said around curling smoke. He was referring to the marble slab in the middle of the basement filled with hundreds of dollops of cooling caramel on a bed of roasted pecans which he had prepared before dipping. Alex's assignment was to separate the dollops, freeing some imprisoned pecans while leaving others attached to resemble the legs and head of a turtle, and lining them up neatly on the pans his father was emptying at an impressive rate.

Making turtles required a full morning of effort:

1. Roast twenty five pounds of lightly salted whole pecans (which his father did at home in the kitchen oven and delivered to the store in the station wagon).
2. Spread the pecans evenly across the slab, touching but not overlapping.
3. Cook five quarts of heavy cream, four pounds of butter and ten pounds of sugar at 425 degrees for thirty-five minutes stirring constantly with the wood paddle.
4. Using a metal cone with a hole in the bottom and a wood dowel, release a dollar-size dollop of molten caramel on the pecans, one after the other in rapid succession until the bed is covered.
5. Separate the cooled union of caramel and pecans into turtle shapes.
6. Hand-dip the turtles.

Step five was currently Alex's responsibility. While boring and hypnotizing, it wasn't a totally vacuous exercise. Some attention was required since a single pecan was likely to be stuck to two dollops, like Siamese twins, requiring a decision as to which dollop the pecan was to be attached to, so they came out looking like turtles. Alex smiled to himself as he worked, recalling the story his father told him about the origin of turtles. The name was copyrighted by the DeMet Candy Company of Chicago years ago requiring his father to call his own turtles Pecan Roasties which evidently didn't hurt sales any because they were his father's biggest seller. DeMet was a shortening of the name Demetriou, a Greek immigrant of his father's generation who settled in Chicago and who, like his father, started a candy business and who, unlike his father, mastered the art of nomenclature.

After ten minutes the muscles in Alex's neck began to ache and he was getting the equivalent of writer's cramp in his wrist. He shook his hands in the air, trying to spring life back into them.

"I'm running out," his father said from the dipping table.

"Coming father," Alex called out, mimicking Henry Aldrich on the radio. He delivered two trays to his dad.

"Is that all? You should have ten pans filled by now."

"I'm dancing as fast as I can, Pop," Alex replied, bristling at yet another cheap shot from his old man. Somebody ought to teach him motivational techniques, like you don't knock over the beehive to get at the honey. Besides, he of all people should understand that if you work too fast you end up with lumpy misshapen hunks that have as much resemblance to a turtle as a piece of lava rock. He went back to the marble slab and did his best to increase production but he was also hampered by troubling thoughts, most important, whether his mother had said anything to his dad about Mary Lou. So far nothing in his demeanor other than constant harping suggested she had. Maybe his mother was harboring the terrible news so she could retain her Champion of Sufferers trophy.

In a perverted way he wished Mary Lou would take it upon herself to call on his parents without him. Their first reaction, apoplectic shock, would be replaced in due course by respect for her courage and strength of purpose, values they wished Alex had more of, figuring that if anyone could shape up Alex, it was this charming woman. He imagined his parents becoming disarmed by Mary Lou's optimism and cheerfulness. Wouldn't it be great to see them getting along? But Mary Lou and his parents would have to keep their rapprochement a secret so Alex wouldn't feel as if he'd been circumvented. They'd pretend it was his initiative that brought them together, and work out a secret plan so that when Alex brought Mary Lou home to what he assumed would be their inaugural meeting, his parents would react at first with theatrical shock, and presently warm up as Mary Lou's glowing personality filled the room. Giving Alex plenty of time to be amazed, they would then burst out laughing at their little joke on him, and everything would be joyous and fulfilling and delirious.... He broke away from his reverie and looked down at the pan he was working on. Only one row. He became conscious of his father slopping chocolate and anxiety gripped him. He started pulling pecans from their caramel moorings with abandon, filling the rest of the pan in record time. He rushed it over to his father.

"What's this?"

"You wanted me to work faster."

"These are no good for the Minneapolis Club."

"Once they find out how good they taste, no one will notice the difference."

"You the one talking quality?"

"You either have quality or you have speed. Which do you want?"

"Both."

Defeat replaced anxiety. "If I'm doing such a lousy job why don't you hire someone?"

"So you can fool around all of the time instead of most of the time?"

"I don't fool around. I go to class, I study. I write papers."

"All that schooling got you a job yet?"

"I have a job," Alex said with a dab of disgust. "I work in a candy store, but I don't get paid."

His father stopped dipping. With thoughtful deliberation he put out his cigarette in the nut can and turned in his chair, its stretchers straining from the torque. He looked up at his son. "You don't get paid?" he repeated in a rising voice. "You drive a car and you don't get paid? You have a room and a bed and you don't get paid? You eat home-cook food and you don't get paid?"

Alex was startled by his father's intensity. It wasn't the message, he'd heard that one often enough, it was the heat. The old man rarely raised his voice. The stoicism that made it possible for him to withstand hours of unrelieved candy making also made it possible for him to control his emotions. The only time his father shed a tear in front of Alex was when he got a letter from Greece informing him that his younger brother Gregory had died on the Haraka trail, and it unnerved the seven-year-old to see his tower of strength, his pillar of security, his rock of permanence cover his eyes and sob.

In the real world though Greeks are emotional, prone to outburst. It's a Mediterranean characteristic to argue, gesture wildly, have strong views and express them openly. But his old man was so reserved, so goddamned Scandinavian. Sometimes Alex wished he could suffer real pain from his father's hand, a slap on the cheek, a fist to the chest, even a black eye or a bruise. Something tangible, clear evidence of punishment - much easier to deal with something physical, something you can feel. Then you can fight back, let out some of your own steam. God knows Alex had stored up enough to power a locomotive.

On the bright side his old man's outburst did give Alex the opening he was looking for. "Pop," he said, "You should get upset more often. It does me good to have you bawl me out. Makes me realize I can't go on like this, sponging off you and mom. It's high time I take responsibility for myself."

Theodore got up from his chair and walked over to the marble slab, holding his dipping hand skyward, and studied the remaining pecan clusters like a general examining troop movements on a battle situation table.

"Dad, are you listening to me?"

"I heard it before."

"This time it's different. I'm moving out of the house."

"Pick up the turtles first."

"Dad, I'm not kidding."

"Neither am I." He went back to dipping.

Upset that he wasn't being taken seriously (So what else is new?), Alex grabbed an empty pan and slammed it down on the slab. Corn starch in the bottom of the pan to keep the candy from sticking rose up and dusted the front of his pants . "Damn," he said. He filled three pans and brought them to the dipping table where his father methodically plopped the turtles upside down in the melted chocolate, turned them over and placed them on a pallet to dry.

"I'll bet your father didn't talk to you like that," Alex said, watching. "What did he say to you when you left for Turkey?"

His father stopped dipping and stared at the chocolate-speckled wall opposite the table as if looking back to his own youth. "He say goodby."

"Come on, Pop, He must have cried, hugged you."

"No."

"You must have cried."

"No."

Alex was awed. "You were only fifteen."

"I know."

"That took courage."

His father went back to dipping. "No," he said, "courage I learn later."

"You don't learn courage, Dad. You either have it or you don't."

"Life teach you courage."

Alex thought about this as he filled more pans. Nothing in his life so far had taught him courage. And what he intended doing, moving out of the house, did not require that either. Grit maybe but not courage. He brought the pans to the dipping table. "You know, Dad, if you had kicked me out of the house the way your father did, I'd be a lot better off."

"What's keeping you?"

Alex ignored the taunt. "Will you help me stand up to ma?"

He had called his father's bluff. Theodore shifted uneasily on his padded seat, worn to his shape like a hollow victim of Pompeii. "Your mother is sick," he said.

"She's always sick," Alex replied. "You really don't want me to move out because then you'll have to deal with her all by yourself."

"We talk about this later. Now is not a good time."

"There is never a good time."

Using his clean hand, Theodore reached for the pack of Luckies and the matchbook on the shelf next to the dipping table. With the skill of long, solitary practice, he pinned the matchbook to the table with his elbow and pulled a match from the cluster, striking it on the carbon strip in one fluid motion. In a second he was puffing smoke in the air. "You think your mother is the problem?"

"You know she is."

His father looked sharply at Alex. "She is sick because of you."

Alex stared up at the ceiling, at the cobwebs hanging in the corner. "I know, I know. I've heard that before."

"How you think she feel after she talk to Mrs. Pappathos?"

Alex sighed. So his mother had talked to dad after all. He returned to the marble slab and filled the last tray. "It was pretty rotten of Tony to rat on me. None of his damned business."

"He's a good boy," his father said, the implication being that Alex was not. He stopped dipping and rested his dipping wrist on the edge of the table. "I don't say much and that's my fault, so pay attention to what I say now. When you were little, Father Trainer came to the restaurant in Waseca. He wasn't interested in my cooking he was interested in you. Ted, he say to me, your boy needs a Christian education but he is not getting one. He say I should bring you to Sacred Heart. So what do I do? I put you in the car and take you to St John the Apostle on the other side of Clear Lake. The Episcopal Church. You remember that?"

Alex remembered it all right, a country church like the kind you see in a Norman Rockwell painting, white clapboard against a field of alfalfa, a narrow steeple with Gothic openings in the belfry, and Gothic shaped windows. Inside, the central aisle had a grate and when you walked over it heat warmed your ankles from the coal furnace in the cellar. The altar was a small stage on which he once participated in an Advent Tableau dressed like a shepherd. He was given a framed picture of Jesus like all the other kids. He still had his. That Advent program was the only time his parents ever set foot in the church.

"Because I go to this trouble when you were little," he continued, "you think I still don't worry you might get mixed up with a Katholiki?"

“I'm not mixed up," Alex said. "Besides what's wrong with Catholics? My best pal in Waseca was Mike Callahan. He's Catholic."

"That's different."

"It's ok to play with a Catholic as long as I don't marry one?"

His father's reaction was just like his mother's. The word marry made him tense. "Forget her, Taki." He used the Greek diminutive for his name. His parents were both appealing to him using boyhood references. They probably never wanted him to grow up, they only wanted to protect him from the dangers and heartbreak of adulthood. They didn't have to worry. After his debacle at Richard's even Mary Lou didn't think he was a grownup.

"You don’t have to worry, Pop, there's nothing between us."

"You no see her again?"

"It's over."

"You promise."

Alex swallowed as he said, "I promise." But he did not promise that he would not dream of her, ache in his groin for her, cruise by her sister's house to get a clandestine glimpse of her. "But I'm still moving out."

"Where you live?" his father asked suspiciously.

"Don't worry, Dad, not with her," (he still could not bring himself to mention Mary Lou's name in front of his parents). Still, he wished he could live with her. No more sneaking around, no more steamed up car windows, no more feeling like an escaped criminal. "I just want to be on my own. I'd be better off living under a bridge than in your house."

"Your house too!" his dad thundered loud enough to be heard upstairs, probably rattling his mother.

"It's not a house, it's a prison. You and ma are the guards and Tony is your informant. I can't do anything right, I can't please you no matter how hard I try. All I hear is criticism. How do you suppose that makes me feel?"

"Don't throw your life away," he pleaded.

"You're throwing it away for me, Pop!"

Theodore snuffed out his cigarette in the nut can and continued dipping in silence until he was finished. He used a putty knife to scrape remaining chocolate from the marble slab and from his dipping hand, dropping the remnants into the double boiler. He bent down to switch off the burner under the table, went to the sink and washed his hands.

THE EURASIAN

MEMORANDUM

From: Commander Destroyer Squadron One
To: Commanding Officer, USS Robert B Sprague DD884
Subj: Squadron Commander's Quarters (Living and Working Conditions in the)
Ref: (a) ComDesRon One Memo to the CO, USS Craig T Sumner
(b) ComDesRon One Memo to the CO, USS Robert B Sprague

1. I wish to inform you that I have noticed no appreciable change in the noise and traffic around my quarters since I shifted my pennant to your ship, and that I have personally made numerous requests on your OOD and various of your personnel to stop this incessant, needless and avoidable noise around my quarters.

2. This is my last request to you in this matter, and I have made my last personal effort to stop this needless noise and traffic on your ship.

3. Take appropriate action.

B. Katz
Commodore

Poulos carried the memo and its carbons to the Commodore's quarters forward of the chart house, from which most of the noise the

Commodore was complaining about had been emanating. He knocked lightly on his door. "What is it?" a voice snarled from within.

"Your memo is ready for signing, sir."

The door burst open and Commodore Katz, a squat man with a perpetual sneer stitched to his mouth, snapped it from Poulos's hand. His stateroom reeked from the smoke of a thousand cigars. One was clamped between his teeth. He puffed on it as he examined the memo Poulos had typed for him. He went to his desk and reread the memo several more times. Poulos wondered if he would spend that much time on a declaration of war. Finally satisfied that it properly expressed his irritation, he signed it with his initials. "Hand deliver the original to Captain Blessing right away and place the carbon in my personal file."

"Should I also put a copy in the ship's file, sir?" Poulos had included an extra carbon just in case.

Katz tore up the extra carbon into small bits and let them trickle through his fingers into his waste basket. "Does this look like I want a copy in the ship's file?" He slammed the door in Poulos's face.

The ships of DESDIV 1 steamed through the Tsugaru Straits. The unit was engaged in joint Anti-Submarine Warfare training exercises with a task group consisting of two submarines, a carrier escort and a British destroyer.

Poulos had the eight to twelve watch in the Combat Information Center. The dimly lit radar room was packed with electronic tracking gear. Chartreuse radar scopes followed the movement of surface vessels. Lines of light swept like second hands around the scopes' faces, illuminating blips in their wake.

Commodore Katz stood over a Plexiglas charting table lighted from beneath. Commander Rauenzahn, the Exec, was standing next to him. They were using grease pencils to mark navigational positions. The ships of DESDIV 1 appeared as four blips on the radar screens, moving in orderly fashion under the command of Commodore Bernard Katz. His code name was Flapper. The warships in the training exercise were not the only vessels being tracked. The radar revealed dozens of other, much smaller blips sprinkled randomly like dandruff on a dark jacket: fishing boats that made navigating in the black, choppy waters hazardous. Some of them were North Korean spy ships tracking the squadrons' movements. Whatever their mission, catching haddock or surveilling warships, they were a nuisance. In order to avoid accidents, each ship had the authority to maneuver independently to keep from accidentally ramming one of the bobbing fishing boats, perhaps igniting an international crisis.

The radio circuits were filled with routine course changes. "Slocum this is Flapper. Have contact zero one zero, four point two miles on a collision course. Will maneuver independently to avoid. Over."

"Flapper this is Slocum, Roger, out."

The boredom was enough to make Poulos doze off on his feet, a trick he had learned from Scotty. Stand at least six inches from the bulkhead with knees locked and lean back, preferably against a vertical radiator. The warmth would move up Poulos's back, relaxing him into a kind of torpor. The large talker's earphones all but hid his face and he was able to fake alertness when he was actually dozing. Whenever someone came on the line, the voice brought him to attention.

During the training exercise, the ships and U-boats were assigned the same code name, Fleming, followed by a different number. Poulos's destroyer, the Sprague, was Fleming 4. The task group as a whole was known as Veritable. The code name for the leader was Magnify, a designation reassigned every twenty-four hours. This night the captain of the British destroyer was Magnify. The task group used a single radio circuit, Screen Common, to stay in voice contact with one another, referring to themselves individually as Fleming and collectively as Veritable, as in "Veritable, this is Fleming 4, execute to follow zero five zero. Standby, execute."

A problem developed because of the dozens of fishing boats that dotted the radar screens. There were so many avoidance course changes announced over the circuit that it was beginning to sound like a fraternity party. Standing jokes developed, and there was more levity than Commodore Katz could manage. Even though he wasn't Magnify, he asserted his presence anyway and announced: "Fleming 4 to Veritable, there must be more circuit discipline and less unnecessary conversation." He ended with "Over" which required each ship and the two U-boats to Roger-that. This cluttered the circuit even more.

As leader, Magnify was obviously miffed. It was the responsibility of the Captain of the British destroyer to monitor circuit discipline, not the Commodore. Magnify responded stiffly. "Fleming 4, your request for circuit discipline is duly noted."

A few minutes later Katz came on the line again, this time to send a routine message to the Captain of the Yarnall, "Fleming 2 this is Fleming 4..."

He was suddenly cut off by Magnify. "Fleming 4 this is Magnify," the distinctly British voice said from the CIC loudspeaker. "Hereafter, any message sent over Screen Common must first have permission from Magnify before transmitting, including inter-division traffic." He added "over and out," meaning this was the final word on the subject and no

Roger was required.

The CIC room on the Sprague went dead quiet. A junior Brit skipper had pulled rank on a Commodore of the United States Navy. Katz was furious. He paced the tight confines of CIC muttering, "Goddamn Limey, who the fuck does he think he is?"

The crew sucked in their stomachs and pushed themselves against the bulkhead to stay out of his way.

Finally, Katz snapped the Screen Common switch open and snarled into the microphone: "Magnify, this is Fleming 4. I wish to continue my message to Fleming 2. Do I have your permission? Over."

The response was immediate and stunning. "This is Magnify. Wait. Out."

The sonovafucking Brit was putting the Commodore on hold!

The strained silence in CIC continued, the only sound coming from the fans whirring heat off the radar screens. The Commodore placed an unlit cigar in his mouth and chomped on it as he waited for Magnify to grant permission.

Presently the radio came alive again. "Fleming 4, this is Magnify. Reference use of Screen Common to send routine messages to ships in your division. Inasmuch as you yourself demanded circuit discipline, we therefore follow your lead and deny your request to transmit. Use signal lights. Out."

Katz became livid. He bit all the way through his cigar and spat out the chewed end into the trash receptacle. "Get the name of that fucking captain," he said to Rauenzahn. "I'll have his ass for breakfast."

"Sir, he's British."

"We beat the shit out of them in the Revolution, didn't we?"

"That was nearly two hundred years ago, sir."

The Commodore had to have the last word. He shouted into the open microphone for all the ships to hear, "Magnify this Commodore Bernard H. Katz of the United States Navy. If I want to talk on Screen Common I'll talk on Screen Common and no chicken-shit captain of a has-been British navy is going to tell me I can't. Got that?"

The message came back stiffly, "Raw-ther."

After the training exercise, the Sprague and her sister ships arrived at dawn in Hong Kong, steaming slowly into the narrow harbor separating mainland Kowloon and the island of Hong Kong in the South China Sea. They entered single file as sampans with roofs of mats came out to greet them. The high-sterned boats darted like water bugs, propelled by dark-skinned oarers who twisted their sculls back and forth. Intermingled with the sampans were junks with bamboo sails. In minutes the sleek gray warships of the American navy were surrounded by the dirty boats bumping one another for position. The Chinese waved for attention and held up signs advertising Harris Tweed Sam Chu Pedder St; American Steak Jimmy's Kitchen nr. Queens Theater; Hong Kong Tours 110 Peninsula Hotel. Chinese boys jumped into the water to dive for coins tossed overboard by the sailors. They wore one-piece trunks made from a single length of cloth looped around their legs. The end piece was drawn up from the crotch and stuffed inside the waistband.

Positioned several hundred yards apart, the quartet of destroyers dropped anchor for their first liberty in nearly two months. They shared the busy harbor with other American ships plus British navy vessels including destroyers, gunboats and carrier escorts, as well as an international armada of freighters. Seen from the decks of the Sprague, Hong Kong was a modern city of gleaming buildings terraced along a hill. It was also a city of refugees. Its shoreline jammed with sampans and a shanty town was eating at its edges--home for the tens of thousands of refugees who had fled Mainland China when the Communists took control.

Poulos had become a minor expert on Hong Kong, having spent a week preparing a twenty-page mimeographed handbook of tips on where to go, what to do, and what to avoid. He had worked hard on the project to get back into the good graces of Ltjg Radinger. Poulos not only wrote and edited the booklet, he also designed the cover. Hong was spelled out across the top and Kong ran vertically down the right border. The letters were curved to resemble Chinese characters. He also drew an outline of a pagoda to frame the name of the ship, USS Sprague DD 884, which was stepped diagonally down the center. Even Captain Blessing commented on how nice it looked.

Poulos used material supplied by the information office of CINCPACFLT, but he rewrote its officialese so it would read more like a travel brochure than a boring naval directive:

Hong Kong today is a haven for hundreds of thousands of refugees from Communist-held China. Since the victory of Communist forces on the Chinese mainland, the population of Hong Kong has skyrocketed from 800,000 to 2,000,000. While the overwhelming majority of the population is Chinese, the government is under the control of the British. As in all foreign ports, you are a guest. The impression you make on your British hosts is an important one. If this impression is positive your host will welcome you warmly and do his best to entertain you. If this impression is a poor one you will probably have a hard time enjoying yourself, and might well end up in a lot of trouble; remember the standards you've been brought up to believe in, and don't do anything or say anything you wouldn't do or say in your own home town. You will find the British are extraordinarily polite, and they will do everything possible to make your visit to Hong Kong a pleasant experience.

The British coxswain swung his water taxi parallel to the Sprague's fantail and threw the engine quickly into reverse. Angry water spewed out from under the sides of the flat-bottom boat as it slipped neatly to a stop, nudging the bumpers protecting the ship's hull. Using his throttle the coxswain expertly kept the taxi close to the sea ladder so that a gaggle of chattering, excited sailors could climb down and jump in. The coxswain displayed a cocky grin. They were a proud lot, these sea drivers, no matter whose navy they belonged to.

Poulos, Witter, Scotty and Browning were in the third wave to catch a water taxi to Star Pier. There was a slight breeze and a sunny sky. The shore-bound sailors wore their summer whites in Hong Kong's sub-tropical climate. Shouts of pleasure and anticipation filled the air as they crowded onto the landing. Instantly they were besieged by rickshaw drivers, peddlers, and children swarming like drones around their queen. Little hands begged for a coin or a cigarette. The sailors had been cautioned about pickpockets and their skill with a razor blade, Every dirty-faced urchin was a threat.

The four sailors pushed their way past Conaught Road, the thoroughfare paralleling the harbor, and into Hong Kong's tenderloin. It seemed that every building they passed was a financial center: Bank of Canton, French Bank, Bank of East Asia, Bank of China, Shanghai Bank. There were other buildings, of course, including fine hotels and government offices, and they all had in common the stiffly proper demeanor one associates with British rule, contrasting sharply with the chaotic mass of humanity milling in the streets and boulevards: pedestrians, red-painted rickshaws with convertible tops, open-air vendors hawking fish and produce, not to mention beggars and traffic police on every corner. White Rolls Royces and Bentleys crawled amongst this flotsam and jetsam, the aristocratic beeps of their horns lost in the noise of the masses.

Poulos considered himself fortunate that he was given liberty after his fracas with Clayton. It was ship's talk for days, in the chow line, on watch, during turn-to hours. He had attained a kind of celebrity status. The attention changed his attitude, and he bore down on his work. The Captain's compliment on the Hong Kong booklet went a long way toward convincing Radinger he should let Poulos visit the city he had written about. This concession, however, did not mean he was no longer on his shitlist.

As for Clayton, the event seemed to mark a turning point. He never spoke much before and now he hardly spoke at all. His attention to detail suffered. He turned in logs and transfer orders, which had to be letter-perfect, with sloppy erasures. He began to miss deadlines. He lost interest in neatness. Instead of shaving every morning he shaved intermittently, sometimes letting it go for a long-enough period so that everyone thought he was growing a beard. He missed meals and became even thinner. His eyes sunk deeper into their sockets and an unhealthy pallor covered his skin. Although he didn't say anything, Radinger was beginning to worry about Clayton's sanity.

No sooner had Clayton retched all over the deck than Radinger and Gildenhall emerged from the fore and aft passageway; Gildenhall tall and neat, Radinger short and rumpled.

"Clear the decks!" Radinger hollered and carefully picked his way around what was left of Clayton's lunch. He led Clayton to the railing in case there was anything else that had to come up. Then Clayton took the slop bucket he had been using to clean the Ship's Office. He sloshed his vomit toward the scuppers which emptied it into the sea. Radinger let him go below to wash up.

Meanwhile Gildenhall pulled Poulos into the Ship's Office. He looked around at the mess. "What the fuck happened here?"

"We got into an argument over the manuals. One thing led to another and pretty soon we were fighting over them."

Gildenhall shook his head in disbelief. "His face was covered with soot."

"I punched the dust bag."

Gildenhall glanced up at the dirty piece of cloth now devoid of its contents, and made a face of disgust. "When was that thing last emptied?"

"Probably never, sir, till now."

"Jesus, no wonder he heaved."

"He kept quoting scripture on me."

"Scripture?"

"Sayings from the Old Testament."

"You don't have to tell me what scripture is, Poulos. Just tell me why you had a fight."

"He was doing it to show me up, Lieutenant." It sounded laughable in the telling.

"Is that why you smeared him with dust?"

"He thinks he's the only one who knows the Bible."

"I suppose you do."

"Well, sir, I studied the Old Testament in a course on comparative religions."

"I warned you not to flaunt your education."

"I had to defend myself, didn't I? All I did was quote scripture back at him."

Gildenhall shook his head. "Is this why I became a naval officer?"

They joined Radinger on the main deck. "What do you think, Lieutenant?" Gildenhall asked him.

"Fighting aboard ship is a serious offense."

"I'm not sure a tug of war over manuals constitutes fighting."

"I'd have to check UCMJ before answering that one."

"I doubt if manual tugging is in there," Gildenhall replied.

Radinger shifted his fleshy weight from one foot to the other. Even though he knew Gildenhall was shitting him, he had to be careful not to reply in kind and upstage a superior officer. There might be other opportunities to get even with him but this was not one of them. "So what do you have in mind?" he asked passing the onus back to Gildenhall. "How about having the yeomen determine their own punishment? Poulos can fill out Clayton's violation report, and Clayton can fill out Poulos's."

Radinger stared at Gildenhall as if he'd been handed a turd.

Poulos and his shipmates sought out Jimmy Loo's tailor shop on Bonham Strand East. Hong Kong was legendary for tailored clothing, and the first thing they wanted to do was get fitted for sport coats and suits which would be delivered to the ship in less than two days. One dollar American was worth $5.50 Hong Kong, and no other place in the world had better silk and wool tweed. Jimmy met them at the door with bottles of warm beer. He was short and round and had a permanent grin on his face. His showroom was filled with bolts of cloth and smelled of moth balls. He specialized in Harris tweed but he also carried camel's hair, cheviot, tropical worsted, sharkskin and whipcord, as well as fine-woven cashmere, silk and shantung. Poulos had himself fitted for a speckled gray Harris tweed sport coat and dark gray flannel slacks. Jimmy and his assistants briskly measured him in front of a three-way mirror, and wrote numbers on a ruled order form. Poulos paid fifty Hong Kong dollars down with another hundred due on delivery, about $32 American. Witter selected a solid blue weave for his sport coat. Anything on him would look good. Scotty and Browning ordered suits and cashmere sweaters. Browning also wanted to order a pair of Hong Kong shoes. Jimmy Loo recommended Peter See Leather Merchant right next door where Browning ordered a pair of ankle-high boots of brown kangaroo leather. Peter See made a tracing of Browning's feet. He admired the Parker 51 pen clipped to Browning's jumper pocket. Browning gave it to him in exchange for the shoes. Their purchases would be delivered tomorrow afternoon to the USS Robert B Sprague, anchorage 16 Charlie.

Out on the street again they searched for a restaurant with an American bill of fare. They asked a group of British sailors for an opinion and the consensus favored Tee-Bone's across from the Kayanully Building. They climbed into two rickshaws and went to lunch. At the restaurant, festooned with brightly colored paper dragons hanging from a waffled ceiling, they ordered chicken livers in cocktail sauce for appetizers, and for the main course, 16-ounce New York steaks smothered in mushrooms. The steaks were fried in fish oil and they tasted awful. Even a bottle of burgundy failed to overcome the fishy flavor. They finished their disappointing lunch with peach melba and coffee.

Outside once again, they wandered along streets named Stanley and Willington, Gloucester and Wardley, and stopped to watch a cricket match being played out on a large field in the center of town. Tall, slender, elegant British subjects wearing immaculate white slacks and white shirts with their sleeves rolled up played almost languidly. The sailors quickly grew bored and headed for the Tiger Balm Gardens where they took pictures of each other with Scotty's Brownie, crouching under fierce-looking gargoyle sculptures hanging over the paths. By now they had left the business district behind them. After wandering around some more, they took a ride on the Peak Tramway, a funicular railway whose summit station provided a breathtaking view of Hong Kong, its neighboring islands, the Kowloon peninsula and the distant mountains of Communist China. What was also painfully visible this high up were the squalid shacks and dirt streets of the refugee encampments. Poulos wondered aloud what would happen to all those people. Scotty said, "You can't worry about them. They're the crap of life."

They walked from the tram station into the countryside and found an abandoned building, a rubbled shell of stone walls. They sat at its base for a while, resting and smoking.

"Anyone want to climb to the top?" Witter asked presently. "We can see Hong Kong better from up there." He pointed to a section that was like a parapet some twenty-five feet high.

Browning studied the piles of stone they would need to climb. "I don't want to mess up my shoes." They were highly polished.

"In Catholic school," Witter said, “we stood close to girls to see a reflection of their bloomers in our shoes.”

Browning maneuvered his shoes till he could see his face shining back at him. "I'll be damned."

“I used to work in a bloomer factory,” Scotty said.

“Really?” Browning said, getting sucked in.

“Yeah, I was pulling down a hundred a week.”

When the guffawing subsided, Poulos asked Witter, "So you're Catholic?" He was surprised that he and Mary Lou shared the same religion. On Witter it did not seem so onerous.

Witter reached inside his jumper and pulled out his name tags. "There's a C under my serial number."

"How come we have two tags?"

"One stays with your records; the other goes home with your body."

"Not mine, I hope."

"What's on yours?" Witter asked Poulos. "O for Orthodox?"

"There's only P for Protestant and C for Catholic." Browning said.

"What about A for Atheist." Scotty said.

"You gotta be a C or a P."

"What if you're a Jew?"

"J for Jack off," Scotty said.

They all laughed.

"Hey, Poulos," Witter said, "you a P or a C?"

"He's a J," Scotty said.

"Fuck you, Scotty."

"Let's have a look, then.”

"It's a P."

"Show it to us."

"I told you it's a P. Don't you believe me?"

Scotty and Browning held out their name tags. There were Ps stamped on theirs. "We showed ours, now you have to show yours." They made leering faces.

"This is kid stuff," Poulos said. He reached inside his jumper and brought out his dog tags. "See?"

"What's that hanging from the chain?" Witter asked. "That’s a wedding ring, small, what a woman would wear."

Poulos wished now he hadn’t been so willing to show his tags.

Browning asked, "Who does that belong to?"

"It's a keepsake."

"Your mom died?"

Poulos let the assumption ride. He stood. "Let's climb up the building."

Witter and Scotty followed Poulos, working their way up a slope of rubble.

Browning watched from the ground. "I don't want to wreck my shoes."

"Nothing will happen to your goddamned shoes," Witter called down.

"Ok, ok, wait up." Browning was slow, studying each step before taking it, careful not to mar his shine.

They reached a wide ledge with notches that once supported wood roof beams. A fire must have burned the wood, leaving the shell of stone, like the ruins of a medieval castle. The building was of Western architecture with arched openings where windows had been. Maybe it served as a warehouse or factory. Poulos knew from his research that Europe opened trade with China 300 years ago although Hong Kong remained a tiny fishing village and a haven for smugglers until the nineteenth century. The building probably dated to that time.

The sailors daringly picked their way along a ledge less than three feet wide and felt the adrenaline rush that comes from taking risks.

"We have reached the summit," Witter announced like a mountain climber.

The full breadth of Hong Kong lay below them. It was a breathtaking sight. Scotty took snapshots with his Brownie. He had difficulty maintaining his balance, and it was nerve-wracking to watch him sway with the camera to his eye. He pretended to stumble.

"Let's get down," Witter said, "before Scotty kills himself."

Browning began to descend and accidentally dislodged a rock that fell to the ground. "Damn! I just scuffed my shoe."

"I'll buy you a shine," Scotty said, and kicked another rock loose to let Browning know what he thought of shoes. This rock was much larger, and tumbled down the slope of rubble below them, clattering as it fell. The sound echoed inside the shell.

"Hear that?" Scotty said and kicked another one.

In a moment, Witter and Poulos joined him, sending rock after rock bouncing to the ground. The echoing made it seem as if the entire building were collapsing. As they played kick the stone, immersed in their fun, a family of refugees suddenly emerged from a corner of the building where the rubble had provided a hidden shelter. Holding their arms over their heads, they ran toward a wooded area some hundred yards away. Poulos counted six people, three of them children. One woman was carrying an infant. They were dressed in tatters and had rags wrapped around their feet.

"There are people down there!" he shouted.

Scotty continued kicking rocks off the ledge. "Shit, I didn't hit a single one."

The sailors descended from the ledge in shameful silence and approached the hill of rubble the refugees called home. A shelter had been dug out of the pile. A lean-to roof was supported by trunks of saplings on which stones were carefully piled. It was so well-camouflaged they never would have seen it if the refugees hadn't run from it. One at a time the sailors bent over and peeked in. There were reed mats on the dirt floor. A vegetable crate served as a table. An unlit candle sat on the crate, secured by its own wax. A bundle was tied in a knot. It probably held their dinner. There was an air of tidiness in the bare surroundings.

"How can so many people live in such a tiny hole?" Browning asked.

"We scared them away." Poulos was filled with remorse. All he could think of was the terrified family running from the big sailors dropping rocks on them. "They had little kids. Did you see the baby?" He pulled Hong Kong bills from his jumper pocket.

"What are you doing?" Scotty asked.

"I'm leaving money." He took a small stone as a weight and left the bills on the vegetable crate.

Scotty shook his head. "We kill gooks in Korea and here you give them money."

"They are not gooks, they are Chinese."

"A gook's a gook."

They walked back to the tram station for the trip down. Nobody had much to say. It was not until they re-entered the bustling city streets and got shoeshines that the sailors loosened up, as though their newly polished shoes had cleared them of guilt. Yet the image of the fleeing refugees continued to haunt Poulos. The last time he left a large sum of money behind was at Richard's, and for the worst of motives: to indulge a bruised ego. Maybe he had redeemed himself a little bit.

"Still thinking about those people?" Witter asked as they walked along the sidewalk.

He nodded.

"They probably found the money by now. How much did you leave them?"`

"A hundred dollars Hong Kong."

Scotty whistled. "They're the luckiest gooks in the Far East."

The sun set over China's mainland. The sky darkened and neon came on all over the city. Bright signs dazzled the eye. Color flashed and pulsated with such intensity they reflected off the faces of passersby. The sailors looked for a place to eat, this time avoiding restaurants boasting

American food. They settled on the Peking Duck in the Hennessey Hotel. The restaurant had a hushed atmosphere with mirrors framed in dark cherry wood, white tablecloths, fine china and silverware. The Chinese waiters wore black tunics and starched shirts and carried folded napkins over their arms. The sailors were on their best behavior, recalling the admonitions in the booklet Alex had prepared about avoiding unflattering nicknames (like gook) or slang expressions (like fuck you).

After dinner Scotty covered his mouth and allowed a discrete belch to escape between his fingers. "Nice meal, and I don't even like Chinese."

In the lobby they bought the Hong Kong evening newspaper and checked the entertainment section for something to do. They had to be back on board ship at 0100 hours and it was only 2100.

"How about this?" Browning said, pointing to an ad for the Hong Kong Jockey Club.

"That's off limits to us swabbies," Scotty said. He read aloud, affecting a snooty British accent: "To participate in the benefits of the Club premises call at the office of our secretary, Windsor House, 2nd floor on the way to request a complimentary badge."

They hooted.

"What about this one?" Scotty said, "Club Lido Dance Hall, Des Veaux Road Central. Get this: Dancing girls furnished per hourly rate."

An animated discussion carried them out into the street where a line of rickshaws waited for fares. They walked to the front of the line.

"Club Lido, my good man," Scotty said to the lead driver, a wiry Chinese dressed in a sport shirt three sizes too large and baggy shorts. Poulos and Scotty rode together and Witter and Browning followed. The dance hall was so close they could have walked. Scotty paid the driver and they went inside. Club Lido was as large as a warehouse and packed with American and British sailors and Chinese girls, all shrouded in cigarette smoke. Somewhere beyond the haze a live band was playing American pop tunes. There was a long bar against one wall and tables around the perimeter of the dance floor. They headed for the bar and got separated in the crowd; Poulos found Scotty but Witter and Browning had disappeared in a sea of white uniforms.

As they stood in line to buy drinks two Chinese girls came up to them.

"You big fella," one said, attaching herself to Poulos. She was dressed in bright red silk. Her waist was so small he could have circled it with his hands. She was barely five feet tall, and did not appear to be very young. The girl who picked Scotty was only slightly taller and had the same flat facial features as her companion.

"Why do Chinks all look alike?" Scotty asked rhetorically.

Poulos's girl clung to his arm. "My name Betty." She pulled him over to a table with two empty chairs. She signaled a waiter and he came right over as if they were in league with each other. "You buy me drink plus two Hong Kong dollar for one hour."

He ordered two gin fizzes.

Betty got up. "We dance now." The floor was crowded and hot.

"You like?" She looked up as if trying to see the top of a skyscraper

"Nice," Alex called down.

After the set they returned to the table and their drinks were waiting for them. As they sipped through straws Betty talked about herself. She was born in Peking. Her parents sent her to Hong Kong in 1936 to escape the Japanese soldiers, only to have them show up in Hong Kong as occupying forces during World War II. She hadn't seen her parents since she was seventeen. She wanted to know the name of his ship and where they were headed after leaving Hong Kong. Poulos was cautious. The handbook was very specific about giving information:

Rest assured that there are plenty of Communist spies around. Not all of these are men. Some of the most deadly and efficient agents are members of the feminine sex. They may seem only innocently curious, interested in your doings, how your ship operates, what kind of weapons it uses, where it came from where it is going. Don't tell them! These bits of information may seem unimportant but they can add up to valuable intelligence which can be used to send you to that well-known locker run by Davy Jones.

Poulos was disappointed the Communists didn't have a better-looking spy than Betty. The waiter brought another round of drinks. Poulos hadn't ordered them. Betty apparently was working the tab. The second gin fizz began to have an effect on his head. It was sweet and strong. The air was stale and smoky. Betty was homely. And he was concerned Scotty might be giving his date an earful. He stood up.

"Where you go?"

"Look for my buddy," he said

Betty followed right behind him. Poulos finally found Scotty at a table near the bandstand. The din made talking difficult. He bent down and shouted in Scotty's ear, "Let's find Dave and A. John and shove off."

"We just got here," Scotty shouted back. He had his arm around his girl. "I paid an hour for her and we've only been here thirty minutes."

Poulos looked at her. "She isn't worth more than thirty minutes."

"When you find them come back to get me."

In Poulos's fizzed state, every American sailor looked the same, just like the Chinese, and after ten minutes he gave up and returned to Scotty's table. "I can't find them."

"Did you look?"

"Shit, how many sailors are in here, a thousand? You think you can find them go look yourself."

Scotty finished his drink. "Never mind, I'm getting bored. Let's get out of here."

Poulos paid for the drinks and his hour with Betty. She tucked the bills into her bony cleavage and followed him out to the sidewalk. "You not like?"

"Too crowded."

She tugged at his arm. "You come back, ok? You come back, ask for Betty, number 56."

As they walked away Poulos asked Scotty, "What was your girl's number?"

"Sixty nine."

They strolled along Des Veaux, past the supreme court building, the Prince's building, a number of banks. They were feeling more familiar with the city and beginning to get their bearings. Behind them was Victoria where they had watched the cricket players and beyond that, in sharp contrast, began the subdivision of squatters' shacks. To their right a few blocks away was the Peak Tram Station and next to it Hong Kong's Church of England Cathedral.

A driver pulling an empty rickshaw drew alongside and followed them as they walked. "Eurasia girls," he called. "Very pretty. Me take." Poulos waved the driver off and kept walking but Scotty went over to him. Poulos stopped and pedestrians flowed around him. He worked his way cross current to where Scotty stood at the curb. The driver wore a huge smile. He was missing several teeth and those that remained were black. He was thin and wiry, typical of his trade. A soiled blue sailor cap with a narrow bill was kept at a jaunty angle over his forehead.

"Those girls at the Lido were ugly," Scotty said. "I'd like to see some decent nookie while I'm here."

"Go ahead. I'll head back to the ship."

"You leaving your buddy behind?"

"Eurasia girls cherry," the driver said.

"Oh sure," Scotty said and winked. He was having trouble keeping one eye closed and the other open.

"How many drinks did you have back there?"

"Not enough to forget how horny I am."

"I'm not interested in getting laid."

"You don't have to. Wait for me in the rickshaw." Scotty climbed in. "Coming? If you know what I mean?"

"Just for the ride." He didn't want to wander the streets alone.

The rickshaw creaked on its springs. The driver made a U-turn and jogged down Des Veaux Road. They passed Victoria Barracks and entered a darkened area.

Poulos started worrying. "Hey, driver, this off limits?"

The driver shook his head. Between breaths he called out, "No worry, no worry. Ok, ok."

Poulos was not sure. At an intersection he spotted two signs: Blue Poole Road and Tsum Wun Street. He remembered that they were among the streets in the out of bounds areas listed in the booklet. The driver went down Blue Poole and the traffic thinned. To their right, a short block away, the edge of the slums could be seen. The hillside of hovels was dark except for an occasional flickering lamp. The driver then turned right on Singwee Road and stopped next to a house with a veranda. Several girls in sheer white kimonos sat on deck chairs smoking cigarettes. Paper lanterns hung at the corners of the veranda and lined the sidewalk leading to the house.

Scotty jumped out and stood by the rickshaw. "You wait here with my buddy."

"Trip here free. Trip back you pay."

"Scotty, this area is off limits. I don't see any other sailors around."

"We're here now."

A Chinese woman of indeterminate age came down the steps to meet them. She was dressed in a heavily brocaded, silk kimono with a high collar. Her hair was pulled back tightly and hung in a long braid down her back. "Welcome to Mama Naffi," she said, bowing.

Poulos guessed Naffi was pidgin for navy. He could see the outlines of her hands joined together under the kimono. "You have no need to worry. I run a clean house."

She walked back to the veranda. Scotty followed, rubbing his hands in anticipation.

The madam turned and said to Poulos: "Very uncomfortable sitting in a parked rickshaw."

She was right. The driver had set his handle bars on the ground and Poulos had to prop his legs to keep from sliding off the seat. He climbed down and joined Scotty on the veranda. Close up, he could see that the girls were very young, some in their early teens. One gave her chair to him. A manservant came out of the house with tea.

Scotty was all smiles and gonads. "What did I tell you? Aren't they knockouts?" He chose a slender girl who looked all of fourteen. They went into the house.

Poulos sat in the still night and sipped tea. It was strong.

The madam said, "You are lonely for a girl back home?"

He thought of Mary Lou but didn't say anything.

"You prefer boys?"

The question was meant to provoke him. "Of course not."

Mama Naffi made a subtle move with her head. The girls rose from their seats and moved languidly past him. One caught his eye. Poulos wondered why Scotty hadn't taken her. Her skin was almost as white as the silk of her garment. When she walked by her fingers brushed his hair.

"You like?"

"Is her name Betty number 56?"

Mamma Naffi was offended. “We are a proud house here, no trashy bar girls. Her name is Natasha.”

"That's Russian."

"She has Russian blood."

Natasha smiled at Poulos. Her teeth were shiny and white. She wore no lipstick.

"The evening is young," Mama Naffi encouraged.

"And so is the girl."

The madam threw her head back in laughter. The girls giggled.

Natasha sat on the arm of Poulos's chair and leaned over. Her breath touched his hair. He felt himself rise. Natasha took notice. She began to massage his shoulders. Her fingers were unbelievably sensitive. Mama Naffi smiled benignly. Natasha took Poulos by the hand and tugged slightly. He got out of the chair and followed her into the house. They walked down a narrow hallway and entered a small delicate room, like a sanctuary, its space separated by an oriental screen. Somewhere a romantic ballad played scratchily on a phonograph. She led him behind the screen and crouched on a mattress. On a low table with a mosaic top a clump of incense burned in a dish. Beside it a narrow chest of drawers inlaid with mother of pearl probably held her feminine needs. Poulos sat next to her. Coal black eyes peered at him. She leaned forward and kissed him. Her breath was surprisingly sweet and made him self-conscious that his own probably smelled of a combination of all the things he had ingested that day. She pulled her kimono from her shoulders. Her nipples were rose-colored reliefs on small soft mounds of pure white. Her thighs were short and rounded. Her belly had creases and her navel was a small dark hole. Her agile fingers freed him from the thirteen buttons that locked his groin in his uniform.

"So-o-o-o big," she said.

"I'll bet you say that to all the sailors."

"We fuck now."

Time is money, he thought, and the thought gave him trouble holding his erection. She played with him till he firmed up. She reached behind him with her free hand and was just ready to push him inside her when all of a sudden Scotty shouted his name outside their private space and Poulos lost it altogether. He went limp as the door burst open and Scotty looked at them around the screen. A leering grin erupted on his face. "Did I interrupt something?"

Poulos scrambled to his feet, knocking the screen over in his haste to cover his dangling penis. "Why did you have to barge in here?"

"You weren't in the rickshaw and I had to find out if you really were fucking one of the girls."

Natasha turned to the wall, exposing her milky-white buttocks. Her thick ebony hair spread across her back like an ink blot. He couldn't tell if she was crying but she had to be mortified, even if she was a prostitute. He felt bad for her. Her private little space had been desecrated by Scotty's sudden intrusion. Even the incense on the small table sizzled out as if Scotty had used up all the oxygen. One last curl of smoke tried to climb the fetid air and hold off the rancid odor of old sex and dried perspiration.

"How can you be such a clod?" Poulos said. "Look at the girl."

"I am. Great ass. Want to finish?"

“Are you kidding?” Poulos dressed as several girls, drawn by curiosity, crowded in behind Scotty. One of them pointed to Natasha lying on her mattress and said something in Chinese. The others snickered. Natasha jumped to her feet screaming epithets. Her delicate breasts wiggled in the wan light. Poulos tenderly draped the kimono over her shoulders. She drew it tightly around her body and crossed her arms.

Mamma Naffi looked in "What goes on here?"

"He didn't get his pussy," Scotty said. "He doesn't have to pay."

"Stay out of this, Scotty."

"I've had more experience in whorehouses than you have."

The madam spoke in rapid Chinese to Natasha. Natasha answered meekly.

"She say you try. So you pay."

Poulos didn't want to argue. "How much?"

"Fifty."

"Borrow me a hundred, Scotty. I gave all my money to those refugees."

"That's twice the going rate."

"Shut up and just give it to me."

Shaking his head, Scotty pulled bills from his jumper pocket and handed them to Mamma Naffi. "You've gone completely Asiatic."

"Wait in the rickshaw. I'll be right out." Poulos pushed Scotty out the door with Mamma Naffi and closed it.

He reached inside his sock for the twenty dollars he had put away for emergency and the ride back to the ship on the walla walla. He held it out to her but she kept busy getting her place in order. She replaced the screen. She opened a drawer in her small chest and removed a box of incense. She dropped a fresh pellet on the small plate and lighted it with a match. As she blew, the incense began to glow and smoke. When the incense was glowing she finally took the money. "You Americans are so rich it's disgusting."

Poulos stared at her.

"Are you surprised I speak your language?"

He felt his cheeks color. "It's perfect."

"My mother was English."

"Where is she?"

"Dead. My parents were killed by the Communists. Mamma Naffi takes care of me now."

"I'm sorry."

"Don't be sorry for me. Be sorry for yourself. You didn't get your sex. You still want it?" Natasha untied her kimono and held it open the way a flasher would. Seeing her naked this way embarrassed him. He averted his eyes.

"Your face is red." She laughed derisively.

"What did the girls say that made you angry?"

"They teased me for not being woman enough to make you come. And I told them you can't get screwed with a prick at half-mast." She was bent on humiliating him. Maybe she was getting revenge for all the insults and degradations she had suffered in her short life. Maybe she felt he was patronizing her. He was an easy target because he had made himself vulnerable by expressing sympathy, rare and unexpected in her world.

"If you feel that way, give me back my money."

"Fuck you, sailor." The words came out as if she were spitting on the ground.

He became infuriated. The final insulting straw had been piled on him. He tried to pull the money from her hand. Natasha swung at him, her tiny fist hammering his side, her blows slamming at his kidney. The pain was like a side ache from running too fast.

Bewildered he stumbled into the hall. The other call girls were lined up along the wall, forming a slit-eyed phalanx for him to walk past. Mamma Naffi stood on the veranda, her arms folded inside her kimono.

He reached the rickshaw and climbed in.

"Where's your hat?" Scotty asked.

"Shit, I left it inside."

He looked toward the house, feeling Mamma Naffi's inscrutable stare.

"Better go back for it. The SPs will pick you up."

He climbed out and walked back to the veranda. "My hat," he said.

"I get." She went inside and returned in a few seconds with his hat. "Real sailor fuck girl."

The rickshaw driver trotted them to the boat landing, his running as regular as a metronome. The streets were less crowded as sailors began returning to their ships and merchants were closing their shops.

"You wasted good money." Scotty said, yawning.

The Communists probably killed her parents because they were Nationalists, and she had to flee for her life to Hong Kong, hungry and penniless, a perfect candidate for Mamma Naffi's teenage brothel. She had to get tough and mean in order to survive. What a despairing biography.

"No it wasn't wasted."

Scotty didn't hear him. He had settled back against the straw cushion and was fast asleep.

THE MATTRESS

Even though Alex's parents were walking on eggshells, Easter came and went without further incident. The family was too busy making, packing and selling candy to think about anything else. April turned into May, and lawns turned green only to be covered by a bumper crop of seeds from the majestic elms that canopied the streets. Lilacs and crabapple trees and bridal wreath bloomed. Screens replaced storms, and the verdant smells of approaching summer filled houses as doors and windows were left open in the soft spring air.

But May turned into June and the weather turned hot. The demand for chocolates dropped as the temperature rose, and Alex's father began turning out summer assortments of vanilla mints, fondants, divinity, peanut brittle, and fruit centers dipped in Nestle's non-chocolate coating which came in white, rose and pastel green.

Alex's morale was as desultory as the weather. Mary Lou was constantly on his mind, but the awkwardness with which they parted in front of Richard's, plus the admonition from his father to stay away from her, dispirited him. Nothing he did had any heart to it.

His resolve to get a job and leave home was gone, wilted like spring blooms. He hardly took notice of time passing; sometimes he forgot what day it was.

Meanwhile his parents maintained a prayerful silence broken only by essential communication such as "pass the butter" or "buy some tuna when you go to the store." So far their prayers were being answered because Alex was coming to work every day. Whether they made the connection between a store that was air-conditioned and a house that was not they did not say.

Unexpectedly, it was Mary Lou who interrupted Alex's stagnant summer by telephoning him. Fortunately his parents were at the store. If they had been home, Alex would have had to say something circumspect like "Hello there, how are you?" and explain to his suspicious parents that it was a classmate taking summer session who wanted to borrow his notes on Mythology in Western Art, a fable if there ever was one.

"Hi, stranger," Mary Lou said.

"I've been meaning to call you," Alex replied, even though this was not true.

"Why haven't you?"

He couldn't tell her about the conversation he had with his old man. "I've been busy."

"Really?" she asked with heightened expectation. "Did you get a job?"

"Well, no. I mean busy at the store."

"Oh," she responded, her enthusiasm slipping into neutral. "So, you were too busy to call." She let the words drop off.

"Not exactly. I...well, I didn't think you wanted to see me again."

"Why not?"

"Don't you remember the things you said?"

"Are you still agonizing over that?" She sounded incredulous.

"You weren't exactly singing my praises."

"Alex, you ought to know by now that I'm not one to harbor anger. Nothing good ever happens when you let anger control your life. If you want to throw your money away to impress that Greek man, what's his name..."

"Tony."

"...Tony, that is your business, but you don't have to suffer tons of guilt over it. You need to learn how to be at peace with yourself. I'm not criticizing, Alex, but you do have such a hard time dealing with life."

"Isn't that criticism?"

Her sigh had a high degree of futility to it. "Never mind. I called to ask you a favor."

"What kind of favor?"

"I rented an apartment."

"You're moving out of your sister's house?"

He felt a twinge of envy. Mary Lou was moving and he was stuck at home.

"Patty is pregnant and Larry is going to remodel my room into a nursery. He's really busy, otherwise he'd help me move, and you have that station wagon." The way she phrased her words between short intakes of breath was stirring his dormant desire. His gonads started aching. "There's not much, just my clothes, the bedroom set, a chest and mattress."

"Mattress?"

"Can't you tie it on the roof of the car? I'll pay you what I would a mover. How does twenty-five dollars sound?"

It sounded like a fortune, and for one night's work. He would not only see Mary Lou again, he would even handle her clothes. His mind picked up speed for the first time in weeks. He had to build a case for breaking the promise he made to his old man. After all, his father's concern with Alex was his personal relationship with Mary Lou. Helping her move was strictly business. How could his father object to that? Especially after Alex told him he was getting paid twenty-five bucks.

Hell, he might go into business as a mover, using Mary Lou as a referral. Maybe she would write a letter of recommendation. His mood was brightening considerably. "When?"

"Tonight."

His enthusiasm suddenly dampened. "That soon?"

"I want to move in by the first which is tomorrow."

He hesitated. He didn't think there was enough time to convince his old man.

"If you don't want to do it I can call someone else."

Who? he wondered. "I'll do it!" he said quickly. His thoughts were racing now. "What time?"

"Seven."

"Ok, I'll see you at Patty's."

He boiled a couple of wieners on the stove, thinking hard. After downing them with ketchup, he screwed up his nerve and called the shop. "Guess what, dad?" he said. "I got a job."

It was so novel his father was immediately suspicious. "Doing what?"

"Helping someone move."

"Who?"

"My advisor at the U." This was the best he could come up with on such short notice.

"I thought he go to Europe this summer."

"His wife stayed behind. They sold their house and she asked me to help her move to their new apartment. I can do it all in one evening, but I need the station wagon."

"How much you getting?"

"Twenty-five dollars."

"I have to see it to believe it."

"You will."

That evening, on his way to Mary Lou's, Alex stopped at a liquor store and bought a bottle of Chianti encased in a woven basket. It was to be a housewarming gift. He hid it under the car seat.

She met him at the door in blue jeans worn white at the knees, a University t-shirt he had given her, and white canvas sneakers scuffed gray. She looked younger than her years and virginally innocent.

"Patty and Larry are out for the evening. We have the place to ourselves." She led him to her room and they began with the closet. She was an orderly person--her heavy winters were stored in garment bags, and her summers hung in neat rows, from light jackets and blouses to skirts and scarves. He felt strangely melancholy as she loaded her belongings onto his arms. He wanted to hug them to his face as the closet grew emptier.

"Can you carry that?"

"No problem."

It took longer than Mary Lou had predicted, even though her new place, The Nicollet Apartments, was less than a mile from Patty's house. Hauling the bedroom set took three trips alone. Alex had all the car windows down so the breeze would cool them as he drove. The apartment building was vintage 1920s: maroon brick highlighted with window sills and cornices of Mankato limestone. It was flanked by a late-night grocery store on one corner and a funeral home on the other.

Alex unloaded in the parking lot behind the building and propped the rear door open with a box of books. Mary Lou's unit was on the main floor halfway down the hall. It had a narrow entry with a closet on one side and a waist-high planter on the other. A galley kitchen had a drop-leaf table at one end. Beyond the small sitting room was the bedroom and bath.

"How much?"

"Fifty-five a month and that includes electricity."

After bringing in the last load, he checked the time. It was past eleven. "Shall I help you make the bed?"

"I have to put my things away first."

"All that work has made me hungry."

"The grocery store down the block is still open. Help me shop and I'll fix us something to eat." The suggestion gave him a feeling of tranquil domesticity, what he hoped his life held in store. They walked to the corner grocery. Alex pushed a little cart down narrow aisles as Mary Lou selected items for her refrigerator and pantry. He helped her pick out two small ribeye steaks for their dinner. When they left, the grocer locked the door behind them.

"I wish we had wine but the liquor stores are closed."

Alex smiled. Throughout the moving process he waited for the appropriate moment and now it had arrived. "I have something for you," he announced, "unless you're afraid of Greeks bearing gifts."

While Mary Lou put away the groceries, Alex brought in the wine from the car.

She loved it. "Now I have a candle holder. I'll let the wax drip down the sides."

"We have to drink the wine first."

The kitchenette was barely large enough for one person. Alex did not mind the inevitable body contact as they squeezed around one another. Mary Lou made a salad. He wanted to nibble the back of her neck as she cut up the cucumber and tomato but he didn't want to startle her with a knife in her hand. He put on the rib eyes. The oven was dated and wedged into a corner of the crowded space but it was clean and the broiler worked fine. They both liked their steaks medium rare and Alex hit them right on the button.

They were having such a good time, they didn't pay attention to the hour. It was well after midnight when they finally sat down to eat. Mary Lou miraculously had found a candle buried in a box and made a temporary holder out of a bud vase. She placed it on the drop leaf table and shut off the lights. Because the table was small, they ate the salad out of the serving bowl, sometimes dueling over the same slice of cucumber. They laughed and drank wine and looked at each other over the flickering candle, its light making Mary Lou's face glow like a chiaroscuro painting.

Alex felt a glow of his own. He could see the bare mattress behind the bedroom door piled high with her personal things--her sweaters and shirts, her underclothes and pajamas, her towels and sheets. He wanted this glorious engulfment in her intimate world never to end. He raised his glass. "Here's to your new apartment, your private haven far from the madding crowd. May it keep you safe and warm."

They touched glasses and drank. Over her rim, Mary Lou's eyes locked on his for a moment. She became pensive.

"A penny for your thoughts," he said, feeling terribly romantic. His own were worth upwards of a dollar.

Mary Lou put her glass down. "Alex..." she began.

"What?" he asked softly.

"There is something I have to tell you."`

"What is it?"

"I've met someone."

His jaw suddenly went tight. "Met someone?" He didn't want to appear overly concerned. "Anyone I know?"

"No. He's a manager in Patty's office."

It was as if Alex had landed with his wheels up. "So your sister is playing matchmaker."

"Hardly. Patty had a dinner party for some of the staff and she included Stanley..."

"Stanley?"

"He happens to be single and everyone else was married and she needed to balance out her table. So she asked if I'd mind being Stanley's partner.

"She's never invited me to dinner."

"Are you jealous?" She seemed to enjoy asking that.

"Why should I be? Your sister doesn't like me anyway."

"The way you act sometimes, I'm not surprised."

"Does Stanley have a last name?"

"Muller."

"Spelled with a u?"

"Yes."

"Is there an umlaut over it?"

"What's an umlaut?" she asked

"Two accent dots over a vowel."

"How should I know?" she said, getting peeved that he was throwing her off message.

"If there is, he's not Greek. There's no umlaut in the Greek language."

"Alex, will you be serious?"

"I'm interested in his nationality, that's all."

"Stanley happens to be Austrian."

"Lutheran?"

"Catholic."

"I should have guessed. Patty would never have anyone but a Catholic in her house."

"My sister is very broad-minded."

"Not about me she isn't. How old is this Stanley guy?"

"He's more mature than you are."

She had meant to smart Alex and it worked. "You didn't answer my question."

"Stanley is in his thirties."

"Where in his thirties?"

"Thirty-seven."

One of Alex's favorite little books was Ring Lardner's essay on aging, Symptoms of Being Thirty-Five. Using Lardner's accounting, Stanley was already walking up the path to the old people's home. "Is he getting gray?"

"Around the temples."

"Temples? Is he bald?"`

"Oh, Alex, really. He's not bald. Just a bit thin on top."

Alex smiled a winning smile. "Is he tall?"

"Taller than you."

"Oh," he said, losing a round on points. He was still looking for the knockout punch. "Is he fat?"

"Thin."

A TKO. Alex envisioned a gaunt Dickensian figure with strands of hair pasted over a shiny scalp sitting on a stool next to a coal skuttle. He was wearing an eye shade and entering numbers in a ledger with a quill pen. Stanley appeared threatening not in the least. "Have you been on a date?"

"He took me to a concert at Lake Harriet."

"Lake Harriet concerts are free."

"He bought ice cream cones."

"Has he kissed you?"

"That's enough, Alex."

"Does he know that I've kissed you?"

"I haven't told him about you."

Alex leaned forward. "Did you ask me to help you move just so you could make me squirm over some guy with an umlaut over his name that Patty set you up with?"

"At least I got your attention."

Alex sat back in his chair. "You're not serious about him."

"I'll know if I am Saturday night."

"What's happening Saturday night?"

"Stanley is taking me out to dinner."

"Where?"

"Harry's."

Harry's was Minneapolis's finest restaurant, one which Alex could not afford. There were three intimate dining rooms, each on a separate floor serviced by a tiny elevator. "Why is he taking you to such a fancy place?"

"Certainly not to throw his money away."

"You had to bring that up, didn't you?"

"You asked for it."

Alex looked down at his plate, at the congealed fat and blood left from the steak--a dreadful metaphor for the mess his life was becoming. There was only one reason why a single man would take a single woman to an elegant restaurant. "Is he going to propose to you?"

"He may."

Alex had nothing left to counter with. "How are you going to answer him?"

She didn't say anything.

He knew that it was up to him to provide her with the answer. If he was truly serious about his desire for her, he had to tell her now or give her up to Stanley. "Don't do it," he said. "Not Stanley."

"Why shouldn't I?"

"He's not for you."

"Is that the only reason?"

"No."

"What else?"

"I..."

"Yes?"

"Because..."

"Because what, Alex?"

"I love you." She finally got him to say the three little words.

"Why has it taken you so long to tell me that?"

"I don't know. I think about you all the time."

"How am I supposed to know that? I had to drag it out of you."

"Maybe I was never taught how."

"It's never too late to learn." She reached for his hand and squeezed it. Her eyes began to glisten in the candle light. "Patty thinks Stanley would be right for me. He has a future with the company. He could be president someday."

"All you want is security."

"And a family."

"There's plenty of time for that."

"There's not! I'm twenty-nine!"

Alex thought about the phrase Greeks use to describe an old maid--tha mini sto raffi, she will remain on the shelf.

Mary Lou slid her hands up and down her thighs. "I have to know if we have a future together."

"I have to graduate and get a job. Then we'll get married."

It was as if he had deflated a balloon. "Alex, do you understand why I rented this apartment?"

"You told me, Patty is going to have a baby."

"I could have moved over their garage. Patty and Larry would love to have me help around the house. But if I stayed I'd become a maid to Patty and a maiden aunt to her child. I don't want to end up like that."

He was unable to meet her eyes. If there were a fifth dimension where time was suspended and space was contained, he would enter it, crawl into its furthest corner and disappear. His father's plea to forget her pounded his skull, driving out the words Mary Lou was waiting--needing--to hear: marry me. "Is the train leaving the station?" he asked.

She nodded. “Will you climb aboard with me?"

"I want to."

"What's stopping you?"

"I'd have to leave everything else behind."

"Like what?"

Alex shifted in his chair. "Everything that's familiar. What I grew up with." He hesitated, unsure if what he was going to say would make sense to her. "My dad made me promise not to see you anymore."

Mary Lou stared in surprise. "Why?"

"Because you're not Greek." Alex decided it was better to describe the problem in terms of what Mary Lou was not rather than what she was, Roman Catholic.

Lines of puzzlement furrowed her forehead. "They're not in Greece, they're in America."

"For them, the train never left the station."

"It went backwards."

Alex felt compelled to defend his parents now that he had left them open to criticism. "They grew up in mountain villages. They're not sophisticated. When they came to America they didn't have anything but their tradition so they hung on to it."

"My parents were immigrants, too, and they blended in."

"They were Catholic."

Mary Lou raised her eyebrows. "What difference does that make?"

"You don't think of yourself first as Croatian, do you? You think of yourself first as Catholic. Greeks don't separate their religion from their culture. They're Greek, period. So it's natural for them to stick together."

"And keep everybody else out? Is that why you haven't introduced me to your parents?"

"They're afraid." he said.

"Of me?"

"Of any Catholic."

"Well, I'm not any Catholic." There was a strained silence. "You're the one who's afraid, Alex."

He poured out the last of the wine and turned the bottle by its neck. "Why is an empty bottle called a dead soldier?" he asked.

"I haven't the vaguest idea."

"Maybe it describes our relationship."

"Empty?"

"No, dead."

"Oh God, Alex, don’t get morbid."

"Did I ever tell you that the name of the senior class play at my high school was Death Takes a Holiday?"

“What on earth made you think of that?"

"Wishful thinking, I guess, because nothing can die when Death takes a holiday, not even love."

"If you aren't able to keep ours alive, don't expect Death to do it for you."

"It was just a romantic thought."

"How can Death be romantic?"

"In the play he disguises himself as a handsome prince and falls in love with a beautiful young girl named Grazia."

"Sounds like a fairy tale. How come you remember it so well?"

"I was in it."

"You? An actor?"

"Fits, doesn't it?"

"What role did you play?"

Alex bowed his head. "Death. Otherwise known as His Royal Highness Prince Sirki of Vitalba Alexandra." He recalled how proud he felt in his royal-red tunic with double rows of shiny buttons and epaulettes that broadened his shoulders, a fourragere under his arm and a stand-up collar that kept his chin tilted in a regal pose. He lifted his wine glass. "Let us drink to beauty, to love, and to ecstasy that is their child."

"Is that from the play?"

He nodded.

"You have a good memory."

"The play was the high-point of my young life."

"I'm sure the girls adored you."

He put his glass down. "Alas, they adored the Prince."`

"But you were the Prince."

"A pretender to the throne. I got the part because I stood out in a school full of blond Scandinavians."

Mary Lou smiled at him. "You got the part not only because you are dark but because you are tall and handsome. I'll bet you could have asked anybody to the prom."

"Too bad you weren't around," he said, "I would have asked you."

"You would have been too young for me when I was in high school." Without intending to, Mary Lou pointed up the glaring difference in their ages. When she was a senior, he was in the sixth grade, not something to dwell on.

"Who asked you to your prom?" he asked.

"Roger Krzmarzchyk."

"Whatever happened to vowels in northern Minnesota?"

"You don't need them to work in the mines."

"If you had stayed in Hibbing, you'd be married to a miner and have six children by now."

She sighed. "Maybe that's what I should have done."

"What happened to Roger?"

"The war started and he was drafted. I never saw him again."

The thought that Roger might had been killed in some World War II action gave them pause.

Presently Mary Lou said, "Who did you take to the prom?"

"I didn't go."

Mary Lou was surprised. "The man who played the lead in the class play didn't even go to the prom?"

"I went to Excelsior Amusement Park instead."

"What did you do?"

"Rode the roller coaster." He didn't want to admit that he was so shy in high school that he could not muster up the nerve to ask a girl to the prom.

"What a sad story." Mary Lou studied his face. "You know what, Alex?"

"What?"

"You're still riding that roller coaster."

The candle between them fizzled and went out. Melted wax had turned the bud vase into an abstract expressionist object. Alex picked at the wax that had stuck on the table surface. It only served to remind him how stuck he was.

"I'm tired of people telling me what to do."

"What people?"

"My parents. Tony. The entire community. There's an incredible pressure to conform. Go to the Greek church, have only Greek friends and, lest we forget, marry a Greek girl. I feel like I'm in a box."

"Break out."

"That's what I've been trying to do."

"You're old enough to vote, you're old enough to fight a war and die for your country. You're old enough to make decisions that make you happy, not someone else."

If only he had Mary Lou's clarity of purpose, her determination. "You make it sound easy."

"It is if you believe in yourself."

"I'd like to go home, pack my bag, and move in with you."

Mary Lou appeared startled. "I hope you're joking."

Alex rose from his chair. He came around to the other side of the table and pulled Mary Lou to her feet. "What if I'm not?" He drew her close but she pulled away.

"It's getting late. You better go."

He glanced around the efficiency wishing he didn't have to leave. "Are you working tomorrow?"

"I'm taking the day off."

"I can come over and help you put your clothes away." He reached under Mary Lou's t-shirt and ran his fingers along her waist. She arched her back. "I like touching you."

"Come back tomorrow and touch my clothes."

"Those, too."

"Goodnight, Alex."

"You know something?" he said, stalling for time, "When I played Death in my senior year, I was good, really good. And now I think I know why."

"What do you mean?"

"I wasn't playing a role. I was Death."

"That's morbid."

"No, think about it. I identified with Death because he was lonely, missing out on life. He yearned to be in a world where he didn't belong."

"Where do you belong?"

"With you."

"Are you sure?"

"I shall take a holiday and not a leaf will fall, nor a star from heaven. No one will die. Nothing will decay. There will be only a springtime of life and growth."

"Is that Death speaking, or you?"

He bent his head and lightly touched Mary Lou's mouth with his, feeling the downiness on her upper lip. "Me." Her breath played against his, causing a stir deep in his groin.

"I think you have more than Death on your mind."

"I have you on my mind." He began to rise.

She pulled her head back and looked up at him. "Is that the only place?"

Alex felt the smooth, warm line of her arched spine. Then he brought his hands to the front of her body and ran his fingers along the edges of her bra, touching the inner part of her breasts.

"Please..."

"You've let me before."

"We are alone."

"Weren't we alone in Patty's living room? The front seat of the car?"

"There was always the risk of being interrupted that kept us under control. But here there is nothing to stop us."

"We can stop."

"We'll regret this, I know we will."

"I can't think beyond right now."

"That's always been your problem."

He found the clasp of her bra and released it, freeing her breasts. Her nipples rose and hardened to his touch. He kissed her and she separated her lips so their tongues could meet. They clung as one, drowning in the liquid sensuality of their bodies. As they sank deeper and deeper, the shimmering surface above them where they could break through and breathe the atmosphere of rational thought was growing fainter and more distant.

Mary Lou's bed, still unmade, was a bare mattress piled with her clothing. They fell onto it, scattering sweaters and skirts as they undressed in a flurry of groping fingers. They were smothering in the inevitable compression of their senses, oblivious to everything but their bodies, delirious and passionate. They fed on each other like starving animals. All Alex was aware of was the overwhelming force of her body as it moved against his, driving him toward some new, unimagined horizon. He reached his destination: the uncharted, virgin territory of Mary Lou's spirit. He felt as if he were meant to be there all along, that it was only a matter of overcoming the delays and diversions along the way. She gave a stifled cry and bit his shoulder as his repeated thrusts grew more frenzied. There was an explosion of such force they were both engulfed in it, their former selves burned beyond recognition in an inferno of their own making.

Alex fell onto his back in the jumble of clothing, dazed and spent. Beside him, Mary Lou placed her hands between her legs, cupping herself to keep from dripping on the mattress. "Oh, god," she cried. Tears fell from her eyes and made tiny rivulets into her ear lobes. Her breasts raised and lowered as she breathed.

He lifted himself on one arm and looked at her. "Do you hurt?"

She moved her head back and forth on a stack of sweaters that had been hastily pushed into a pillow at the height of their love-making. "I didn't want it like this, like a pair of rutting animals."

No, Alex thought, not rutting animals. Exotic animals, the kind woven in medieval tapestries or painted on classical frescoes or scratched into cave walls. "It was beautiful," he said.

"You call this beautiful?" Mary Lou held up her hand and opened her palm. It was lathered with his semen and her blood. She struggled to a sitting position. Under her, Alex noticed a fresh pink stain; the traditional symbol of virginal love was permanently affixed to the satiny pastel blue fabric of the mattress. She rose unsteadily to her feet still cupping herself. Alex watched as she walked in crouched half steps across the room, her buttocks trembling, to the bathroom. She shut the door behind her.

He looked down at his greasy penis, lying on its side across his thigh, and his matted pubic hair. In the aftermath he felt a growing unease. The nakedness he had groped for only moments before was now an embarrassment. He got up, dug through the layers of tossed-about clothing for his shorts and began to dress. As he pulled his t-shirt over his head he felt a dull soreness. He checked his shoulder. There was a welt where Mary Lou had broken through his skin with her teeth; the quid pro quo of their love-making, a mark just like the mattress stain. What if his mother saw it? He almost shuddered as he pulled on his pants and buckled his belt. His mother had power over him, like Death.

Death. The unfortunate comparison brought to his mind the final moments of his senior class play when Death announces his love for Grazia.

Grazia's mother pleads with him to leave her daughter behind when he returns to his shadowy kingdom.

Death says to her: "A mother cannot stand in the way of true love."

Then he turns to Grazia: "We are going far away, to a land that will be all strangeness and mystery to you."

Grazia shivers. "Why is everything so dark? There ought to be lights and music..."

The toilet flushed behind the bathroom door. "Alex, hand me my robe," Mary Lou called.

"Where is it?"

"Look for it. It's white terrycloth."

Alex eventually found the robe among scattered clothing and tapped on the door. Mary Lou opened it just far enough to take the robe from him. A minute passed and she came out, the robe wrapped tightly around her body. She was outwardly composed but an air of profound sadness had enveloped her. She sat on the edge of the mattress and noticed the stain on the ticking. She picked up her abandoned t-shirt from the floor and began wiping the stain with it, slowly at first and then more rapidly as she realized how futile her effort was.

"Nothing will take this damned spot out. Every time I get in bed I'll know it's there, reminding me how reckless I was. Why did I let this happen?" She seemed to be talking to herself. "My fear of getting old took over. I knew I was on dangerous ground but I couldn't stop myself. Maybe that's how nature works, how it guarantees that life goes on."

"What are you talking about?"

"What do you think I'm talking about? Do you want me to draw you a picture?"

"Everything is ok," he said, trying to hide his own nervousness. "Nothing happened."

"We didn't protect ourselves. We didn't do anything."

Alex sat next to her on the bed and tied his shoes.

"I'm scared," she said. "What if I get pregnant? You'll stand by me, won't you?"

"Of course."

"No matter what your parents say?"

Alex felt a stab of anxiety cut through his intestines.

"If you made me pregnant, Alex, you have to marry me. I won't let you shame me."

He rubbed her shoulders, trying to convey unity and support. For a time, they were lost in their thoughts. Mary Lou folded her arms and gripped her body as though she suddenly had a chill. She bent over and touched her chin to her knees. She stared at the floor. Alex looked down at her back, now an unflattering convex curve, the opposite of the sensual concave curve that had excited him so.

"How does the play end?" Mary Lou asked. Her voice was muffled by the terrycloth pressed to her mouth.

"What?"

She straightened.

"The Prince and his girlfriend, what was her name?"

"Grazia."

"What happens to her?"

"They go away together," Alex said.

But what he didn't tell her was that the Prince goes back to being Death again, his holiday is over and the world resumes its obsession with his finely tuned craft.

"Like you said, it's a fairy tale."

That's what she wanted to hear, had to hear. "So they live happily ever after?"

"Isn't that how fairy tales end?"`

THE DRUNK

"Did you get screwed?" Ensign Porteous asked when Poulos checked in at the quarterdeck. Porteous was a raw ROTC ensign younger than Poulos. He wore the OOD's silver-plated Colt .45 on his hip. He looked like Billy the Kid with his cocky smile and adolescent beard.

"No, I didn't get screwed!" Poulos snapped.

"You don't have to get huffy about it."

Scotty went below but Poulos didn't feel like turning in just yet. He went into the Ship's Office and sat down, tilting his chair into the corner where the bulkhead and filing cabinets came together and put his feet on the desk. A light rain had started falling and water was coming in through the porthole. The clipboard holding the week's Plans of the Day was getting wet but he just stared at the sheets getting soaked. He was too preoccupied nursing his bruised ego. His side still ached. He pulled up his jumper to see if Natasha's powerful little fists had also bruised his skin. There was a telltale redness, and he thought about the red welt Mary Lou had made on his shoulder. No Mary Lou this time. Just Poulos and his thoughts about Natasha. He hated to admit it, but the biggest blow to his pride was his failed attempt at, as Porteous so indelicately put it, getting screwed. All the way back to the ship he fantasized about Natasha--not about screwing her, but about saving her, rescuing the pretty girl-child with the intelligent eyes and perfect English from her life of misery. He gave her money and what did he get in return? Insults. He had to laugh at himself. He was so naive. Natasha is a whore, he had to remind himself. He was trying to idealize her, turn her into something she was not, nor ever could be. She didn't get that way singing in a choir.

"Why do you have such a soft spot for gooks?" Scotty asked on the crowded walla-walla back to the Sprague.

"You fucked one, didn't you?"

"I was horny."

Poulos rationalized that it was probably a good thing he didn't screw Natasha. He might have caught the clap like Powell, the deckhand who spent minutes at a time in the head pissing drops of red-stained urine. But then it was Powell's own fault for not taking a penicillin pill. That's why Ensign Porteous grilled every sailor returning from liberty. If the answer was yes, you went to sick bay for a dose of penicillin. Poulos suspected that some sailors said yes even when they didn't get laid because they didn't want their manhood questioned. Maybe he should have, too. Mamma Naffi's accusation that he was a faggot still rang in his ears. Not till the breeze blew rain on his shoes did he bother to get up and close the porthole, securing the lugs till the round window was tight. He sat back down and surveyed the crummy little space he worked in, the desks and the two Underwoods, the gray metal filing cabinets; the green bulkheads, the corner plates showing signs of rust. His attention was drawn through the open doorway to the midship's passageway. Because of the rain, Ensign Porteous had ordered Avery Fiveash, the Master at Arms, to move the quarterdeck into the shelter of the passageway. Fiveash carried in the portable desk with the OOD's log and set it on the boat winch, the cranking machinery used to haul the Sprague's gig out of the water. The boat winch surface was round and the desk teetered when Porteous wrote on it, but at least they were dry. Porteous took off his navy-blue raincoat and removed the waterproof cover from his dress hat. He refastened the khaki web belt that held the silver .45 in its brown leather holster. Following Naval pecking order, the Master at Arms carried a billy club on his belt, a shiny, blonde-oak bludgeon shaped like a baseball bat.

Witter and Browning checked in from liberty and popped their heads into the Ship's Office. "We looked all over for you."

"It was too smoky so we took off."

"Where'd you go?"

"A rickshaw driver gave us a ride."

"Sightseeing?"

"In a way."

"What's to see at night?"

Poulos figured he should tell them first, before Scotty gave his version of their visit to Mamma Naffi's. "Girls."

Their eyebrows raised with surprise and disappointment. "You went to a whorehouse and didn't tell us?"

"It was the Scotsman's idea."

"You get laid?"

"Not quite."

"Not quite?" Browning said. "You either get laid or you don't."

"I was ready to screw her but Scotty barged in on us."

"I wish I'd been there to see that."

"It wasn't funny."

Browning and Witter thought it was. They walked off howling with laughter.

Porteous stuck his head in. "What did I miss?"

"Nothing," Poulos said, feeling grumpy.

Another boatload of sailors arrived and Porteous went back to the quarterdeck to check them in. Poulos sat in his chair, ignoring the noise of the drunken sailors milling about outside the door of the Ship's Office until he heard a familiar voice giving the OOD a hard time.

"Stop leaning on the desk," Porteous was saying, "you're making it tip."

Poulos looked out to see Clayton, his elbows on the desk reading the log sheet, but it was a man he did not recognize. His whites were dirty. There was a streaky red stain on his pants as though he had wiped a bloody knuckle on it. His left eye was puffy and discolored, and his shoes were scuffed. He was also hatless. "Check me in. Firs' Division."

Porteous stepped back from Clayton's breath. "You're checked in, Clayton. Go below."

Clayton reeled back against the bulkhead, ignoring the ensign's command to go below. "Why you holed up in the midship's passageway? Stopped raining. Look at me, dryza bone." He swept his bleary gaze around the passageway and caught Poulos staring at him. "Well, looky here. If it ain't Yeoman Poulos, keepin the Ship's Office open after hours. What are y'doin, checkin in liberty passes?" he asked, using a hillbilly patois as if he were purposely debasing himself. Clayton reached into his jumper pocket and pulled out his laminated liberty card. "Check mine in." He spun it at Poulos's head, and it zipped across the air like a missile, bouncing off the bulkhead.

Poulos ducked. "You almost hit me!"

Clayton smiled crookedly. "I didn't even come close."

Sailors waiting to check in exchanged glances. Ever since the fight over the manuals, everybody wondered if Clayton had the balls to get even. He might be drunk enough to try something right now. Early money had the unexpectedly aggressive Clayton at eight to five.

Porteous didn't want trouble on his watch. He straightened himself as if he could exert authority more effectively by appearing taller. "One more word out of you, Clayton, and I'll put you on report."

Clayton brushed aside the OOD as he would a pesky fly and stepped into the Ship's Office, crowding Poulos against the file cabinet and filling the air with the smell of dried sweat. The glare of the overhead bulb made Clayton blink. He seemed to be losing some of his belligerence in the bright light. He struggled to focus his eyes and looked down the length of his body. He spotted the bloody stain. "Fell down." He rubbed his head, surprised not to find his hat sitting there. "Had it when I left."

"You're lucky you didn't run into SPs," Poulos said, recalling how he almost forgot his hat at Mama Naffi's.

"SPs run into me!" Clayton laughed at his cleverness. "They brought me back." He leaned unsteadily against the filing cabinet. "I didn't fall down," he said as if needing someone to talk to. "I got in a argument with a Brit. He poked fun at the way I talked, said my ancestors had a choice: go to America or go to prison, gaol he called it. I wasn't taking that lying down, so I told him we were kissin' cousins and that made him mad, real mad. So we went outside to a parking lot to settle it. The SPs came and broke it up."

Clayton gently touched the puffy skin around his eye. "This is where he got me."

"Maybe Cooky's got some raw meat in the locker. Why don't you go look for him."

"How about you and me sit a while and talk?"

"Tomorrow when you're sober."

"You saying I'm drunk?"

"I'm not saying you're anything."

Clayton's eyes grew sad. "You saying I'm not anything?"

"Stop twisting my words." Clayton's body odor was beginning to foul the office. Poulos reached over and turned on the fan.

"Why you doing that?"

“Clearing the air.”

“What for?”

"You need a shower."

Clayton sniffed an armpit reflexively. His putty-colored cheeks turned pink. "You never smell?" He lifted his jumper and pulled out a flat pint of Canadian Club he had hidden in the waistband of his bellbottoms. He uncapped it and took a swig, wiping his lips with the back of his hand. He teetered slightly as he put the bottle away.

"Better watch it, Clayton. You know you can't drink on board."

Clayton's eyes narrowed into slits. "I said, you never smell?"

"That's enough, Clayton."

Clayton stood his ground. "Does your shit stink?"

Poulos was no longer willing to suffer Clayton's goading. "Not any more than Radinger's."

Clayton's eyes, heavily veined from too much liquor, made an effort at staring. "What is that supposed to mean?"

"You kiss Radinger's ass often enough, you oughta know if his shit stinks."

Porteous was at the door, a knot of sailors gathering behind him. "Clayton, go below will you?" he said almost pleadingly.

Clayton turned, paying attention to the Officer of the Deck now that he needed him. "Hey, Mr. Porteous, you're just in time to answer a question. You ever seen me kiss Lt. Radinger's ass?"

Porteous stared blankly.

"Does that mean yes or no?"

Porteous motioned to Fiveash. He'd had enough. "Get him below."

Fiveash came over and put his thumbs in his web belt. "I don't want any trouble from you, Clayton."

Clayton stumbled out of the office and stood among the sailors. He pointed at Poulos. "He's the trouble, can't you see that?"

"Stow it, Clayton."

"Hates the navy, hates me. Made me eat dust, now he says I stink."

Porteous said, "For the last time go below. Either willingly or the Master at Arms will drag you down."

"Gotta straighten things out with Poulos first."

Poulos was not willing to get trapped again with Clayton's smell. He swung the door and slammed it in Clayton's face. He turned the lock for good measure. On the other side he could hear Clayton yell in sudden fury.

"You can't lock me out, I work here! This is my office!"

There was scuffling and a confusion of noises in the midship's passageway. After a while, it became quiet. A voice called out, "You can open up now, Poulos, it's over."

He opened the door and looked out. Ltjg Armstrong was at the quarterdeck. Baker was Master at Arms. The watch had been relieved.

Poulos stepped into the passageway and saw Lt. Gildenhall on the main deck leaning against the railing, his arms crossed.

He motioned to Poulos. "Let's talk."

The rainclouds were breaking up and a three-quarter moon cast a rippling river of reflected white on the black water. The harbor was dotted with the riding lights of ships at anchor, and in the distance Hong Kong twinkled.

"What about?"

"Why did you lock Clayton out?"

"You could see he was drunk," Poulos said defensively.

"Is that an excuse?"

"It's been a long night."

"It's going to be even longer. Tell me what went on."

"Look, Lieutenant, Clayton even took out a bottle and drank from it. Isn't that against regulations?"

"Clayton is falling apart and you're the only one who doesn't see it."

"I'm trying."

"Not hard enough." Gildenhall sighed. "It was a mistake letting you two write each other up. Radinger has been riding my ass about it ever since."

"Your idea was innovative, Lieutenant, I'll give you that."

It had taken the rest of that Sunday to clean the Ship's Office before Poulos and Clayton sat down with the violation reports in front of them. There was a period of awkward silence. Finally they decided to write apologies to each other with cc's to Lt Gildenhall and Ltjg Radinger.

Clayton's read: I shouldn't have prevented Seaman Poulos from cleaning the shelves. I'm sorry. (signed) RB Clayton, YN2, USN.

Poulos wrote, I apologize for arguing with Yeoman Clayton during clean-up of the Ship's Office. (signed) A. Poulos, SN, USNR.

No mention was made either of the dust or the fight.

"I've never known anyone with so much pent-up resentment," Gildenhall said.

Poulos couldn't agree more. "You don't have to work with him every day the way I do."

Gildenhall straightened and planted his feet. He was as tall as Poulos and their eyes met on the same latitude. "I'm not talking about Clayton, I'm talking about you. He was a model sailor before you came aboard. Now look at him, drunk and disorderly."

"Is that my fault?"

Gildenhall looked across the harbor to take in Hong Kong's glittering skyline. He bit his lip as though pondering something. After a moment he said, "Do you own civvies?"

"I bought a Hong Kong suit. It'll be delivered tomorrow."

"Good. When we hit Tokyo meet me at the Imperial Hotel and I'll buy you a drink."

"You and me? An officer and an enlisted man?"

"No, just two guys having a drink together. I think it might be useful to get away someplace where we can let our hair down. You know the Imperial?"

"I read about it in school. Frank Lloyd Wright's hotel."

"His masterpiece as well as an engineering marvel. Survived the earthquake of twenty-three."

"You sound like an architect."

Gildenhall nodded. "I was one till the Korean War put me on hold."

Just when the conversation was starting to get interesting, an all-too familiar voice interrupted them. They turned. Clayton was back in the midship's passageway. "Goddam strong-arm tactics!" he shouted.

"Didn't you take that bottle away from him?" Poulos called to Baker.

"What bottle?"

"In his waistband."

As if being reminded that he had a bottle, Clayton pulled it out and held it in the air. "Anyone want to join me in a toast to Poulos, who's trying to take over my job?"

Baker grabbed the pint from Clayton and threw it over the side. There was a small splash.

Clayton stared angrily at Baker. "What did you do that for?"

Baker drew his billy club from his belt as a warning.

"Let me talk to him," Gildenhall said. His voice was calm and conciliatory. He walked over. "It's been a long day, Clayton. You really must be tired."

Clayton looked at Gildenhall, his bloodshot eyes glazing over. "What do you want?"

"Be careful, Lieutenant." Baker was ready to hammer Clayton on the skull if he tried anything.

Gildenhall spoke softly in Clayton's ear so no one else could hear. Clayton periodically nodded. Finally he and Gildenhall walked to the hatch leading to the fore and aft passageway. As they stepped over the sill, Clayton looked back at Poulos. He lifted his middle finger and jabbed the air with it.

Gildenhall returned five minutes later. He conferred briefly with Armstrong and then rejoined Poulos by the railing. "Still up?"

"I had to find out what you said to Clayton."

"I told him what he wanted to hear."

"Which was?"

"That you are an asshole."

Poulos looked down at his shoes. "Fucking navy."

"You volunteered for it."

"Thanks."

"Did you expect sympathy?"

Poulos shrugged. "I don't know. Understanding maybe."

"I understand all too well."

Inquiry in the case of CLAYTON, R(only) B(only) YN2, USN

Charged with the following offenses:

1. Disrespect for an officer
2. Bringing alcohol aboard ship
3. Drinking alcohol aboard ship
4. Conduct to the prejudice of good order and discipline

The inquiry was held 12 August 1952 by Commodore Bernard Katz, USN, on board the USS Robert B. Sprague (DD884) in the ship's wardroom. The accused and all witnesses were duly reminded of their rights under UCMJ.
The statements of the various witnesses is presented herewith:

Testimony of Ens. Porteous
I was the OOD on the 2000-2400 watch, when at approximately 2345 hours Clayton appeared on the quarterdeck drunk, unkempt and missing his hat. He had been escorted back to the ship by two SPs. He was in a bad temper and threw his liberty card at Seaman Poulos who was in the Ship's Office. Clayton had words with Poulos. I ordered him to go below but he wanted to confront Poulos again, and Poulos locked the door on him. Clayton went berserk and pounded on the door to be let in. Lt Armstrong and Chief Baker appeared on deck to relieve the watch. It took all of us to subdue Clayton. Baker helped Fiveash escort Clayton below.
Q: What was Clayton's physical condition at the time of the incident?
A: His face was flushed, his eyes were glassy, his speech was slurred.
Q: How would you describe his mental state?
A: He was very agitated, even paranoid. He had the idea that everybody was out to get him, especially Seaman Poulos.
Q: Can you explain why?
A: Clayton was still smarting over losing the fight he had with Poulos in the Ship's Office.

Testimony of Ltjg Armstrong
When I came to relieve the watch, Clayton was pounding on the door of the Ship's Office. Ensign Porteous and the Master at Arms were having trouble containing him, so I stepped in. It wasn't until Chief Baker showed up that we were able to get Clayton under control. Baker and Fiveash escorted him below.
Q: Did Clayton have a bottle?
A: Yes.
Q: What sort of bottle was it?
A: It was a flat pint bottle of brown colored glass, the kind whiskey comes in.

Q: Do you know if it actually contained whiskey?
A: If Clayton's behavior is any judge, it sure as hell, excuse me, it certainly was alcohol.
Q: What happened to the bottle?
A: The MAA threw it over the side.
Q: What was your impression of Clayton's condition?
A: Very intoxicated.
Q: What was his mental state?
A: Extremely provoked.
Q. Was this usual or unusual behavior for Clayton?
A. Unusual.

Testimony of A. Fiveash, BS1
Clayton was in bad shape when he came aboard. He argued with Ensign Porteous. He was ordered to hit his rack. He wouldn't go on his own so Chief Baker and me dragged him down. He was an armful. Baker relieved me of the watch and I went below to my own rack.
Q: Did you know Clayton had a bottle with him?
A: No, sir.
Q: How would you describe his behavior?
A: Some drunks are happy, some are mean. Clayton was mean.
Q: Have you ever seen Clayton drunk before?
A: First time for me.

Testimony of Ltjg Radinger
I was not a witness to the incident relating to the night of 12 August but as Clayton's Division Officer I can attest to the fact that I have never seen Clayton in any condition whatsoever but cold sober. In fact, I was shocked when I heard what happened. I still can't believe it. I am convinced that this deviation from normality is directly attributable to the fight he had with Seaman Poulos when Poulos dumped the dustbag on his head. (Let the record show that Ltjg Radinger is referring to the altercation between Clayton and Poulos in the Ship's Office on 7 July which was witnessed by several of the crew.)
Q: Why do you think the fight in the Ship's Office is related to Clayton's behavior on the quarterdeck?
A: Clayton was humiliated when he threw up all over the main deck. Half the ship's crew saw it. After that his work began to suffer. He lost interest in personal grooming and he was given to periods of depression.
Q. Does Clayton's alleged drunkenness come as a surprise?
A. Shock is a better word.
Q: Why does it shock you?

A: Clayton was a very religious person. He used to attend Sunday services without fail and quoted the Bible. Ever since the dust fight, he does neither.

Testimony of Lt Gildenhall
I was called to the quarterdeck and found Clayton being restrained by officers Porteous and Armstrong, as well as the two MAAs. His strength reminded me of people you read about who, with sudden superhuman effort, are able to lift a car to save someone trapped underneath.
Q: But Clayton was not trying to save someone.
A: He was trying to destroy someone.
Q: Who?
A: Himself.
Q: But you managed to calm him down. What did you tell him?
A: That I sympathized with him. He just needed someone to talk to.
Q: Have you seen Clayton agitated like this before?
A: No.
Q: Lt Radinger mentioned Clayton's change in behavior after the so-called dust fight with Poulos. Can you also verify these changes?
A: Yes.
Q: What are your observations?
A: Clayton lost his ability to concentrate. He withdrew even further into himself. He became confused and distant.

Testimony of A. Poulos, SN, USNR
I returned from liberty about 2330 hours and went to the Ship's Office. After Clayton checked in he came into the Ship's Office. He was drunk and argumentive.
Q: How did you react to his presence?
A: I turned on the fan.
Q: Why?
A: He smelled.
Q: Is your nose overly sensitive?
A: Have you ever set foot in the Ship's Office?
Q: I'm asking the questions, sailor.
A: All I meant, sir, is that the Ship's Office is cramped, not a place you'd like to be with anyone who smells.
Q: How did Clayton react when you told him he smelled?
A: He wanted to know if I ever smelled.
Q: Do you?
A: I guess we all do, sir.
Q: Don't be a smartass, sailor.

A: Well, sir, he was trying to get back at me. Why he even said...
(at this point the witness stopped talking)
Q: Why did you hesitate? Said what?
A: Nothing important, sir.
Q: I'll decide if it's important or not. What else did Clayton say?
A: He said, I suppose your shit doesn't stink.
Q. I see. Even though this borders on unpleasantness, it may help to better understand Clayton's state of mind which is what this inquiry is all about. Therefore I will pursue this line of questioning. So, sailor, how did you respond to Clayton when he asked you if your, ah, shit didn't stink?
A. I told him he ought to know.
Q. Know what?
A. That he is an expert at...sir, do I really have to answer that?
Q: You have to answer.
A: Ok, sir, if you insist. I told him he was an expert at smelling shit.
Q. Why did you say that he was an expert at, ah, at this sort of preoccupation?
A. Will you repeat the question?`
Q. You heard me, sailor. Just give me an answer.
A. Yes, sir. I told him he knew what shit smelled like because he was good at kissing ass.
Q: When you said that, did you have anyone's particular ass in mind?
A: Yes, sir.
Q: Speak up, sailor.
A: Yes, sir!
Q: Whose?
A: Lt. Radinger's.

Findings
The charges against Clayton are too serious to be ignored. Such behavior is prejudicial to the maintenance of naval discipline and cannot go unpunished. However, Clayton's excellent record and the unusual personality changes he suffered recently are mitigating factors that need to be considered. I am therefore ordering Clayton to undergo a military psychiatric evaluation, the results of which will determine what disciplinary action is to be taken. The Captain of the Sprague is hereby ordered to transfer Clayton to the Yokosuka Naval Base Hospital for treatment.

USS ROBERT B. SPRAGUE (DD884)
P16-4/MM
Serial: 0003718840

From: Commanding Officer, USS Robert B. Sprague (DD884)
To: Chief of Naval Personnel
Via: Commander Cruiser Destroyer Force, Pacific Fleet
Subj: CLAYTON, R(only) B(only), 276-33-90, YN2, USN
Ref: (a) BUPERS Pers-B211k-ds-24
Copy to:
BUPERS (advance copy)
COM 13
COMSERVPAC
COMWESTSEAFRON
COMCRUDESPAC

1. Reference (a) directs this command to transfer subject named man on or about 1 September as assigned below.
2. CLAYTON is to be transferred to the Commanding Officer, USS Kearsarge, to await placement in the US Naval Hospital, Yokosuka, Japan, psychiatric unit.
3. Upon evaluation of subject's mental condition, CLAYTON will await disciplinary action by the Judge Advocate General.
4. Commanding Officer, USS Robert B. Sprague, and Commander, DESDIV 1, will be informed of findings of the hospital psychiatric panel.

K. B. BLESSING

THE UNCLE

Alex loaded the last of the cases of fluorescent tubes into the cargo bay of the paneled 1940 Ford delivery van whose odometer was stuck at 138,147 miles. He slammed the doors shut and the porthole windows rattled. The van had a big oval grille. The headlights were mounted on round beefy fenders. The V8 engine was called an 85 because it once delivered 85 horsepower. Alex renamed it a more realistic 65. It had been repainted recently and sported a shiny gray finish that belied its years. The van also had a new clutch which is why Alex liked to drag race at semaphores. Sitting up high in the cab he was able to look down at unsuspecting drivers who thought the old Ford was a beater. When the light changed to green, he popped out the clutch and the van snapped to life in a bravado show of acceleration. It didn't last long. Surprised drivers squealed their tires to catch up, and roared past this insolent truck driver with delusions of grandeur, leaving Alex far behind as the van labored through the rest of its gears to get up to speed.

The tubes were bound for Mound Metalcraft, maker of scale model vehicles called Tonka Toys. The plant was located in a converted schoolhouse on Lake Minnetonka, and Alex had to drive through the swanky village of Wayzata to get there. The town's main street ran along the north bay of Lake Minnetonka, the most fabled of Minnesota's ten thousand. On the inland side of the street were the toney shops catering to the area's wealthy, but on the lake side was a tawdry rail yard with mile-long freight trains, smoking steam locomotives and rumbling diesels which hid the beautiful bay from view. Legend had it that James J. Hill, who built the Great Northern railroad to the west coast, was pissed because Wayzata's town council did not grant him the right of way where he originally wanted it, so he laid his track along the shoreline he owned in a nose-thumbing gesture of unmitigated gall.

The many bays of Lake Minnetonka sprawled for more than two hundred miles of shoreline. So extensive was it that both the wealthy and the poor could engage in their life styles completely segregated from one another. Alex passed Bracketts Point, the walled-in estate of the Pillsbury family, while across the road was a collection of modest lake cottages with screened porches in front and fish houses sitting on trailers in back.

He hummed as he drove, feeling pretty good that he finally got off his ass and found a job. Nothing spectacular mind you--delivering lighting supplies--but it gave him a sense of pride. He was making a sincere effort to turn his life around since he and Mary Lou went all the way.

He was so tired after he left her that night that he nearly fell asleep at the wheel. The streets at three in the morning had been watered down by a tank truck, and the slapping of his tires on the wet pavement helped keep him awake. His groin was sticky and beginning to itch. He looked forward to climbing into the shower and flopping into bed. Wearily he turned off Excelsior Boulevard and saw a police car parked in front of the house. The lights were blazing in the living room. A sudden shot of adrenaline squirted him awake.

Jesus, he thought, his mother had a stroke or his father had a heart attack. Why else would there be a cop car parked in front of the house at three o'clock in the morning? Ruefully he pulled into the driveway, cut the engine and sat behind the wheel trying to get his breath. His lungs felt like punctured balloons. He climbed out of the station wagon and walked across the grass to the front door. His mother and father were sitting on the sofa in their bathrobes.

Standing over them were two of St. Louis Park's finest, holding their hats. They wore dark blue uniforms with revolvers and billy clubs hanging from wide black belts. Their imposing presence shrank the living room.

"Mr. Poulos?" the younger of the two said when Alex came in. He wore his blond hair in a crew cut.

The cop looked familiar. Alex recognized him from high school. He was a grade back and played varsity basketball on the team that went to the State Finals. What was his name? Carlson, Nelson, something like that.

Alex wondered if the young cop remembered him. He hoped not. Right now he yearned for total anonymity.

"What's wrong?" Alex asked his father.

"Your mother is worry sick."

"Is that why the police are here?"

"We thought you have an accident," his father said.

"Accident?"

"Look at the time. You been gone all night."

The older officer, a paternal gray haired man, said, "Your parents did the right thing by calling us."

Alex's embarrassment was mixed with anger. "Don't you have more important things to do, like catching burglars?"

The older officer was not amused. The younger one, eyeing Alex, said, "Say, weren't you in the senior class play?"

Damn, Alex thought, I've been ID'd.

The officer smiled admiringly. "You were very convincing as Death."

His mother, who had been sitting as someone hypnotized, suddenly lurched.

"Sorry, ma'am," the officer said. "I was only talking about the play."

The older officer cleared his throat and put on his hat. "We'll be going." He looked scoldingly at Alex. "Next time give them a call."

Alex backed up the Ford to the dock next to a tractor-trailer and began unloading the cases of fluorescent tubes. When he finished he walked onto the factory floor and watched presses stamp out toy chassis and cabs, and then followed them to the paint room where they were suspended from hooks and sprayed the familiar Tonka yellow. Most interesting was the assembly line, where women took the various parts and fitted them into realistic looking, scale-model dump trucks, graders and power shovels. He was fascinated by industrial technology and thought he would enjoy working in a place like this, but what could he do besides assembling? He didn't know anything about design or engineering or marketing. He certainly wasn't an inventor, not in the traditional sense, anyway. What he was good at was inventing himself, not necessarily a skill he could put on his resume. He had to be good at something, though, but what? Pretty soon, he'd have to deal with that.

What he couldn't deal with, though, was his mother's rocking back and forth in a regular rhythm after the cops left. She would have impressed the time-and-motion experts at Tonka Toys.

"Why you so late?" his father had asked.

"I told you, Pop, moving furniture."

"Don't Pop me. You're not twelve years old anymore."

"You treat me as if I was. How do you expect me to act?"

"Like a grownup."

If his father only knew that's exactly what he was tonight. He fished out the bills Mary Lou had given him and tossed them on the coffee table. "I made twenty-five bucks, not bad for a night's work."

"You should be paid more for moving furniture till three o'clock in the morning."

"We got hungry so we stopped to eat."

"Where?"

"Where? In her apartment."

His mother stopped rocking.

"You alone with the professor's wife having midnight dinner in her apartment?"

"What's wrong with that?"

"A married woman?"`

"We just ate. We sat at a table and ate."

"Candles," his father asked. There was a sense of fatalism in his question.

"What?"

"Candles on the table?"

"One candle," Alex replied, sighing heavily.

Weariness sagged him into the wing chair by the window. The wood was stained honey blonde and the upholstery fabric was printed in pastel tropical flowers and palm trees. The colorful pattern did nothing to ease his sense of foreboding. "After dinner I helped her wash the dishes. That's why I'm late." He wished he had the guts to spill out the truth rather than feed them a trickle of lies they didn't believe.

"She put her best china out?" his father asked sarcastically.

Alex's mind was befogged. "She used paper plates."

His father leaned forward accusingly. "You wash paper plates?"

"No, I mean...I helped her unpack." Alex stood. He wanted to scratch his groin in the worst way. He was carrying Mary Lou's orgasm--her blood, her sweat, her tears.

His mother suddenly shouted, "Eisan mazi tis!" You were with her!

Alex drew back, startled. Was his mother smelling Mary Lou?

"You lie to us!" his father cried. "You weren't with some professor's wife. You make that up so you go see afti Katholiki!"

"I just helped her move, Pop, it was business."

"Monkey business!"

Alex threw up his arms. Let them assume the worst. Hell, they didn't have to assume anything. They knew. He went to the bathroom and stripped off his sticky love-scented clothing. He drew the shower curtain and turned the handle all the way, hoping the spill of hot water would wash away his anguish. He soaped his groin, rinsed, and soaped again. He stood under the shower till the hot water ran out. He climbed out dripping, his skin pink. Heavy steam covered the mirror and ceramic tile.

He dried himself off and wrapped the towel around his waist. He picked up his clothes and opened the bathroom door. He walked past the living room to go upstairs to his attic room, forgetting that his shoulder was exposed. A shriek split the air.

"Look!" his mother cried pointing at the welt Mary Lou had made with her teeth. His mother covered her face and sobbed, grieving the death of her son.

The foreman said it was ok to use the office phone to call Mary Lou. Alex was told by the newspaper's third floor receptionist that Miss Stachich was not at her desk and would he leave his number. Alex told her he was en route and would call back. He waited ten minutes and redialed.

An anxious Mary Lou came on the line. "I just missed your call. Where are you?"

"Mound. I delivered a load of fluorescent lights. This is my last delivery. How was your day?"

"Taking dictation. Mr. Rand is doing a presentation for the annual meeting on Friday. Luckily he won't need me then. Have you told your parents?"

"No."

"Aren't you going to?"

He couldn't tell her that his mother was in a catatonic state and his father was an iceberg.

"Are you certain about this? There's no turning back."

He lowered his voice so the foreman couldn't hear him. "I want to stay with you tonight."

"Not till after we're husband and wife."

Now she was Miss straight-laced. "I won't try anything."

"So what's the point? Have you made the appointment for our blood tests?"

"I haven't had a chance."

"You haven't done that yet?" Mary Lou was perturbed. "What about Mike Callahan? Did you get in touch with him?"

"He was surprised to hear from me after all these years. You know what he's doing? He finished Billy Mitchell and is working at his dad's law firm in Waseca."

"I don't care what he's doing, Alex. Will he be a witness?"

"Mike will drive down and meet us at the justice of the peace at two."

"Can you borrow the van?"

"Mr. Parsons said it was ok."

"Then it's just the blood tests. Oh," she said abruptly, remembering something else. "The rings." This was Mary Lou's assignment since she had the $35 needed to buy them. There was a moment of silence as Alex waited for her to scribble a note on her calendar pad. "Make the appointment for the blood tests and I'll get the rings, and we'll be ready," she concluded, her voice filled with anticipation. "I only wish you would tell your parents."

"When we get back. By the way, how are you feeling?"

"If you mean did I get my period the answer is no."

Alex stared into space, his mind clogged with the terrible possibility that Mary Lou may be pregnant.

"That gray panel yours, buddy?" A man in coveralls was glaring at him.

"Oh, yeah," Alex said, holding the receiver away from his mouth.

"Clear the space. We need to load a semi."

Alex said into the phone, "I have to go."

"When can you call again?"

"In the morning when I get to work."

Getting a job--any job that paid--had been Alex's first order of business after that early morning confrontation with his parents. Over coffee the next day he studied the help wanted ads in the morning paper, circling those that read "Immediate Openings." That afternoon he was hired by Parson's Electric as a delivery man. The boss let him drive the van home since the warehouse was way out on Stinson Boulevard.

His mother hated the van. It was an eyesore and leaked oil. Most of all she hated what it represented: her son's freedom. Alex enjoyed an independence he never had before. He had money of his own, a job that kept him away all day. He ate his meals at the Pylon, a drive-in on Highway 12 owned by one of his high school buddies. Alex used the house for changing clothes and sleeping. And why should he spend any more time there? The atmosphere had all the charm of an oozing sore.

He drove home to change out of his uniform. He got off Highway 7, took Alabama to 39th, and drove up Xenwood Avenue, past the neat rows of modest two-bedroom bungalows built after the war by the same developer, Tom Motzko. They all looked alike except for variations on the front entrance. Deluxe models had stone, Semi-Deluxe had brick. His parents had brick. Since Alex was approaching in the opposite direction from the one he usually took, he didn't see the big Packard parked in the driveway until he turned into it. There was only one person rich enough to drive a luxury car like that. Uncle Gus. Well, not really his uncle--his mother's first cousin. He was called Uncle out of respect.

There was only one reason Uncle Gus would have driven from Worthington, a two-hundred-mile trip: to shake some sense into Alex, who now wished he had seen the Packard and driven on. Too late, he realized he was trapped, the van's noisy exhaust had announced his presence, and there was no backing out of the driveway. He killed the engine and climbed out of the van. He entered through the back door of the kitchen, removed his work boots and placed them on the landing to the basement. His mother did not allow shoes in the house unless, of course, they happened to be Uncle Gus's Florsheim wingtips.

The smell of paragemistes domates, stuffed tomatoes, baking in the oven comforted him. At least he would have his favorite meal. Isn't that what wardens served doomed convicts--their favorite meals? Of all the difficulties he had with his mother, he could not fault her cooking. That's what he would miss most. Mary Lou was not at home in the kitchen. He padded across the linoleum in his stockinged feet and opened the swinging door to the dining room. The carved oak table was set for dinner with his mother's best china.

The table and chairs were the only furniture his parents brought from Waseca, and they held special memories for him. As a child he sat under this table when his mother made dough for spanakopita. She covered the tabletop with a folded bed sheet, placed the ball of dough in the center, and pulled it out with her fingertips until it was paper-thin and hung nearly to the floor. He remembered watching the filo slowly descend like a theater scrim.

Gus was sitting across from Alex's parents, his ample backside two sizes larger than the chair seat. Everything about him was ample: chin, stomach, arms, thighs. His suits were tailored. You couldn't buy that size off the rack. On this day he was wearing a three-piece black-worsted suit, perfect for a funeral. Alex's fashion statement consisted of dark green pants and a matching shirt with a lightning bolt stitched across the back.

Gus labored to his feet. "I heard you drive in. Sounded like a tank." He laughed at his joke and gave Alex a bear hug. Alex could almost feel claws digging into his shoulders. Gus's shiny cheeks smelled of after-shave.

He squeezed the muscle on Alex's upper arm. "Your job is making you strong." He looked approvingly at Alex's mother. "Isn't that right, Chrysoula?"

She forced a wan movement of her lips as she gripped the edge of the table to control her shaking.

"He can use toughening up," his father said.

Gus poured Mogen David, the only wine his parents kept, from a silver decanter, and lifted his glass in a toast. "To Alex and a bright future."

Alex barely tasted the sticky sweet wine because it gave him a headache.

Gus pulled out the chair next to him. "Sit down, sit down."

"I have to change first."

Alex's mother did not allow work clothes on her brocaded chairs.

"Be as you are, my boy," Gus said expansively. "We waited quite a while for you and I'm hungry. Your mother knows my weakness, paragemistes domates. It is well worth the drive just to taste her cooking. You're lucky you can enjoy it every day."

"I haven't been eating many meals at home lately," Alex said.

His mother dropped her gaze.

"A pity," Gus said.

"How long will you be in town?" Alex asked guardedly.

Gus wore thick lenses, and his eyes appeared as if they were on his glasses, not in his head. "That depends."

Alex knew not to ask, depends on what?

Alex's mother drew herself up to a standing position and shuffled into the kitchen.

"Gria, thelis voithia?" Old woman, do you need help? his father called after her.

"Theodoros," Gus tut-tutted.

Alex's father looked at him questioningly.

"You don't hear yourself anymore."

"What did I say?"

"You know what you said," he admonished. "It's so automatic you don't even think about it. Call her Chrysoula. It's a beautiful name."

Alex watched his father's cheeks turn crimson. He felt sorry for him. His dad was always several steps down from Gus. He smelled of chocolate, Gus smelled of expensive cologne. He had one good suit, Gus must have a dozen. He drove a Chevrolet station wagon he bought used, Gus traded each year for a new car. His father went as far as the fourth grade. Gus went to Seminary.

Alex's mother brought in a steaming platter of baked tomatoes. Uncle Gus had three helpings, eating with gusto, dipping his mother's homemade bread in the juice. After dinner, his mother made Turkish coffee for the men in a small copper pot. Using one hand to steady the other, she poured the thick, unstrained brew into demitasse cups. Then she returned to the kitchen to wash dishes.

Gus unwrapped a Garcia 'y Garcia and snipped the tip with a silver clipper he kept in his vest pocket. He lit the cigar carefully, first holding the end to the match flame and then, with the cigar in his mouth, rolling and puffing till there was a perfect, round glow. Smoke billowed and drifted toward the ceiling. It was as heavy as incense.

They sipped coffee.

"Tell me, my boy," he said, "how do you like your new job?" The question came from behind a cloud of smoke.

"Like you said, it's building me up."

"How much do they pay you?"

"A dollar fifty-five an hour. Dollar ninety with overtime."

"What about school?"

"It's on hold for now. I plan to go back winter quarter."

Gus made a face of disappointment. "Be sure you finish. Make us proud. Nobody in my generation went to college."

"You went to Seminary."

"Yes, but I didn't become a priest, I became a restaurateur."

"What's wrong with that?"

"All right for my generation but you can do better. When I was your age, I opened the Sweet Shoppe." He puffed contemplatively. "I can't believe that forty years have gone by since then."

"You've been very successful."

"Success is relative, Alex. One of my regrets is that I didn't get married and have a family of my own." He made an inclusive sweep of his arm. "You are my family." Gus looked at his cigar as if it held the answer to life itself. "Remember the last time I went to Greece?"

Even though Alex was seven he remembered it clearly. Gus drove a big black Buick then, with spare tires on both front fenders, just like the cars in gangster movies. No one in Waseca had a car like that, not even Mr. Priebe who owned the Buick agency. "Sure I remember."

"I asked you what would you like me to bring back from Greece, and you said..." Gus hesitated, prompting Alex.

His mother came in from the kitchen to hear better.

"I asked you to bring me a piece of marble from the Parthenon."

Uncle Gus slapped the table, milking it for all it was worth. "Not an evzona doll from a souvenir shop, but a piece of marble from the Parthenon! A symbol of the glory of Greece! You made me very proud of you that day, Alex. Where is it?"

"On my dresser upstairs." Alex made as if to get up and fetch it but Gus put his hand on his arm.

"I can see it later. The point I want to make is, that as a seven-year-old boy, you already appreciated the significance of your heritage. You understood even then how privileged it is to be Greek."

If the truth be known, Alex didn't feel privileged at all. He now had deep misgivings about the small piece of gray marble he so blithely asked for when he was seven. Whatever part of the Parthenon it came from--a step, a lintel, a column--it was wrong to help yourself to a piece of magnificent architecture. What if every tourist did this? There wouldn't be anything left.

"A son sensitive enough to ask for a treasure like that could never dishonor his family." Gus was cruising in high gear now, talking and smoking--what Greek men did best.

"I am planning another trip to Greece. This time I would like a traveling companion, someone who appreciates the same things I do."

"Sounds good to me," Alex said, presuming Gus was talking about his father.

Gus glanced at Alex's parents as if to say, See? That wasn't so hard.

He shifted his attention back to Alex. "I knew I could count on you." He smiled generously, as if he were handing over the keys to his new Packard.

"You want *me* to go with you?" Alex asked.

"Who did you think I was talking about?"

"Dad."

There was a puzzled look followed by a moment of embarrassed silence. "Well...I guess he could come, too."

"You know I can't leave your mother," his father said gruffly.

"Bring her along," Alex said blithely. What a splendid idea--everyone gone while he and Mary Lou started out their new life together, but they looked at him as if he had taken leave of his senses. "Ok, it was just a thought."

"Dream with me for a moment," Gus said, picking up the tempo again. "I'll take you to the Parthenon and show you where I picked up the marble I gave you. We will go to Delphi, Olympia, Naphplion, Agamemnon's tomb--you will see all the glories of Greece." Gus was in a glory of his own, speaking fervently of the land he had left behind. "Our trip will culminate in Niata where your mother and I grew up. We will gather figs from the trees, eat freshly slaughtered lamb and warm yogurt, drink goat's milk, swim in the Mediterranean, bask in the sun."

Alex was getting married in two days, and his uncle was talking about getting a tan. He had to give his parents a lot of credit, though. They had brought in the heavy artillery, the Big Bertha from Worthington, to get him out of here, as far away as possible--a culture and a world far away from Mary Lou. That will cool his ashes.

"I don't know..." Alex started to say.

"I am not young anymore," Gus interrupted. "My knees bother me. I need someone young and strong, someone I can depend on. Most important," he emphasized, "I want to travel with someone who knows the classics, who can look at a ruin and understand the history that is buried there."

Alex couldn't help being intrigued. He would love to walk among the Hellenic treasures he had only read about. Maybe he and Mary Lou could postpone their elopement. "How long a trip are you talking about?"

"Two months."

Alex pulled back. "Two months?"

There was a shift in the posture of a man who did not plan to lose. Gus balanced his cigar on the edge of the ashtray and leaned forward as far as his girth would allow. "You and I have never spent much time together, Alexandros. This is an opportunity for us to get to know each other better."

"Two months is a long time."

"What's to keep you here?"

He couldn't tell Gus what was keeping him here was the woman he was going to marry. "My job."

"Driving a delivery truck?"

"I also have school."

"You just told me you weren't going back till winter quarter."

"I have to finish my thesis."

"You've got the rest of summer and the entire fall to do that." Uncle Gus patted Alex's hand. "What is most important right now is to discover your roots. You have to know where you came from in order to know where you are going."

"I know where I'm going."

"Do you?" Gus asked with feigned admiration. He looked at Alex's father. "I envy the certainty of the young, don't you, Theodoros?"

Alex's father was clearly awed by Gus's performance. Gus was an actor, all right. He locked eyes on Alex. "I need your decision." A level tone of firmness had replaced the seductive cantor of his sales pitch.

"When are you planning to leave?"

"Two weeks."

Alex relaxed. "It will take a lot longer than that to get a passport."

Gus smiled. "You forget you are talking to Gus Pantoflas. I called Senator Thye's office in Washington and he will expedite your passport. All we need is a photo and your birth certificate."

Alex rubbed the claw foot under the table with his stockinged foot.

"Well?" Gus asked.

"What's the rush?"

Gus's cigar was growing shorter and so was his patience. "Your parents are worried, very worried."

Alex looked at their lugubrious faces. "That's what they do best."

"You can't blame them for being concerned about your relationship with this..." He let the sentence go unfinished. Everyone understood who he was referring to.

The gloves were finally off. "Uncle Gus, I'm twenty-two-years old. I shouldn't even be here listening to you."

"Siopi!" Shut up! Alex's father warned across the table. "Don't talk to your uncle like that!"

Gus raised his hand for order. "Now, now, Theodoros, emotion is healthy. We should not suppress Alex's feelings."

One thing about Uncle Gus: he was smooth.

"Now then, my boy, tell me about this woman you've been seeing."

"What about her?"

"Is she a local girl?"

"She moved here from Hibbing."

"What about her parents."

"They're both dead."

"What about brothers, sisters?"

"A sister who lives in town."

"Is she educated?"

"Well...business college."

"And what did she learn in business college?" His tone implied that all she learned was typing.

"She's executive secretary for the publisher of the Star and Tribune." Alex said in defense of the woman he loved. "That's a responsible job."`

"She is attractive?"

"Of course."

Gus winked like one of the guys. "I know you wouldn't go with a girl who wasn't."`

"Thanks for that."

"Alex, you really have to understand that I see this from your point of view as well. Every young man has to have a fling."

"Is that why you drove all the way up here? Because of a fling?" Alex said testily. "Then you wasted a long trip."

Gus exchanged glances with Alex's mother. She turned and went into the kitchen. Water ran in the sink.

"You don't know what this is doing to her," Gus said in a low voice.

Alex was getting a headache, either from the Mogen David or the thumb screws Gus was boring into his skull. "I need time to think..."

Gus turned the black onyx Masonic ring on his pudgy finger. It reminded Alex of the Secret Decoder Ring he got years ago with a Wheaties box top. "Are you willing to give up everything you value?"

"Like what?"

"Tradition. That is what makes us who we are, Alex. Our tradition goes back thousands of years, long before there was a Catholic church."

"I wouldn't give up anything I didn't want to."

"Oh, no? Catholics obey only one man, the Pope. You would have to renounce everything you hold dear--not only your beliefs but also any children you may have." Gus placed his palms together and looked at the coffee dregs in the bottom of his cup. Greek fortune tellers read them to predict the future. Alex didn't see anything down there but congealed blackness. "Have you talked to her about these things?"

"Not exactly."

"Then you need to."

"Ok, I will," Alex said, straightening his back.

Gus picked up his cigar. It had gone out. "And while you're at it, ask her if she minds if you to go to Greece with me."

Alex cleared nervous phlegm from his throat.

"Will that be hard for you to do?"

"Why should it?"

Gus smiled knowingly. "Because deep down you know what her answer will be."

"You sound awfully sure of yourself, Uncle Gus."

Gus relit his cigar. He puffed till the round glow had returned. "I have four thousand years of Greek heritage to back me up," he said through the smoke. "I have Homer, Plato, Socrates and Aristotle on my side."

THE RAID

The four destroyers of DESDIV 1 steamed out of Hong Kong harbor Wednesday morning, the cloud-banked mountains receding as the ships' turbines turned at full speed. The Squadron had received orders from COMCRUDESPAC, and the scuttlebutt was that they were heading north of the 38th parallel to shell Wonsan Harbor, a strategic seaport on the eastern coast of North Korea.

Before getting underway, Clayton was transferred to the Kearsarge. The carrier's launch threw bubbles from under its hull as it pulled alongside the Sprague to pick him up. The coxswain idled his engine as two SPs scrambled up the accommodations ladder. Poulos climbed up to the O1 deck and stood by the portside three-inch fifty gun tub, where he could look down without being obvious. The quarterdeck was subdued, a shipmate was being carted off in the company of SPs. Clayton showed up crisp and neat in a fresh pair of dress whites, his seabag on his shoulder. He had a small bandage over his eye. Clayton set his seabag at his feet. The two SPs flanked him. He wanted everyone to see what a good sailor he was. He stood at attention and saluted the Executive Officer as he was handed his orders. His arm came up smartly. His elbow stuck straight out and the tips of his fingers just touched the rim of his hat. Clayton then made a precise about face and saluted the ship's pennant and the American flag fluttering high on the ship's mainmast. Poulos was so spellbound by the scene that he neglected to hide behind the gun armor and Clayton spotted him staring down. Their eyes locked for a split second. The intensity of feeling was in stark contrast to that minuscule lapse of time.

One of the SPs nudged Clayton and broke his concentration. Clayton tossed his seabag into the launch and climbed down the ladder.

He sat on a slatted wood bench running fore and aft and the SPs positioned themselves on either side of him. The coxswain rang the bell one time as the launch pulled away and chugged across the water to the Kearsarge.

Poulos did not notice Scotty next to him till Scotty nudged him and broke his concentration. He jumped. "How long have you been standing there?"

"Did I surprise you?"

"You scared the shit out of me," Poulos said, collecting himself. "I was watching Clayton leave."

"Good riddance." Scotty grinned, and his acne scars made tiny crevices along the sides of his mouth.

"No need to be hard on him now."

"I didn't see you run down and shake his hand."

Poulos felt bad. "The navy was his life."

“Feeling sorry for him now?"

"Why kick him when he's down?"

"Isn't that what you did when you dumped the dust bag on his face, kicking Clayton when he was down?"

"Is that what you think?"

"That's what everybody thinks."

"Everybody?"

"The whole fucking ship, officers and men. You got rid of him, just like you planned."

"I didn't plan anything," Poulos said, taken aback.

Scotty patted him on the shoulder. "Hey, don't worry about it. We're all glad to see the bastard go."

Poulos stared at the launch receding in the distance, wishing now he had done something, anything, before Clayton was hauled off, apologize, ask forgiveness. He shook his head in remorse. Too little and too late, the story of his life.

"Who's moving in with you?"

Poulos looked at Scotty "Oh, Ernie Klein."

"From engineering?"

He nodded.

"Looks like you're in charge now. El Bosso. Lead-o Yeo-man-o."

"Can it, Scotty."

"Will you be standing watch?"

"Of course."

"Clayton didn't."

"I'm not Clayton."

The four destroyers met a weather front and the wind picked up causing the Sprague to pitch and roll disagreeably. The sailors spent the better part of a day adjusting their sea legs. The most difficult task was keeping down a supper of gummy chicken a la king on cold toast. The movie was cancelled with little complaint. No one relished sitting in a pitching messroom redolent with the odors of a hundred thousand chow downs, even to watch Mitzi Gaynor. On the second day out, the seas calmed and life aboard ship returned to normal.

That night, after the eight o'clock reports, Poulos went to the chart house to see Witter and Browning and check out their Hong Kong purchases. The chart house was on the Ol deck and shared a common passageway with the Commodore's stateroom. The sailors were very sensitive to noise ever since the Commodore's scolding memo to Captain Blessing. Apparently the memo wasn't enough because the Commodore ordered the Captain to include a notice in the Plan of the Day shortly after the Sprague put to sea:

There is still (underscore still) entirely too much loud and completely unnecessary noise on the O1 level in the vicinity of the Commodore's Cabin. Most of this noise originates in one of the following locations:

a) The chart house
b) The mess line
c) The serving line
d) The scullery
e) The scullery passage
f) The wardroom pantry
g) The ship's galley

This noise is of the following type:

a) Slamming of doors
b) Playing of jazz phonograph records
c) Running up and down ladders
d) Singing and whistling
e) Banging and dropping utensils
f) Yelling "HOT STUFF!" when carrying pans of food from the galley

Personnel who create loud and unnecessary noise in the vicinity of the Commodore's Cabin will be awarded ten hours extra duty for each offense.

The crew was in a foul mood.

In the chart house, because of the Commodore's directive, Browning had his record player turned down so low Poulos and Witter could barely hear the strains of Pachuco Hop. The map table was covered with their Hong Kong purchases. Every item they tried on fit miraculously.

Browning was especially enamored of his new shoes. He slid them on and rocked on the balls of his feet. "How do you like them?" he asked, barely above a whisper.

"They squeak," Witter whispered back.

"What?"

"I said, they squeak. Can't you hear it?"

"That'll go away after a while."

"You'll have to walk all the way from San Diego to Portland to get rid of that problem."

"Maybe some engine room grease will help," Witter said.

"What?"

"I said...never mind."

"All new shoes have to be broken in." Browning decided to start right now. He stepped into the passageway and walked up and down on the rubber mat. Poulos and Witter stuck their heads out and watched. Suddenly the door at the end of the passageway flew open. The Commodore stood in the doorway of his cabin fuming.

"What the fuck is that noise?" he thundered. A cigar was clamped in his teeth and smoke exploded from its tip.

Browning stood frozen in front of the Commodore, his arms locked to his sides, his eyes unblinking and staring at an imaginary point above the Commodore's bald head.

"Have you got a tongue?"

"Aye, aye, sir."

"Speak up, sailor, why are you whispering?"

"I said, aye, aye, sir."

"What's this aye, aye bullshit? Can't you answer yes or no?"

"No, sir, I mean yes, sir."

Poulos thought Browning was going to faint standing up.

"I didn't ask for a sentry at my door. Why the fuck are you marching up and down the passageway?"

"Trying out my new shoes, sir," Browning stammered, his eyes bulging in fear.

The Commodore looked down. "Is that where the noise is coming from?"

"Yessir."

"Where did you get those goddamn shoes?"

"Peter See the Leather Merchant in Hong Kong, sir."

"They sound like a squadron of rats."

"That's why I was walking up and down the passageway, sir. To break them in so they don't squeak."

"Walk, goddamnit, so I can hear them again."

Browning marched down the length of the passageway. He about-faced and marched back. His new shoes squeaked impressively.

"Don't waste your time. You'll never break those in. Toss them overboard."

"I traded them for my Gold-Tip Parker pen, sir," Browning pleaded.

"You traded a Gold-Tip Parker pen for those fucking shoes?" The Commodore shook his head as if lamenting the future of a navy that had to depend on sailors who make deals as dumb as this one. "If I hear another sound from those shoes, I'll put you on report. Dismissed."

Browning stood at attention.

"I said dismissed!"

Browning was nearly in tears. "Sir, if I move, my shoes will squeak and I will be put on report."

The Commodore chewed on his cigar as he pondered the stalemate created by his order. It was not good discipline to rescind a command. But if he didn't Browning would have to stand in the passageway till his bladder burst.

Poulos had an inspired idea. He said to Witter, "Let's give him a lift."

The two stepped forward and took up positions on either side of Browning. On the count of three, they raised him off the deck by his stiffened arms and carried him into the chart house.

"Good thinking, sailor," the Commodore said to Poulos, smiling around his cigar, relieved to be taken off the spot by a fast-thinking enlisted man. Maybe the service's future wasn't in jeopardy after all. "What's your name?"

"Poulos, sir."

"You'll go far in the navy." The Commodore slammed his door.

Ernie Klein came up from engineering to work with Poulos until a new yeoman could be transferred from DESPAC. He was delighted to work in such a big space. He normally spent his days in a cubbyhole aft of the boiler room. It was so narrow the typewriter had to be positioned athwart ships. In heavy seas the carriage tended to return on its own, messing up his typing.

Klein was the antithesis of Clayton--easy-going, friendly and uncritical. The two yeomen worked together in such harmony they became remarkably efficient. Things got done on schedule. Radinger's birthmark remained a cool pink and the officer even managed a compliment now and then. As nice as Ernie was to work with he had one aggravating fault. It had to do with personal grooming. To be sure, his nails were trimmed, his teeth were bright, and he didn't smell. The problem was that he never washed his hair. It laid on his head like a mannequin's wig, and it always looked as if it needed dusting.

After they got to know each other better, Poulos asked Ernie if he was allergic to shampoo.

"No, why?"

"Because you never wash your hair."

Ernie carefully ran his fingertips along his part, checking to make sure every follicle was in place. "I don't want to mess it up."

By the time the destroyers reached the east coast of North Korea, the temperature had dropped thirty degrees; Siberian winds were biting cold. Boatswains and deck hands and anyone else who had to stand watch in the open wore foul weather jackets and knit stocking caps. The Communist coastline was visible from the sea, a landscape of forbidding brown hills under menacing gray skies. The Sprague was first in line to relieve the USS Walke of DESDIV 12 from duty in Wonsan Harbor. The other destroyers in the Sprague's squadron had changed course to join the carrier Yorktown for plane guard duty in the Japan Sea. In two weeks the Sprague would be relieved by the Meredith. After that the Yarnall would take her turn, and then the Sumner. After all four ships completed their cycles, they would head for Yokosuka, home port in the Far East, for an extended break from sea routine.

Destroyers are fast and highly maneuverable firing platforms whose five-inch cannon can knock out truck convoys and supply trains, repair crews and bridges--anything within a five-mile range. The city of Wonsan was a major port and rail junction located in a harbor so large that it was possible to make sweeps along the shoreline, bombard the city and steam full speed back into open water, hoping to outdistance the range of enemy shore batteries. The skies over Wonsan were considered safe, not because the Russian-built MiG 15 jets were better than American F86s, but because the North Korean pilots were so lousy.

The Sprague cruised into position outside the harbor entrance and maintained just enough headway to keep from drifting. It was overcast and foggy. There was scuttlebutt that the Walke had received a direct hit on the last day of her mission. The Sprague's decks were crowded with hands waiting for the Walke to make an appearance. Presently, her silhouette emerged from the wide mouth of the harbor and headed slowly for the Sprague, coming to a stop off her port beam. Men from both ships stood in somber silence staring at each other across the water. Just above the Walke's waterline a hole the size of a shell was punched into her metal skin. The jagged edges of the circular hole could just be made out. That was bad enough but what was even more sobering were the seven evenly spaced lumps of canvas on the Walke's fantail.

The Sprague's gig was lowered and the Doc went over. The sailors watched him lift the edges of each canvas shroud and look at the bodies underneath. Then he conferred with the Walke's pharmacist's mate. When he returned he went to the wardroom for a meeting with the officers. Word spread like lightning. Seven men died when an armor-piercing shell went through the hull and ended up in the Walke's engine room. It didn't go off but sliced open one of the boilers and the escaping steam cooked the men like lobsters. One of them, Poulos learned, was the Walke's lead yeoman, who happened to be walking by the engine room hatch in the fore and aft passageway when an 800-degree woosh of high-pressure steam shot out of the opening and engulfed him. He was the only one who didn't die instantly.

Everyone talked about the irony of getting killed by a dud. Poulos's thoughts went further. He wondered about the yeoman. What was he doing near the engine room hatch in the first place? Why was the hatch even open? The Walke should have been at General Quarters when the shell hit, which meant that the hatch should have been secured and the yeoman at his battle station. Maybe the ship wasn't at GQ, maybe the skipper thought they were out of range. Maybe the RNK had a Russian gun that could fire shells further. Whatever the reason, that poor yeoman paid the ultimate price for being in the wrong place at the wrong time. Maybe it's true about your number being up. Sitting behind a pile of sandbags eating fish heads, the Commie gunners never knew they had scored a direct hit that scorched seven Americans to death. There was no telltale explosion or smoke.

So who are these guys, this enemy we can't see, these gooks we're supposed to hate? There wasn't a sailor on the Sprague who had ever laid eyes on a North Korean. Even if he had, how could he tell the difference between him and a South Korean? The Sprague's token South Korean was an ROK ensign, Boo Doo Phiel, and the only difference between him and his cohorts to the north was that he spoke pretty good English.

The Walke limped away, setting a course for Sasebo for repairs, and the Sprague entered Wonsan harbor, staying well clear of enemy shore batteries. The mood on the ship was gloomy. The usual levity in the chow line was missing. Sailors waiting their turn to eat stared at the bulkhead or lost themselves in a shit kicker. Anything could happen in the next two weeks. The Walke's crew probably thought they were home free when the shell hit. The Sprague went on alert status; her gun covers were removed and gun crews went through silent drills, spinning their mounts and raising and lowering their barrels. No one was allowed forward of the break because mount 51 turning suddenly could knock you overboard. On the O1 deck, the clack-clack of the three-inch fifty loaders was heard above the ceaseless hum of the ventilators. A symbiotic relationship existed between a gunner and his weapon, Poulos realized, as he saw the care that was taken to clean and oil the guns. It made sense, of course, when your life depended on a properly functioning weapon.

This was his first exposure to the grim reality of war or, as the politicians called it, a police action. Whatever name you gave it, somebody could really get hurt out here. Poulos's closest exposure was a few weeks earlier when an AD launched from the Yorktown flamed out and fell into the ocean. Poulos was in the Ship's Office when the Sprague unexpectedly picked up speed with the immediacy of a car shifting into first gear. He came out on the main deck, gripping the railing, to see what was going on. A helicopter off the port bow was hovering over three heads bobbing in water streaked with fuel oil. The helicopter lowered a line and rescued the pilot, the most valuable of the three, leaving the radar man and aerologist for the Sprague to recover. Drifting in the water with the men were bits of detritus from the plane, including a glove, a flare, and a square of Plexiglas from the plane's canopy. As the second division tried to lower the whale boat, it became abundantly clear that the crew was not very adept at sea rescue. In their earnestness, they managed to jam a line in a pulley block and the boat, hanging free of its moorings, kept banging against a stanchion. There'd be hell to pay for that. As the ship came alongside the downed airmen, Baker, a coolheaded World War II veteran whose cruiser had been sunk at Midway, tossed a lifebuoy over the side and plucked the men out of the water one at a time. The grateful fliers were cold and their flight jackets were stained with oil. They were hustled to sickbay to be checked over by the Doc. In the meantime, the helicopter returned from the Yorktown, its rotors thumping the air. The pilot held up two fingers as the craft hovered next to the ship. Two, did you rescue two? he signaled. All the sailors on deck held up two fingers and nodded affirmatively. Satisfied, the pilot dipped the nose of his helicopter as he flew away. Later, the Sprague came alongside the Yorktown to transfer the men by high-line. In return, the Sprague received a dozen gallons of freshly made ice cream, compliments of the skipper.

There won't be any ice cream on this trip, Poulos thought, looking at the leaden sky above Wonsan Harbor. He was standing the 0800 to 1200 watch on the bridge, communicating on a sound-powered telephone with the other battle stations on the ship, by now routine, but the first time he stood watch he really fucked up. It was during a firing drill in the Japan Sea three days after coming aboard. When the practice was over, Poulos received a message from fifty-three, the aft twin cannons mounted on the fantail. The gunner was a Southerner and talked as if he were chewing a mouthful of grits. "Mount fifty-three requests permission to clear the deck of cotter pins."

Poulos approached Captain Blessing. He was on the flying bridge, leaning on the azimuth smoking a cigarette. "Mount fifty-three requests permission to clear the deck of cotter pins," Poulos told him.

Blessing looked at Poulos, something he rarely did. It was not his habit to notice enlisted men, especially the new ones. They were simply objects needed to operate his ship, like the polaris or the engine revolutions indicator. "What was that?"

"Fifty-three requests permission to clear the deck of cotter pins, sir."

The Captain straightened. He was tall and rangy with the slouchiness of an athlete who has let his body go soft. He lifted his hat by the bill and scratched his head. "Tell fifty-three to repeat that message."

Poulos did as told and reported back to the Captain. "Sir, the gunner said he wants permission to clear the deck of cotter pins."

Blessing was getting worried. Poulos could tell he was mentally flipping through the ship's blueprint, trying to figure out what the fuck was coming apart. "How many cotter pins?"

"Bridge, fifty-three. How many?"

"Gotta be a dozen or more. They're rolling all over the place."

"A dozen or more, sir."

Blessing was getting concerned. "Tell him to repeat his entire message...slowly."

"Bridge, fifty-three, the Captain wants you to repeat your entire message...slowly."

"What's the fucking problem? Don't you speak English up there?" He enunciated every word. "Request permission to remove pow...der...kegs."

"Powder kegs! I thought you said cotter pins."

There were loud guffaws on the line. The sailors and officers in the pilot house tried not to snicker. The Captain, however, was far from amused. He stood nose to nose with Poulos. "Are you hard of hearing?"

"It sure sounded like cotter pins." Poulos retreated to a corner of the pilot house trying to hide his embarrassment.

The morning wore on. Scotty's voice broke the tranquility.

"Gooks working on the beach."

"Bridge, Control, repeat your last."

"We got gooks working on the beach."

Poulos approached the Captain. "Control says there are gooks working on the beach."

"Where?"

"A road bearing three one zero, sir."

Blessing checked the polaris, grunted and looked through his binoculars at Wonsan's skyline some four thousand yards away. Most of the city's buildings had been bombed or shelled, leaving misshapen spires of brick and masonry here and there. The only intact structure, left purposely so, was a factory smokestack the navy used to establish coordinates. "How many?"

"Control says a few, sir."

"How many are a few?" the Captain demanded.

"Control, bridge. How many?"

"Shit, now I have to count them?" It was ok for Scotty to speak his mind because he was tucked away alone in the round tower above the pilot house. He began counting out loud and stopped at twenty.

"Control says twenty, sir."

"Tell control when he sees fifty to let me know. Projectiles cost money you know."

Time passed quietly. The sun followed its accustomed path across the sky, oblivious to the trivial activities of life at sea. Suddenly Scotty came on the line, his voice filled with excitement. "Trucks, looks like trucks, maybe a convoy."

Poulos relayed the message.

The Captain visibly brightened. "Let's see how good we are." He went into the pilot house and had General Quarters sounded.

"Man your battle stations," was announced several times on the PA and throughout the ship sailors dropped what they were doing and ran to their assigned positions.

The Commodore appeared on the bridge wearing a life preserver over his uniform, and a helmet with the straps hanging free. Binoculars were suspended from his neck. "What's up, Commander?" The Commodore asked, stuffing cotton in his ears.

"Our first engagement with the enemy, sir," Blessing explained.

"What's that?" The Commodore asked, cotton sticking out of his ears.

Blessing raised his voice. "We're attacking a truck convoy north of

Wonsan."

"Excellent," said the Commodore, rubbing his hands. "What we came here to do."

"Engines ahead one-third," the Captain called.

"Engines ahead one-third, aye." The sailor at the engine revolutions indicator moved the needle forward and then back till it rested on one-third.

"Left full rudder," the Captain ordered the helmsman.

"Left full rudder, aye." The helmsman spun a metal disc rimmed in wood the size of a bicycle wheel. He kept his eyes glued to the gyrocompass as the ship heeled slightly to starboard. The men in the pilot house planted their feet.

"Bearing, Captain?" the helmsman asked.

"Two-one-three."

"Two-one-three, aye."

The helmsman watched the compass needle approach the new heading, and then reversed direction a couple of turns with practiced hands, making smaller and smaller adjustments until the ship was steady on her new course. They were moving at eighteen knots.

"Steady as she goes."

"Steady as she goes, aye."

"Gunnery report."

Poulos had the various mounts call in. "All mounts loaded and ready, sir."

"Mount fifty-two fire one!" the Captain shouted.

Poulos repeated the message into his phone and the gun mount closest to the bridge fired a round. A massive concussion shook the wood grate on which they stood and a terrible noise assaulted their ears. Flames spewed a foot from the right muzzle of the five-inch cannon. A perfect smoke ring billowed into the air and for an instant Poulos heard the high-pitched whine of the shell spinning away. The officers and men of DD884 waited in anticipation. In the distance a puff of smoke appeared and Scotty's voice came on the circuit. "Left one hundred, drop fifty."

Adjustments were made and mount fifty-two fired again.

"Left fifty, drop ten."

The next projectile hit the target.

"No change, no change!" Scotty shouted.

The Captain ordered all mounts to commence firing. The big guns boomed, shuddering the Sprague as she continued on course. The Captain beamed with pride and pleasure.

The firing stopped. "Bores clear. No casualties."

"Engines full," the Commander roared. "Let's get the fuck out of here!"

The Commodore stood on the flying bridge looking through his binoculars at the receding target. "Any better shooting than that, by god, and they cast us in bronze."

Excitement ran throughout the ship. On the bridge discipline was temporarily suspended as officers and enlisted men slapped one another on the back. Phone talkers hooted and howled over the circuit at the Sprague's success--here's one for the Walke. Scotty was especially proud because he directed the firing of the five-inch mounts. Poulos listened to the happy, congratulatory sounds coming over the circuit. Suddenly there was a shout of alarm and a brief scream.

Poulos called to the various stations to check in. Scotty did not respond. "Bridge, Control!"

Poulos shouted. "Check in!"

"Bridge, what's going on?" a voice on the circuit asked.

"Don't know. Can't raise Scotty."

"Probably fell asleep," someone suggested. There was laughter.

"Scotty," Poulos said, "get on the line, will you?" Nothing but silence. Poulos approached the Captain. "Sir, I'd like to check the main battery. Scott isn't answering."

"Hanson," the Captain said to another sailor on the bridge, "Take the phones."

Poulos climbed the ladder to the top of the pilot house. The main battery was a cylindrical tower six feet high. It extended another six feet down between the pilot house and the Captain's sea cabin in a cranny jammed with equipment. Access to the main battery was through a hatch at the top of the tower. Poulos had to climb another set of metal rungs to reach it. He looked inside. Scotty should be perched on a steel seat above a complex of range-finding gear but he wasn't there. His ear phones were dangling by their cord. Poulos heard moaning and stuck his head in further. He saw the top of Scotty's head. He was wedged between cables and hydraulic motors at the bottom of the tower.

"Scotty, what happened?"

He grunted from pain. He had fallen a good ten feet. "I stood up. I was so fucking excited I stood up. My leg is busted."

Poulos shouted for help.

It took half an hour to extricate Scotty from the tight confines of the tower. A makeshift harness was lowered. The tower was too small to hold another person and Scotty had to slip the harness under his arms by himself. It was amazing that he didn't pass out. Poulos stayed with the rescue team and called out encouragement as Scotty was slowly hoisted out of his prison. As soon as his upper body appeared through the hatch, the Doc injected morphine into his shoulder, right through his shirt. By the time they got Scotty onto a stretcher, he was in a daze. It must have been quite a dose. He was carried down to the wardroom, which served as a dressing station during GQ, and laid on the broad, green-felt dining table which had been covered with padded plastic and a sheet. Poulos peeked through the wardroom porthole to see the Doc rip Scotty's dungarees up the seam and expose the damaged leg. His ankle was dark red and swollen and his foot was turned inward at an excruciating angle, revealing a splintered shard of bone. Poulos was surprised there was not a lot of blood, just an oozing gelatinous claret along the gash in his skin. He had to turn away. The Doc ordered ice from the reefer to hold down swelling. It was all he could do.

Even without x-ray equipment the Doc was able to diagnose the full extent of the injuries. "There are severe fractures of the right tibia, tarsus and metatarsus. The right knee appears to have suffered compression, which suggests that the anterior and middle fibular ligaments have been ruptured. In other words, it ain't good."

"Do I get a purple heart?" Scotty asked groggily.

"You better rest," Poulos said. Scotty stretched out his arm. "Don't leave."

Poulos looked at the Doc and he nodded his head.

"What's going to happen to me?" Scotty asked.

"You're going to the Yorktown. We're heading out now to meet the helicopter."

"I bet the Commodore isn't too happy about that."

Scotty lay on the sickbay examination table covered in blankets. Poulos leaned a metal chair against the bulkhead and watched as Scotty slept until he slept too, waking up once to hear him mumbling, "Sorry, Mom, I didn't mean to." Shortly after reveille, Scotty was carried to the fantail where mount 53 was turned athwart ships to get the guns out of the way for the helicopter. A sea detail transferred him onto a wire-mesh stretcher which had a bright yellow life ring attached to the frame. He was secured with straps.

Witter and Browning joined Poulos to wish him well.

"Will I see you guys again?" Scotty asked through the haze of morphine.

"You'll be back," Poulos said.

"Not too sure." He looked at his buddies as though he was saying goodby for good. "Dumb, wasn't it? Subconscious desire to get out of the navy."

The helicopter whirred into view and pushed swirling air down on them. The trio stepped back so Scotty's stretcher could be hoisted up. He raised his fingers in a ta-ta motion just before disappearing inside the cabin of the helicopter.

Scotty was right. Commodore Katz was not happy. Ready to draw more blood from the Commies, the Sprague instead steamed out of Wonsan Harbor like a dog with its tail between its legs. She had lost twenty-four hours out of her mission because some fuckhead failed to follow regulations during General Quarters. Katz made a mental note to tell Blessing to put that stupid sailor on report.

He was so pissed losing precious time, not to mention face, that he came up with a grand strategy to gain back the initiative: make a daring raid on Munch-On, a non-strategic city tucked inside a narrow inlet in the upper reaches of Wonsan Harbor. A Commodore had seniority over the Captain of a fighting ship but it was rare if not unheard of to take over his command unless the Captain was incapacitated or there was a dereliction of duty, but no one had the balls to look up the appropriate sections of UCMJ and point them out to the Commodore. Thus unchallenged, Katz ordered officers to the wardroom to outline his daring plan: steam full speed through the inlet, shoot up Munch-On and anything else that stuck its head above the ground, and steam out again in less than five minutes. Here was a mission no American ship had ever attempted before, and for good reason. The inlet to Munch-On was known as suicide alley. This did not deter the Commodore; in fact it challenged him. He was determined to prove his mettle. This was his final tour and he aimed to end it with his finest hour, the prospect of which terrified everyone on the ship.

Like a kid in a candy store, Katz pored over charts on the map table with the skipper who showed little enthusiasm for the mission. Information on this part of the harbor was not reliable since sounding depths dated back to the eighteen-nineties. The Commodore was convinced that if the Sprague stayed in the middle of the inlet there would be no problem, as it was shown to be deep enough for a submarine. Two rivers flowed into the channel behind the promontories and the Captain was worried about the build-up of silt over the years. He did not think it very probable that the North Koreans dredged the channel. Nothing went in or out but fishing boats. Besides, and this was the most ticklish point, there was nothing strategic about Munch-On.

"That's what makes my plan so beautiful," the Commodore said. "The Commies won't expect us to hit them there. They will still be pulling up their loincloths by the time the Sprague is out of range."

There was spirited discussion in the wardroom; officers were cautiously expressing their reservations. The Captain enlisted the help of the Korean Ensign Boo Doo Phiel, to try to convince the Commodore that even the South Korean navy would not try something like that in its own back yard. The most outspoken was the Sprague's navigator, Lt. Hendershot, who did not trust the water depths on the charts. But the Commodore ordered Hendershot to lay out a course where he was certain the waters ran deep. The major concern, the Commodore insisted, was not water depth but the element of surprise. The Commies had to be caught completely off guard or the Sprague would get blown out of the water.

The Commodore made the announcement to the crew over the PA system. He was introduced by the Captain. "Attention all hands, this is the Captain. The Commodore has an announcement to make." There was a noted lack of enthusiasm in his voice.

"Officers and men of the Robert B. Sprague," the Commodore began. "Except for that sailor who broke his fucking leg, I am extremely proud of the way you handled yourselves in our recent combat operation. Each of you will receive my personal commendation on your record."

Poulos groaned. More typing.

"Now that you have shown your courage, we will test it again. This time our target will be Munch-On."

At this point the entire ship's crew groaned.

"Until now, Munch-On has been spared naval bombardment because of its isolation. But no longer. The Commies can't hide from the guns of the Sprague. Late tomorrow night we will take our position at the entrance to Munch-On Bay. Before the first light of dawn, we will steam through the inlet and lay devastation upon the surprised Commies. We will catch them in their cots, we will catch them in their crappers. We will be out of there before they can load a single shell. Division Officers will brief you at 1645 muster. That is all. Good luck. God bless you, and God bless the United States of America."

Disbelief spread through the ship. Everyone was convinced the Commodore had completely lost his marbles. There was no earthly reason why a city that no one ever heard of was worth a single American life. Poulos cornered Gildenhall on the Ol deck. "Shouldn't he be relieved of command?"

"On what grounds?"

Poulos was reading Witter's copy of The Caine Mutiny. "Queeg was relieved of command to save the Caine from sinking in a typhoon."

"There's no typhoon, unless you count the one inside his head."

That night Poulos lay in his rack thinking about Scotty safely on the Yorktown. Better to be injured than dead, even if you spend the rest of your life walking with a limp. And what about Clayton? He too was safe, no doubt sleeping in a comfortable bed with clean sheets, listening to Armed Forces Radio, and being attended to by nurses. No need to feel guilty over Clayton. Poulos may actually have saved his life.

At 0300 the Sprague hove to at the mouth of the inlet, facing two dark land masses set against a background of sea and sky only slightly less dark, when reveille was held at 0330, two hours earlier than usual, half an hour before the duty cook is normally called. Instead of piping reveille, the chiefs of the various Divisions went through the compartments and shook the sailors awake. There was an unnerving silence as the men climbed out, hoisted their racks out of the way and drew on their clothes. The only lights were from overhead lamps--red bulbs glowing eerily in metal cages. The sailors quietly shuffled through the galley for a breakfast of sandwiches and black coffee. No cream and sugar were allowed because the Commodore worried that spoons would make too much noise clanking against the mugs. Sailors throughout the ship were dying for a cigarette, but the smoking lamp was out.

On deck it was clammy--cold and misty. You could see your breath. The men put on battle gear and went to their stations, being careful not to run up and down ladders because the sound of shoes hitting steel treads would echo across the water. Poulos climbed to the bridge, careful not to slide his shoes on the ladder. From the storage locker he got a life preserver, flak jacket, and a steel helmet almost as large as a punch bowl. It had to be, in order to fit over the the earphones that stuck out several inches. His shoulders sagged from the weight of the vest of woven ball bearings meant to stop shrapnel. He was sure the added weight of the flak jacket would cancel out the buoyancy of his life preserver and he would drown anyway.

Shadows moved around the bridge and the pilot house: the Commodore, the Captain, the Exec, the navigation officer, the pilot house crew. Speaking quietly into his transmitter, Poulos told everyone on the circuit to check in. The new man in the main battery director was Bubba Schamberger who traded watches with Scotty. He would serve double duty until a new man could be transferred to replace Scotty.

The odds were better than even that someone would get killed, most likely on the bridge, the most vulnerable spot on the ship. The longest odds were those placed on the likelihood of the Sprague sinking but if she went down there wouldn't be anyone to collect the money. There were even some pollyannas who hoped the ship did sink because survivors would get 27 days home leave. It didn't register to them that those who didn't die would end up POWs and the North Koreans were not known for their hospitality.

Poulos studied the Commodore. In the mist of early morning he saw only the burning eyes of a zealot. Normally, the Communists would not expect an American destroyer in their private pond but then, as is true of any military operation, each side has its own psychopath. Behind those hills somewhere, there had to be a North Korean commander whose eyes were burning with the same intensity as the Commodore's. He was waiting for his moment of glory, too, waiting to sink a US destroyer with all hands on board.

At the first light of dawn, the Sprague would charge full speed through the channel with the port and starboard anti-aircraft guns firing a continuous fusillade of fifty-caliber bullets into the nearby hills. As soon as the Sprague was through the channel, she would turn and fire broadside, all six five-inch guns raining death and destruction on the sleeping city. When her turn was completed, she would speed back out of the inlet, anti-aircraft guns once again providing cover for the ship's escape into open water. Total elapsed time calculated at four minutes thirty seven seconds. On the plotting table in CIC it sounded terrific.

The Sprague suddenly sprang to life, her screws churning the water. She picked up speed so quickly, unprepared crewmen fell to the deck. In seconds the ship's four three-inch fifties opened up, their tracers splitting the brightening sky. The machine guns were firing at such a rapid rate they sounded like the continuous roar of a waterfall. The pilot house was in a frenzy. Poulos was having trouble sorting out the voices on the circuit. Everyone was hollering. It was mass confusion. As the Sprague reached the narrow channel, flashes of light appeared on the far shoreline. The North Koreans the Commodore said would still be in their crappers had somehow managed to pull up their pants and fire back.

Voices on the line shouted that the ship was being fired upon.

"Christ, don't you think I can see it up here?" Poulos shouted back.

The Captain ordered the Sprague hard to port. Shells off her starboard bow exploded in a shower of water.

"They're locking us in!" the Captain shouted.

Meanwhile the Sprague's three mounts came about and pointed toward Munch-On as enemy shells hit the water fore and aft of the Sprague's position. When Poulos saw the flumes of water getting closer, he believed it was all over, the ship was doomed. The next volley will explode on the ship itself. Limbs will fly, blood will splatter, men will scream and die; the ship will catch fire and sink. But curiously he was not afraid. He couldn't understand how he could feel so fatalistic over the prospect of dying. Without warning a long, shuddering vibration tore through the ship. Someone shouted, "This is it!"

Poulos closed his eyes and started reciting the Lord's Prayer in Greek as he was taught to do as a child kneeling by his bed.

"Call the engine room!"

Poulos was busy mouthing silently in Greek.

"Goddamnit, didn't you hear me? Call the fucking engine room!"

Poulos's eyes snapped open. The Captain was standing in front of him with his arms akimbo. "Find out what the fuck is going on and don't tell me it's cotter pins!"

Saliva spattered Poulos's face. "Bridge, engine room!" Poulos shouted into his phone. "Report in!"

"Water coming out of the bilges!"

Poulos reported to the Captain who was extremely agitated. "Get the fire room. Find out if they're ok."

"Bridge, fire room, anything going on down there?"

"Shit man," came a harried voice, "we got water comin' in all over!"

"Fire room has water too."

The Commodore was clinging to the corner of the pilot house. The Captain gave him a dirty look. "Turn hard about," he called to the helmsmen, "and keep your fucking foot on the gas!"

The Sprague made a tight U-turn, heeling well over. Poulos hung on convinced she'd tip into the sea. The ship's mounts were spinning and their five-inch cannon were jerking up and down as Bubba in main battery control was vainly trying to lock on the ever-shifting target.

He shouted over the phone, "What the fuck is going on? I can't get a fix if you keep turning so fast!"

Poulos reported Bubba's frustration to the Captain. "Tell Schamberger to fire a salvo! Get something off so this fucking raid isn't a total disaster!"

But none of the guns could fire. They were turned in so far, their shells would have hit the ship's superstructure. The bay behind the Sprague was pock-marked with explosions that fell further behind as she retreated into open water. Relief coated with humiliation spread through the pilot house. The mission was a fiasco. While not a single round was fired at the enemy, the Commie shore batteries had a field day taking pot shots at the Sprague. They probably hadn't had this much target practice since Perry opened the Orient in 1852.

The Captain was fuming and cursing. His ship was taking on water at an alarming rate; she was listing badly and vibrated above fifteen knots.

When they were safely out of range, the Captain ordered all engines stopped.

"Thirty-four, bridge," the gunner from one of the anti-aircraft batteries reported in.

"Bridge, thirty-four, go ahead," Poulos replied.

"Oil slick off the port beam."

"Thirty-four reports an oil slick off the port beam, Captain."

"Shit," Blessing said more to himself than to the those in the pilot house. He called the engineering officer on his bridge-engine room communicator. He turned the telephone crank several times and, in the eerie silence of a ship riding swells without her engines turning, it sounding like a banshee wailing. "Have a repair party find the leak off the port beam. Get me a damage report on the double."

Half an hour later, it was established that numbers three and four fire rooms were taking on water at an estimated rate of 300 gallons a minute. Number five forward engine room was taking on water at an estimated rate of 500 gallons a minute. The leak was traced to a fuel line rupture and repaired.

The Sprague had run aground on its charge into Munch-On, ripping her hull in at least two places. The screws must have struck bottom causing the blades and the 100-foot shafts to bend. This would explain the vibration at upper speeds. Bilge pumps and eductors were managing to keep the flooding under control, but they could not keep the Sprague from leaning at a seven-degree list.

THE NEGRO

It was Saturday morning and Alex and Mary Lou were heading south on Highway 65 to Mason City. It was raining hard. The downpour was so heavy he expected to see catfish jump out of the water. He turned the van's wipers to fast. They worked feverishly but could not keep the windshield clear. He slowed down. Mary Lou wanted him to pull off the road and wait till the rain let up, but the shoulder was so narrow he thought it was safer to keep driving rather than risk getting rear-ended by an unsuspecting driver.

"I just hope the water doesn't kill the engine," he muttered. Fortunately, the rapping on the van's un-insulated roof was so deafening Mary Lou didn't hear him. No sense making her more nervous than she already was. The unexpectedly heavy rain was delaying them. The Cerro Gordo County Courthouse in Mason City closed at noon and they had to pick up their license. They also had to find a motel and change clothes, get their Wasserman tests, and meet Mike Callahan at the Justice of the Peace at two o'clock. Mason City was the Upper Midwest's equivalent of Reno where couples can get married without a waiting period. Mary Lou had convinced Alex it was the only decent thing to do, get married as soon as possible, given the uncertainty of her condition. So, using a pay phone, he called the Mason City Chamber of Commerce and was given the number of Frederick R. Shaffer, Justice of the Peace.

"Are you over 21?" his secretary asked.

"Yes, ma'am."

"Is the girl over 18?"

"Yes," he said. No problem there.

Alex had asked Mr. Parsons for Friday afternoon off to prepare for his elopement. He was so anxious to finish his deliveries, he kept making bonehead mistakes like delivering the wrong order and forgetting to get a customer to sign an invoice. He had to backtrack twice and didn't get to Mary Lou's till three-thirty.

"I thought you were taking the afternoon off."

"I am."

"Then why are you so late?"

"Isn't it enough that Mr. Parsons is letting me use his truck over the weekend?" he snapped, finally realizing how thin a thread his emotions were hanging from. “Sorry,” he added. “Guess I’m nervous.”

“Join the club,” she replied, and gave him a bucket of sudsy water to wash the van.

Feeling waves of guilt--for being short with Mary Lou, for lying to Gus, for the hurt he was about to bestow upon his parents--he occupied himself by sweeping the floor, whisking the seats and wiping the dashboard and the windows clean of years of accumulated grime. The old Ford truck came out looking surprisingly good. It had better. It was to be their wedding coach. He felt an added stab of regret. No limousine. No guests to throw rice; no best man, attendants or ushers; no clergy, organ or soprano singing Oh Promise Me.

He drove home pretending he had worked the whole day. "It's about time they cleaned that truck of yours," his father said when Alex walked into the kitchen. There was an air of expectation as the family sat down to dinner. His mother had made chicken pilaf, another favorite.

"I'm leaving Sunday," Uncle Gus said.

"Really?" Alex replied, feigning disappointment. "So soon?"

"Not till afternoon because of church." He made a gesture of inclusivity with his arms. "We'll all go together."

A lump formed in Alex's throat. By Sunday morning he and Mary Lou would be Mr. and Mrs. Alex Poulos.

"I'd also like to visit a travel agent Saturday," Gus said. "We need to plan our trip."

Alex stopped chewing. "Saturday?"

"How does ten sound?"

"Can't make it."

"All right, how about eleven?"

"Can't make that either."

Gus was admirably patient. "You name the time."

Alex's mind flew into high gear. "We have inventory and Saturday is the only day everyone can get together."

"All day?"

"Looks that way."

"I hope you are not doing inventory on Sunday," he said with a hint of sarcasm, "because I expect to see you in church."

On Saturday morning, in case anyone in the family was up at 5:30 to see him, Alex dressed in his uniform to prove the lie and, on the way to Mary Lou's apartment, pulled over on a quiet street, crawled into the cargo bay and changed into travel clothes he had stashed away earlier, a short-sleeve shirt and Chino pants.

Even though this was not going to be a church wedding, far from it, Mary Lou insisted that it can and should be dignified, and so Alex dry-cleaned his dark blue suit and bought a new shirt and rep tie at Dayton's Kenwood Shop. Mary Lou found a white silk pleated dress in the Oval Room with a half-price sales ticket. She also insisted that their wedding clothes hang in garment bags rather than be folded into a suitcase so they would be fresh and wrinkle-free for the ceremony. Alex suspended the garment bags in the van's cargo bay from a metal strip supporting the roof.

"You sure they'll be safe?"

He wiggled the bags. "They can't fall off."

"All set," she said with crossed fingers.

The rain began slowly at first. By the time they reached Owatonna, it was coming down in sheets. Alex stopped at a four-way intersection.

"See that highway?"

Mary Lou squinted into the driving rain. "Barely."

"That's County 14 to Waseca."

"Where you grew up?"

"I'll take you there someday."

The rain squall pushed north as they drove through it and when they saw the border sign for Iowa the sun started coming out. It raised their spirits, and gave Alex hope that things would work out after all. "Remember the rich uncle I told you about?"

"The one who lives in Worthington?"

"He's in Minneapolis visiting my parents. He drove up three days ago."

Mary Lou looked at Alex. "Have you told him about me?"

"Yes. He wants to meet you." That was true enough.

"It's about time someone in your family wants to meet me."

Alex kept his eyes on the two-lane highway ahead of him. "Tomorrow, you'll meet them all tomorrow."

They arrived in Mason City just after eleven, and drove down main street to a large central park graced by majestic elms. Steam rose from the drying pavement. Alex found a diagonal parking space around the corner from the courthouse. They climbed a marble staircase to the second floor where they picked up their marriage license from the Department of Licenses. When they came out again the sun had heated up the van.

"Open the windows," Mary Lou said. She looked through the small oval window in the partition separating the cab from the cargo space. "What about our clothes? Maybe we should find a motel now and get them out of the truck. It's steamy back there."

"We'd better get our Wassermans before the clinic closes." He got directions to Park Clinic.

On the way Mary Lou said, "This is really a waste of time. I don't have syphilis."

"Maybe I do," he teased.

"If I don't you don't."

"Pretty sure of yourself."

"Pretty sure of you."

They found the clinic on the edge of town, a one-story cinder block building. Inside, they were escorted to a small room. A nurse sat by a table with syringes.

"Why do I have to be tested as if I were a, well, you know," Mary Lou asked the nurse.

Mom would have finished the sentence, Alex thought bitterly.

"It's the law," the nurse replied. She drew blood from Mary Lou's arm, and then repeated the procedure on Alex.

"How does this work?" he asked.

"We test your blood against that of a syphilitic. If it comes out negative, you're fine."

"And if it doesn't?"

"You don't get married today."

They were charged seven dollars.

"Isn't that a lot of money to pay for something you didn't need in the first place?" Mary Lou asked.

Alex studied the receipt. The word Premarital was stamped across the top. "I'm going to save this," he said, folding it into his wallet.

"I'd rather not be reminded that we had to be tested for a social disease."

"It's part of the record of our wedding." He put his arm around her shoulders and squeezed. "Someday we'll look back on this and laugh."

Mary Lou was having a hard time relaxing. "I hope so."

The clinic's receptionist gave them directions to a motel where they could change into their wedding clothes. It was called Fair Oaks and lived up to its name. The grounds were thick with mature oak trees, their gnarled branches bending every which way, interlacing one another and creating welcome shade.

"I'll bet it's in the eighties," Mary Lou said, fanning herself with her hand. She waited in the van while Alex checked in.

"A single please," he said to the owner, a man in his retirement years.

The owner looked out the big lobby window at Mary Lou sitting in the van. "Here to get married?"

"Yes."

"Staying overnight?"

"Just for the day. We need a place to change."

"You still have to pay for an overnight." He slid the register toward Alex so he could sign it. "If you do decide to sleep over you'll have to show me your marriage certificate. I run a decent place." He gave Alex the key to unit twenty-seven, around the corner and down an asphalt lane. Alex parked in front of the unit. He opened the rear doors of the van. Moist heat poured out. The wire hangers were wedged so tightly in the metal strip that it took a while to free the garment bags. He carried them into the room. They seemed to have weights in the bottoms.

"Don't lay them on the bed," Mary Lou said from the bathroom. "Hang them in the closet."

Alex unzipped the bags and let them slide to the closet floor. He looked down. Water was oozing out of the crumpled plastic. He checked their wedding clothes. They were soaked and stained a dull red.

"Jesus."

He went outside and climbed into the back of the van and ran his fingers along the metal roof frame. Moisture collected on his fingertips. The old truck couldn't keep the heavy rain from coming through. The coat hangers had channeled rusty water down their clothes to the bottoms of the garment bags. That's what made them heavy. He came back in and knocked on the bathroom door.

"Mary Lou, honey."

The toilet flushed and she opened the door. "You never called me honey before. What's wrong?"

"We have a problem..."

She looked alarmed. "What happened?"

"Our clothes..."

She rushed to the closet and felt her dress. "My god, it's soaking wet!"

She brought it to the window so she could examine it in the light. "There's rust on the shoulders!" Tears formed in her eyes. "My beautiful dress is ruined." She held it out as if imploring Alex to make it clean again. He took it from her and hung it back in the closet.

She shook her head in dismay. "How could this have happened?"

"Water leaked through the roof in the heavy rain."

"Why did we take that old heap? Why didn't we rent a car?"

"To save money."

Frustration creased her forehead. "This is what you call saving money?"

"I'm sorry."

Tears formed in her eyes. With incredible self-control, she held them in check so they would not ruin her mascara. Mary Lou was nothing if not disciplined. Did her religion have anything to do with it? He wondered.

She sniffled. "Get me a Kleenex."

He went to the bathroom. "There isn't any." Nothing seemed to be going their way.

"Bring me some toilet paper then." Mary Lou touched the corners of her eyes with the paper, then blew her nose and wadded the paper into a little ball. Alex took it from her and dropped it in the toilet.

He heard a sigh as though she was trying to bolster her spirits. "Into each life a little rain must fall, I guess."

He came out of the bathroom. "A little? That was a rain of Biblical proportions." He could have bitten his lip.

"Are you saying that God was sending us a message?"

"Heavens, no!" He couldn't seem to clear his brain of religious metaphors.

"Seriously, was it wrong to come here? Are we going against His will?"

"You're being superstitious." His mother was so superstitious it literally frightened him. He hoped Mary Lou wasn't like that.

"Looking to God for answers is not being superstitious." She stared at him. "I need reassurance. Is that too much to ask?"

He wrapped his arms around her. "We weren't the only ones who got rained on," he said. "Farmers are thanking the same God for all that rain. If you want to call it something, call it a blessing."

That's what she wanted to hear. She checked herself in the dresser mirror, at her everyday frock she drove down in, a cotton print of pale polka dots and a white fake-leather belt. "I'll have to wear what I've got on, and you will, too."

They stood side by side in front of the mirror and stared at their reflections, an unlikely couple, one dark, the other fair.

"How do you like my hair? It's a new color." She was pleased that at least her hair looked good. “Clairol calls it Autumn Auburn.”

"It matches your freckles."

"Clairol does not do freckles." Mary Lou leaned forward and ran her finger along her cheek. "Do you like them?"

"One of your most adorable features." And also, he thought to himself, because freckles are as common in Greek women as blue eyes.

"I was called Freckles when I was little."

"Can I call you that?"

"Not unless you want a quick divorce."

"We're not married yet."

Mary Lou's resolve wavered a bit. "I so wanted to look like a bride."

"You do to me."

She patted her tummy. It looked really flat to Alex.

"How are you feeling?" he dared to ask.

Her shoulders sagged. "How am I supposed to feel?"

A vaguely depressing stillness filled their small motel room. It was in keeping with the plastic laminated furniture, the heavy green drapes, and the Emmett Kelly circus print on the wall.

Alex checked out and paid the bill for the night they did not use.

"Sure you won't change your mind?" the owner asked. "You're throwing away good money."

As they headed downtown, the sun baking the van, Alex began to wonder if he should have kept that room after all, in spite of its sad reminders. He and Mary Lou could have spent their first hours as man and wife in a town where nobody knew them, away from everyone and everything familiar, where their passion could be unfettered from the pressures awaiting them back home. He paid for a bath tub they did not use--where they could have soaped each other in all the right places--and a bed they only sat on--into which they could have fallen dripping wet--a private paradise where he would have come, fallen asleep still inside her, only to wake up and come again. What's a honeymoon for if it isn't to find out how many times you can make your bride cry out Yes! Yes! Yes!?

"Alex!" Mary Lou shouted. "Isn't that our turn?"

He slammed on the brakes. A driver following too closely honked in anger. He passed Alex on the right and gave the Minnesota driver the Iowa finger.

"Up yours, too, asshole!"

"Try not to be vulgar, Alex."

The offices of Frederick Shaffer, Justice of the Peace, were above the Green Mill Cafe at 119 1/2 North Federal Avenue. The entrance was under the restaurant awning, next to a miniature windmill painted bright green. Alex parked in front. They were fifteen minutes early and so they crossed the street and sat on a park bench in the dappled shade of a giant old elm. Looking across the street at the entrance to Shaffer's office Alex began feeling jittery. The wings of romance were losing their lift, weighed down by the significance of what he was about to do. Unhappy as he was at home, he was far from certain that where he was heading was any better. Just where was he going anyway? The needle on his emotional compass was no longer pointing north. He was embarking on an uncharted course, waving goodby to a father who handed over money, a mother who ironed his underwear, an uncle who promised him the trip of a lifetime...

Sensing his anxiety, Mary Lou asked, "Getting cold feet?"

He looked down at his shoes. "Too warm for that."

"You can still back out."

He stared at her.

"I don't want you to marry me if you're going to resent it the rest of your life."

He was beginning to wonder if resentment hadn't already set in. "Why are you saying this to me now?"

"I just want you to know that what we're doing is forever. I don't believe in divorce."

"Well, neither do I."

"I'm glad we agree on something at least."

"I'm just worried that we can't afford a baby."

"You should have thought of that before you made love to me."

"You were a willing partner as I recall."

"Stop making excuses."

"The truth remains that I can't support a family delivering light bulbs."

"You have time to finish school and look for work before the baby is born." She made it sound like a cold fact.

"Oh, sure, in nine months I'm supposed to finish my thesis, graduate from school, and find a job that pays five thousand a year."

"I have faith in you."

He turned to face her. "What is this absolutism about faith that you have? Faith in God, faith in me, faith in faith itself. What if I back out? What happens to your faith then?"

"There is Stanley."

Alex scoffed. "What would Stanley do?"

"Marry me."

"Even if you were..." he did not finish. The possibility that she might be pregnant was ever-present and ominous. Instead he made light of it. "I wouldn't want a kid of mine growing up with an umlaut over his name."

"It's better than having no name at all."

"There is another way."

"What?"

"You know...a way out."

Mary Lou tensed. "Are you suggesting that I get an abortion?" She measured her words. "Even in my darkest moments, Alex, I will never, never have an abortion."

A heavy silence spread between them like a stream overflowing its banks, Mary Lou on one side, Alex on the other, breached only when a Chrysler Town & Country with wood paneling, fat whitewalls and a harmonica grille turned the corner and parked in front of the restaurant. The driver cut his engine, got out and looked around. He was tall and slender, and well-dressed. It was Mike Callahan.

Alex stood and waved.

"How long has it been?" Mike asked when Alex and Mary Lou joined him on the sidewalk. He had playful gray eyes, a square jaw, and thinning sandy hair. "Eight years?"

"At least."

Mike reached through the open window of his car and brought out a bouquet of long-stemmed roses wrapped in cellophane. "Is this the bride-to-be?"

Having forgotten his manners between his brittle conversation with Mary Lou and Mike's arrival, Alex hastily said, "Sorry, this is Mary Lou Stachich."

"Enchante", Mike said and presented the roses so deeply red they were almost the color of blood.

Mary Lou's hurt glance reminded Alex that he had not only forgotten to introduce her, he had also forgotten flowers, not even so much as a carnation. She held the roses to her bosom. "These would have looked beautiful with my wedding dress."

Mike was obviously puzzled. "Did the invitation say casual dress?"

Alex pointed to the van. "The roof leaked and our wedding clothes got wet. We have to wear what we drove down in."

Mike did not question their mode of transportation because it fit the seemingly ad hoc nature of the event. "In that case," he said, "I'll get casual, too." He removed his jacket and tossed it into the backseat; then loosened his tie and unbuttoned the top button. "How do I look?"

"You look like you took off your jacket and loosened your tie."

As they stood awkwardly, the door leading to Shaffer's office opened and a young couple walked out holding hands, obviously just married. Also obvious was the girl's condition, she was pregnant.

"I guess we're not the only ones getting married today," Alex said with a nervous laugh.

Mary Lou blushed. It was clear that Mike assumed she was in the same condition, only not showing yet. Why else do people elope?

Mike looked at his watch. "Shall we go up?" He held the door for Alex and Mary Lou.

They climbed a narrow flight of stairs to the second floor hallway, the wood treads worn down by a multitude of couples on the same mission. There was a heaviness in the way Mary Lou moved her hips, like a woman weighed down by grocery bags. Ahead was a dark-stained door with pebbled glass on which black letters were outlined in gold:

Frederick B. Shaffer
Justice of the Peace
Marriages Performed

They stepped into a stuffy reception area that reminded Alex of an Edward Hopper painting. A paneled desk sat diagonally by an open window. A partly raised shade flapped in the hot breeze. A green filing cabinet stood next to a wood partition. A middle-aged woman in a one-piece dress with a white collar came out from behind the partition. She went to her desk and referred to a typewritten list. "Alexandros Poulos and Mary Lou Stay-chich?"

"Stah-shish," Mary Lou corrected.

"Sorry, honey. Say, that's a nice bouquet. You hardly ever see flowers around here."

"I'm not surprised," Mary Lou said.

The secretary shifted her glance to Mike. "Are you a witness?"

He nodded.

She looked at Alex. "One witness? Where's the other one? You need two."

Mary Lou looked at Alex. Her face was getting mottled.

"Why two?" Alex asked.

"You know how it is," she said conspiratorially. "A lot of couples that come here are teenagers. They think running away is the answer to their problems, but they don't realize how serious marriage is. When they have to bring two witnesses along, it winnows out the impulse buyers."

The cellophane covering on Mary Lou's roses began to rustle.

"Don't worry, honey, I can see you are a responsible adult. Mr. Shaffer will find someone to sign as a second witness."

The secretary ushered them down the hall through double doors into a large room that resembled a Masonic Lodge. Several rows of metal folding chairs were set up on either side of a makeshift aisle. Wood-slatted blinds were pulled over the windows to block out the noonday sun, leaving the room dark and shadowy. It took a while to adjust to the diminished light. Down front, facing the rows of chairs, was a metal folding table. Behind it sat the Justice of the Peace in shirt sleeves because of the heat. Sweat stains appeared along the suspender straps on his shoulders. Silhouettes of a man and a woman stood facing Shaffer.

"I want to sit here," hissed Mary Lou, and moved into the back row. Their eyes finally adjusted, they could see the couple in more detail.

"Oh my God!" Mary Lou whispered loud enough to be heard beyond their row.

Alex leaned toward her. "What's the matter?" he whispered.

"That man." She pointed at the groom. "He's colored."

Alex had trouble determining the shade of his skin, it blended with the darkened room. But he was tall with narrow hips and his hair shone like black enamel. "So what?"

"Look at the woman he's marrying. She's white!"

Shaffer closed a well-worn book he held in his hand and removed wire-rimmed glasses from his head. "By the power vested in me by the County of Cerro Gordo, State of Iowa, I now pronounce you man and wife." He shook hands with the mixed-race couple.

The man and woman turned and faced each other.

Mary Lou clutched her breast. "Oh my God, they're going to kiss!"

"That's what you do when you get married."

Another couple, both white, rose from the front row and hugged the bride and groom. They had to be the witnesses. They all began walking up the aisle, smiling and chatting. The woman who just got married had an orchid corsage pinned on her shoulder. She was beaming. As they got closer, she saw Mary Lou. "What beautiful roses," she said, obviously wanting to share her good feeling with someone else about to get married.

Mary Lou pretended not to hear. She looked down, pressed her knees together and pulled her skirt tightly around them.

The woman stiffened and walked out. She hadn't even got to the end of the aisle and already she was being snubbed for marrying a black man.

Alex exchanged brief glances with the groom, his dark face in sharp contrast with the white of his shirt collar. Even the whites of his eyes served to emphasize his blackness. So what happens to him now with a white woman at his side? Will he be strong enough to withstand the slights, slurs, hostile stares that will hound him the rest of his life? They already had a preview of things to come.

Alex wished he had handled himself better and congratulated them as they walked out, perhaps neutralizing the cold reaction from Mary Lou. Yet he also understood the greater context. Just like the black man and white woman, Alex and Mary Lou chose to marry in the chambers of a justice of the peace, away from the prying eyes of a disapproving society. She probably considered this yet another bad omen--like the heavy downpour and her ruined wedding dress. Alex felt a wave of regret. If anyone in this room had a right to look lovely it was Mary Lou who was in her traveling clothes--an ordinary dress--reason enough to shy away from a well-dressed woman wearing an orchid corsage.

"Next?" Shaffer was looking at them.

Alex and Mary Lou got up and walked down the aisle with Mike a step behind. They lined up in front of the table. Mary Lou's roses began to shake again.

"Would you like to put those down?" Shaffer asked gently.

"I'll hold them."

"No need to be nervous," he said. "Your first time?"

"My only time!" Mary Lou snapped.

He smiled like an indulgent father. He no doubt was used to women like Mary Lou. "Glass of water? It's plenty warm in here."

"Can't you just marry us?"

Shaffer looked at Alex with an expression that implied, I hope you know what you're getting into. "You are the groom?"

Alex handed him the marriage certificate.

"Then I take it the young man next to you is a witness."

Mike nodded.

"Sign here." Shaffer pointed to the lower left hand corner of the certificate. Under the legend, Marriage Solemnized In The Presence Of, there was space for two signatures.

"Which line do you want me to sign on?"

"Either one."

Mike wrote his signature on the bottom line.

There was a stir in back. Shaffer peeked out between Alex and Mary Lou. They turned to see who it was. The black man was standing in the doorway.

'Scuse me," he said, "but your office is closed and the secretary is gone. I wanted a copy of my marriage certificate."

"I'll mail it to you," Shaffer said. "Oh, by the way, Mr. Washington, as long as you haven't left yet. We need another witness."

Mary Lou stiffened as if she were suddenly cast by a spell. Even her flowers stopped shaking.

The man came forward and took the pen from Shaffer. He bent over the table and put his face close to the paper as he signed. The back of his neck glistened from sweat. The back of his shirt collar was stained yellow. He laid the pen down and straightened. Like Stepin Fetchit, he smiled and backed before turning. Then he walked up the aisle and was gone.

Mary Lou stared down at the black man's signature, scrawled for all time on the legal document that recorded her marriage. His name was a scribble except for the capital W writ so large it actually crossed into the sacrosanct space of her name printed on the form--an ugly gash through the elegant calligraphy. The symbolism was inescapable. Mary Lou was now irrevocably bound to the very woman she had earlier scorned for not conforming to convention. Mary Lou was no different. The two women were outcasts together--each bound by a social contract of their own making. Mary Lou's knees began to wobble. Alex put his arm around her waist and held her against his side.

"Sure I can't get her some water?" Shaffer asked.

"We'll be all right," Alex said, although he wasn't speaking from a position of confidence.

Shaffer cleared his throat. "Shall we start, then?" He put his wire spectacles back on and began reading from the small, well-used book with the black cover. The corners of the pages were finger-smudged from frequent turnings. When he came to the part about anyone having "reason that these two should not be joined in marriage," doubt roiled Alex's stomach. He glanced over Mary Lou's head at Mike, who was staring solemnly down at the floor. Alex wished Mike would hold up his hand and say, "Maybe we should think about this a little more." But Mike was silent, absorbed in his own thoughts, and the ceremony continued.

When Shaffer got to the exchange of vows, Mary Lou responded in a tinny, almost imperceptible voice. Alex's was not much better. Shaffer asked for the rings. Alex pulled out the tiny manila envelope from his pocket. At least he hadn't forgotten the one thing Mary Lou had entrusted to him. They slid the rings onto each other's fingers. His went on with difficulty. Mary Lou had to push hard to get it over his scar.

Shaffer's closing words, "I now pronounce you husband and wife," seemed to Alex like the end of something rather than the beginning.

He bent to give his new wife the traditional wedding kiss.

Her lips were cold.

THE SCOTCH

The Sprague was difficult to steer, wanting to circle in the direction of her list. She steamed toward the center of Wonsan Harbor in relative safety from the shelling of shore batteries. Harmless geysers hitting periodically several hundred yards away reminded the crew that they had stirred up a hornet's nest.

His mission in shambles, Commodore Katz was in a sweat. He had made an egregious miscalculation and sent the Sprague into unsafe waters. Blessing could barely contain his anger as he barked orders. Not only his ass and career were on the line, there was also danger of an air raid. No doubt enemy communications were crackling all the way to Siberia: a renegade American warship stupidly made a dawn attack on a non-strategic city of the People's Republic of Korea. If there was an occasion to scramble Russian MiGs this was it. They could be over Wonsan harbor in a matter of minutes for target practice.

Blessing was in radio contact with the Skipper of the Yorktown far out in the Japan Sea. "Big Dipper this is Flapper, we are nearly derelict after striking an underwater obstacle and request air cover in the event of MiG attack, over."

"You struck something in Wonsan Harbor?" came the surprised response. The North Korean harbor, even though huge, was well-charted and the waters ran deep.

"We were in the bay of Munch-on."

There was a moment's hesitation as the Yorktown's captain took this in. Munch-on was not part of the task force's operations plan. In fact no one ever heard of it. "State your present position, over."

"Heading 307 degrees true east."

"We will send air cover. Any casualties?"

"None."

"Have you determined damage to your ship?"

"It appears we punctured the hull in two places on the starboard side and are at a seven degree list. Maximum speed is thirteen knots due to excessive vibration. Number three and four fire rooms and number five forward engine room are taking water but we are managing to stay afloat."

"Do you need a tow?"

"We can steam under our own power."

The Sprague leaned like a drunken sailor as she headed toward the harbor entrance to rendezvous with the Yarnall. Overhead, screams of F86 Sabre jets split the air. They were providing cover in case any MiGs showed up to finish off the wounded warship. Radio chatter was constant. The Sprague had to undergo major repairs. Depending on the availability of dry-dock facilities it would be either Sasebo or Yokosuka.

"Sasebo can't handle a bent propeller if that's what's causing your vibration," the carrier's Skipper radioed to Captain Blessing. "So we'll get CINCPACFLT to clear a space for you at Yokosuka." Yokosuka was the main naval base for the Far East, on the eastern side of Japan, a neighbor of Tokyo. It was a long drive. "Think you can make it?"

"We'll make it," Captain Blessing said, his wounded pride unable to admit to anything else.

Three hours later, the Sprague made a rendezvous with the Yarnall in the mouth of the harbor. The Commodore prepared to transfer his pennant. A cheer erupted from the Sprague's crew when the announcement was made. The whaleboat detail went to work immediately, checking every knot, the turn in every line, the operation of each pulley, to make sure the boat would be launched without a hitch. The sailors were highly motivated to make sure the transfer of the Commodore was as pleasing to him as it was to them.

But he was not in a pleasing mood. Much had to be done in a short time. Files, uniforms and personal effects had to be packed and brought to the main deck by 1400. Moreover, an inquiry was inevitable and he would have to justify his decision-making before a panel of tough admirals. He may not have been in deep water in Munch-on harbor but he sure as hell was now.

Seeing the Yarnall waiting for them reminded Poulos of the day the Sprague replaced the Walke. Now it was his ship that was limping out of the harbor. Both the Walke and the Sprague were damaged by duds--one an unexploded shell and the other a Commodore of the United States Navy.

On the signal deck Witter hauled down the Commodore's flag and folded it neatly. It was presented to Katz by Captain Blessing during a short ceremony on the main deck. Officers not on duty were present, as was an honor guard dressed in blues. It was a waste of time but no one objected. Everyone was delighted to see the bastard go. The whaleboat was lowered as smartly as anyone could remember, and there was a lot of crisp saluting as the Commodore climbed down the sea ladder and into the boat for his ride to the Yarnall.

"Tough shit, Yarnall," someone in the ranks shouted after the boat was out of earshot.

Poulos had a brief conversation with Gildenhall on the O1 deck. "What's going to happen to the Commodore?"

"Nothing."

"Nothing? Isn't the navy going to nail his ass?"

"The worst thing that will happen is retirement. Katz will live out his life sitting in the sun smoking cigars."

"What about the Captain?"

"He will probably get a reprimand on his record and a slowdown in advancement, but he'll survive."

It didn't seem right to Poulos. "At least they should give Katz a psychological evaluation."

"You mean like Clayton?"

"Clayton was drunk and disorderly. Katz nearly sunk the fucking ship."

The Sprague set a new course and next morning she limped past the Yorktown whose flight and storage decks were crammed with F86s, ADs and a handful of Grumman Hellcats left over from World War II. The giant carrier had amenities that made the Sprague's crew drool with envy: a soda fountain, movie hall, recreation room, a deck big enough to play football on. She also had a well-appointed sick bay, operating room, surgical dressing room, dental office, pharmacy, laboratory and x-ray room.

Scotty was in that floating city somewhere. Witter flashed a PVT on his signal light to Scott Karl from his buddies on the Sprague. The Yorktown was nearly out of sight when a tiny white dot of light flashed on the horizon: Three attempts to set bone no luck transfer to Yokosuka Scotty

"Scotty's going to the naval hospital in Yokosuka," Witter called out. "We'll see him again!" He flashed his thanks: TKS. The Yorktown flashed back: DMI (Don't Mention It).

Poulos had to type a clean copy of the deck log remarks about the incident cleverly written by the officer of the watch:

'Twas an unpleasant day on Korea's east shore
And we steam for Japan steering one-forty-four.
We've been to Wonsan on northern patrol,
But it's south for us now where warm waters roll.

The speed that we make comes from 2 and 3 boilers.
Split plant operation in terms of the oilers.
Eleven point two is the best we can make
For both screws were bent in yesterday's wake.

Baker is set in all spaces below
And flooding in hand, though progress is slow.
As one o'clock sounded we came to the right
To course 215 for the rest of the night.

We changed speed to nine as two o'clock went
To arrive 0800, our latest intent.
We found more speed needed at zero-three-twenty
So we gave half a knot which proved to be plenty.

ComDesDiv One is S-O-P-A.
Yokosuka is next in Tokyo Bay.
As cold winds blow and swirl 'round here,
The watch looks forward to pretzels and beer.

Poulos last saw Tokyo Bay when he arrived on a troop ship nine months ago. He stood at the railing when the Sprague entered the massive harbor, as awed now as he was then by its sheer size. After a few minutes he went back to work, distributing a mimeographed memo about expected behavior in Japan:

1. The Sprague will be in Yokosuka for an extended period due to repairs on the ship's hull. Consider yourselves guests of a foreign country. Remember--Japan is no longer occupied. We have no power over her people. The Japanese are not slaves or hirelings. Treat them courteously.

2. Any man who gets into trouble with the Japanese Armed Forces Police or anybody else on the beach will not go ashore again while in WESPAC. The Communists take great pleasure in publicizing

embarrassing incidents.

3. You are not a bunch of hillbillies, cowboys, or zoot suiters. You are members of the US Navy who wear a uniform prescribed by regulations. Wear what is correct and you will not be bothered by the Shore Patrol.

4. Don't waste your money on tailor-mades. They stick out like a sore thumb and you won't get ashore in them. The same goes for Asiatic dungarees and wide leather belts.

5. It is against the law to take anything but Military Payment Currency or yen ashore. The Communists will go to great lengths to get hold of greenbacks.

6. Japan is probably the easiest place in the world to make out and also the easiest place to get VD. Ok, the penicillin pills will stop it. But remember penicillin is good for gonorrhea. If the gal has some other disease and you get it, all the pill does is postpone the effects for a short period. Don't forget your family back home. VD may recur at a later date, it may make you sterile and it can be transmitted by you even after the doctor says you're cured. It can have horrible results on a baby born to an infected man. If you do have sexual intercourse get some penicillin tablets immediately and log in at sick bay. Failure to do so is subject to disciplinary action.

7. Japanese whisky has caused death and blindness. If you must drink, drink at the EM Clubs.

Most of the ship's memos ended up in the sea, either rolled into balls and thrown overboard or made into paper airplanes and launched from the fantail. This one was no exception.

The Sprague sat at anchor most of the morning awaiting a dry-dock berth. Yokosuka was the only facility in WESPAC where four-bladed propellers could be repaired. Orders were finally received to proceed to Section XI, Drydock 4. A pilot came out in a harbor boat to take the Sprague in. The crew pulled up anchor and the ship moved at a snail's pace through the heavy sea traffic of the Bay, a curious spectacle to all who noticed her seven-degree list and her bilge-pump hoses pulsing sea water over the side.

By midafternoon, she reached her destination. Two tugs stood by to nudge her into a concrete caisson, much like a lock in a canal. Two giant metal gates closed behind her while deckhands secured the ship by looping three-inch-thick hawsers around heavy iron capstans. Sailors used to roughing it stood on deck to watch, fascinated by the prospect that their ship, a bobbing cork at sea, was soon to be motionless; inert as a dead volcano.

The dock was a beehive of activity, the bees being mostly diminutive Japanese men and women dressed in baggy trousers, loose-fitting shirts and woven straw hats. They wore sandals on their bare feet, and there was a lot of gesturing and scurrying about.

The Sprague was inside a concrete shell some four hundred feet long by seventy feet wide, centered between rows of thick timbers set at angles to stabilize her keel. When it was finally determined that she was properly positioned, water was drained out of the caisson. It took several hours to expose enough of her hull to determine just how extensive the damage was.

USS ROBERT B SPRAGUE (DD884)
Fleet Post Office
San Francisco, California
DD884/KBB/ap
Serial: 007264
From: Commanding Officer, USS ROBERT B. SPRAGUE (DD884)
To: CINCPACFLT
Subj: Touching underground object(s), USS ROBERT B. SPRAGUE (DD884), report of
Ref: (a) US Navy Regulations 1948, Article 0727
Encl:(1) Certified copy of Ship's Log for 14 September 1952 (0400-0800)

(2) Certified copy of Quartermaster's Note Book for 14 September 1952 (0400-0800)

(3) Certified copy of Bearing Book entries for 14 September 1952 (0400-0800)

(4) Certified copy Fathometer's Log entries for 14 September 1952 (0400-0800)

(5) Certified reproduction of chart being used during incident

(6) Certified copy of Engineering Log for 14 September 1952

(7) Certified copy of Bell Book for 14 September 1952

1. In compliance with reference (a), it is hereby reported that at approximately 0546 on 14 September 1952, the USS ROBERT B. SPRAGUE (DD884) touched uncharted, submerged object(s) while engaging the enemy in the northern sector of Wonsan Harbor.

2. Commander Blessing had the conn, the Navigator was navigating, the Chief Quartermaster was at the polarus, and the fathometer manned. The original approach was 285 degrees T. This was corrected to 288 degrees T at 0530 and again to 295 degrees WT at 0540, to correct for a set to the south.

3. An attempt was made to take a bearing on Point Peret, but due to the many rocks off the point, it was impossible to determine just where the tangent was. A rough bearing put the ship slightly eastward of the plotted location. These two objects were used almost exclusively to establish the ship's course. Bearings were taken by the Chief Quartermaster and by the Navigator and were corrected by two degrees to compensate for the two degrees easterly gyro error. As the ship moved both polaruses were used on Point Peret. All bearings showed the ship was in the center of the channel where depth contours and soundings indicated adequate safe passage.

4. At approximately 0546 a vibration was felt throughout the entire ship and flooding was reported in both the forward engine room and the fire room. It was apparent the ship had struck something and it was necessary to abort the mission and disengage from the enemy.

5. Damage to the ship is as follows:

a. A thirty-seven (37) inch by five (5) inch longitudinal split, frame 76 between longitudinals no. 3 and no. 4, forward fire room. Shoring was installed to prevent additional buckling.

b. A six (6) inch split at frame 109 between longitudinals no. 4 and no. 5 forward engine room under the fire and bilge pump.

c. Bulkhead 110 is buckled between longitudinals no. 3 and no. 5 to a height of three (3) feet above the bottom plating. There was leakage of fuel oil from B-10 1/2-F into the forward engine room.

d. The fire and bilge pump in the forward engine room is out of alignment but still operative.

e. There is a four (4) foot crack along no. 3 longitudinal at frame 119, after fire room. Shoring was installed and flooding was negligible.

f. Thief samples taken from fuel tanks indicate no water except in B-10-F.

g. Both propellers and shafts were damaged due to excessive vibration above 100 rpm.

6. This is a preliminary report made in compliance with reference (a).

A letter report, including details of the mission which resulted in the damage, will be submitted as prescribed by CINCPACFLT Instruction 3040.1.

K. B. BLESSING
Commander

There was jubilation over the bad news. Damage to the hull was nothing compared to bent six-foot propellers and hundred-foot shafts. Extensive repairs that would take at least two months to complete, providing everything went smoothly--an oxymoron in the navy. The sailors not only got full sea pay, they were also landlocked in the best port of the Far East. Repairs were conducted in an atmosphere of American knowhow and Japanese primitiveness. Laborers constructed a network of bamboo scaffolding tied together with lengths of palm fronds, inventing it as they went along. They worked in twelve hour shifts. Arc lights illuminated the work at night and it was amazing the sailors got any sleep at all. Acetylene torches burned through the damaged steel plates, hissing and spitting as they cut open the Sprague like a whale being gutted.

Poulos liked to watch the dozens of diminutive Japanese laborers working tirelessly in the massive concrete cavern beneath him. He marveled at their industry and discipline, and understood better why it had taken nearly four years to defeat them.

No sooner were hull plates removed than enterprising greasers discovered how easy it was to smuggle booze on board. The hole in the fire room was large enough for sailors to sneak on and off the ship without detection. It came to be known among the enlisted men as the Prisoners' Gangway.

The inquiry into the grounding was going on in a building in the vast sprawl of the naval base and it seemed no longer to have any connection with the Sprague. The Captain and the navigator, Lieutenant Hendershot, went ashore to testify, as did the Chief Quartermaster. Poulos wondered if he might have to testify since he was the Captain's bridge talker, but he was not called. Just as well. A board of inquiry did not need his testimony to confirm what was already obvious to everyone: it was the Commodore's own fucking fault.

Mail was delayed because everything addressed to the Sprague was sent to DESDIV 1 via the Yorktown, still at sea. Finally it was transferred back to the base with three sacks of mail turning up in one day containing letters that had left the states a month ago. Browning got a box of stale gedunk which he shared with his buddies over coffee in the pilot house, which had become the enlisted men's hangout once the ship was in dry dock.

The pilot house quickly took on a lived-in look. The windscreen panes were removed to let the breeze flow through. A laundry line was strung between two stanchions. The Captain's leather flying chair was now a chaise lounge for anyone who got to it first. Someone scrounged a canvas deck chair and set that up in front of the polarus which served as a makeshift ottoman. Feet hung out of open portholes. The wood grating was littered with cigarette butts, candy wrappers, wax paper, and crumbs of cookies packed whole by loving mothers and sweethearts back home. The atmosphere was so relaxed, now that the Commodore was gone, that Browning was back to breaking in his Hong Kong shoes. No officer came within a ladder of the bridge. For the time being it was enlisted man's country.

Witter looked up from a copy of LIFE magazine his mother sent him. He whistled. "Check this," and turned the magazine for them to see. "Burt Lancaster and Deborah Kerr are kissing on the beach." The full page, black and white photo was a scene in From Here to Eternity, the hot new movie everyone was talking about. The actors were lying in Hawaiian sand with frothy surf washing over them.

"Lancaster's toes are curled."

"I'd have more than that curled."

"You get any mail?" Witter asked Poulos.

"No."

"You don't get mail if you don't write to someone. Haven't you at least got a girl friend?"

Poulos had a lot of free time to kill. When the Sprague was at sea his work day was twelve hours long including watches. Every third week he had to be on duty sixteen hours a day. He averaged five hours of uninterrupted sleep a night. But now, with the Sprague in dry dock and no watches to stand, he was enjoying the life of Riley. He wished it could stay like this until it was time to go home.

"Radinger been bugging you?" Browning asked.

"Ernie and I get the work done and Radinger stays out of our hair." Even if work didn't get done, Radinger would for sure stay out of Ernie's hair.

"Heard anything from Clayton?"

"Why should I?"

"You worked together for Chrissake."

"That doesn't mean he wants to make contact. He was probably dishonorably discharged anyway."

"Easy enough to find out," Browning said. "I can call BUPERS on ship-to-shore as long as it's official business. They'd have a record of him."

"Clayton is official business?"

"He's in the USN, isn't he?"

"If you want to call someone, call Scotty. He's in the USN, too."

Much to Poulos's relief, Browning snapped his fingers and said,

"Great idea!"

They slid down the ladders and headed aft to the quarterdeck. Ensign Porteous was on duty.

"We want to call Scotty," Browning said.

"What about?"

"Official business. See how his leg is doing."

"Be my guest."

Porteous, whose attempt at growing a beard was falling woefully short, handed Browning the ship-to-shore telephone which had been hooked up by SeaBees. Browning got through to a Chief Yeoman at BUPERS and was given the telephone number of the base hospital.

"I'm trying to reach Gunners Mate Second Class Scott E. Karl from the Robert B. Sprague, DD 884." He listened a moment. "He was transferred from the Yorktown ten days ago with a broken leg." He pressed the handset to his chest. "They're switching me to physio-therapy."

Browning got a ward station and spoke to a nurse who eventually found Scotty and brought him to the telephone. Poulos and Witter crowded close and Browning held the receiver away from his ear so they could all hear.

"Hi, Scotsman!" they shouted in unison.

"You guys get my signal from the Yorktown?"

"We were nearly over the horizon but we saw the light. How's your leg?"

"I got more pins in me than a bowling alley and I'm up to my crotch in plaster."

"But are you going to live?"

"The doc says if this didn't kill me, nothing will. Say, are you guys back in port already?"

"We got excused early."

"How come?"

"We hit bottom on the high seas."

"I don't get it."

They started to explain but in their eagerness to tell the story they kept stepping on each other's words.

"Hold it, just one person talk."

Because Poulos had been in the pilot house and an eyewitness to Katz's downfall, he was elected to be the reporter. As the story unfolded, Scotty laughed and howled with pleasure.

"Schamberger didn't get off a single round? I'd've blasted those fucking gooks out of their jockey straps. And the hull got sliced?"

"Like a giant can opener did it. The screws got bent too."

"Talk about lousy timing. The Sprague is in drydock, the Commodore is gone, and I'm in the hospital."

"How long?"

"Six weeks in this cast. It wasn't worth breaking my leg just to get off the Bobbie Bee."

"We'll come see you."

"How about Saturday night? This place is loaded with nurses."

"Can't you take care of them by yourself?"

"Not in this cast, but they do have sensitive hands."

Their interest level suddenly shot up.

Scotty called to someone. "My buddies are coming to see me Saturday night. Tell them about your sensitive hands." They heard what sounded like a squeal and then a slap. Poulos and Witter squeezed closer to the receiver Browning was holding.

"Hello?" a female voice asked. "Are you friends of Scotty's?"

"We sure are," Browning said.

"Then you're not friends of mine." She laughed. "It's a good thing he's in a cast." Her voice was firm and professional, yet there was something in her crisp manner that hinted at playfulness. "Just a second, Scotty is pulling on my arm." They could hear his voice muffled in the background. The nurse came back on the line. "Scotty wants you to introduce yourselves."

They did.

"What's your name?" asked Browning.

"Tammy Sanders."

"Do I have to get sick to meet you?"

"It would help."

Porteous was making faces at them but the trio shrugged him off.

"Did one of you say your name is Poulos?" Sanders asked.

"That's me," Poulos said, taking the phone.

"Is that a Greek name?"

"Unfortunately."

"There's a nurse here who's Greek."

"Small world," he replied without enthusiasm. Poulos never understood why people assumed Greeks automatically wanted to meet each other. He was ready to hand the phone back to Browning who was frowning at him.

"Can't you see she's giving you an in? You want to blow this for all of us? Keep talking. Find out about that Greek gal."

"Ok, ok!" Poulos said.

"What?" Sanders asked.

"I was talking to my buddy. So tell me about this Greek nurse."

"Her name is Jenny Betheras. She's cute."

How unusual, Poulos thought. "Put her on."

"She's on duty. If you're coming to see Scotty, you can meet her."

"Fine."

"Don't forget us!" Witter and Browning shouted in unison.

"There are a thousand sailors for every nurse in Yokosuka. What makes you so special?" Sanders asked.

"We've been seasick two straight months."

She laughed. "You guys sound more desperate than ill, but when you get here we'll take your temperature."

Porteous was fuming in the background. This call got out of hand a long time ago.

"Official business now," Browning said to Porteous. Then he talked into the phone, "Can you help us locate another shipmate who was transferred two weeks ago for psychiatric evaluation?"

"That's what you should all be having. Let me give you the building number for the psychiatric unit." Browning wrote it down on the quarterdeck note pad and ripped off the sheet.

Poulos gave him a hard stare. “What the fuck are you doing?”

“Just in case you want to say hello.” Browning tucked the note paper into Poulos's shirt pocket.

"I don't want to say hello."

"At least you know where he is in case you change your mind." Browning handed the phone to Porteous. "Thanks."

Porteous was all smiles now. "You ignorant swabbies. You think you're gonna make out with some nurses?"

"Why not?"

"They're naval officers, you idiots. You better be careful what you salute them with." He laughed so hard he almost gagged.

Yokosuka, still recovering from the saturation bombing of World War II, was a sprawling collection of dirt streets and jerry-built shanties, single story houses, and open-air shops. The sewage system was a network of open channels that had to be jumped over in order to cross the street. Traffic moved opposite to that in America and most of it consisted of motor scooters and pedal bicycles that jockeyed about in congested mayhem. Except at intersections. The white-gloved traffic cops who stood on platforms were strictly obeyed, preventing massive tie-ups that otherwise would occur.

Poulos had accepted Gildenhall's invitation to meet him at the Imperial Hotel for a drink, and he walked to the Metro to catch the commuter train to Tokyo. He changed into his Hong Kong Harris tweeds in the men's room of the station and stowed his navy clothes in a locker. The train was crowded but fast, and in half an hour it pulled into Tokyo Central right on time.

He was early and wanted to see some of the city, and so he went from taxi to taxi in the lineup till he found a driver who understood English. Tokyo was jammed with tinny cars with funny sounding names such as Mitsubishi, Subaru and Mazda. Poulos had always thought that Mazda was a light bulb. The most popular American car on Tokyo streets was the Studebaker. He wondered why. Honking was constant. The diminutive Japanese seemed oblivious to the noise as they headed purposefully to some important destination.

The taxi driver took him past the Diet, Japan's parliament building, a stubby tower standing back from the bustling streets on a large open plaza. They drove over a narrow arched bridge into the Ginza. Garish neon signs blazed even though it was still afternoon, and prostitutes lingered suggestively on the sidewalk. When his taxi stopped for a light, a girl came over and leaned into the back window. Her breasts were squeezing out of a low cut dress to suggest they were larger than they really were. She wore thick makeup and, in pidgin English, made the universal pronouncement of availability. "You like, sailor?" Poulos recalled Natasha and her fragile beauty. This girl was a pig by comparison. The driver shouted some rapid Japanese out his window; then looked over his shoulder at Poulos and shook his head. "No good, no good." The light changed and they moved on. The taxi pulled up to the Imperial Hotel. Poulos paid his fare with military scrip. He had three one dollar bills in his pocket and tipped the driver with one of them. The driver bowed his head half a dozen times and repeated over and over, "Arigato." Poulos thought the man's broad smile would squint his eyes completely shut and blind him as he drove off.

He stood for a moment at the curb and admired Frank Lloyd Wright's historic landmark with its distinctive cantilevered construction. Two flagpoles flanked the entrance, one flying the Japanese flag, the other American. It was strange to see the bright red-orange sphere and the Stars and Stripes fluttering side by side. How unpredictable life is. Here he was in Tokyo, the target of Jimmie Doolittle's raiders in April 1942. He remembered vividly the movie based on the raid, Thirty Seconds Over Tokyo, made two years later. He was only fourteen, and he watched with pounding heart as Van Johnson's B-25 sat on the aircraft carrier waiting for takeoff, its engines whining at redline rpms, its brakes barely holding the trembling bomber. Then, just when Poulos thought the plane was going to shake apart, the launch coordinator points his flag to the deck and the heavily laden B-25 with split rudders lumbers down the wet carrier deck with 400 feet of takeoff distance, only to dip perilously close to the sea as it finally, frighteningly, agonizingly pulls up. In the cockpit the copilot sighs with relief as he tells Van Johnson that he had forgotten to set the flaps. At the end of the film, Poulos was in such a state that tears fell from his eyes as Johnson, having lost his leg in the raid, jumps from his wheel chair when he sees his wife, played by Phyllis Thaxter, and falls flat on his face to the hospital floor. Poulos looked up at the sky where those B-25s once flew and marveled at the sweep of history that brought him here. But Doolittle's raid was puny compared to the armadas of B-29s that firebombed Tokyo to the ground in 1945. He was grateful that Wright's masterpiece survived. He could not imagine a pilot telling his bomber wing, "Don't hit that hotel down there, it was designed by Frank Lloyd Wright."

There was a lot to engage the eye. The hotel blended with elegantly landscaped grounds. Wings, terraces and planters flowed naturally into each other. He searched for a word to describe what he saw. It finally came to him. Harmony. Form and material in harmony with nature.

Poulos walked inside. Gildenhall told him to meet in the Cabaret Restaurant. He crossed a soaring lobby of brick and stone. Balconies and bridges seemed suspended in air. Everywhere he looked there was a dramatic view. Wright had pulled out all the stops.

The restaurant was not busy. He stood in the entrance a bit self-conscious in his new suit, feeling like a farm boy visiting the city for the first time.

"Impressive, wouldn't you say?"

Poulos turned. Gildenhall had come out of the lounge, a drink in his hand. He was the essence of naval officer, his starched khaki dress shirt crisply creased in the appropriate places. The tip of his tan tie was tucked into his shirt between the second and third buttons. His ribbons were in neat rows over his flapped pocket.

"I saw you come in but I didn't want to interrupt your obvious thrill at being in Wright's monument."

"It's a monument all right."

"It's not pure Wright any longer. The army used it after the war and made changes that brutalized it. Wright was asked to bring it back to its former glory but he turned them down. Pity. If he has lost interest in the Imperial I fear for it."

"Why?"

"Land is precious here. The hotel takes up a lot of space. And it represents a past the Japanese would sooner put behind them. Mark my words, it will be gone someday."

Poulos ran his fingers along the burnt-umber bricks. Their surfaces were rough and sharp enough to snag material, even cut skin. "What are these bricks made of?"

"Lava. And the white columns are oya stone."

"You know what this architecture reminds me of?"

"What?"

"A Roman bath. I can picture senators in long robes and curled hair taking the cure."

Gildenhall smiled appreciatively. He led Poulos into the Cabaret lounge, an intimate surrounding of high-back sofas, cane chairs and tables, and a ceiling shaped like the keel of an inverted ship. They sat down. "I'm having Scotch, how about you?" He called the Japanese waiter over. "Glenfiddich on the rocks."

The drinks came and they settled back in their chairs.

"First time I've seen you in civvies," Gildenhall said.

Poulos tried the Scotch. It was smoky and smooth.

"Do you like my drink preference? It's a single malt whiskey. I don't care for blends."

Poulos realized that Gildenhall didn't wait for an answer but kept talking. Perhaps his officer training made him that way. Additionally he was sitting with an enlisted man who was clearly ill at ease, who did not know what a single malt whiskey was and didn't want to give himself away. "I don't either."

Gildenhall surveyed the architecture with appreciative eyes. "It's hard to believe that the young architect who worked as a draftsman in Louis Sullivan's office in the 1880s would someday create this splendid palace."

"Do you like Sullivan?"

"Yes, but Wright belongs in the pantheon compared to Sullivan."

"There's a Sullivan bank in Minnesota."

Gildenhall nodded. "The National Farmers Bank of Owatonna."

Poulos raised his eyebrows. "You know it?"

"Sullivan collaborated with George Elmslie who designed the terra cotta and plaster ornamentation. Elmslie was the subject of my graduate paper at the University of Chicago. I visited the bank in 1940. I took the 400 from Chicago to Minneapolis and then a two-car train called the Doodlebug to Owatonna."

Poulos laughed. "The Doodlebug came to Waseca, too."

"Waseca?"

"The town where I grew up, thirteen miles from Owatonna."

Gildenhall leaned forward. "You mean in 1940 we were within a few miles of each other?"

"I was only ten, but I remember my dad driving me in his '32 Nash to Owatonna to visit a Greek friend whose restaurant was right across the street from the bank."

"Did you ever go inside?"

"No."

"You missed the wrought iron grillwork and the chandeliers and the frescoed arches--all the things Elmslie did that gave the bank its uniqueness." It was clear Gildenhall was genuinely disappointed.

"I'll go there someday."

"What a coincidence that we nearly crossed paths. You could have been in that restaurant when I was in the bank studying its architecture."

"It's possible," Poulos said, unconvinced.

"There has to be a universal power that directs our lives."

Poulos was wondering where Gildenhall was going with this. "Like a God you mean?"

"More like fate. I'm a believer in the philosophy of inevitability. Take you and me, for example. In 1940, we could have met except the circumstances weren't right. Twelve years later, thousands of miles from our first near-encounter, circumstances that didn't fit then fit now--and we find ourselves drinking excellent Scotch together in an incredible setting." Gildenhall's eyes widened. "We were destined to meet. Owatonna was simply a dry run."

"You're getting pretty philosophical, there, Lieutenant."

"Call me Bill."

Poulos looked around as if concerned someone might have overheard them. "I can't call you by your first name."

"You would in Owatonna."

"I'm in the Navy now."

"You'll never get rich you sonovabitch, you're in the Navy now," Gildenhall sang and threw back his head in laughter. "I guess my warning to you had the desired effect."

"I wasn't on board the Sprague five minutes and you told me I better not forget I'm an enlisted man."

"We're off the ship now."

"You're still in uniform."

"Drink some Scotch, that'll help put you at ease." As though following his own advice, Gildenhall drained his glass. He leaned back. "You really have a love-hate relationship with authority don't you?"

Poulos drained his glass, too. "Does it show?"

"You can't hide hostile ambivalence." Gildenhall signaled the diminutive Japanese waiter for another round. "Ever had a mentor?" he asked after the drinks arrived.

Poulos looked at the slender wrist and tapered fingers, trying to visualize the young architecture student in the lobby of the Sullivan bank, as romantic as a castle. "No, have you?"

"Not when it counted." he said, stirring the ice in his glass. "But if you thought the navy was going to be your mentor, you were dead wrong."

"Do you think that's why I went on active duty?" Poulos swallowed some Scotch and set his glass on the table. "Ok, I will."

"Will what?"

"Call you Bill."

"And I'll call you Alex."

The last vestige of formality between them collapsed.

"I made a shitload of mistakes," Poulos said.

"We all do."

"Not the kind I've made."

Gildenhall's eyebrows peaked with curiosity. "What did you do, rob a bank?"

"Yeah, the Farmers' Bank in Owatonna."

They broke up with laughter, not so much that the joke was funny but that the Scotch was starting to have its effect.

"What could be worse than robbing a bank?"

"Getting caught."

"Doing what?"

Poulos picked up his glass again and studied the amber fluid. It reminded him of a urine specimen. "Getting caught with my pants down."

"Are you simply being clever or drunk?"

"I never thought it was simple to be clever."

Gildenhall frowned. "You use humor as a shield from criticism. It's a gift to be quick-witted but it gets in the way of self-evaluation."

"I self-evaluate all the time."

"You self-deprecate all the time." Gildenhall crossed his legs, the point of his glistening shoe just grazing Poulos's shin. "Have you ever stopped to think how selfish that kind of behavior really is?"

Poulos squirmed.

"What are you afraid of?" Gildenhall asked. "Clayton?"

Poulos paused. "There is something about him, I don't know what. It's as if he has power over me."

"I'd say it was the other way around."

Poulos took his drink and swallowed too much too fast. The Glenfiddich burned his stomach. It made him think about how much his insides burned when his mother forced her famous hot water enema on him. His bowels were just another part of her cleaning regimen, like her floors. His childhood was fraught with memories of her obsession with cleanliness. He couldn't smell Lysol without having to puke. She scrubbed his pants with a hard-bristle brush. His clothes didn't wear out from use, they disintegrated from scrubbing. Why was she like that? Was he some kind of blot on her character? Let three days go by without a bowel movement and his mother forced upon him her secret ritual of pain and humiliation--toh klizma.

Out came the hot water bottle and the enema tip lubricated with Vaseline. Trembling, he dropped his pants, got on his knees and bent down to expose his rectum. Heated lubricant swelled his insides. Terrified of spilling on the bathroom floor, his sphincter became the strongest muscle in his body.

Gildenhall was leaning toward him. "What's the matter?"

"You want me to come clean?" Poulos thought he was being hilarious.

"Are you going to let me in on your little joke?"

"It's not a joke. That's why I'm laughing so hard."

Gildenhall sat back in frustration.

"Ok, I'll tell you," Poulos said. "The burning Scotch reminded me of another burning sensation." He held up his glass as if toasting his candor. "Enemas."

"Enemas?"

"My mother's torture machine. She was always giving them to me."

Gildenhall shook his head. "Mothers have a way of getting even."

"For what?"

"For wanting to have sex with their sons."

Poulos stared in confusion. "What the hell are you talking about?"

"Your mother was using you to satisfy her own sexual need."

"That's crazy."

"Think about it. She penetrated you to make up for her own lack of it."

Poulos drained his glass. He looked down into it. It was like his soul, empty.

"Want another?" Gildenhall held up two fingers. They waited quietly till the drinks were served. "Arigato," Gildenhall said, and then to Alex, "There is a strong sexual attraction between mother and son. That would explain her obsession with seeing you squatting before her."

Poulos could accept the analysis but not him as the victim in a case study of a mother's sexual perversion. "The literature is full of it," he admitted, "from Oedipus on. But not my mother."

"Why not?"

"She's old."

"She was young once."

Gildenhall's comment jogged Poulos's long-ago memory of the naked woman climbing into the tub as he sat on his potty watching her. It stirred him.

"Well, it's of no matter now. All this was part of another time, another life."

"So the navy was your escape from that other time and other life?"

"That's part of the equation."

"So what's the other part?"

"I was never good at algebra."

"There we go again, another smart-ass answer."

Poulos moved uncomfortably in his chair and the caning rustled under him. He wanted to talk about Mary Lou but held back. It somehow did not fit the tenor of their conversation.

"How much leave have you accumulated?"

"Seven days."

"When we get back to San Diego I'll authorize two weeks."

"Radinger will be furious."

"Fuck Radinger. A trip home as a sailor on leave will give you a new perspective, and when you return you won't be the defensive, angry person you are now."

"Wait a minute, Lieutenant..."

"Bill, remember?"

Even the Scotch wasn't helping now.

"One of my jobs on the Sprague is to maintain discipline. You are one of the most undisciplined sailors I've ever known. If you go home on leave and settle your problems, or at least face up to them, it will make my job a helluva lot easier. And it will be a helluva lot easier for you, too, returning home as a sailor. If you wait till you're a civilian again, you'll be just another veteran trying to get his life back together. But if you go home in your uniform with your ribbons on your chest, everybody will think of you as a hero."

"I thought you had to do something brave to be a hero."

"For you, going home will be an act of bravery."

Gildenhall settled back in his chair. "I'm talking like a Dutch Uncle."

"So did Polonius."

"Polonius?"

"Hamlet's Dutch Uncle."

"There you go, showing off again."

"It's the Scotch."

"Everything's the Scotch--from your shit to your Shakespeare."

That evoked laughter.

"Try to understand that you are not the only son who had problems with his mother."

"I don't know any others."

Gildenhall set his glass down. "You do now. Your mother reminds me a lot of my own."

Poulos had trouble meeting Gildenhall's gaze. It was one thing for an enlisted man to open up to his officer but not the other way around. It was like the patient listening to the psychiatrist on the couch. "You have my sympathy," he said noncommittally.

Amusement played briefly in Gildenhall's eyes. "She didn't force enemas up my ass if that's what you're thinking."

"Doesn't it concern you that this is getting too familiar?"

"Are you?"

"What happens when we get back to the ship?"

"I'm confident that anything said between us will not go beyond this room."

"You're trusting an ordinary seaman."

Gildenhall smiled. "You are far from ordinary and I trust you more than most officers."

"Including Radinger?"

"Especially Radinger."

Poulos smiled. "At least we have that in common."

Gildenhall held up his glass as if solemnizing the faith he had placed in Poulos, and began his story: "My mother was twenty when I was born. My father was considerably older, forty-eight. He was a broker on the Board of Trade and she was his secretary. He came from a prominent Chicago family. My mother was from Bristol, a tiny Wisconsin town just on the other side of the Illinois border. So you can imagine the consternation on Lakeshore Drive. It was common knowledge that they got married because they had to. My mother was already pregnant. But my father's family couldn't stand to have their perfect little world disrupted, and so they had my birth date altered to make it look as if I was born legitimately six months later. I'm sure all it took was a case or two of bootleg whiskey to bribe someone in county records." Bill snapped his fingers. "And just like that I lost six months of my life."

"You can make it up."

"How?"

"Die six months later."

Gildenhall laughed. "I'll see what I can do. Sadly, though, this indiscretion of my father's was nothing compared to what happened a few years later. He had an affair, which in itself was not as bad as it might have been except that it was with a man." He hesitated, awaiting Poulos's reaction. When he saw there was none, he continued. "He thought he could maintain a double life, but my mother finally found out. She was devastated and filed for divorce. Her main concern was to protect me. There was a nasty court proceeding. It was in the newspapers. This was one time the family could not hide the truth. The scandal was too great. Three months later my father killed himself."

"That must have been tough. How old were you?"

"Seven. My mother tried to shield me by telling me that he died in a car accident. Any suicide is terrible but the way in which my father took his life was gruesomely symbolic. He put a shotgun between his legs and blew off his groin."

Poulos winced. "His groin?"

"Everything...penis, testicles, half his lower intestine. It was his way of destroying the instrument of his perversion. It revealed how much he loathed what he had become."

As repulsive as this was, Poulos was too far into the tale to back out now. "You didn't know any of this?"

"Not till high school, old enough to start questioning what happened. I went to the public library and looked up the newspaper file. It was there, everything in gory detail."

"Did she know that you found out?"

"I never told her and she never asked."

Thin shadows of Frank Lloyd Wright's leaded windows moved across the gray carpet. The geometric patterns were distended by the deep angle of the late afternoon sun. Poulos looked at his watch. "I have to be going."

"Stay and have dinner with me."

"I'd like to, but I'm meeting Witter and Browning. We're going to see Scotty at the hospital. He's lining us up with some nurses." As soon as Poulos said this he wished he hadn't.

Disappointment clouded Gildenhall's words. "So you prefer a nurse's company over mine."

How should he answer?

It wasn't just dinner. It was dinner in a hotel, and not an ordinary hotel but an architectural wonder which was not only historic, it was also seductive. There would be wine and dessert; a second cup of coffee, a digestif, a cigar. And, following dinner, then what? After what Gildenhall had told Poulos about his father's tragic life--and horrible death--the balance of the evening would hang in the air like an unanswered question.

"Does my dinner invitation make you feel uneasy?"

"I hate to turn you down."

"I'll withdraw it."

"I'm sorry."

"Don't be. Are we still friends? We won't be wearing our navy uniforms forever and I was looking forward to seeing you again after the war. I'm thinking to myself, wouldn't it be interesting to meet at the Sullivan bank in Owatonna."

THE PRIEST

The drive back to Minneapolis was dismal. Mary Lou sat next to Alex in the van as impassive as a store mannequin. Her arms were folded tightly across her chest, which lifted occasionally in a heartsick sigh. Her feet pressed so hard on the floorboards he expected them to go through the rusted old metal. She looked straight ahead even when he addressed her. There was no conversation as such; his efforts at conciliation were met with an occasional grumble. Mostly she was deep in thought; submerged like a deep sea diver--so many fathoms down it would take her days to decompress.

After the ceremony, Shaffer had offered his congratulations but Alex could detect misgivings in his handshake. He probably figured the black man and white woman had a better chance at their marriage. At least those two appeared happy, confident and in love. Mary Lou led the way down the stairs as she had led the way up, but this time her heels were striking the wood risers with sharp blows that echoed around them. They came out on the sidewalk and marshaled next to the miniature windmill in front of the Green Mill restaurant. To a casual observer the newly married couple was in a state of inertia, perhaps even shock.

Mike Callahan tried to make the best of it. "Everything was beautiful."

"What's beautiful about a dark, sweaty room?" Mary Lou snapped, looking about like someone who had misplaced her car keys.

Alex smiled at Mike apologetically. "Let's have something to eat," he said, nudging Mary Lou in the direction of the Green Mill's entrance. "How about joining us for a wedding breakfast, Mike? Just the three of us. I'll order 7-Up in stemmed glasses and we can pretend it's champagne." He was hoping his attempt at lightheartedness would be contagious, but Mary Lou reacted as if it were a disease he was transmitting.

Suddenly she gripped his arm. "They're in there!" she cried.

"Who?" he asked.

"That negro couple."

Alex turned to look. It did not surprise him that, even though the bride was white, Mary Lou referred to the couple as black.

She yanked his arm. "Don't! They'll see us!"

"So what?" he asked, finally losing his patience. Through the plate glass he saw the black man sitting in the booth with his new wife and the couple that witnessed the ceremony. He was enjoying himself, laughing and gesturing, and pushing his shoulder lovingly against his mate. What is it about that man that made him so joyful and spontaneous? He felt a twinge of envy.

"Let's go somewhere else," Mary Lou said. "I don't want them to see us."

"They're so involved in each other, they won't even notice."

"Yes they will. What if he asks us to join them?"

"Why would he do that?"

"He signed our marriage certificate, didn't he?"

Alex was embarrassed for Mike who had done him a big favor by participating in this fiasco. "Maybe we should do a raincheck."

Mike smiled understandingly. He was too polite to show it but Alex knew he was relieved. "I'll be in St. Paul starting in October. Leave a message at Billy Mitchell and I'll get back to you." He got into the plushy Chrysler and fired up the big cast-iron V8. He waved as he backed out.

Alex watched the big sedan turn the corner knowing he would never see Mike again. On their way out of town he stopped for gas and had the oil checked. It was down a quart. When he paid his bill, he bought a Three Musketeers candy bar. In the van, he tore open the wrapper and offered a section to Mary Lou. "Have a bite of candy."

"What kind?" she asked absently, staring straight ahead.

"Three Musketeers," he said, hoping humor might still save the day. "Athos is vanilla, Porthos is strawberry, and d'Artagnan is chocolate. I know you like chocolate."

"Chocolate?" Mary Lou retorted. "After what I went through, you expect me to eat chocolate?"

Alex gave up. He ate all three sections, and wadded the empty wrapper into the ashtray. He got on highway 65 and headed north. Mason City receded behind him in the rearview mirror like a flattened raccoon.

Her attitude reminded him of something equally disconcerting, the way single Greek men thought of single American women. They called their fairer-skinned dates "white girls," a demeaning mix of sexism and reverse racism, a piece of white ass, a fling as Uncle Gus put it. Alex angrily pushed the old van till it began to vibrate. He couldn't tell how fast he was going since the speedometer was broken. He didn't give a damn if he was pulled over; he was in that kind of mood.

When they reached Owatonna, he decided to calm his nerves by driving past the Sullivan Bank. He hadn't seen it since he was a kid living in Waseca 14 miles away. He detoured off 65 and drove around the town square to the bank. He slowed to a crawl. The corner building was so richly ornamental it looked like a chapel--a great venue for a wedding. It made him sad thinking about it.

"Mary Lou," he said.

She roused herself as if from a deep dream. "Where are we?"

"Owatonna. I wanted to show you this building."

She looked at the fanciful brick work; at the stained glass in the arches, at the terra cotta keystones. "What is it?"

"A bank."

"Too ornate for a bank."

He got back on the highway. They had the lane virtually to themselves. Everyone else, it seemed, was home. To their left, the sun began to lower over the uninterrupted flatness of the plains as they passed farm towns named Dundas, Webster and Elko. When they were a dozen or so miles from Minneapolis, Mary Lou finally began to open up.

"That hall we were married in," she rambled, an occasional tear falling to her blouse like a raindrop. "It was so dreary. And that justice of the peace. Did you see how bored he was? He wasn't interested in us. He just wanted to get it done. Why did he ask that negro to sign the certificate? Where was Shaffer's secretary? Why didn't he call her in?"

"She was gone, remember? Besides, Shaffer probably wanted a man to be a witness..." he stopped too late.

"What's wrong with a woman's signature?" Mary Lou asked with reignited irritation. "Aren't women good enough to be trusted? It was a wedding, wasn't it? Why didn't Shaffer ask me if I minded? I felt so cheap." She looked out her window. "I'm glad now I wasn't wearing my new dress." She turned and gave Alex an accusing stare. "Why didn't you come up with a second witness like you were supposed to? Don't you have any other friends? Don't you know anyone besides Mike Callahan?"

"It's only a signature."

"It's a symbol of everything that went wrong, everything that was seedy about our wedding. I wish my mother were alive," Mary Lou said. "I need her to tell me everything will be all right."

"Everything will be."

"When you talk that way you sound so patronizing, like you want me to shut up so I won't bother you." She sighed heavily. "It's been a long day."

"Tomorrow isn't going to be any shorter."

They descended into the Minnesota River Valley, crossing the marshy plain on a narrow bridge supported by wood pilings driven into the shallow river bottom. Against the hazy north horizon they could just make out the Minneapolis cityscape punctuated by the architectural exclamation point called the Foshay Tower, at 32 stories the tallest building west of Chicago. They were nearly home, but the word had a strange ring to it. Where was his home now?

He dropped her off at a quarter past five. He carried in her suitcase and her soiled wedding dress. "What do you want me to do with Mike's roses?"

"Put them in the sink. I'll get a vase."

Mary Lou had arranged her new apartment with personal mementos: her Beatrix Potter ceramic figures, her fancy perfume vials, a gilded, rose-pattern chocolate set of her mother's, a small wedding portrait of her parents in a sterling silver frame.

"If you have any ideas about staying with me tonight, you're mistaken."

"Will you go to the Greek church with me tomorrow?"

"I'm not backing out if that's what you're implying. I have to meet your family sometime." Mary Lou hung her soiled wedding dress in the closet. "I was going to wear this tomorrow, too, but now I'll have to think of something else." She began sorting through her wardrobe, holding up a dress or a skirt by its hanger and reflecting on it.

"Be sure to wear something modest."

Mary Lou looked at him sharply. "Are you afraid I'll embarrass you?"

"No, no, of course, not. It's just that Greek women are catty. They always look for something they can whisper about behind your back. I don't want to give them any ammunition, that's all."

Mary Lou slammed the closet door. "I'll wear what I wear to church. If it's good enough for Catholics it ought to be good enough for Greeks."

"That's all I meant."

"On our first day as husband and wife you'd think we would be happy and proud, and not give a damn what someone else might think about us. Why can't we act like we're on our honeymoon instead of worrying if I'm going to embarrass you?" She was fighting back tears.

"I'll pick you up at ten."

"Six forty-five."

"Six forty-five? Why so early? The service doesn't start till ten-thirty."

"We're going to seven o'clock mass."

"Mass? In a Catholic church?"

"Where else do you go to mass?"

"Can't this wait till another time? We just got married."

"Exactly! Do you expect me to miss church after what I went through today? First my wedding dress was ruined by the rain and then my wedding ceremony was ruined by some black man...and on top of all that I have to be ready to meet your family."

"Is that priest going to be there?"

"What priest?"

"The one you told everything to, at confession."

"Alex, sometimes you really do try me."

"I'll be uncomfortable."

"Too bad."

"What am I supposed to do?"

"The same things you do in your own church. Or has it been so long since you've been in it that you've forgotten?"

Maybe because he was beginning to feel the weight of his broken promises that her putdown really stung him. "I will mend my ways."

"Fine. You can start by taking me to mass in the morning. Then I'll be ready to face that Greek crowd of yours. You want your mother to be proud of her new daughter-in-law, don't you?"

When Mary Lou said daughter-in-law, panic hit him. The word was like an arrow that pierced his body. He couldn't remove it. Even the hyphens were barbs. Why hadn't he realized this before? It never occurred to him that the woman you marry is not only a wife, she's also a daughter-in-law.

His heart raced as he drove home. It eased up only a little when he saw that Uncle Gus's Packard was not in the driveway. At least the old fart was gone. Wishful thinking had him heading back to Worthington, but that's all it was, wishful thinking. He'll be back. Alex parked at the curb. If he had to leave at six-thirty in the morning to pick up Mary Lou he sure as hell wasn't going to get trapped in the driveway behind Gus's limousine.

Alex opened the back door and went in. The house was dark except for the stove light. "Hi, Ma, hi Dad," he sang out. No one answered. He went through the house.

So where is everybody? he wondered.

He went back to the kitchen and turned on the ceiling fixture. Then he saw a note Scotch-taped to the refrigerator door. His parents never did that. What's going on? In a neat script the note read:

> We waited and waited. Having
> dinner at the Rainbow Cafe.
> Join us.
> Uncle Gus

Gus probably was feeling guilty for all those meals Alex's mother labored over for him. He breathed a sigh of relief. He had walked in totally forgetting he was still wearing his dress shirt and shoes. How could he have explained those anomalies after lying about working all day? God--or someone--must be looking out for him. As if reminding him these weren't his only lapses, his finger began to itch. Jesus, he remembered. His wedding band! What if his mother spotted gold gleaming from his left hand. He tried to twist the ring past his knuckle but it wouldn't come off. He went to the bathroom and lathered his finger with Camay, and finally wrestled the band loose. He looked at his hand. Blood was oozing out of his scar. "Shit," he said out loud, and tore open a Band Aid. He wrapped it around his ring finger. Rather ironic, he told himself, substituting his wedding band for a bandage. He put the ring in his pocket along with his change, and started to breathe easier. Actually things were turning out better than expected. He had time alone to get ready for tomorrow. One good note deserved another, and so he left his own next to Uncle Gus's:

> Had a busy day. (No lie there)
> Went to bed early.
> Alex

He returned to the bathroom and shaved, scraping off his whiskers as close as he could. In the morning he was going to wash up and brush his teeth at the kitchen sink and piss behind the garage. He hoped to sneak out of the house with no one the wiser. He climbed the stairs to his attic room and laid out everything he was going to wear. He set his Seth Thomas for six a.m. and put it under his pillow so only he would hear it.

Around eight p.m. the deep-throated rumble of the Packard reached his ears. Soon, voices speaking Greek drifted up the stairwell. The television in the living room went on. Around ten-thirty water ran in the bathroom. At eleven the house became still; not even a joist or rafter creaked. Every now and then he turned in his bunk bed just to create sound. Sleep was marred by an anxious dream. Something deep in his subconscious was bubbling up and he fought to keep whatever it was submerged. Tonight, though, it very nearly broke the surface. A membrane as smooth as vellum wrinkled and charred at the edges as though it was about to catch fire. The unsettling image made him shiver even though he was sweating.

It seemed as if only moments had passed when the alarm sounded in his ear. He groped under his pillow to shut the bell, and rubbed sleep from his eyes. His nose was oily. He carefully dressed and made his way down the stairs, staying close to the wall where nails held the treads firm. He pushed open the door and looked out. Across the dining room was the short, transverse hallway that led to two bedrooms, one where his parents slept and the other where Gus slept. The bathroom was between the bedrooms, too close to use. He waited with bated breath until he was satisfied no one was stirring, not even a mouse.

In the kitchen he took out the baking powder and made a slurry with water and rubbed it on his teeth. Then he washed his face with Arm & Hammer dish powder from under the sink. It was gritty and hurt his skin but that's all he had. He dried himself on the hand towel his mother folded over the oven handle. He went outside and left footprints in the dewy grass as he walked behind the garage to piss. When he buttoned up, his stomach grumbled--reminding him he hadn't eaten since that candy bar on the road from Mason City. He'd have to wait until after mass to have breakfast. There would be plenty of time before the Greek service started. He and Mary Lou might as well kill it in a restaurant. He returned to the kitchen to leave another note, the last alibi he'd ever write, he promised himself. He got a pencil and a note pad from a drawer and sat at the table, his mind going over the words he would use--something like,

Got up early. Going to breakfast.
Don't wait for me.
I'll meet you at the church.
Alex

That sounded pretty good. He began writing. Suddenly the hackles in his neck tingled. He spun around and literally jumped from fright. A mummy-like figure had materialized in the doorway, wrapped in a threadbare bathrobe and a white skullcap which framed a gaunt face and a pair of sunken eyes as cold as death. The wraith-like presence was other worldly, from a time and place that bore no relationship to the here and now--hailing instead from a dark age of superstition, ignorance, rigidity, false piety--aspirin-devouring, self-denying, piteously medieval...

It was only his mother. He was surprised she wasn't shaking; he certainly was. "Ma, don't scare me like that."

"Pou pigainis?" Where are you going? Her voice was hollow as though coming from a crypt.

"Out...for breakfast."`

"Tora?" Now?

"I couldn't sleep."

He waved the piece of paper he was writing on. "I was leaving you a note. I guess I don't have to now." He squeezed it into a ball and dropped it in the ashtray by the telephone that his father used.

She stared at his hand. "What you have on your finger?"

For an unnerving, desperate second he thought he was still wearing his wedding ring.

"Oh, just a Band Aid. My scar started bleeding, that's all."

She kept staring at the bandage.

"What's wrong, ma?"

"How you do that?"

"Stacking boxes at work." He laughed lightly. "Because the boxes are filled with fluorescent bulbs, they are reinforced with metal bands. Must have cut it on one of those. I should be more careful. Those edges are really sharp."

"Pseftis!" Liar! The word crackled like a smoldering fire that had suddenly reignited. She stepped into the kitchen and closed the door behind her. "I know you not at work. We call there."

"You called?" he asked, feeling snares closing around him.

"Gus did."

Alex had been blindsided by his uncle. He should have anticipated this. Unlike his parents, whose lack of sophistication and fear of the truth--that their son was, in fact, a pseftis--caused them to live in a state of tormented resignation. Uncle Gus was not so intimidated.

"When he call, nobody answer."

Of course nobody answered, Alex thought, the goddamned warehouse was closed. His usually nimble mind was now completely stalled. He didn't want to argue with her. He didn't want to defend himself. He just wanted to escape.

"Ok, I was with her. I was with Mary Lou. Are you satisfied?"

"From six in the morning to six at night?" His mother's breathing shallowed. She started to shake. "What you do? Tell me what you do!"

Alex looked at his watch, concerned about the time. Mary Lou said six forty-five and he was going to be late if he didn't leave right away. He rose from the kitchen chair and moved toward the door. "I'll see you in church."

"We go to church together. You promise your uncle."

"What difference does it make? We're going to end up in the same place."

"Panagia mou," My God. She crossed herself three times. "She blind you and you don't see it."

"Ma, if you're blind you don't see anyway." The absurdity of his comment was a metaphor of the madness around him. He left the house and marched to the van. Behind him he heard the screen door pull against its spring and slam. He turned. His mother was following him down the driveway, her bathrobe flowing behind her and her nightgown clinging to her barren Venus mound.

"For Christ's sake, ma, get back in the house before the neighbors see you!"

"Poulaki mou!" she cried.

Again she was calling him her little bird. He shouted over his shoulder, "I told you I will meet you in church."

She stumbled toward him, her arms outstretched, and fell to her knees on the front lawn, her hands clasped together as if beseeching the Lord to stop her son.

He climbed into the van, cranked the starter and threw out the clutch so quickly he killed the engine. He tried again, fearing he might have flooded the plugs. Don't fail me now, he pleaded. Finally the engine caught and sputtered to life. He pulled away from the curb. Out the big rear view mirror mounted on the fender he saw his father and uncle in their pajamas hurrying down the driveway. As he sped away, he caught a final, indelible sight of two elderly men lifting a hysterical woman to her feet and guiding her back to the house, their ashen faces turned toward the receding van.

He drove like a madman, forcing the gears and braking hard at stop signs. The rational side of his psyche was warning him to take it easy but the lingering vision of his mother begging on the lawn in front of God and everybody threw him into a frenzied state. He was bewildered and lost, cut from reality like a cow is cut from the herd and led to the slaughterhouse. Nothing made sense anymore. What had been a clear vision of how he would conduct himself was now blurred and distorted and excruciatingly painful as if acid had been thrown at his eyes.

When he pulled up in front of Mary Lou's apartment he couldn't remember how he got there. She was waiting in the vestibule, behind the wrought iron door. When she saw him she hurried down the sidewalk, her high heels clicking on the concrete. It was his habit to lean across the seat and open the door for her, but she was at the curb before the van had come to a full stop. She climbed in and slammed the door. The sheet metal echoed like a tin drum. "First you're late and now you don't even open the door for me. Is this the way it's going to be now that we're married?"

Alex gritted his teeth but said nothing.

"Let's get going. We just have a few minutes to make it." As he turned the steering wheel to pull away she noticed the Band Aid on his finger. "Why aren't you wearing your wedding ring?"

"It was rubbing my scar. It began to bleed."

"So where's the ring?”

"In my pocket."

"Fine," she said, "already you've pocketed your wedding ring. Do you have any other good news?"

There was other news, all right, but none of it good.

As the two of them stewed in the front seat, Alex drove absent-mindedly down Nicollet to 38th and turned right. He stayed on 38th till he reached Grand Avenue. St. Cecilia's dominated the intersection. You didn't have to be Catholic to know it: the imposing red brick church, the large school and playground, the convent hidden behind a high brick wall were all familiar landmarks. He expected to find plenty of parking spaces in front of the church this early in the morning but he was mistaken. Catholics take their religion seriously. He asked if she wanted to be dropped off in front of the church entrance with its imposing steps but she said she'd walk with him. He drove to the end of the block, made a U-turn over the streetcar tracks and parked behind a long row of cars.

Mary Lou sat in the van till he came around and opened the door. She climbed out. They waited for a streetcar to rumble past and then crossed Grand and walked down the sidewalk, barely conscious of the freshness of this September Sunday--the first full day of their married life. The weather front that had sucked the hot, moist air from the gulf and caused the downpour and humid temperatures on their wedding day had moved east overnight, and a high pressure system was bringing down the cool, dry Canadian air that made Minnesota autumns so special. When they stepped into the narthex, Mary Lou's demeanor changed. An aura of serenity suddenly enveloped her. Alex felt blocked out by it. Mary Lou draped a black crocheted mantilla over her head and he finally took notice of what she had on: her properly conservative gray suit with the subtle pinstripe she wore to the office. On her feet she had black pumps, and in her hand a small, black soft-leather purse. He was relieved. This should show the Greek critics that his new wife was a proper lady.

He nearly bumped into her when she stopped and dipped her fingers in the holy water font. She crossed herself, leaving a tiny dot of moisture on her forehead. He was going to wipe it away for her when she began walking down the central aisle of the vaulted nave. He fell in a step behind and hesitated by a back pew, hoping to park there, but Mary Lou marched resolutely to the second row from the front. He caught up to her as she genuflected in the aisle. Then she pushed herself into a pew that was nearly full. Annoyed worshippers had to slide over to make room for her and Alex as they squeezed in. He felt exposed so far down in front, certain everyone was staring at him.

Mary Lou pulled the kneeler out, got on her knees and prayed silently into her folded hands. He wondered if he should do the same. Apparently it was the thing to do this morning--even his mother did it on the front lawn.

In a gesture of compromise, Alex leaned forward and braced his forearms on the pew in front of him. He kept his eye on the activity behind the chancel rail where a squad of God's soldiers was preparing for the observance of the holy sacrifice. There were altar boys in white surplices and assistant priests in black cassocks helping the priest who was draped and girthed in the brocaded trappings of his exalted position. He wore gold-rimmed spectacles down on his nose so he could peer over them at his flock. His nose was heavily veined. Alex speculated that he polished off a lot more wine than what was left in the communion cup.

When Mary Lou slid back onto the pew so did Alex. She folded her hands in her lap and became absorbed in the Latin incantations coming from the altar. Meanwhile he busied himself studying the embellished architecture that was intent on smothering him--the wall frescos of scowling saints and chubby puti, the pilasters of fake marble, the gold leaf capitals, the arched clerestory windows, the frescoed ceiling.

There was a break in the proceedings, and the priest climbed the steps to the carved oak pulpit a good seven feet above his parishioners to deliver his sermon, blessed in its brevity. His topic was fidelity. If we believe in One Catholic God, he intoned, we must also believe in One Catholic Spouse, and ruled out passage to God's Kingdom for those who marry outside their religion. Alex gave Mary Lou a sidelong glance, not to get her attention but rather her reaction to a sermon whose message was hitting very close to home. She was listening intently. It was almost as if the priest had fashioned his words to make their greatest impact on her. Alex's mind wandered. Was this the same priest Mary Lou admitted confessing to, describing her secret sex life in graphic detail on the other side of the screen? What about their Big Night on the Bare Mattress; did she tell him about that, too?

Every time the priest swept his gaze over their pew, Alex looked down, convinced he was being singled out as the prosecution's Exhibit A.

The sermon ended in a prayer, heads bowed, and the language went back to Latin as the mass continued amidst the heady aroma of smoldering incense and the hypnotic tinkling of little bells. Presently, the large bells in the belfry announced Communion, pealing and vibrating as the Priest held the chalice over his head and enjoined parishioners to come forward and partake of the blood and flesh of Our Lord and Savior Jesus Christ.

Why is everyone so profoundly moved? There is nothing unique about Communion. Every religion since the dawn of man used sacrifice as its centerpiece, and Christianity was only the latest incarnation. Just new wine in old bottles, and Alex was not convinced it was that superior a vintage.

Mary Lou rose and pushed against his thigh so she could get around him. He jumped into the aisle, his shoulder knocking an elderly woman's wide brimmed hat askew. He apologized quietly but profusely, his cheeks burning as the woman re-secured her hatpin and gave him a look that suggested she wanted to stab him with it. He sat again, all alone now as everyone rose to take communion. He felt as shunned as a leper.

At the altar rail Mary Lou accepted the host and wine with bowed head and outstretched hands. When he saw her munch the wafer his stomach ached. Maybe he should have gone with her just to get something to eat. The mass mercifully ended and parishioners streamed out in a rush to have breakfast. Alex was in complete sympathy.

"Let's go," he said, bacon and eggs dancing in his head.

Instead of turning up the center aisle, Mary Lou began walking down it. "Follow me."

"Where?"

"We're going to see Father Bassagni."

Everyone had poured out of the church and the large nave, empty of sound-absorbing bodies, ominously echoed her words.

"I already saw him. I even listened to his sermon."

She stopped in front of a door that blended so well with the rococo plasterwork he hadn't noticed it before. "Father Bassagni wants to meet you."

As if on cue, the door opened and Father Bassagni poked his head out. "Ah, there you are. I was in my office and when you didn't show up I thought I'd better come looking." He motioned like an usher. "Come, come, we mustn't keep God waiting."

Alex came forward like a dog expecting to be leashed.

Father Bassagni had shed his brocade. He was in his black cassock. A ring of white collar was nearly covered by the sagging wattles under his chin. He gripped Alex's hand way up the palm and shook it firmly. "Welcome to St. Cecelia."

He led them down a hallway that connected the church building to an office annex where he directed them into a well-appointed office and closed the door. He possessed the rosy confidence of a man completely at ease in his milieu--the diametric opposite of Alex's demeanor who felt as though he was on another planet. The priest sat behind his desk and motioned them to sit opposite.

They were surrounded by oak and leather. There was a prayer rail in the corner. Above it a small, white-marble sculpture of the Virgin Mary was flanked on either side by gold sconces holding white candles. A shelf behind them was packed with books and files. On the wall above Father Bassagni's head was a painted portrait of a female saint wearing a halo and a beatific expression while holding a violin.

"That is St. Cecilia," the Father said, following Alex's gaze, "the patron saint of music. We are quite well known for our music program here. Our ten o'clock service today will be Haydn's Mariazeller Mass with members of the Minneapolis Symphony performing with the choir. It will be quite extraordinary." He opened a drawer and handed Alex a printed folder. "You might be interested in our church schedule for the year."

"I usually go to Northrop Auditorium to hear extraordinary music," Alex said without glancing at the folder. He was so provoked he didn't care who knew it. The priest left the folder lying on his gleaming desk. He leaned back and leather crinkled. He folded his hands across his stomach and studied Alex over his glasses. "Now, then, shall we get down to business?"

"Will anyone tell me what's going on?"

Father Bassagni looked at Mary Lou as though they were the only two people in the room.

"Have you discussed this with him?"

"Discussed what?" Alex asked, turning his head as if he were at a tennis match.

The priest held up his hand. "Let me explain..."

"Explain what?"

"Mary Lou called me..."

Alex steadied his gaze on Mary Lou. "You called him?"

She nodded. "To tell Father Bassagni that we eloped. And he asked to see us right after mass."

"If you will allow me to get back into the conversation," the priest interrupted, "let me say that I am not sitting in judgment of your decision to elope. I am sure you are convinced your reasons were the right ones.

But now that you have taken that step, you cannot assume you are married in the eyes of God. The vows you exchanged in Mason City are meaningless unless they are consecrated by the church. That is why I told Mary Lou I wanted to see you right after mass. This matter must be taken care of before it is too late."

"Too late for what?"

Father Bassagni leaned forward to emphasize the delicate nature of his subject matter. "Before you engage in conjugal relations..."

"You mean making love?"

Father Bassagni, his cheeks blending with the pink of his nose, leapfrogged over Alex's comment. "...which constitutes a mortal sin unless the church blesses your marriage in the eyes of God."

"What's a mortal sin?"

"It is a sin that puts your soul at risk of going to hell."

Alex looked at Mary Lou. "Am I missing something or haven't you told him that we already committed a mortal sin?"

Mary Lou shot him a glance that could have melted the candles over the prayer rail.

"Are you referring to Mary Lou's confession?"

"Confess, tell--what's the difference?"

Father Bassagni measured his words as if the blasphemous Alex had been sent to test his faith. "There is a world of difference. Whatever is shared in the confessional is not a subject of casual conversation."

"Even if the confession involves me? I was sinning, too, you know."

Mary Lou crossed her leg and the toe of her elevated foot was making angry circles in the air.

"Confession is a private conversation between priest and confessor with God as the mediator. It is a personal act of contrition, allowing the sinner an opportunity to repent, and thereby saving one's soul."

'What about my soul?"

The priest smiled confidentially. "I'd be happy to help you with it."

"Not a bad deal. Every time I sin, I can go to confession, repent, and sin all over again."

Mary Lou's toe was in a virtual tailspin.

The priest cleared his throat. "Believe me, Mr. Poulos, I am not afraid to take you on in a theological debate, but I don't have the time. However, I am concerned how your attitude is affecting Mary Lou. She is in a vulnerable state right now. I cannot express to you how important her faith is to her. It is the very foundation, the very essence, of her existence..."

"Who did she marry, me or the church?"

The priest patiently plodded on, confident that the angels were on his side. "In a Catholic marriage there is no difference."

It's Orwellian all right, Alex thought.

"That is why you must honor Mary Lou's wish to bless your marriage. Then you will be at one with God. I'll perform the service in the chapel. It won't take long. We can do it before the next mass."

"Right now?"

"You are here." Father Bassagni placed his fingers to his chest, "and so am I."

"You're here because you have to be."

The priest laughed indulgently. "Because I am God's shepherd and this is his lea."

"Not mine. I belong to the Greek Orthodox Church." For the first time Alex found himself defending his religion.

"God looks over all of His flock."

"Does that mean Mary Lou can also graze in mine?"

"If you are asking, can she partake in the body and blood of Christ at your church? The answer is no."

"But can she still visit the Greek church?"

"Only as your true and virtuous wife."

Despite his beleaguered state, Alex began to understand what this was all about. "And the only way she can be my true and virtuous wife is if I agree to this blessing you are talking about?"

The priest nodded.

"So, in effect, you're saying I need to be vaccinated before she can enter my church?"

Mary Lou had kept her silence till now, but this was too much. "In my entire life I have never heard anyone speak so disrespectfully to a priest!"

Alex looked at his wife. She was so different he barely recognized her. A muscle in her cheek twitched and her lips were set in such a hard line he could not discern their color.

Jesus, but he was tired! His reserves of energy were registering on empty--dissipated first by his mother and now exhausted by this formidable team of Bassagni and Stachich, with God coaching on the sidelines. Alex wished he had the strength of Hercules and the wisdom of Socrates, not to mention a plateful of food. He sighed. "All right, let's get it over with."

The priest opened a file in his desk drawer and withdrew a form. He handed it to Alex, all business now. "Look this over."

At the top was the imprint of the Catholic Archdiocese of Minnesota and a list of the church hierarchy from Archbishop to Coadjutor, like attorneys in a law firm. There was a bold-face heading, SOLEMN

AGREEMENT, and under it a subhead: To Accept the Precepts, Principles, and Canons of The Roman Catholic Church.

What is this? Alex asked himself, the church's Good Humping Seal of Approval? He began reading the paragraphs of small type. He was so lightheaded from hunger the lines began to undulate. There was a lot of high-tone, doctrinaire language backed up by quoted scripture about the Church's position on such matters as birth, baptism, moral conduct, and death. Practice of birth control other than the rhythm method was strictly forbidden. No sexual intercourse Saturday before Communion on Sunday. Mass was mandatory on Sunday and encouraged other days. No meat on Friday, Holy Days and Lent. Children must be baptized and confirmed in the Catholic Church. They must study the Catechism. At death, Catholics were to receive the Last Rites of the Church, but not if death was the result of suicide. That was a sin.

Alex wondered if starvation was a also sin. "Ok, I've looked at it. Now what?"

"Sign at the bottom."

Alex was looking at Mary Lou when he said, "Can't we just sit down and decide this by ourselves?"

"When you borrow money from a bank you sign a promissory note," Father Bassagni said. "This is a promissory note to God's bank." He handed Alex his gold fountain pen. It was long and thin, tapered like a fine candle.

Alex hesitated, his hand poised over the document. He was no different from the black man who happened to be in the wrong place at the wrong time and signed a document he was not meant to sign. "And if I refuse?"

Father Bassagni and Mary Lou exchanged concerned glances.

Alex twisted his mouth into a wry smile. "I don't get to eat, right?" He scratched his name across the bottom. It didn't look like his signature. He laid the pen on the document and slid it across the shiny surface of the desk. Father Bassagni rolled a curved blotter over the wet ink. Then he took a velvet bag from his desk and removed a gold plated stamp, like the kind notaries use, and pressed the church seal over Alex's signature.

THE NURSE

Poulos climbed into a taxi in front of the Imperial Hotel, his bloodstream astir with Glenfiddich and his head with uncertainty. On the way to the train station he thought about the sense of incompleteness in his afternoon with Gildenhall--like a three-act play with the third act yet to be written. Gildenhall had revealed his sensitive side, the side he necessarily had to hide on the ship, the tough-guy persona is a natural by-product of life at sea, but in the sublime atmosphere of the Imperial's bar, he was able to pry out of Poulos the personal things they had in common, among them artistic sensitivity and domineering mothers.

Gildenhall's inordinate interest in his personal life made Poulos uneasy, especially after he told his scotch-fueled enema story, because he felt the officer wished to unlock a door to a more intimate relationship. Poulos had never before given a second thought to how he related to other men, or how they related to him. Take Witter, for example. He found him attractive because the guy looked like a muscled Doryphoros, not because he was interested in him sexually. At least, that is how he thought he felt. The afternoon with Gildenhall had stabbed a thorn of doubt into his otherwise comfortable male skin. Strange how complicated personal relationships can get.

On the speeding train back to Yokosuka, the scotch began to wear off. Poulos watched the Japanese countryside whiz by his window--rice paddies glistening in the setting sun, blue-gray hills silhouetted against the sky's waning light, villages of thatched roofs and dirt paths, wagons and mopeds waiting at lowered gates for the train to pass.

The Yokosuka station was crowded with American servicemen hurrying to make connections for Saturday night liberty. Poulos changed back into his dress blues in the station's men's room and stored his civvies in the locker, then took a navy bus to the base hospital, a gridded complex of two-story, wood-frame buildings uniformly painted naval gray and trimmed in white. The grounds were landscaped with neatly clipped grass and hedges. The navy had plenty of cheap labor, sailors doing brig time, to keep everything spick and span.

It was six-thirty, a half hour to kill before meeting his buddies. He pulled out the piece of paper on which Browning had written Clayton's building number. He had kept it since the day Browning gave it to him. He might grow to regret not making an effort to find out what happened to Clayton. He walked around till he found MNP-13, the number written on the paper. A wood sign below it, screwed to the siding, read Neurology and Psychiatry, the very same words that so angered his mother the time he took her to the University Hospital. As he stood on the sidewalk wondering about this strange coincidence, the lampposts came on, as if signaling him to make a move. Struggling to put his self-doubt aside, he removed his hat and walked in. A nurse in the starched white of her profession sat behind a reception desk reading Saturday Evening Post under the light of a goose-neck lamp. There was a Rolodex on her desk and a PBX switchboard on a stand against the wall. He expected to hear the screeches and moans of the insane, but it was eerily quiet.

She looked up from her magazine inquiringly.

"Excuse me, I was wondering about RB Clayton, yeoman second class. He was transferred here for psychiatric evaluation from the Robert B. Sprague."

She flipped her Rolodex to the Cs. "Carson, Chezwik, Clayton."
She consulted a file in her desk and pulled out a folder. "I have a copy of his orders."

Poulos leaned forward with curiosity.

"He was released pending final review by the Judge Advocate General."

That was promising. Sounded like Clayton was going home.

"Are you a friend of his?"

"We served together on the Sprague."

The nurse lifted the top sheet and referred to the Final Destination entry on page two. "Well, then you'll be happy to hear that Clayton is on temporary billeting aboard the USS Hampton at the Harbormaster Pier. He's going back to the Sprague."

Poulos was stunned. "He wasn't discharged?"

She returned the file to the drawer. "No. Isn't that great? You'll be seeing him again."

He went back outside and angrily pulled his hat over his forehead.

Great? he asked himself. You call that great? Clayton is coming back to the Sprague? Who decided that? Some pseudo-psychiatrist? Why didn't he ask Poulos how he felt about it? He could tell him what a terrible mistake this is. He looked up at the darkening sky, beseeching the gods to explain how the navy could make such a stupid blunder, but all he got for his efforts were a gibbous moon just beginning to stake out its position in the darkening sky and stars coming out of their daytime hiding places.

When Poulos got to Scotty's building, he was hardly in a sociable mood. A cohort of the nurse in MNP-13 was sitting at a reception desk with a telephone console, the only difference was that she was reading Stars and Stripes. He was probably scowling at her because she looked at him cautiously.

He did his best to smile. "I'm here to see Scott Karl, Gunner's Mate Second. He's a patient..."

"I know Scotty," she interrupted. "We all know Scotty. Upstairs to room 230. Your shipmates are already there."

The highly polished linoleum treads squeaked under him as he climbed the stairs. The second floor was a ward for patients in various stages of recovery. Through open doors he saw sailors in traction with casts on their arms or legs, sometimes both. Others walked the hall, pushing rolling walkers or using canes. More than one man was missing a limb. They all wore light gray bathrobes with USN stenciled on their backs. It was quiet until Poulos came to room 230 where unbridled laughter and loud talk came out of the doorway. He looked in. Browning and Witter were leaning against a window sill. Scotty was stretched out on his bed, his hands behind his head. Above him was a steel frame of hollow tubing supporting a collection of pulleys, cables and rings that looked like something a trapeze artist would train on. One leg of his hospital pajamas was cut off for a thick cast which ran from his crotch to his toes.

"There he is," Scotty said, when he saw Poulos. He hoisted himself to a sitting position with the rings above his head. "You're late. I thought you were going to stand us up, which is more than I can do."

"I got lost. All these stupid buildings look alike."

"What's the matter? You act like you got a rod up your ass."

"Does it show?"

"Something is bugging you," Browning said.

"I did what you told me to do. I went to see Clayton."

They all came to attention.

"How is he?"

"He was released from the hospital."

"Medical discharge?"

"Nope." Poulos waited a few seconds to build suspense. "Clayton is coming back to the Sprague."

Scotty whistled. "I thought you said the navy got rid of psychos."

"Unless his doctor is a bigger one."

"Clayton is no psycho if he's getting a second chance," Witter said.

"Dan is always defending that Bible thumper," Scotty said. "At least he's not my problem."

"I wish I was in your shoes," Poulos said, without thinking.

"They're in the closet. Help yourself."

Poulos felt his cheeks redden. "Sorry, Scotty, I didn't mean it that way."

"What's a limp between friends?"

The mood in the room got serious. "What do you mean?" Poulos asked.

"Looks like a twenty-five per cent disability. I'll get fifty bucks a month for the rest of my life."

The sailors pondered the trade-off. Even though none expressed it out loud, no amount of money was worth a permanent disability.

"Hey, don't look so down," Scotty said, trying to revive the party mood. "You came to conquer nurses, not bury your buddy."

"Fine with me." Browning said, looking around. "So where are they?"

"They'll be here any minute. Bonnie is showing up with that Greek nurse."

Poulos was bothered by Scotty's offhand reference to "that Greek nurse" as if she were a non-entity, someone not worthy to be called by name.

"So where are the gals you promised me and A. John?" Witter asked.

"Downstairs in the lounge. The nurses fixed up the basement. They even have a juke box and a dance floor down there. Wait till you see it."

"Is there a bar?"

"This is a hospital!" Scotty laughed. "But don't worry. Someone always shows up with a bottle."

There was a tap on the jamb. They turned. Two nurses stood in the doorway--one blonde, the other brunette. They wore light gray slacks and sweatshirts with the navy seal and the words Healer Dealer silkscreened in pink.

"Are we interrupting anything important?" the blonde asked.

"Nothing more important than you," Scotty said with a familiarity obviously intended to impress his buddies.

The blonde wore her hair cropped short like a tomboy revealing tiny jeweled earrings in her pierced lobes. She was athletic with a strong neck and shoulders, and looked as if she could beat most men at arm wrestling. She had a cheerful smile and her cheeks were rosy either from rouge or a naturally healthy complexion. By contrast, the dark-haired nurse appeared reserved, even shy, her Mediterranean coloration more pronounced in the presence of the blonde. She was taller and thinner than the blonde although hippier--a sure sign of heavier things to come, Poulos thought. Her black hair was straight and cut short, but not as short as the blonde's. She parted it on the left side and there was a cowlick where her part ended. She had a strong nose but what dominated her face were her eyes, irises so dark they blended with her pupils, creating shimmering opaque circles that reflected back at him.

"Fellow shipmates," Scotty said in his best Emily Post manner, "I want you to meet the woman in my life--Bonnie Sanders." Then he added, "This is Jenny Betheras,"

Poulos did something with his face hoping it came out looking like a smile.

"The square-jawed guy is Dave, and the glasses belong to A. John."

"What does the A stand for?" Bonnie asked Browning.

"Guess," Browning said.

"Abner."

"No."

"Alonzo."

"No."

"Abercrombie, Artimus, AskmenoquestionsI'lltellyounolies."

"No, no and no!"

Everyone was laughing except Poulos who was still waiting to be introduced. "Hey, my name starts with A, too."

"Oh, yeah, here's Alex, the Greek gob."

"Gob?"

"You sure as hell are no Greek god."

The evening was not off to an auspicious start.

Fortunately, Witter changed the subject. "Are we supposed to salute or shake hands?"

"Shaking hands will do," Bonnie said.

Scotty broke in, "Did you hear the one about the guy who brought a pair of dead squirrels to a taxidermist?"

"I don't want to hear it," Bonnie said.

He was already laughing. "The taxidermist asked him if he wanted the squirrels mounted and the guy said, shaking hands will do."

Bonnie rolled her eyes. "Do we have to take him along?"

Scotty slid his cast over the edge of his bed. "You're not leaving without me."

"Careful, or you'll fall down," Bonnie said as though dealing with a child. "Get a chair will you Jenny?"

Jenny left the room and returned pushing a wheelchair. She locked one of the footplates in the upright position, and the two nurses helped Scotty into the seat. They worked well together from long practice.

Bonnie pushed Scotty down the brightly lighted hallway to an elevator, Witter and Browning walking alongside, Poulos and Jenny bringing up the rear. Even though they were acutely aware of one another they were not exchanging glances. He wanted to check her out more fully but he kept his eyes straight ahead, conditioned by years of feeling tentative in the presence of a Greek girl. When the elevator came, he caught a glimpse of her ankles below the cuffs of her slacks. Not bad, he thought, wonder how the rest of her looks? The elevator slowly transported them to the lower level. The door opened onto a carpeted hallway that led to the lounge. Instead of the harsh fluorescent tubing on Scotty's floor they were treated to subdued indirect lighting from green enameled ceiling fixtures. Above the entrance to the lounge was a hand-painted sign: The Nite N Gals. A large room opened up before them with tables and chairs forming a perimeter around a small dance floor. The tables held candles and napkin dispensers. Music was coming from a 100-play Wurlitzer. The walls were painted plush red. Black netting stretched across the ceiling from one supporting post to another.

A Japanese man in a white apron stood behind a table selling pop, pretzels and potato chips.

"Nice place you have here," Witter said.

"We decorated it ourselves."

They pulled two tables together to accommodate Scotty's wheelchair. Like Bonnie and Jenny, most of the nurses in the lounge were casually dressed. A few were in their whites, probably because they had just got off duty or were going on. Except for the sailors from the Sprague, all the men present were patients.

"Where did you get the juke box?" Poulos asked, finally managing to think of something to say.

"From a USO warehouse left over from the occupation," Jenny replied in a voice that was softly southern. "We managed to get all the phonograph records, too." She smiled. Vertical lines formed at the corners of her mouth, not dimples but slight indentations that reminded him of the Giaconda smile--enigmatic and mysterious.

Inevitably he compared her to Mary Lou. Jenny was taller and bonier; Mary Lou shorter and zaftig. Jenny used very little make-up. Mary Lou used a ton of mascara and eyeliner. She also plucked her eyebrows into perfect arches. Jenny left hers alone. They almost grew together. He kind of liked that. Even if she was Greek, he wanted to find out about her--why she joined the navy, where she lived, what books she read. As he compared her to Mary Lou, a pang of guilt crawled out of his subconscious. Oddly, he didn't react this way when he was with Natasha. Mary Lou didn't even enter his mind. In his system of moral equivalency, a prostitute didn't matter simply because she was, well, a prostitute, but being with a woman he could compare to Mary Lou made it much more personal.

He began to rationalize that he was not cheating on Mary Lou. After all, he was talked into coming here by Scotty and that Betty Boop nurse, he was at a naval hospital, not in a bar looking to pick up a woman, he was in the company of naval personnel who were not only female but also officers, for Christ's sake! The fact that he had just spent an afternoon in a bar with an officer, albeit male, supported his rationalization because he was once again in the company of an officer who happened to be a woman, far less incriminating than being with a civilian woman and, what was most significant, a civilian woman who was also Greek. So why should he suffer recriminations and not simply enjoy himself?

The subject of officers stayed forefront in his mind, as good a place as any to start a conversation, he decided. "How come there aren't male officers here?" he asked.

"They have their own clubs."

"Ever been to one?"

"No."

"You're an officer, aren't you?"

"I just can't walk in, I have to be escorted." Jenny looked around the lounge. "Besides, what's wrong with this place?"

"It's filled with enlisted men, like me. I just thought you'd like to hang around with your own kind."

"My own kind?" she asked, sensing correctly that Poulos was baiting her. "Just what is that supposed to mean?"

"Officers are a privileged class."

"Believe me," she said, "nurses are not a privileged class. You should spend a few days here and see what we do."

Poulos had to admit that he liked to hear Jenny talk. Her accent was pleasant, not at all like the southern drawls he heard on the ship; like the gunner's mate who wanted to clear the deck of cotter pins. She spoke clearly and with a lilting cadence, accenting her syllables with a delicate nuance that was melodious, even welcome, to his ear. Nevertheless he could not resist the urge to argue. "But you can still go to an officer's club if you want to."

"No one has asked me." Her cheeks reddened slightly as she realized she gave the impression that she didn't consider herself pretty enough to be asked on a date.

Poulos understood that Greek women tended to be self-conscious about their sex appeal, conditioned as they were by the fact that gentlemen, especially Greek gentlemen, preferred blondes. But Jenny didn't have to take a back seat to anyone. He did, in fact, find her pretty enough. "Date a doctor," he said, "the place is crawling with them."

"Doctors do not see nurses as anything but the help."

"Ok, then, forget doctors. What if a line officer asked you out, would you go?"

"Just because he's an officer?"

"Sure."

She shrugged. "It would depend..."

"Whether or not he's Greek?"

A knowing smile spread across her face. "What you're really getting at is that the reason I'm here with you is because you happen to be Greek. Am I right?"

"I was only curious why an ensign would be seen in the company of an enlisted man."

"It doesn't matter to me if you're a one-stripe seaman or a four-stripe admiral."

"As long as I'm Greek?"

She studied him a few seconds. "The reason I'm here is because of Bonnie. She invited me to come along because she likes Scotty and she wanted his friends to have a good time."

"But that doesn't disprove my point. She didn't set you up with Dave or A. John. She set you up with me. When she found out I was Greek, the first thing she said to me was that I should meet the Greek nurse on the staff."

Jenny placed her elbows on the table. "May I ask you a question?"

"Go ahead," he said with feigned innocence.

"Why are you so combative? You've been on the attack ever since we came down here. It's as if you have to beat a Greek girl into submission before you can be comfortable with her."

"I'm just wondering why Bonnie assumed you and I wanted to meet each other, that's all."

"Is that so strange? Look at all the things we have in common..."

"Like what?"

"For one thing we have a rare language that only eight million people in the whole world speak. We share a beautiful tradition that goes back thousands of years. We're like family..."

"That's just it."

"What is?"

"Family. It's incestuous."

She stared at him as though she could not believe what she was hearing. "Incestuous?"

"Sure. When you go out with a Greek girl you might as well be dating your sister."

Disappointment registered on her face. The condescension was a common putdown among Greek men of Poulos's generation and it was not lost on Jenny.

Scotty felt the glacial cold crawling across the table. He swung his wheelchair around. "Having a good time?"

"We're still getting acquainted."

"Why do you need to get acquainted? You're both Greek, aren't you?" Scotty tried to read the frustrated expression on his buddy's face. "Did I say something wrong?"

"Forget it."

Scotty made a gesture like a traffic cop. "Why don't you two dance?"

Bonnie said, "Leave them alone, Scotty."

"If I can't dance, I'd like to watch somebody who can."

Witter and Browning came back from the bar bearing bottles of Coke with glasses hanging upside down over the tops, and passed them around. "We're going to sit with those gals over there."

Scotty smiled approvingly. "Two sailors and six nurses. That's what I call sandwich dates."

"Yeah," Witter said, "club sandwiches." He followed Browning across the dance floor. They dragged empty chairs from another table and squeezed in.

Poulos broke off with Jenny to watch the sailors blend easily into the casual, undefined atmosphere of the group. No need to feel responsible for someone else; just have fun. He looked longingly at the crowded table filled with laughter and talk. His concentration diverted, he poured Coke into his glass too high and foam sloshed over the side.

"Go join your friends if you want to," Jenny said, getting irritated with him.

"Why would I want to do that?" he said, pulling a napkin from the dispenser and wiping up the spill.

"Because I make you nervous."

"Me, nervous?" he denied, but, as he balled up the wet napkin, he saw it as a visual metaphor of the mess he was making of his date with Jenny.

She really wasn't bad, not for a Greek girl. He had to say something conciliatory, but in a manner that would show he was still in charge, an attitude Greek men tend to assume is their birthright. He leaned back, hoping to strike a casual pose. "What makes you think I want to break in on that crowd?"

Jenny's eyes flashed with renewed grit. "To get away from your sister?"

"I don't have a sister," he lobbed back

"I'm glad to hear that. I can't imagine you being a brother."

"Touché." He held up his glass in salute to a worthy adversary. "I'd much rather talk to you."

"Do I take that as a compliment?"

"Please do," he said. "because I want you to tell me why you think two people can fall in love when they are stamped out of the same mold."

"Do you really think Greeks are stamped out of the same mold simply because they share a common ancestry?"

"I'll give you an example. Look at how they abrogate their right to choose for themselves."

"You mean proxeinya?"

"Yes, why should someone else pick out who I want to marry instead of deciding for myself?"

"We may not be mature enough to make a lifelong decision. My parents' marriage was arranged. They grew to love each other."

"What about love at first sight? Do you think that can happen?"

She shook her head. "Infatuation maybe, physical attraction maybe, but not true love, the kind that grows and lasts a lifetime."

"Have you ever fallen in love?" he asked her bluntly.

"My you work fast."

"It's just a question."

She ran her fingers through her hair. It flowed like wheat in the dark of night.

"Not yet," she answered.

"Shouldn't love be the determining factor in whether or not you marry someone?"

"You think love conquers all? After the allure fades and you see your wife in curlers, what then? That's why having shared values like religion and culture are so important."

"But you can't always dictate whom you fall in love with. What if Mr. Right comes along instead of Mr. Rightopolis?"

"That's not likely to happen."

"So you're going to hang around hoping some Greek guy will ride up on a white stallion and sweep you off your feet?"

"He doesn't have to be on a horse."

"My mother once told me she hoped I would marry a Greek girl whose mother came from the same village as she did. I can only think of four, and two of them happen to be sisters."

"There's that word again."

They laughed together, reducing the friction between them. It was verbal sparring after all and they both knew it, had it happen to them before, and was part of the ongoing search for meaning among first generation Greek-Americans, a ritual meant not to alienate but to dig deep even if it hurt.

Jenny finally got around to pouring her soft drink. Small bubbles collected where the Coke met the glass. "Have you ever been to Greece?" she asked, sipping.

He shook his head. "I was invited by my godfather to go with him but I turned him down."

Jenny's eyes widened. "You did? Why?"

Poulos shrugged, trying to appear nonchalant but inside he was suffering pangs of regret at what might have been. Had he accepted Gus's invitation how much better off he would be right now. "Something came up. I couldn't make it."

"I would jump at the chance to go again."

His regret deepened. "You've been to Greece?"

"My parents gave me a trip as a graduation present. It opened my eyes and my soul...Delphi and Olympia, Agamemnon's tomb, Sounion where Lord Byron scratched his name on a marble column..." She spoke with such ardor, goose bumps formed on his arms. "I finally understood why my parents were so proud of their heritage. They knew that if I saw where they were born, I would be as proud of Greece as they are."

Jenny's words were so close to those of Uncle Gus that he was nearly despondent. He had let an opportunity of a lifetime slip through his fingers. And for what? Love at first sight?

"You seem sad," Jenny said.

"I was thinking that we only begin to see when we have to look back."

"You are a man of contradictions."

Poulos straightened himself. "I'll get to Greece someday."

"I'm glad to hear you say that because you have to be there to know what Greece is really like. The experience will change you." There was a hint of challenge in her eyes. "I'd like to meet you again after you go to

Greece just so I can say, see, what did I tell you?"

Someone punched up Stardust on the Wurlitzer. The poignant words drifted into his ears. He looked into the deep-dark of her pupils and felt that if he stared at them long enough he would become obsessed. He wondered what it would be like to put his arm around her waist. Would she dance if he asked her? He decided to chance it and got to his feet. "Would you like to dance?"

"Are you declaring a truce?"

He held both hands in the air. "Unconditional surrender."

She smiled at him and stood up. They walked onto the dance floor as Scotty rapped his cast with his knuckle and shouted, "Wish I could do that!"

Poulos angled Jenny toward the rear of the floor to lose themselves behind the other couples who were moving slowly to Hoagy Carmichael's melody. Most of the time he didn't mind Scotty's raw intrusions but right now he wanted to be alone with this bright and self-possessed woman so he could get to know her better. He had enjoyed their verbal sparring. Perhaps it was her very Greekness that was so intriguing. He had prepped himself not to like her, to write her off because she was Greek, and yet it was this very quality that fascinated him. Jenny was right. He was full of contradictions.

Stardust came to an end and they waited for the next number to come up on the juke box. It was Gershwin's Long Ago and Far Away. They began dancing to the poignantly romantic lyrics:

> Long ago and far away,
> I dreamed a dream one day,
> and now that dream is here beside me.
> Long the skies were overcast,
> but now the clouds have passed;
> you're here at last...

The poetry was so agonizingly tender, so beyond his reach, that he ached with sorrow. He wished he could start over; redo the last year of his life.

The song ended and they waited for another record. An instrumental version of Cole Porter's Night and Day gave them an opportunity to talk as they danced.

"What do you do when you're not on duty?" he asked in her ear.

Jenny pulled her head back to look at him. "Go to the base movie. Read. Write letters home."

"Do you write to a boyfriend?"

"My parents and my sister."

"Aha," he said, "a sister!"

"And she's happily married to a Greek."

"What does your father do?"

"Fruits and vegetables. He owns a produce company. What does your father do?"

Poulos was always embarrassed when asked this question. "Nothing much, a candy maker."

"Nothing much? I would think candy making is an art."

"Mostly it's hard work."

"Running a produce company is hard work, too."

"Where did you go to school?"

"Randolph Macon Woman's College in Lynchburg, Virginia."

He imagined a campus shaded by Spanish moss hanging from magnolia trees. "What was your favorite subject at Randolph Macon Woman's College?" The words rolled off his tongue like iambic pentameter.

"Shakespeare."

"Shakespeare and nursing? An odd combination."

“After graduating, I took nurse's training at Columbia General, in Columbia, South Carolina, where I live."

"But what has taking care of injured sailors got to do with Shakespeare?"

"You can learn a lot about the human condition from Shakespeare. Besides..." Jenny hesitated a moment.

"Besides what?"

"My father wanted me to learn a profession."

She didn't have to elaborate. He knew what she was referring to. Greek women had to be able to support themselves because their marriage options were so limited. If there was no Greek waiting at the altar, there was no walk down the aisle. A Greek tragedy--a modern Greek tragedy.

Uncle Gus compared unclaimed Greek women to unsold merchandise sitting on a shelf. Tha mini sto rhafie, he would say.

Poulos could not imagine Jenny like that, sitting on a shelf. He felt a need to come to her defense. When he left the fold for Mary Lou, there was one less bachelor available for a Greek girl to marry, creating a ripple effect that could even reach Jenny. What he did could ruin Jenny's chances for marriage, allowing this Greek girl whom he was beginning to like to languish in spinsterhood. Given his propensity to project his own problems onto others, not to take responsibility for them where none was either needed or expected but rather to assume their burden, he added more weight to his bag of guilt now almost too heavy to bear.

"You can't spend the rest of your life alone," he said plaintively.

Jenny stopped dancing and looked up at him. "Why do you think I will?"

He dropped his arms from around her. "The system," he stammered, "it's working against you. You should be able to marry anyone you want, and no one should condemn you for it."

"Who's being condemned?"

When he didn't answer she said, "You need to justify something for yourself, not for me."

Poulos wasn't surprised at how perceptive Jenny was. "Would you ever run away and get married?"

"Elope you mean? Why, whatever for?"

"Say your parents didn't approve of the man you loved and the only way out was to run away."

"I would never do that. Would you?"

If he were to answer her, he would have to say not that he would, but that he had. "What would you think of a Greek man who ran away and got married?"

"To an American girl?"

He nodded.

"I'd feel sorry for him."

"Oh?"

"I think he would live to regret his decision."

Maybe she was reading his mind. It was time to talk about something else. He put his arm around her and they began dancing again. "How long have you been in the Far East?" he asked.

"Two years."

"So that means your tour is nearly over?"

"This is my last weekend in Japan."

He just met her and had no right to assume that she had any interest in him. But now that he learned she was going home, the option of seeing her again was denied him. After tonight she was out of his life forever.

Jenny said, "I can't believe I'm going home."

"What will you do?" he asked, wanting to appear only casually interested. "Continue nursing?"

"Not right away. I need to get reacquainted with myself as a civilian first. Then I might go back to school. I have this silly notion of becoming a doctor."

"What's silly about that?"

Glenn Miller's Sunrise Serenade came on, and Poulos was suddenly overwhelmed by a sense of loss, of being left behind. Even though he had met Jenny only tonight, he felt as if he had known her a long time because she was Greek and therefore not a stranger. Jenny was right, after all. They didn't have to go up the blind alleys that are typical of a blind date. They knew where they stood with each other from the beginning. Maybe there was something to the commonality of a culture after all.

"It's your turn," Jenny said.

"For what?"

"Telling me about yourself."

"Oh," he said again. What was there to tell? What was there he could possibly tell?

"What were you doing before the navy?"

"Driving a truck."

She looked at him in surprise. "You don't talk like a truck driver."

"You should hear me on the ship."

"You're too intellectual to talk like a truck driver or a navy man."

"I went to school."

"Where?"

"University of Minnesota."

"What did you major in?"

"Humanities. I took every humanities course under the sun."

Her eyes brightened. "That sounds more like you. I couldn't imagine you making a career driving a truck."

"I was pretty good at it."

"I have a feeling you'd be pretty good at anything you tried."

Her compliment warmed him. They were more relaxed with each other.

"Have you read anything by F. Scott Fitzgerald?" she asked.

"Just about everything."

"He came from Minnesota, didn't he?"

"Grew up in St. Paul, lived in a row house on Summit avenue with his parents during the time he wrote his first novel, This Side of Paradise. When he got the letter from Scribner's that his book was accepted, he ran into the street and stopped cars to tell everybody about his good fortune."

"You know a lot about him."

"Local boy makes good. He's also one of my favorite writers."

"Mine too."

"His wife, Zelda, was a Southern belle, like you."

"And Fitzgerald was a Minnesotan, like you."

Poulos laughed. "Have you read any of his short stories?"

"Just his novels."

"You should read The Ice Palace about a soldier from St. Paul who meets a southern girl while he's stationed in Alabama."

"Like Zelda and Fitzgerald."

"I'm sure that's what gave him the idea. The story opens with Fitzgerald describing the languid air, the smell of azaleas and the buzz of insects so well you can feel the heat. The girl is attracted to the soldier because he is so different from her, and she accepts his invitation to visit St. Paul in January when the Winter Carnival is in full swing. She never saw her breath until she got off the train. He takes her to the Ice Palace which is built out of big blocks of ice cut from a frozen lake. She gets lost in the maze of rooms. To her one wall of ice looked like any other I suppose. He finally finds her huddled in a corner, crying and shivering. Needless to say she takes the first train home."

"Can you blame her?"

"What's interesting to me is the way Fitzgerald used climate extremes to draw a distinction between the north and the south. And I think he also used it as a personal metaphor for the differences between him and Zelda."

"Are winters there really that cold?"

"Colder," Poulos said proudly. He was no different from any other Minnesotan who held bragging rights for living in the coldest state in the union. "Did you know that Minneapolis is on the same latitude as Milan, Italy, but has the winter temperatures of Moscow?"

"Brrr," Jenny said, "I definitely wouldn't live there."

The look on her face made him wish he hadn't been so frank. "Summers are nice, though."

"They'd have to be, wouldn't they, or no one would want to live there."

They continued dancing until the music stopped. Then they stood in front of the brightly colored Wurlitzer and watched the record return to its slot and another take its place. The tone arm lowered and The Modernaires began singing:

> To you, my heart cries out Perfidia,
> for I found you, the love of my life,
> in somebody else's arms.

A wave of remorse hit Poulos as he listened to the lyrics of unfaithfulness. Mary Lou was never far from his mind after all. He was an idiot to think he had any right getting interested in someone else.

"The melody is pretty isn't it?" Jenny said.

"But the lyrics are sad."

When the record ended they walked off the floor holding hands.

Poulos wanted to go outside, find a bench and talk about things he had never talked about with Mary Lou--literature and authors and ideas. "I'm having a good time," he said.

Jenny responded by rubbing her thumb along the palm of his hand. She felt his scar. "What's this?" she asked, turning his hand up.

"An old burn."

Her manner suddenly became professional. She moved him under a ceiling fixture and held his hand to the light. "This is deep," she said, expressing medical interest. "When did this happen?"

"A long time ago."

She ran her fingers along the white, leathery tissue. "A third degree burn."

"Is that bad?"

"As bad as you can get."

"I thought first degree was as bad as you can get."

"If you commit a crime, maybe."

He smiled but it didn't feel natural. "Maybe I did."

"How did this happen?"

"I reached for the flame on the kitchen stove."

"How old were you?"`

"Around the time I learned to walk. At least that's what I was told."

Jenny shuddered involuntarily. "You burned yourself nearly to the bone. See how the scar tissue webbed your two middle fingers?" She tried to straighten them out. "No flexibility," she said. "In burns of this severity the edges, called the eschar, are pulled toward the center and that's why your middle finger is pulled down like that. You lost the full thickness of your skin, as well as the underlying fat and muscle and the nerve endings."

"How come you know so much about burns?"

"I'm a nurse, remember?"

She ran her nails along the scar.

"Do you have any feeling here?"

"No. It only bothers me when the skin breaks and it bleeds."

"I don't suppose you can wear a ring on that hand."

The comment jarred him as he remembered trying to get the ring off so his mother would not see it. "Not easily."

"What are you going to do when you get married?" she joked.

He pulled his hand away.

"You can do what men in Greece do." Jenny held up her right hand. "They wear their wedding rings on their right hands."

"I'll have to remember that," he said. Under his jumper Mary Lou's wedding ring seemed suddenly to grow heavy.

"You said you reached for the flame on the kitchen stove?"

He nodded. "I do dumb things, and that was one of them."

"There has to be a reason."

"I was fascinated by the flame--or so I was told. My mother was cooking dinner. I saw the bright, flickering yellow on the stove and I reached up. Even then, I was playing with fire."

Jenny took his hand again. "But look at how concentrated your scar is. Think how small your hand was as a toddler. When you reached for the burner flame your entire palm would have been burned, including your fingers...not just the center like from a pilot light." She looked at him. "Are you left-handed?"

"Yes."

"How does your mother feel about it?"

"Being left-handed? It doesn't fit into her high standards of perfection."

"Have you ever considered surgery?"

"I remember going to a doctor when I was seven or eight. But he said nothing could be done."

"New procedures were developed during the war. One of them is called a Z-plasty where the burned tissue is cut in a z-pattern, like using a pinking shears, and the diagonal pieces are shifted and sewn together." She drew an imaginary zigzag line with the nail of her little finger on his scar. Even with what little feeling he had, it tingled pleasantly. "You may be able to open your hand wider, but there is not much that can be done about the webbing."

"I'm used to it."

They were standing close to each other so they could hear their voices above the music and the laughter and the occasional shouts. The group Witter and Browning were with had grown substantially. There were now a dozen sailors crowded around the nurses. One of them was spiking Coke from a whiskey bottle in a twisted paper bag. Another was passing around Melmac bowls filled with pretzels and potato chips. Above them cigarette smoke collected on the ceiling like a weather cloud.

"Let's get some air," Poulos said.

Jenny checked her wristwatch. It had a large face like a man's watch. "I have an early call."

As they walked out of the room, Scotty shouted, "Where you going?"

"Outside for a while."

"Didn't I tell you?" Scotty winked broadly. "Greeks know each other so well, they make out on their first date."

Poulos waved, privately delighted with Scotty's flagrant presumption. "Don't pay attention to him," he said.

"It's hard not to," Jenny said.

They walked out a rear exit into the night air. They breathed deeply to clear their lungs and fell into step on a sidewalk that led to the front of the building. Above them the moon was reaching its zenith and stars twinkled. They strolled past a motor pool bordered by a chain link fence. Behind it jeeps and troop trucks and sedans and ambulances were lined up in neat rows. They came upon a bench under a street light. As if reading each other's thoughts, they sat down. Poulos placed his hat next to him.

"What do you look like in your uniform?" he asked.

"In my starches and Red Cross shoes and white stockings?" Jenny asked. "Not very stylish."

"If you were dressed like that now would I have to call you sir or madam?"

"Ensign."

He snapped his arm up in a salute. "Aye, aye, Ensign Betheras."

"I like Jenny better."

"I was thinking..." Poulos said.

"About what?"

"Too bad we didn't meet sooner."

"I had the distinct impression you didn't care."

He looked at her. "People change."

"In one night?"

"Why not?"

"Anything is possible, Alex."

This was the first time she used his name. It made him tingle. "Would you have time to see me again?"

"Probably not. I leave in a week."

Mary Lou again invaded his thoughts. "Maybe it's just as well."

Jenny seemed disappointed that he gave up so easily.

"It wouldn't be a good idea to get to know each other and all of a sudden you're gone."

She nodded. "I suppose you're right."

They were silent for a moment.

"Why did you ask me about my mother?" he said presently.

"When?"

"In the lounge, remember? You wanted to know if it bothered her that I was left handed."

"You know how it is with nurses, always asking questions like How are we feeling today?"

"If you were asking my mother that, she'd have to say, Not very well."

"What's wrong with her?"

"She has Parkinson's disease. Shakes like a leaf."

"I'm sorry," Jenny said, genuinely moved. "It's hard to see our parents get sick. We want them to be strong and vital like they were when they came to America with just a cardboard suitcase and a bundle tied with twine."

Poulos thought about the early photographs of his mother and father when their hair was dark and their faces were unlined. It seemed as if life had cheated them both. "Did you speak Greek around the house when you were little?"

Jenny nodded.

"Me, too."

"They spoke Greek so they would feel at home in a strange new world. Imagine what it was like living in two different cultures simultaneously. Especially for the women."

"Men, too."

"But they had their businesses to go to; they learned English and the ways of America. The women stayed home. Most of them never learned to read or write English. All they had was the culture they left behind and they hung on to it."

"But it was a culture based on ignorance and superstition."

"How can you say that?"

"My mother is a perfect example." He couldn't tell Jenny about his mother's enema fetish but he could tell her about another one. "I remember her washing my left hand when I was little really hard, like she was trying to scrub my scar away."

"Then you can appreciate why she might have been bothered by your left-handedness. In Greece men used their right hand for clean activities like eating and for wearing their wedding rings, and their left for unclean things..."

"Like going to the toilet. I'd never be invited to dinner over there would I?"

"Things are different now."

"Not with my mother," Poulos said, beginning to heat up. "She's superstitious, vindictive, revengeful, bigoted..."

"I don't think we should talk about her anymore."

"She was always good at killing a conversation."

Jenny searched his face. "Have you ever considered talking to someone about your feelings?"

"My feelings?"

"Toward your mother, I mean."

"I know what my feelings are. I just told you."

Jenny stood abruptly. "It's getting late. Do you mind walking me to my barracks?"

Poulos put on his hat and rose from the bench, confused and uncertain. They began walking down the sidewalk in a veil of silence. Finally Jenny said, "Now that your ship is in dry dock for a while you'd have time to talk to someone here."

"Here? You mean the hospital?" In his mind, Poulos saw Scotty all wrapped up in plaster. "There's nothing wrong with me."

"I'm talking about your anger toward your mother."

"I know why I'm angry at her."

"Do you?"

"Sure."

"The burn on your hand..."

"What's that got to do with my mother?"

"A psychiatrist could help you answer that. I know just the right one. His name is Steiner. I can cut through the red tape before I leave and make an appointment for you."

A strong, nearly paralyzing sense of deja vu suddenly blocked his thought process. In his bewildered state he heard his mother cry, Crazy, you think I'm crazy? when she ran out of the psychiatry building at the University. He didn't realize it but he was repeating her words out loud: "Crazy, you think I'm crazy?"

"No, no!" Jenny replied anxiously. "Of course you're not. You have conflicting emotions and unresolved hurts...many people have these problems. They don't mean you're crazy. Dr. Steiner is an expert at helping sort these things out. Just talk to him, tell him what you told me." Jenny saw the panic in his eyes. She rubbed her forehead. "Oh, my god," she said, "what have I done? I'm sorry, Alex. Please, let's just drop it."

They walked side by side but no longer connecting. The spiritual distance between them, having narrowed as they got to know each other, was now moving the other way, growing wider by the step. When they reached Jenny's barracks, they were totally disengaged, strangers once again.

THE MOTHER

Alex and Mary Lou had to wait in line fifteen minutes before they got seated at The Hasty Tasty on Lake and Hennepin. He had not expected the restaurant to be so busy this early in the morning. He guessed it was packed by Catholics who went to six o'clock Mass just so they could be the first ones to get a booth. The restaurant dated from the 1930s and he occupied himself by studying the Art Deco interior it was noted for--the quaint half-moon mirrors etched with geometric patterns, the tiered green-and-gold chandeliers, the quasi-classical columns--but his stomach was in such a tight knot he could barely concentrate. Once in a while his view of things turned white as he rocked on the balls of his feet behind the Please Wait to be Seated sign. Finally it was their turn and he fell into the booth with a heavy thud.

When the waitress brought menus and water Alex ordered an orange juice and doughnut for immediate delivery. He was nearly hyperventilating when his pre-breakfast snack arrived.

Mary Lou watched Alex wolf down the doughnut.

"Are you that hungry?"

As his head began to clear, he was able to reconstruct the pivotal events of their morning. After the raid on his espousal rights in Father Bassagni's office, they adjourned to a small chapel behind the chancel, a curved alcove of Pipestone granite with tall, thin stained glass windows and frescos of Baroque putti floating on clouds. They kneeled before a dainty altar while Father Bassagni invoked the blessing. Obviously in a hurry, the priest read from a limp-cover missal as rapidly as an auctioneer--what am I offered for the success of this union? Not very much evidently since the ceremony was over in less than five minutes.

Nothing that went on at St. Cecilia's--the mass, the signing of the document, the blessing in the chapel--nothing was more important to Alex than getting something to eat.

The waitress stood over them for their breakfast order. "What'll you have, miss?"

Alex expected Mary Lou to flash her wedding ring to let the waitress know she was a Mrs. "Whole wheat toast with a pat of butter separate, a three-minute soft-boiled egg, a small orange juice, and black coffee."

"How many eggs do you get with the Hasty Tasty Super Breakfast Special?" Alex asked.

"Three."

"Ok, I'll have that."

"How do you like your eggs?"

"One sunny-side, one over easy, one scrambled."

She looked at him, her pencil poised over her order pad.

"Really, Alex," Mary Lou said.

"It doesn't sound any fussier than your order."

The waitress let out an impatient breath. She was busy.

"Ok, scrambled," he said and handed back the menu.

"What comes with the eggs?" Mary Lou asked.

"American fries, sausage patty, two strips of bacon, and three buttermilk pancakes."

"Are you sure that will be enough?"

"The last time I had anything to eat was that candy bar in Mason City."

At the mention of Mason City Mary Lou bit her lower lip as though it was too painful to recall something as recent as only yesterday.

The waitress delivered an insulated pot of steaming coffee and two mugs. Alex poured. "You know what I look forward to?"

Mary Lou shook her head, her autumn auburn curls waving slightly.

"Waking up in the morning and having breakfast together."

"You're never very far from that bed are you?"

"Doesn't breakfast usually follow bed?"

She made a face.

"What's the matter? Haven't I done everything you wanted me to do?"

Mary Lou unfolded her paper napkin, the size of a war map, and laid it across her thighs. "You still don't understand what's bothering me, do you?"

Alex shrugged.

"Do I have to repeat it?"

"My memory is still foggy."

She sighed impatiently. "When Father Bassagni talked about mortal sin, you had the nerve to say, 'Isn't it a little late to be worrying about that?' I was so mortified, I almost got up and walked out."

He almost wished she had. "Didn't we commit a mortal sin when we made love on your mattress?"

"Keep your voice down."

"So what difference does it make?"

"You have a lot to learn about the Catholic religion."

"What I've learned so far has been an education, believe me."

Mary Lou pressed her lips together. "One thing I will not compromise is my religion."

"You compromised me! You should have told me about that paper I had to sign. I don't even get to raise my own children."

"That's not true. The church gives us guidelines on how to do it, that's all."

"Guidelines? Sounds more like 1984 to me."

"We'll be grandparents by 1984."

"1984 is a novel."

She was getting exasperated with him. "What has a book nobody ever heard of got to do with a religion people all over the world believe in?"

"First of all, 1984 is a classic. Second, I am not a believer."

"Do you believe in anything?"

"I'd rather believe in myself than have Big Brother do it for me."

"What Big Brother?"

"A character in 1984 who controls people's thoughts just like your Pope."

She stirred her coffee with the vigor of a cement mixer. "It's a good thing I pray for you. You really need it."

His eyes widened. "You pray for me?"

"Every day."

"Pray for the Ethiopians. They're having a drought."

"So are you...a drought of the spirit."

"With you, prayer is like waving a magic wand...poof and all of your problems disappear. Is it ok to ask what you pray for me about?"

"I pray that God eliminates the bad things from your head, like that book you just mentioned."

Alex felt his pulse quicken. Uncle Gus's warning was beginning to sound like a prophesy. "Mary Lou, you can't pray great literature out of existence."

"What goes on inside that busy brain of yours needs a lot of work.

You need to balance the things you learn at the University with the true meaning of Catholicism. I'll help you with your religious instruction. We'll study the catechism together. She patted his hand. "After that it's up to you."

"What's up to me?"

"When you decide to become a Roman Catholic."

"When?" he asked lamely. "Whatever happened to if?" He shook his head. So it had come to this--a battle for his soul. He thought back to that winter afternoon and their chance meeting at Dayton's. Or was it chance? Uncle Gus had warned him about Catholicism's goal of world domination. Maybe that's the way the church does it--one victim at a time. In Alex's case it was a sexy missionary who trapped him. "Would you mind taking off your jacket to see if this sweater will fit Larry?" That's all it took, the touch of her fingers on his shoulders.

"Someday," Mary Lou said, "you will appreciate the one true church."

If there was anything to appreciate it was the one true breakfast the waitress brought him--a platter loaded with what he needed most right now: carbohydrates. He ate with the abandon of a starving man--too much and too fast. As the food coursed through his body without benefit of digestion he remembered reading somewhere that a condemned man--which is how he now viewed himself, eating his last meal--dies with his pants full of shit. He excused himself and rushed to the bathroom.

When he returned Mary Lou was on her second cup of coffee. She was quite composed; the canary sitting in the catbird seat. "Do you feel better now?"

"Not much."

After breakfast they had time to kill so they walked down to Lake Calhoun and followed the arched portico of the bath house to the beach. A flat-bottomed boat with a gas engine for removing pilings was tied to the partially dismantled dock, a sign of approaching winter. Alex watched ducks and coots bobbing offshore. Well-meaning people fed them. So instead of migrating in the fall, they hang around fat and sassy, drifting in the ever-tightening open water as ice forms on the lake. Sometimes a bird gets caught, frozen in the ice, a victim of bad timing, just like Alex.

"Shouldn't we get going?"

"I guess so."

They walked back to the van and climbed in. He headed east on Lake Street, letting the tram rails steer the van.

"Hold on to the steering wheel," Mary Lou said, "let's not have an accident."

As far as he was concerned, an accident had already happened.

St. Mary's Greek Orthodox Church sat at the corner of Tenth Avenue and East Lake Street--a small, dark-brick edifice with an oblong dome that looked as if giant hands had squeezed the juice out of it. A temple-like pediment protecting the entrance gave the otherwise Byzantine architecture a schizoid quality, as though its designers had wanted to incorporate a bit of Greece's ancient glory with the orthodoxy that prevailed later. The building looked forsaken because it was surrounded by commercial property--immediate neighbors were a sprawling Sears warehouse and retail store and a used car lot with a huge billboard that proclaimed: Bud Nolan Your Lake Street Angel. Extending above the sign was a big cutout of an angel with a neon halo flashing bright yellow. It was as if Bud Nolan had decided to extend the church's purview to include car advertising.

Alex approached the Greek church wishing he was making a delivery to St. Paul instead. Then he would simply drive by, giving the building where he had given up so much of his youth a quick nod, and head for St. Paul, crossing the Mississippi River and getting on Summit Avenue so he could drive past the house where F. Scott Fitzgerald wrote his first novel. In spite of Fitzgerald's tragic life, Alex nevertheless envied this famous Minnesotan who had written, at the tender age of 23—near Alex's own age by the way—a masterful piece of fiction.

"Isn't that the Greek church?" Mary Lou asked, looking over her shoulder at the receding dome.

"What?"

"Did you change your mind?"

Maybe he had and wasn't willing to admit it. "I'll circle the block." He drove all the way to Cedar Avenue.

"Aren't we going a little out of our way?"

"We're early."

He turned left and drove by the Cedar Avenue Cemetery. In his mind every marker had his name on it. He turned left again at 29th Street, a narrow one-way that paralleled a railroad trench, and he even longed for a freight train to rumble by so he could throw himself in front of it. When he reached Tenth Avenue, he turned left a third time--was he going around in circles?--and pulled up to the Sears loading dock.

"Why are we parking way back here?" Mary Lou asked.

"This truck is such a wreck, I don't want anyone to see it."

"You weren't concerned about that when we went to St. Cecilia's."

Alex killed his engine and sat in the driver's seat looking at the parking lot next to the church. His uncle's Packard was nowhere in sight. He was hoping the family was already inside so that he and Mary Lou could sneak in and sit in back unobserved till the service was over.

"What are we waiting for?"

Mary Lou certainly wasn't making things any easier.

He got out and walked around to open the door for her. She clambered down, and lifted one leg and then the other, checking the seams in her nylons over her shoulder. "How do I look?"

"Great," he said, watching for the Packard.

"I wish you'd pay a little attention to me. This is just as hard for me as it is for you."

"I said you look great." Maybe they weren't coming after all.

Mary Lou took Alex's arm and they crossed to the other side. "Am I walking too fast for you?"

At the end of the block, a bright yellow streetcar ground to a halt. Under the carriage Alex saw two pairs of legs step down from the opposite side. The car trundled off, and Alex saw to his dismay that they belonged to Tony Pappathos and his mother. They stood at the far curb, looking up and down the street for a break in the traffic. A flicker of recognition shone in Mary Lou's eyes.

"Who are those people?"

He pretended not to notice. "Where?"

"Crossing the street toward us."

"Greeks."

"The man...he looks familiar. I remember now, he's not wearing an apron. The nice bartender...what's his name?"

"Tony."

"And the woman?"

"His mother."

"Why is she wearing black?"

"She's a widow."

"I'm sorry..."

"Don't be. Her husband died twenty years ago."

"He's staring at us." Mary Lou waved and called out, "Yoo-hoo, Tony!" She dropped her arm from his and clicked her heels faster. By the time Alex caught up, Mary Lou was already shaking Tony's hand.

Tony was in a state of shock. Seeing Alex with Mary Lou at Richard's was one thing but in front of the Greek Church? Beyond the pale.

"Is this your mother, Tony?" Mary Lou said, looking down warmly at her. "I met your son where he works," she said to the little lady. "He is such a gentleman."

Mrs. Pappathos stared impassively.

Alex leaned close to Mary Lou's ear. "Save your breath. She doesn't understand English."

"Well, then," Mary Lou said, her frustration on the verge of boiling over, "talk in Greek and tell her who I am."

Alex stood dumbly, his panic now in full control.

“Ei Katholiki?” Tony’s mother finally found her voice.

Mary Lou understood that much. She froze a smile on her face and adjusted her hair making sure that her wedding ring flashed in the sunlight.

Tony stared at the ring open-mouthed. Finally he managed to blurt out, "Are you and Alex married?"

"Yesterday," Mary Lou said pointedly.

His mother noticed the ring, too, and she crossed herself rapidly three times.

"Do your parents know?" Tony asked Alex.

"We want to surprise them."

"Oh, they'll be surprised, all right." As they walked to the entrance, Tony asked Mary Lou, "Are you going to change religions?"

"If anyone changes religion," she snapped at him, "it won't be me."

Her answer determined Tony's next move: he ran ahead, opened the door for his mother and followed her into the church, letting the door close on the newlyweds.

“Some manners,” Mary Lou said under her breath as Alex caught the door on its return swing and held it open for her. She stepped inside as gingerly as entering a haunted house. Filled with candle smoke, the narthex did have a kind of spooky atmosphere, and the wheeze of a pump organ from the choir loft above sounded eerily like a wailing ghost.

Mary Lou stood transfixed at the scene unfolding before her. Through the gloomy light she looked upon an interior grayed by a half-century of candle soot. In the nave, a clutter of bentwood chairs like the kind used in ice cream parlors was separated by an irregular center aisle; men sitting on the left, women on the right. The psalti, the cantor, wearing a black robe stood behind a reading stand in a corner. The altar screen was a series of panels, each featuring a scowling saint. At the center of the screen was the royal door, the Agias Pilas, opening to the Iero, the holy inner sanctum. The altar was draped in white linen with the sacred letters ΧΘΨΣ embroidered in gold. The Paten and Chalice atop the altar were protected by a brocaded silk cover in anticipation of the Holy Eucharist. Candles were everywhere--floating in bowls of translucent red glass, standing in gold-plated candlesticks, hanging in chandeliers, poked into sand-filled trays.

Mrs. Pappathos had just poked one of those candles into the sand and hurriedly crossed herself in front of an icon of the Virgin Mary. Then she fairly flew down the aisle to escape the evil behind her. She went straight to the icon of St. Peter painted on the altar screen and began praying and crossing herself in front of it. The congregation stirred. Everyone assumed someone had died. Mrs. Pappathos finished her prayers with an audible sigh and took a seat in the front row of the women's section. Tony sat in the men's section across the aisle from her.

Mary Lou had barely adjusted to the surreal scene before her when an awful smell of garlic assailed her nostrils. The odor of skorthalia, the garlic paste Greek men liked to slather on their breakfast toast, exhaled from their lungs and floated up to the choir loft, causing an occasional flat among the sopranos in the front row.

The priest, a stern figure with a full beard, came from behind the Royal Door and faced his congregation. He wore the full regalia of his profession. Long cleric sleeves overlapped his midsection. As he recited the Litourgia, his attention was drawn to the red-headed woman in back holding her nose.

"Let's sit down," Mary Lou whispered to Alex. "He's staring at me."

"We can't sit together."

"What?"

"Didn't you notice? Men are on one side, women on the other."

"Oh my God."

"Old-world custom."

“Why didn’t you tell me?”

“I’ll sit across from you.” He pointed to an empty aisle seat in the women's section under the choir balcony. Mary Lou hurriedly sat down. The woman Mary Lou sat next to gave her a studied up-and-down look, examining the alien ensemble of amber hair, freckles and, in the opinion of the Greek woman, garish makeup. She scraped her chair away from Mary Lou. The sharp sound caused a turn of heads that spread through the women's section like an ill wind.

Father Karfatsis cleared his throat with a pronounced loosening of phlegm to get the women back to the business at hand: Sunday worship. He chanted, "En eirini Kiriou Theothomen," In peace, let us pray to the Lord.

The psalti intoned a Kirie Eleison.

Mary Lou turned and mouthed the words, When are you going to sit down?

Alex was frozen with indecision. Now that he had walked into the sacred bosom of the Greek community with a woman who was not just his wife but his Catholic wife, he was gripped by the enormity of what he had done. In the abstract coming here seemed like a good idea, but in the concrete, with the hard and cold glare of reality, his feet were hardened in it. Before he could force himself to move, the door opened behind him and someone bumped his arm. He turned. It was his cousin Coula and her mother whom he had not seen since Christmas.

"Hi, stranger," Coula whispered.

Her mother, a large, fully proportioned woman, planted an oily kiss on his cheek and then, to demonstrate her displeasure at not seeing him in such a long time, boxed his ears. Alex clenched his eyes from the pain. There was so much ringing, he could barely hear Coula whisper, "Your mom and dad are coming."

"They're not here yet."

"I just told you. They're getting out of your uncle's car. Glad to see you in church. You should come around more often."

Not very likely after today, he thought, his hearing beginning to return. He was ready to sit across from Mary Lou when the door swung open again and Uncle Gus appeared. He held the door for Alex's mother to shuffle through. Right behind was his dad holding his mother's arm to keep her from lurching forward. She was wearing her Sunday best, a black silk suit with tiny white polka dots, and on her head a black straw hat with a veil. When the trio saw Alex standing there as if he had been waiting for them, relief registered on their faces. He was telling the truth after all. His mother went to the icon of Jesus, lit a taper and stuck it in the sand. She stepped back and crossed herself three times, offering her thanks to God for answering her prayers and delivering her son. His father seemed embarrassed, as though he did not expect to see Alex ever again and now had to own up to his lack of faith. Apparently Uncle Gus suffered no such doubts because he was beaming. Alex could read his thoughts: It took all of our effort to get your mother here, but it was worth it because you kept your word. The Poulos family is together again.

Mary Lou, half-turning, watched the reconciliation from her chair. She could not take her eyes off the frail woman with sunken cheeks and stooped shoulders.

Alex saw her eyebrows go up questioningly. He gave her a quick, affirming nod. Yes, this is my mother.

"Follow me," Gus whispered.

"I'll sit in back," Alex said.

Gus took Alex by the arm. The pressure was unmistakable. He was giving the orders. Alex hoped Mary Lou would understand he couldn't sit close to her. Actually, he thought, desperately seeking sense out of chaos, this was probably better than his original plan. By waiting till after the service, when everyone had an injection of religion, introductions could take place in a more forgiving atmosphere. Mary Lou should be able to see the wisdom of that, shouldn't she? His mother's heart couldn't stand another shock right now, anyway. Hell, his couldn't either.

Uncle Gus started down the aisle. When he came abreast of Mary Lou, they exchanged momentary glances. Uncle Gus hesitated for an instant and continued walking. It didn't take a Philadelphia lawyer to figure out that he knew who the redhead was. Alex watched carefully for his parents' reaction. Would they suspect anything? He needn't have worried. His father was too preoccupied holding Alex's mother as she executed her slow stagger-step. And she kept staring at the floor, not only to keep from falling but also to avoid noticing the inevitable stares her shuffle generated.

Alex had to assure Mary Lou he was not abandoning her, that he was only altering strategy, as in battle when generals can't predict the enemy's movements precisely. As he came alongside her she started to move into the aisle assuming she was to join him, but he nudged her back. Alex whispered hurriedly out of the corner of his mouth, "Stay here till after the service."

Mary Lou could not have been more stunned if Alex had twisted a grapefruit into her face the way Cagney did to Mae Clark in Public Enemy. The brief exchange was not lost on those nearby. There was a lot of nervous breathing which only served to raise the level of garlic odor. Several women took out their handkerchiefs and covered their faces. An epidemic of coughing broke out. The choir was also affected. As the smell drifted upward, musical attacks became more ragged. Something was in the air, all right.

Gus picked a row near the front. After helping Theodore seat his wife onto a chair behind Mrs. Pappathos, Gus moved in and motioned Alex to sit between him and his father. Before sitting, Alex glanced back. He wanted to give Mary Lou a positive sign--a smile, a nod, a gesture--something to let her know everything was going to be all right. In the sea of Greek faces staring at him she was easy to single out--a peach in a box of plums--but her face was not peachy, it was fiery red. Her cheeks flamed and her eyes burned. Even from where he sat, Alex felt the heat.

Gus put his lips to Alex's ear. "Have you gone insane?"

"What's the matter?"`

"You brought her *here*? Into the *church*?"

The service proceeded in an atmosphere of impending doom. Everyone seemed aware of the alien presence except Alex's mother who was deep into herself as she always was in church, sitting with her head bent not so much in prayer but because she couldn't straighten her body.

Alex's father sat with arms crossed and eyes straight ahead--for him church was the place where you saw no evil, heard no evil and spoke no evil. The angelic hymn to announce To Megali Eisothos could not relieve the awful pressure on Alex's brain. When Father Karfatsis stepped forward bearing the gifts of consecration, Alex prayed: If there is a sacrifice, let it be me.

Then came the readings of the epistle and the Holy Gospel. Alex rose and sat, rose and sat, like an automaton. He did not have the nerve to look back to see how Mary Lou was faring. The priest consecrated the host and wine while the choir sang Se ehmnou, Se ehmnou men. We praise, we praise You, and the psalti chanted his response.

The communicants came forward to accept the body and blood of Jesus Christ. Alex got into the aisle and waited in line to accept the bread and wine from Father Karfatsis's sweaty hands. On the way back to his seat he glanced at Mary Lou. She was standing in front of her chair--a shroud of ineffable sadness enveloped her body and her joyless eyes were asking, why have you forsaken me?

Father Karfatsis blessed the Prosforo and the choir sang Axion esthie Aleistho. Truly it is proper to call You Blessed. The voices were more spirited now because the hymn marked the end of their labors. All that was left was the Dismissal Prayer and the sermon which had its own prayer: may it not go on forever. The congregation settled into their chairs. The priest emerged from the Iero. As he proceeded to the pulpit, a determined clicking of high heels suddenly hit the polished wood floor like rim shots. The sound echoed from the inverted bowl of the elongated dome and around the nave. The priest stopped dead in his tracks. Everyone's attention was suddenly riveted on the figure marching resolutely down the aisle. People gawked, and an awesome silence fell over the congregation. Mary Lou's patience had finally run out. Deep-down Alex knew it couldn't last. He had abandoned her to shift for herself through an interminably long and unintelligible service while fighting off hostile stares. When he rose to take communion, she no doubt assumed he would rescue her from this hate-filled place but instead he returned to his seat. That was the final straw. Her seething resentment lifted her like a hot air balloon. Now that she was airborne, she had but a single flight plan: land next to her mother-in-law, crash land if she must, but land no matter what. Alex watched with a mixture of horror and admiration as Mary Lou dragged a vacant chair over and sat down next to the other Mrs. Poulos. Alex's knees began to shake as if he were expecting a tornado. The atmosphere was certainly ripe for it. But his mother was deep in prayer--her head lowered, her eyes closed, her shoulders moving in a rhythmic oscillation--and she did not sense the sudden drop in barometric pressure. Now the entire congregation could look straight at Mary Lou without surreptitiously turning their heads. All they had to do was crane their necks. She was getting radiated from all sides by those whose Sunday worship she had so flagrantly despoiled.

Whispers fell from the choir as the singers finally were able to see the curiosity that had been hiding under their loft. Mrs. Pappathos grumbled out loud in Greek. Father Karfatsis harrumphed several times. Mary Lou was now close enough to smell not only his garlic breath but also his nervous sweat. There was a look of fierce determination on her face. She wasn't going to be locked out of the Poulos family any longer. Alex held his breath as his mother finally opened her eyes. Slowly she became aware of a foreign presence next to her. Confusion marked her features. She pushed her glasses up on her nose and swept her gaze from Mary Lou's legs to her face.

"Pi eisai? Den sou xsero." Who are you? I don't know you. Even though her words were whispered, they echoed around the nave like a death knell.

The congregation sat spellbound. Only Uncle Gus had the gift of movement. He rose to his feet, his imposing girth commanding the space around him. Men moved their chairs to let him pass. He crossed the aisle and stood over Mary Lou. She looked up at him, determination turning to apprehension. Who is this fat man and what does he want with me? her eyes were asking.

Gus leaned over, a difficult feat for a man so round, and whispered something in Mary Lou's ear. Recognition spread across her features.

"I don't care who you are," she said defiantly. "You can't make me!"

Alex had never heard anyone talk to his uncle like this before. His mother hadn't either. Her eyes widened as she scrutinized this strange woman even further.

As though she were fighting off a rapist, Mary Lou crossed her legs and squeezed her thighs together. When Alex's mother saw that, awareness cleared her face like a lifting fog. No self-respecting Greek woman would ever cross her legs in church.

“Ei Katholiki!” she shrieked. The ear-splitting cry nearly lifted the dome off the church.

Mary Lou cringed in horror--trapped on one side by a deranged woman and on the other by a hovering pig.

"Alex!" she called out. "Help me!" Her words hit the church like a mortar shell. Alex had the distinct impression that several people actually ducked.

The time had come for him to make a heroic move. He struggled out of his chair as if overcoming a magnetic field. He looked down at his father. The top of his head, under his thinning gray hair, was beet red. Sorry, Pop, Alex thought, this isn't the way I planned to make introductions.

He crossed the aisle and stood next to Mary Lou, took a deep breath, the deepest breath of his life, and said, "I'd like you to meet my wife, Mary Lou Poulos." Alex fully expecting that the oxymoron of an American name next to a Greek name would cause gasps of horror, even outcries of rage, but instead there was only stunned silence--the only sound coming from Mrs. Pappathos' handkerchief as she flapped it across her cheeks.

Alex's father finally managed to rise from his chair and come over to stand by his wife--his strong, peasant shoulders drooping from the burden of his son's total and abject humiliation. The entire congregation--his friends, his enemies, the priest, even God Himself--was witness to his utter failure as a father.

Gus pressed at his stomach fighting off, no doubt, a gastro-intestinal attack. "We will talk about this outside." He gripped Mary Lou's upper arm and tried to pull her to her feet.

"Don't touch me!" Mary Lou cried out, wrenching herself from his grasp.

Father Karfatsis stepped forward.

"Please!" he called out. "This is a house of worship."

"Really?" Mary Lou snapped. "I wasn't so sure."

This time there really was a gasp, and not just one. The entire congregation began to growl like a mob, ready to rise up and assist Gus in throwing out this Jezebel Alex had brought into their midst. Wife, indeed! Alex's mother--her body shaking as if the earth itself were splitting under her feet--suddenly lunged at Mary Lou, her gnarled fingers spread like claws and her nails groping at Mary Lou's face.

Alex saw what happened next through the slow-motion frames of a terrified witness, frozen in his tracks, unable to alter the course of human events. As he watched, his mother's nails drew a perfect line of carmine red across Mary Lou's left cheek. Mary Lou jumped back and a shrill yowl of pain and astonishment came from her throat. She touched the scratch and stared in horror at the blood on her fingertips.

Pandemonium ensued. There was a scramble as parishioners jumped up, their chairs sliding and banging into each other. Father Karfatsis was yelling at everyone to sit down. Arms reached out seemingly from everywhere to ease the elder Mrs. Poulos back into her chair.

"Se kataromai!" Alex's mother shouted. Her face glowed in triumph like someone who, having spent her life drinking bitter gaul, had finally reached the moment she had craved to try just once: the sweet taste of victory.

"What did she say?" Mary Lou cried plaintively at Alex.

Before he could reply, nor did he wish to, his mother shouted, "You don't know what I say because you not Greek! So I tell you to your face that I curse you for robbing my son, I curse your life and every life you try to make!"

Everyone stood fast like figures in a wax museum. Even Father Karfatsis was immobilized by the hateful words that spilled forth in this holiest of places.

Tears poured down Mary Lou's cheeks, mingling mascara with her blood. "Alex," she begged, "get me out of here."

Before he could react, his mother reached out and grabbed him by the sleeve. He tried to shake himself free but her fingers had the strength of talons. As she clutched him, her shaking set his own arm in motion and it began to move in synchrony with hers. It was a frightening spectacle.

The man Mary Lou had fallen in love with, the man she married, the man she thought would comfort and protect her for the rest of her life, was shaking just like his mother.

"For god's sake, Alex!" Mary Lou cried. "Can't you see what she's doing to you?"

As if on cue, blood began dripping from his mother's nostrils.

"Call a doctor!" someone shouted. It was Tony Pappathos. He finally found something to say.

"Relax, Tony, it's only a nosebleed." Alex pulled out his handkerchief and dropped to his knees. He applied pressure to her nose as Alex's father cradled her head in his hands.

Mary Lou stared in disbelief at the gruesome tableau of the Poulos family coming together in their time of crisis.

"Alex," she begged one last time, "are you coming with me?"

"Can't you see she's bleeding?"

Mary Lou touched the scratches on her cheeks. "What about me? Isn't this blood, too?"

She was surrounded by madness. It leered down from the scowling apostles on the walls. It flickered in the light of the smoking candles. It glared from the eyes of the angry Greeks. It dribbled from the nose of Alex's mother and bubbled gas inside Gus's stomach. It pushed down on the shoulders of Alex's father. It rested in the crumbs on the priest's beard. Most of all it gripped Alex, making him incapable of coming to her rescue, and strangling forever whatever love she had left for him.

"All right!" Mary Lou shouted at his mother. "If you want him that bad, you can have him!" She pulled off her wedding ring and held it between her thumb and forefinger, looking at it one last time, at what might have been. Then she hurled it with all her might. It pinged along the floor like a stone skipping across water. It caromed off Father Karfatsis's shoe, rolled through the Royal Gate into the sacristy, and disappeared under the drapery of the altar table.

Mary Lou spun on her heel and stormed out of the church, slamming the door behind her.

THE BROTHER

Poulos walked forlornly in the dark. A navy bus came along but he didn't run for it. He'd rather not sit next to a snoring sailor with vomit on his jumper and his head bouncing against the window pane. He was so deep in thought he didn't notice an officer strolling ahead of him, and passed him on the left.

"Sailor!"

Poulos stopped, jolted back to the moment, and faced the officer, a short, tightly put-together career man. "Yessir?"

"Don't you fucking-well-know you're supposed to ask an officer 'by your leave' when you walk past him?"

Poulos wanted to tell the little fart too bad he wasn't taller and then maybe he'd see him, but common sense prevailed and he brought his right hand to his temple as smartly as he knew how. "By your leave, sir!"

He found saluting difficult because second nature made him want to use his left hand. He stopped under a street light to look at it. With shadows playing off the ridges, the bleached skin of his palm looked like a miniature moonscape. The burn had stunted the growth of his fingers. The middle finger was half an inch shorter than the one on his right hand. He loved football, and in tenth grade wanted to try out for junior varsity. He had a good arm but he couldn't grip the laces. Instead of spiraling, the ball wobbled as if it were leaking air. It didn't make any difference, though, because his mother nixed the idea of playing football, worried that he might get hurt. She always worried that he might get hurt.

Now that Jenny had opened the floodgates of memory, other instances of growing up drifted through his mind like floating debris. His private collection of events that preserved the past was filled with melancholy. Nothing he could conjure up was light or happy. Not only that, he recalled everything as though he were watching a black and white movie. The grass and sky and flowers and dandelions and butterflies of his childhood were colorless. He grew up painfully shy, terrified of speaking to anyone.

The one time he screwed up nerve to communicate turned to disaster. A regular customer at the Crystal Cafe, a kind and unthreatening sales woman, was having her usual lunch when Poulos whispered something profound, like hello, into her ear. She turned suddenly, surprised by his presence, and he knocked her glasses into the mashed potatoes on her plate. He was so mortified he ran through the kitchen and out the back door where his father found him hidden in the rear seat of the old Nash parked at the curb.

Alex walked on regretting that his date with Jenny had ended badly. If only she hadn't brought up that psychiatrist, Steiner. If she hadn't done that everything would have been all right.

"Shit!" he said, "Everything turns to shit."

When he got to the main gate, he flashed his liberty pass and took a gin rickshaw to the station, telling the driver to wait while he went inside and fetched his clothes. By the time he got back to the Sprague it was after midnight. Strings of lights hung from the ship's superstructure, illuminating her like a giant Christmas display. Out of water, she was no longer the deadly skimmer of the seas. She was as exposed and vulnerable as a beached whale. He crossed the gangway. The quarterdeck was quiet. Ltjg. Armstrong was OOD. His blond hair and eyebrows blended perfectly with his officer khaki.

"You get laid?" he asked routinely.

"I was with a Greek girl tonight," Poulos said, as if that explained everything.

He went below to his rack. The snoring was loud and explosive. A night light illuminated the tight quarters gloomily. It didn't help his mood. He lowered his rack and began to undress.

"Poulos? That you?" a voice in the semi-dark called out.

"Yeah."

"Com-meer." He followed the sound of the voice. It belonged to the Sprague's radioman, Ned Skycloud, a Nez Perce Indian from Coeur d'Alene. He was pointing to a snoring sailor in a lower bulkhead rack. "Look at Pugh."

Poulos stared down at the lanky figure lying on his side with his mouth open. Howard B. Pugh was the most decorated sailor on the ship--his body was covered with tattoos.

"What about him?"

"Look at his prong."

Pugh's penis had slipped through the slit in his shorts.

Poulos bent over. Pugh stirred and crotch odor drifted up. Poulos stepped back. "I don't see anything."

"He got the head of his dick tattooed."

Curious now, Poulos peered more closely. Sure enough, Pugh's penis was black and blue as though it had been bruised. A scabby outline covered the tip.

"What is it?"

"A butterfly."

"A butterfly?"

"Wings and all."

"Looks like a caterpillar to me," Poulos said. "It probably turns into a butterfly when he gets a hard-on."

They laughed.

"What?" Pugh slurred.

"Nothing, Howie," Skycloud said. "Just admiring your tattoo."

Pugh smiled proudly and went back to sleep.

Poulos returned to his rack. He stripped down to his shorts, slipped on his clogs, and took his towel and ditty bag to the forward showers. He was alone. He lingered under the water, wishing it would clean away his troubles, his mind haggard from the questions Jenny raised about his mother. He had traveled nearly halfway around the world to get away from her but she stuck to him like a piece of flypaper. He got out of the shower, dried off and returned to his compartment. He draped his damp towel over the pipe frame to dry out, and climbed in. He tossed about; the dead air in the compartment pressing on him like an extra blanket. He finally dozed off and began dreaming. Jenny had awakened more than thoughts of his mother, she had aroused his dormant sexual juices but it was Mary Lou he dreamed about. She was kneeling over him, her legs astride his body, her breasts hanging free. She wet her lips with the tip of her tongue. He came alive in an instant. She touched her moistened lips to his penis. He groaned. She opened her mouth and wriggled her tongue. He squirmed. Then she slid him inside her mouth, burying it as deeply as she could and began sucking. He moaned. Suddenly he started ejaculating and woke up in a state of confusion as he squirted on his mattress. He grabbed his towel and pressed it against himself until the spasms subsided.

A sleepy voice said, "Who's jerking off?"

The base courier delivered mail around ten-thirty, carrying his leather pouch like a postman. He parked his jeep on the pier with the motor idling. Ernie took the mail and began sorting it: personal mail by division; official mail stayed in the office for processing. Poulos was in a desultory frame of mind. It had been three days since his date with Jenny and he thought about her all the time. Like a stuck record, he kept playing over and over in his mind the things she had said. What disturbed him more were the things she didn't say. He felt as if he had started reading a mystery and when he got to the final chapter the last two pages were missing. The more he brooded, the more he developed a case of anxiety. He needed Jenny to finish the story for him, tell him who did it.

Since there was not a lot to do in the office he took his moodiness to the chart house. Witter got so fed up that he told Poulos to "go take a fucking happy pill or something."

But Jenny wasn't his only problem. He had also worked himself into a lather over Clayton. Every time he heard heavy steps on the gangway, he peeked anxiously out the office porthole, expecting to see Clayton with his seabag on his shoulder. But it would turn out to be a deck hand carrying stores or the courier with his mail pouch. Gentle Ernie, as patient a soul as ever lived, was also getting tired of Poulos's jumpiness. "Clayton will turn up when he turns up," he said, as profound a statement as Ernie ever made.

Ernie held up an envelope from the stack he was sorting. "This is for you."

"Me?" Poulos said, surprised.

"Looks official. Who do you know in high places?"

"Nobody."

"Well, it's addressed to you."

A. Poulos, SN
USS Robert B. Sprague DD884
Section X1 Drydock 4
Yokosuka Naval Base, Japan

There was an imprimatur in the upper right corner: WESPACYKSA 762/52. Interbase delivery, no postage required. In the left hand corner was the navy seal and the acronym NAVOP. Above the return address were handwritten initials in lower case: jb. It was a moment before he realized what jb stood for. He tore at the envelope like a madman.

"You want the letter opener?" Ernie asked.

"This is fine." He removed a sheet of navy stationery. He was so excited his fingers shook as he read:

Dear Alex:

i've been thinking about you a lot, wondering how you are. When my orders came yesterday i realized it was my last chance to get in touch, so i decided to send this. i want to apologize for upsetting you.

You really are a nice guy and i hope you meet an equally nice girl someday. Greek, of course.

jenny

P.S. You may wonder why i don't capitalize the personal pronoun.

i refuse to be a party to ego-driven convention.

Poulos chuckled.

"Good news?" Ernie asked.

"The best."

He ran up the main deck, and climbed the ladder four rungs at a time. He was nearly out of breath when he turned the corner and burst into the chart house. Browning was updating sounding markings on a map spread out on the table.

"Look what I got today!"

"Anybody that happy has his discharge in his hand."

"Very funny. I got a note from Jenny."

"That nurse you met?"

"Here, look for yourself."

Browning held the letter to his nose and sniffed. "You are right...essence of ether."

"Read it."

Browning perused it and handed it back. "I had a feeling that dark-haired wench was warming up to you. I saw her read your palm. Are you going to have a long life?"

"That's what I'd like to know. Help me place a call to her will you?"

"The Exec passed the word. No more personals from the quarterdeck. Only official traffic."

"I have to talk to her."

"Just answer her fucking letter."

"She won't get it in time. Her tour is almost over."

Browning drummed the table with his pencil. "Maybe Skycloud can help, but it will cost you."

"Whatever it takes."

They found Ned sitting in the radio shack doing the crossword puzzle from Stars and Stripes. His smooth, adobe-colored forehead was furrowed.

"What's a four-letter word for Love God?" he asked, polishing the tip of his pencil with his tongue.

"Fucker," Browning said.

"That's six letters. And it starts with E."

"Eros," Poulos said.

Skycloud filled it in.

Poulos promised the Indian a week's pay and a pledge to deep-six any mail addressed to him from a collection agency. Ned faked an emergency call and patched his equipment through to the base hospital. It took several hookups to reach Jenny.

Skycloud handed Poulos his microphone.

"This is Jenny Betheras," came a harried voice out of the receiver.

He was so excited he blurted, "I just got your letter."`

"Who is this?"`

"Alex Poulos.

There was hesitation as though she were collecting her thoughts.

"How did you reach me? You must have important friends."

He smiled at Browning and Skycloud. "I do."

"I'm on duty. I have to go."

"I'll save time by talking in lower case."

She laughed, easing the difficult moment.

"I want to see you again."

"I doubt it. I'm running out of time."

He held the mike so tightly his palm began to sweat. "I have to talk to you, even if it's for a few minutes."

"I don't think it's a good idea."

"Then why did you write?"

"You read my note, to apologize."

"I'm the one who should apologize."

"I'm down to hours, Alex. The nurses are throwing a party for me tonight and I leave day after tomorrow at six in the morning."

"A few minutes, that's all I ask. Pick an hour and I'll be there. Promise."

She thought about it. "Can you come over tomorrow night?"

"What time?"

"Seven o'clock. Go to the lounge and I'll meet you there."

"Great!" He jumped up.

"Watch it!" Skycloud shouted. "You'll tear out my cable."

Poulos and Browning returned to the chart house. They found Witter drinking coffee. The three sailors joked and shot the shit--about Jenny, about the nurses Witter and Browning met, about Scotty and Ensign Sanders. Six bells sounded, more than an hour since Poulos had left the Ship's Office.

"I'd better get back," he said. "Ernie will wonder what happened."

He was rereading Jenny's letter as he sauntered down the main deck, in no hurry now.

"Hey, Poulos." Ensign Kuder was leaning against the OOD's desk. He rested his hand on the Colt .45 protruding from his hip.

Poulos folded Jenny's letter into his shirt pocket. "What?"

"Clayton is back."

"He's what?"

"Back. I just checked him in."

Poulos looked into the midship's passageway and felt the blood drain from his face. There was Clayton's seabag leaning against the bulkhead by the office door, his name stenciled on the gray canvas. He suppressed an urge to return to the sanctuary of the chart house but he thought about seeing Jenny in a little more than 24 hours, and felt anxiety subside. Besides, Clayton was only an irritant now, nothing more than a gnat buzzing in his ear. Poulos was even able to turn a set mouth into a smile as he stepped over the sill to welcome Clayton back.

Clayton was wearing a smile of his own--a curious grin as if he were the only one getting the joke. His light, blue-gray eyes didn't waver as they used to when Poulos looked into them. They were devoid of expression--the eyes of a stranger.

His head had been shaved, and his hair, growing back, was still in the fuzzy stage. He had gained weight--a little thicker in the neck, a little broader on the shoulders, a little rounder at the waist. He was wearing his dark blues but there was something not quite right about them. Then Poulos saw what it was. Clayton's chevrons and rating badge were missing from his shoulder.

"Surprised to see me?"

"I knew you were coming back." Poulos's voice was unexpectedly gargly. He cleared his throat.

"Who told you?"

"I went to the hospital but you moved."

"They put me on a transit ship until they thought I was ready to go back to active duty. "

"You missed the action in Munch-on."

"They told me about it at the hospital. Tore up the ship pretty good."

"At least we got rid of that asshole Commodore."

"I liked him."

Poulos knew Clayton would say that.

Clayton pointed to faint needle marks on his sleeve. "I got busted."

"So I see."

"You're in charge now." His voice was flat, unexpressive, on the verge of boredom. "You're ranking yeoman now that I'm busted."

"I'm only a seaman."

"I'm nothing."

"Talk to Radinger about who's in charge. It won't be me."

"They gave me shock treatments," Clayton said without transition.

"That couldn't have been much fun."

"I got an anesthetic, so I don't know if it was fun or not." He dragged his seabag over and unlaced the cord. He withdrew a manila envelope and handed it to Poulos.

"What do you want me to do with this?"

"Check me in. Form 17/A, Record of Transfer Complete. Make two carbons." He hoisted his bag onto his shoulder and took the main passageway aft.

Kuder came over. "What do you think?"

"It's not Clayton anymore. It's somebody else."

Radinger showed up after chow. "Clayton is back," he announced as if it was news.

"I saw him."

"He's busted, so you're in charge now." It was obviously distasteful for Radinger to say that.

Poulos had all morning to come up with a solution. "Lieutenant, why don't you put Ernie in charge of the Ship's Office?"

"Klein?"

"Sure."

"So you can fuck off all the time?"

"That is not my intent, Lieutenant."

"Bullshit."

"You could transfer me to the Engineering Division." Poulos would be happy to work down in the heat to avoid Clayton.

The lieutenant slid his hat back on his head. "What the fuck do you know about boilers?"

"Nothing."

"What the fuck do you know about pressure gauges? Engine revolutions?"

"Nothing."

"Well, then, Poulos, what the fuck?"`

Poulos ran into Gildenhall outside the wardroom. The noise of welding torches nearly drowned out their voices.

"Clayton doesn't care about anything."

"Shock treatments will do that. So how was your Saturday night?"

"Fine. How was yours?"

"Lonely, but the food was good. How is Scott?"

"He's getting out. Twenty-five per cent disability. Permanent limp."

"Too bad. We lost a good man." Gildenhall nudged Poulos with his elbow. "Did you meet any nurses?"

"Couldn't help it. They were all over the place."

Gildenhall smiled. "I have something for you. Wait here."

Poulos leaned against the railing and waited for Gildenhall. He returned with a hardcover book. "A friend back in the states sent this to me. I just finished reading it."

Poulos looked at the dust jacket: The Catcher in the Rye by JD Salinger.

"What's it about?"

"Read it and we'll talk." He put his hand on Poulos's arm. "Don't tell anyone I lent it to you."

Poulos went to the Ship's Office and sat in the far chair, tilting it against the file cabinets. He opened the book to the title page. There was an inscription in flowery handwriting: To Bill from Carl. I know you'll love this book. The word love was underscored twice. Poulos started reading.

Later that afternoon, just before sweep down, Clayton came in and looked over Poulos's shoulder. "What's the book about?"

"A kid trying to get his screwed-up life together."

"Like me."

"Not exactly." Poulos returned to his reading.

"Does he get his life together?"

"Who?"

"The person in the book."

"I'm not finished yet." Poulos wished Clayton would leave him alone.

"What do you want me to do?"

"Do? Whatever you want. Why ask me?"

"You're lead yeoman."

"Shit." Poulos closed the book. He put his chair back on all fours and pushed the wire in-basket in Clayton's direction. "Help yourself."

Clayton sat quietly.

Poulos shook the basket. "Type up your Record of Transfer. Get tomorrow's log ready. Change the ribbon in the typewriter. Take your pick."

"You pick for me."

"Is this the way it's going to be from now on? Clayton brush your teeth, Clayton take a shit?"

"Why don't you like me?"

"What?"

"I asked you why don't you like me?"

"I think I'll get some air." Poulos stood and squeezed himself between Clayton's chair and the file cabinets. He stared down at the shaved head and wondered what it felt like to be jolted by enough electricity to fry your brains. There ought to be burn marks somewhere. Clayton felt Poulos's gaze. He jerked his chair forward to let Poulos pass.

Station muster was at 0750 and the Third Division marshaled on the port quarterdeck. The rising sun shone through the tall cranes and cast shadows across the deck that resembled giant praying mantises. Poulos lined up in back so he could lean against the bulkhead and finish The Catcher in the Rye. He couldn't put it down. He saw himself reflected in Holden Caulfield, the troubled teenager on a quest for life's meaning. And he loved the way Salinger wrote. There was such a strong sense of immediacy and verisimilitude. The characters came to life before his very eyes.

Ltjg Radinger, standing in front of the men with his back to the sun, was calling the roll, checking off names on his clipboard. The crew had grown accustomed to shipyard noise but Radinger still had to yell loudly.

"Poulos!"

Poulos was buried in his book. Heads turned. He looked up to see what the fuss was about and realized it was about him. "Yo!" he called back.

"Will you put that shitkicker away?"

"Sir," Poulos shouted over the heads of the men lined up for muster. "This is not a shitkicker, this a great novel."

Radinger approached him after the Division was dismissed. "I like my men to read serious novels to keep their minds stimulated. Let me see it." He held out his hand.

Poulos shielded the book with his body, remembering what Gildenhall had told him.

Radinger's birthmark reddened. "Show me that fucking book or do I have to rip it out of your hands and throw it over the side?"

"Into the dry dock?" Poulos asked.

"No, I'm going to cross the gangway, walk down the pier, and toss it into the fucking bay."

"It isn't mine. It belongs to somebody else."

Radinger smiled menacingly. "Who, the Secretary of the Navy?"

"Not quite that high, sir."

"In that case, I'm sure the owner won't mind."

"I'm sure he will sir."

Radinger's anger began to spill over. "I'm giving you an order, Poulos. Let me see that fucking book or do I put you on report for insubordination? You won't get off the ship for a week."

Poulos thought of his date with Jenny. With great reluctance he handed the book to Radinger who looked at the dust jacket. "The Catcher in the Rye," he said with bemusement. "Is this what all the fuss is about?"

"What did you expect, Lieutenant?"

"A porn book. Something to get your jollies off on." He began leafing through the pages. "Any dirty pictures?"

Radinger was about to hand it back when Poulos, who now felt obliged to defend Salinger's art, said, "It's about a troubled teenager."

"Troubled teenager, eh?" Radinger said with renewed interest. "What happens to him?"

Poulos, too eager to please, decided to tell Radinger about the prurient parts that he thought would titillate him. "A pimp sets him up with a prostitute."

"Really?" Radinger said.

"His English teacher makes homosexual advances."

"Well, maybe I should read it, too."

Poulos realized his mistake. "It's really too juvenile for you, sir."

"Wait a minute," Radinger said, "what is this?" He had the book open to the title page. "To Bill from Carl,'" he read, "I know you'll love this book. Who is Bill?"

Poulos feigned ignorance with a shrug.

"You don't know who Bill is and you're reading his book?"

Poulos spoke Gildenhall's name as softly as possible.

"What?"

"Lt. Gildenhall," he repeated more loudly.

Radinger's eyes opened wide. "An officer, a senior officer at that, lent a book to an enlisted man?" He displayed a got-you-by-the-balls leer. He closed the book and held it at his side with his clipboard. "Carry on, sailor."

Poulos hesitated. "But the book."

"I'll return it."

"You, sir?"

"Don't you think I'm perfectly capable of returning a book, especially to another officer?"

If only the book had been Midway, the Battle That Turned the War Around; or Bull Halsey, Biography of a Naval Hero; or Pearl Harbor, the Ultimate Villainy--but no, it had to be a book about a 16-year-old kid with all of his pimples erupting.

Radinger waddled up the main deck to the wardroom, on his way, no doubt, to grab Gildenhall by the short hairs. Poulos had betrayed the only officer he respected. He returned to the Ship's Office filled with despair.

Clayton was sitting at the far typewriter doing clean logs. He looked up when Poulos dropped disconsolately into the other chair.

"What's the matter?"

"Radinger took my book from me."

"Now that you don't have anything to read you can help me get some work done."

Poulos angrily yanked open the file drawer so far it jumped off its track. He cursed and struggled to get the rollers back in position. The drawer was heavy and hard to manage.

"You have to line it up."

"I know that." Poulos could feel perspiration breaking out on his forehead.

"I can see from here that it's crooked."

"It has to be crooked because you lift it first before you can set it down again." Poulos puffed from exertion.

"Let me help." Clayton got off his chair and wiggled the drawer.

"Leave it alone, will you?" He pushed Clayton's hand out of the way.

Clayton acted as if he didn't hear. He went back to wiggling the drawer.

This time Poulos struck the back of Clayton's hand. It was an unexpectedly sharp blow. Clayton shrank away and rubbed his hand. Poulos grunted and cursed and finally got the rollers positioned. He slammed the file door shut. He heard sniffling. He looked at Clayton, who was wiping his cheeks with his shirtsleeve.

Poulos felt contrition for the benighted sailor. "I guess I hit you kind of hard."

Clayton rose from his chair and tried to get past Poulos, not waiting for him to move out of the way. He lost his balance and fell over, pinning Poulos to his chair. He tried to lift himself, using Poulos for a brace, and pushed Poulos's head down to his knees. Poulos was trapped, unable to free himself.

Meanwhile Marcos, the Filipino who operated the laundry across the passageway from the Ship's Office, looked over and shouted, "They're fighting again!"

When the OOD came around the corner, Marcos pointed at the two intertangled bodies.

The OOD threw up his hands. "Shit!"

Sailors hearing the commotion gathered round. Odds were quickly shouted back and forth but before any bets could be laid down, Radinger came charging down the deck. "Clear the passageway!" he shouted as he pushed his way through the knot of sailors and into the office. He helped

Clayton up.

"I think my spine is fractured," Poulos said, favoring his back as he rose to his feet.

Radinger placed a fatherly hand on Clayton's shoulder and gently led the teary-eyed sailor out of the office. With tender voice he said, "Leave us alone for a while, will you Clayton?"

He closed the door, then leaned over the desk and lugged the porthole shut. They were closed off from the rest of the ship. Other than Radinger's heavy breathing the only sound came from the fan.

"You got away with it last time, you asshole, but you won't now."

"Got away with what, Lieutenant?"

"Fighting."

"It's not what you think."

"How do you know what I'm thinking?"

"Your birthmark is turning red."

Radinger glared. "You got a real death wish, haven't you?"

"If you'll just let me explain."

"Shut up! I'm doing the talking now, understand?" He lifted a thick thigh onto the desk. His crease disappeared. "It took a while but I'm a patient man," he said, swinging his leg back and forth. The only thing lacking was a riding crop. "I never did cotton to reservists and you are the letter Able why. You came aboard without ever going to Boot Camp, so you never had your civilian shit knocked out of you. If it was up to me, I would have cut the high-line while they were transferring you off the Chemung. You don't belong on a combat ship. You don't belong at sea. You don't belong in the Navy. You lack self-discipline, and you are the most insubordinate fucker I've seen in my entire career."

Poulos opened his mouth to speak.

"Keep your trap shut! This isn't your pal Bill Gildenhall calling the shots now." Radinger grinned as if remembering a particularly raunchy joke. "I wish you could have seen the look on his face when I gave his book back to him. Now I know why he let you off the hook after you dumped that dust bag on Clayton. He was protecting his sweetheart. Well, you can kiss that relationship goodby, if you know what I mean."

Radinger rubbed his hands sadistically. "And now you are mine, Poulos. You are my personal crusade. I am going to turn you into a navy man or die trying. From this moment on until I say otherwise you are a Prisoner at Large, confined to the main and below decks only. The bridge and the chart house where you like to hang out with your friends are off limits. You violate your rules of confinement, and you won't go ashore until we're out of dry dock."

"That's a month from now!" Poulos blurted.

"Didn't I tell you to shut up? Make that San Diego."

Poulos took a sheet of paper and anxiously wrote, Let me talk. Then wisely added, Sir.

Radinger smiled his catbird smile. "All right, what is it?"

"Let me go ashore tonight."

"What's out there, a piece of ass?"

"I have to see someone. Then I promise I'll do whatever you tell me to."

"You don't make promises, Poulos, you follow orders."

"Give me a break, Lieutenant, please."

"Why should I give you a break?"

"I have a date tonight. She's leaving for the states in the morning. I won't see her again."

Radinger slid his butt off the desk and began filling out a violations report on top of the filing cabinet. "You want to screw her one more time, is that it? Well, pretty boy, if it's a screwing you want, you're getting one right now."

Rauenzahn and Armstrong were playing cribbage on the green-felt table in the wardroom. A metal spill-band ran around the edge to prevent anything from sliding off in rough seas and messing up pristine officer khakis. Behind the table a built-in cherry wood credenza held a silver service. Gildenhall was by it pouring himself a cup of coffee as Poulos watched him through the window on the port side. As if feeling Poulos's stare, he turned. Consternation spread over his face when he saw him. He put the cup down and came out on the deck.

"I want to apologize," Poulos said.

"Follow me. It's too open out here."

Poulos trailed Gildenhall forward, through the sea break to the forecastle, and opened the hatch to the ammunition storage room for mount fifty-two. "No one will bother us here."

They stepped into the tight space. Five-inch shells sat on racks above sealed lockers that had DANGER EXPLOSIVES stenciled on them.

"Radinger had a smirk as big as a Mack Truck grille when he handed over the book. Now he suspects something prurient is going on between us. I told you to be careful."

"I really fucked up."

"I'll say you did. He couldn't wait to tell me he put you on report."

Poulos nodded. "I'm a PAL till we reach San Diego. The irony is that Clayton and I weren't even fighting."

"Does it matter?"

"Not any longer. I have a date with a nurse. I have to see her. She's going back to the states in less than 24 hours. Since Radinger won't let me go on liberty the only thing left for me to do is to jump ship."

"What are you talking about? Jumping ship in wartime is desertion."

"I'm going to the hospital, not off the base. I'll sneak out after muster and be back before anyone knows I'm missing."

"You can't get off the ship without someone seeing."

"I'll use the Prisoners' Gangway."

"The what?" Gildenhall asked.

"You don't know about it?" Poulos could not believe the crew was able to keep this a secret from the officers. "The opening in the hull, it's a perfect way to sneak in and out."

Gildenhall gave a grudging smile. "You have it all organized, haven't you? But if Radinger catches you you'll get brig time. Six months at least plus a dishonorable. Why are you taking such a huge risk? She has to be really special."

Poulos ran his fingers along the rifling of a shell that made it spin as it hurled from the gun barrel. "I can't explain it to you. Hell, I can't even explain it to myself. Things she said. I have to see her."

Gildenhall interrupted. "I hope you know what you're doing. Remember, there is absolutely nothing I can do for you if you get caught."

The afternoon crawled like a snail on concrete. Poulos got in the early chow line. He sat in a corner of the mess room with a divided metal tray of green beans, fried steak, hash browns, and cherry cobbler. He left the cobbler; it had the consistency of rubber. He scraped his leftovers into a large galvanized-iron pail and handed the tray to a deckhand on skullery detail. The scullery was where Poulos felt most like throwing up. He ran up the ladder to escape the steamy, stinking environment. He returned to the Ship's Office to wait for the 1815 PAL muster.

Clayton came in, some cobbler crumbs sticking to his mouth. "Lt. Radinger put you on report," he said as though reporting the news of the day.

Poulos stewed without answering.

"One thing I learned at the hospital is not to take things so hard."

"Radinger won't let me off the ship. How am I supposed to take that?"

"You should talk to Dr. Steiner. He would tell you how to take it."

Poulos suddenly went taut. "Steiner?"

"He's the top navy psychiatrist in WESPAC," Clayton said proudly. "He's the one who treated me."

Poulos shuddered. That was the doctor Jenny told him to see.

Clayton was watching him. "You look kind of pale."

"I'm all right," Poulos said, but he wasn't. He had to see Jenny more than ever now in order to have her explain this hideous perversion, the doctor she told him to see was Clayton's doctor as well.

"Move your chair."

"Where are you going?"

"I have a date with a nurse."

"You're restricted. You can't go on liberty."

"I'll go anyway," he said recklessly. He was giving away too much information but he couldn't help himself.

"You'll be AWOL. I thought you were smarter than that."

"Smart enough."

"I can go on liberty and you can't, so who is smarter? You or me?"

It was a bitterly distasteful paradox.

Since he was not leaving the Base he could wear his dungarees and his shipboard white hat frayed at the edges. He slipped a copy of Clayton's orders inside the NAVOP yellow envelope that Jenny's letter came in and slid it in his waist band. If stopped he would say he was delivering Clayton's orders to the base hospital because he missed the courier pick-up--a deliciously clever twist, using Clayton for an alibi.

As he walked down the fore and aft passageway to the engine room hatch, confusing images stirred in his head--images of the house he lived in as a child, the kitchen with the shiny yellow walls, the narrow table with two chairs tucked under it, dark-stained drawers and cupboards, the bin for storing flour, the old-fashioned stove. A metal logo stamped on the oven door said Peerless. The mental image filled him with terror.

He waited till the passageway was clear, then climbed down the vertical ladder to the catwalk below. He found himself in a subterranean world of turbines, dials, wheel valves, asbestos-wrapped pipes and boilers. It was quiet--no throbbing engines, no hissing steam, no oppressive heat. Strings of incandescent bulbs provided uneven lighting. Deck plates had been removed to expose the bilge. A residue of black slime emitted an unpleasant odor. He could see where the propellor shafts had been unbolted from the turbines leaving gaping holes.

He followed the catwalk, stopping every few steps to make sure he didn't come upon someone by surprise, and stepped through a hatch into the fire room where most of the damage occurred. On the port side of the keel two rectangular holes had been cut in the hull plates. He approached the nearest one and dropped through it to the concrete below. He looked around.

Sections of replacement steel were leaning against the wall of the caisson, ready for welding. In case he was stopped here he had another excuse: Radinger said he could go below decks, why not the engine room? He duck-walked below the hull to the aft section of the ship. After a few yards the hull started making an upward slope to the fantail and he was able to stand upright. He came to the rudder, an impressive eight-foot trapezoid. Beyond were the monster caisson doors holding back the harbor waters.

Poulos did not bother to consider how bizarre or brazen his actions were. He was on his own, fully responsible for his folly. Maybe that's what was urging him on, a need to flaunt authority. He didn't want anyone telling him what to do--not Radinger, not his mother, not his uncle, not Clayton.

He monkey-climbed the scaffolding. Even in his anxious state, he was able to appreciate the ingenious network of bamboo poles held together at their joins by strips of leather. It served as a convenient ladder for an easy twenty-foot climb to the fantail. He reached for the Sprague's flagstaff and peeked over the rear deck between the depth charge racks. He didn't see anyone. Nothing went on back here. He gripped the top of the caisson wall and hoisted himself up. Water lapped on the opposite side, a once-familiar sound that had faded into memory after the ship entered dry dock more than a month ago. He looked around. There was limited activity on the pier at this time of evening: a few sailors and workers moving about; one or two trucks driving by. To them, Alex was just another gob doing his job.

Ahead was the cast-concrete control tower used by the caisson operator to open and close the gate. Once on the other side of the tower, Poulos could make his way to the bus stop undetected, out of sight of the OOD and the MAA standing watch at the midship’s quarterdeck. He was breathing easier now. In half an hour he would be with Jenny, and she would clear the confusion in his head.

As he came abreast of the tower a figure suddenly emerged from behind it. Poulos stopped, frozen still. It was Clayton. He had changed into his dark blues, a sailor on liberty. The rim of his white hat rested low on his eyebrows. "I figured this is where I'd find you."

Poulos looked past him expecting to see the Master at Arms with his billy club at his side. "Did you tell the OOD I was off the ship?"

"I can handle this myself."

"Handle what?"

"Violation of UCMJ, Article 86, section 3, which states: Any member of the armed forces who, without authority absents himself from his unit, organization or place of duty, shall be punished as a court-martial may direct."

"You memorized that?"

"I had plenty of time in the hospital to study the UCMJ."

"What for? To find out how to nail me?"

"You've already nailed yourself."

"So what's it to you?"

"If you get caught off the ship, the punishment will be severe."

"You want me out of your hair anyway, don't you?" It was the wrong metaphor, given Clayton's shaved head, but Clayton didn't seem to mind.

"Not after talking to Dr. Steiner."

The mere mention of the psychiatrist made Poulos feel as if he were standing naked in a crowded room. "Why do you keep bringing him up?"

"He helped me understand some things about myself."

"Such as?"

"I had faith in God but after we had that fight it was like he never existed. I kept wondering why, and then it came to me."

"What are you talking about?"

"God put us together to test us, like brothers."

"Brothers!" Poulos snorted. "Who, Orville and Wilbur?"

"I figure more like Cain and Abel."

"Well figure this: which one of us is Cain and which is Abel?"

"That is for you to decide. Go back to the ship and everything will be all right."

"Clayton, this is not a life and death situation. I'm taking a quick bus ride to physio-therapy."

"Isn't that where Scotty is? You going to see him, too?"

"I won't have time, I'm AWOL remember?"

Clayton brightened. "I have an idea. Why don't I go for you? I can tell that nurse you're restricted from leaving the ship and visit Scotty at the same time."

Nothing could be more odious than to have Clayton call on Jenny. "This is a personal matter."

"Looks official." Clayton pointed to the manila envelope in Poulos's waistband.

Poulos looked down, caught off-guard.

"What's in it?"

He stepped back. "Just papers."

"What kind of papers?"

Poulos's cheeks burned the way they did when his mother confronted him. He fought down the knee-jerk reactions that characterized his defiance of her: deceive, defraud, lie, cheat, flee, hide, avoid responsibility, do whatever it took to escape her accusing stare. He couldn't do this any longer, not to his mother, not to Clayton. He pulled the envelope out of his pants. "They're your transit orders. I just borrowed them in case anyone stopped me. I could say that I was delivering them to the base hospital. Make it look official, you know? I was going to put them right back." It sounded lame and silly. "I'm sorry."

Clayton stood quietly as though uncertain of Poulos's sincerity.

"I said I was sorry."

"What about the dust bag?"

Poulos was getting anxious. He might miss the bus and seeing Jenny was more important than ever now. "I'm sorry I dumped the dust bag on your head. I'm sorry for saying bad things behind your back, I'm sorry for making your life so fucking miserable."

"Do you really mean that?"

"Yes! As God is my witness, I mean every word of it!"

Clayton beamed. He came forward and hugged Poulos, who was so taken aback that he stood stock still and allowed Clayton to lift him and spin him around as though celebrating a great victory. He dropped Poulos and stepped back, extending his arms skyward. "Thank you, Jesus, for answering my prayers!" he cried, his eyes toward heaven. The heel of his shoe caught in the O-gauge railroad track for moving cranes. His uplifted arms suddenly began whipping air as he disappeared over the caisson wall. There was a heavy splash. Poulos ran to the edge and looked down at the murky water below. Clayton was thrashing up an eddy of hysterical whitecaps. A rusted metal ladder was set in concrete a dozen feet away.

"Swim for the ladder!" Poulos hollered and ran onto the pier, waving at Porteous, the OOD, who was staring at him from the quarterdeck. "Aren't you supposed to be on report?"

"Man overboard!" Poulos shouted.

Porteous looked over the railing into the empty caisson.

"Not there!" He pointed, "In the bay!"

He ran back. Clayton had floated away from the wall, his white hat bobbing next to him, his dark blues dragging him under. Poulos dove in.

Oily salt water stung his eyes as he surfaced. He swam to Clayton and felt his limp body just below the surface. He pulled Clayton's head above the water and cupped his hands under his jaw, the angular mandible he had always found so unpleasant--only now it provided a grip to hold Clayton's head up. Poulos flipped on his back, sliding Clayton's body over his, and started kicking. It was arduous work. He heard shouts and a light splash. He turned to look. Someone had tossed a life ring into the water. He was making slow but steady progress. Rescue was within his grasp when Clayton came to and twisted around, their faces now inches apart. He blinked, trying to focus, when suddenly his eyes burned bright hot like a dying meteorite. "Cain!" he screamed. "Are you Cain?"

"It's me, Poulos!" he sputtered, confused by the unexpected reversal of Clayton's euphoria, as if a switch had been turned from on to off.

His panic at full throttle, Clayton began hitting Poulos's head with his fists. "Cain rose up against his brother!"

Poulos tried to ward off the blows but he couldn't and keep Clayton afloat. In spite of the battering, cushioned only slightly by splashing water, Poulos couldn't help but wonder if the electro-shock therapy hadn't short-circuited the rational side of Clayton's brain, causing him to hallucinate. In a life and death struggle perhaps this was his salvation--believing he was Abel, the brother who paid with his life. Was this the real fight that Poulos and Clayton had been rehearsing ever since they met--this final, inevitable struggle for...what? Their souls? The harder Clayton hit Poulos the weaker he became, and it appeared more and more likely that this fight, simply because of its Old Testament precedent, was coming true.

Sailors lining the caisson were shouting support, not betting this time but cheering the rescue, and for a hopeful second or two Poulos believed he could still reach the life ring, but Clayton's flying fists finally were too much, and Poulos felt his grasp slip. As Clayton began to sink, his eyes met Poulos's one last time. They seemed to be asking, almost begging, did it have to come to this?

BOOK TWO

THE DOC

"Do you want this fucking medal or don't you?"

The Commodore's words boomed out of the microphone, echoing and re-echoing in the empty caisson like a donkey's bray off a canyon wall. Even though their cheeks turned crimson, the assembled dignitaries remained at rigid attention--a tribute to a lifetime of discipline which decrees that a naval officer never acknowledges a breach of conduct by another striper, not even a fart. But it didn't take a mind reader to know what they were thinking: That birdbrain Katz has done it this time. We gave him the benefit of the doubt when he ran the Sprague aground. At least his fighting spirit was in the right place. But this highly inappropriate comment--as well as his use of salty language--during an awards ceremony, of all things, was an unforgivable embarrassment. Katz was not only around the bend, he was closing in on the next one as well.

As would any good newsman witnessing a rare opportunity unfold, the photographer for Stars and Stripes pointed his Speed Graphic and caught the instant the Commodore dangled the Silver Star in front of Poulos's face. He imagined his photo being picked up by UP, AP as well as REUTERS, and reprinted in all the major magazines back home--maybe LIFE itself--with the intriguing cutline: "Do you want this (blank) medal or don't you?" leaving the reader's imagination to figure out what the fuck the blank stood for. This is what every news photographer dreams of, capturing the decisive moment as Cartier Bresson once put it. The picture had the Pulitzer Prize and Newspaper Photographer of the Year Award printed all over it.

Murmurings spread among the crew standing at attention on the decks and gun mounts. Their ranks became ragged as sailor after sailor turned his head one way and then the other, exchanging shit-eating grins with those on either side. A few even had the audacity to snicker if not laugh outright. Captain Blessing had seen action both in World War II and the Korean Conflict but he had never experienced anything like this. His career appeared to be ruined if not on permanent hold. His dreams of commanding a heavy cruiser or even a carrier were dashed. He'd be lucky to end up managing the PX at Pearl. His division officers were in a state of shock save one: Ltjg Radinger. For him the debacle was vindication that Poulos could not be trusted. See? his eyes were saying, didn't I warn you about that fucking idiot?

Even the Commodore understood he had finally overreached himself. If ever the Sprague needed a hero, she needed one now. He stared hopefully at the young sailor whose name he had forgotten in the glare of his embarrassing faux pax. The Silver Star turned slowly from its ribbon as he leaned forward and whispered in Poulos's ear, "Got any ideas?"

Poulos could not help but feel proud. For the first time in his life he had made a decision to be honest, even though it would cost him his hero status. It was more important to stand your ground for what is right than worry about what others think.

"Is it all right if I say something?" he asked.

The Commodore turned to Blessing. "Is it irregular to let the recipient speak?"

"Have you seen anything so far that wasn't?" the Captain shot back.

The ranking admiral stepped forward. "I see nothing wrong with the sailor's request, Captain Blessing." He obviously wanted to get this mess over with.

"Go ahead, Poulos," the Captain said resignedly. "I guess it can't get any worse."

Poulos moved to the microphone.

"Captain Blessing," he said, "you said that the Sprague needed a hero. I couldn't agree with you more, sir, but I am not the hero you're looking for. The real hero is RB Clayton. I know RB would not have been an obvious choice because he was quiet and shy, so if he's looking down on us, I'm sure he would be embarrassed to hear me talking about him. But it's important to let you all know that Clayton loved the navy and respected its tradition."

The photographer set his Speed Graphic down on the gangway and began taking notes for his cutline.

"It was my fault Clayton got in trouble and was transferred to the Base Hospital. He not only had to suffer shock treatments, he got busted too. He didn't deserve any of this. He just wanted to do his job. So if you're going to judge him, judge him by what he would have been had he lived--a fine person, a good sailor and, as I found out too late, a brother." Poulos stepped back from the mike.

The ship was absolutely still. Rear Admiral Jensen joined Poulos at the microphone. "Commodore Katz," he said, "may I have the medal?"

Katz was only too happy to hand it over. The Admiral leaned close to Poulos.

"First name?"

"Alexandros, sir."

The Admiral spoke into the microphone. "Acting on behalf of the Secretary of the Navy of the United States, I hereby award this Silver Star to Alexandros Poulos and, posthumously, to RB Clayton. This medal is to be shared by both men as a tribute to the memory of one and the forthrightness of the other."

The Admiral slipped the ribbon over Poulos's head. The photographer grabbed his Speed Graphic and the strobe flashed another time as the Silver Star came to rest on Poulos's chest. Deep down, the photographer knew that this was the only picture the navy would allow him to use.

The Admiral brought his right hand up. Poulos returned the salute. Then the Admiral shook his hand and a cheer erupted from the men.

Repairs on the Sprague were completed ahead of schedule; the Japanese shipyard workers did not know the meaning of the phrase screwing off. A floating crane lowered the two new screws into the caisson. They were welded to the gleaming shafts, and the Sprague was ready to return to sea. Three weeks after the ceremony, the scaffolding was dismantled and small floodgates were opened. Steel cables were tied around the wood beams that cradled the Sprague's hull and, as the water rose and the ship started to float on her own, the beams were pulled out. When the water level in the caisson was level with that of the harbor waters, the big gates swung open and tugs pulled the Sprague free of her imprisonment. Everyone was happy. The sailors were looking forward to getting back to sea. The Captain was absolutely right, being in drydock was a lot like being impotent. The Sprague went on a three-day shakedown cruise before heading back to the States. The other ships of DESDIV 1 had already set sail for their home port of San Diego. Steaming by herself, the Sprague proudly showed off her colors as she followed the open channel of Tokyo bay out to sea--her howlers blasting woop Woop WOOP and black smoke flowing out of her stacks.

Her paint fresh, her bright work gleaming, the Sprague was the antithesis of the destroyer that had limped in at barely five knots two months before, listing badly from her self-inflicted wounds. She turned north and followed Japan's east coast at a respectful distance up to Honshu and back. The ocean greeted them with deep, groaning swells. Unaccustomed to motion, the men fought to regain their sea legs. Seasickness was rampant. Sailors hung over the main deck rail on the leeward side throwing up breakfast, lunch and dinner. The ship's store quickly ran out of soda crackers. In spite of it all, morale was high. The bridge and CIC were beehives of renewed activity. Gunnery crews removed canvas covers on their barrels and fired practice rounds. It was exhilarating. Even Poulos got caught up in the headiness of going back to sea, the throbbing of the new screws under his feet, the endless horizon, the invigorating air, the waves crashing over the bow, the salty spray hitting his face.

Three days went by fast. The Sprague returned to Tokyo bay and dropped anchor at an outer marker; the ship and crew pronounced seaworthy. Excitement filled the air as sailors got ready for their final liberty in the Far East. In less than twenty-four hours, the Sprague would weigh anchor and head for her home port of San Diego; returning to the states for the first time in eighteen months. The first and third sections got first liberty; second and fourth sections the second. CPOs and First Class had till 2400; other enlisted had till 2300.

Browning and Witter talked about going ashore to say goodby to the Scotsman. Deep down they knew it was the last time they'd see him, even though they had made grand promises to look each other up after they all got out of the navy. It was unlikely any reunion would occur once the sailors got home and took up their civilian lives again. Because of missed opportunities, especially the one with Jenny, Poulos was in no mood to visit the physio-therapy building again. If he went to the base hospital with Browning and Witter, he would only be reminded of her soft southern accent, her incredible eyes, her wit and intellect, and reawaken the regret he was trying so diligently to bury along with his other ones.

Browning and Witter bugged him constantly while the Sprague was on her shakedown cruise. "You're feeling sorry for yourself because you blew it with that nurse."

"What crap," Poulos said, upset that they would use Jenny to embarrass him into coming along. The goading went on till liberty was announced. Browning and Witter caught one of the first water taxis and waved their fingers at Alex as the taxi eased away, loaded down with shore-bound sailors. Poulos went back to the Ship's Office and sat down.

There was no activity except for PALs unloading stores for the trip home. That afternoon, he began to have a change of heart. Maybe he should see Scotty after all. Jenny was long gone, only the memory of her remained. And she was in his head, not on the Base. Besides, he was getting bored sitting around doing nothing. He went below to change into his dark blues and then checked himself out at the quarterdeck. He stood by the railing and waited for the next water taxi.

"Clouds forming in the south," the OOD said to him. "Looks like weather's coming."

The taxi arrived and Poulos dropped into the bottom of the LST and huddled under the narrow deck so as not to get hit by spray. There was a handful of sailors riding with him but he was the only one from the Sprague. The trip to the landing took fifteen minutes. The waves were choppy and he was glad to reach shore without getting soaked. He climbed into a taxi driven by a Japanese (only Japanese who spoke English were allowed inside the Base) and directed him to the naval hospital. It was late afternoon by the time he arrived. He had plenty of time; he didn't have to be back on board till 2300. Poulos found Scotty alone in his room sitting in a chair. He was wearing a smaller cast now, from the knee down.

"Where are the guys?"

"They've come and gone."

"How's the leg?"

Scotty wiggled his exposed toes. "Good enough to be shipped back to the states next week to the naval hospital in Alameda."

"We'll be in Dago. Maybe we can see each other again."

There was not much enthusiasm. Without Browning and Witter around, the visit was limp, uninspired.

"I saw your picture in Stars and Stripes. Shaking hands with a fucking admiral. I never even laid eyes on one."

"They've got so much gold braid on their sleeves you wonder how they lift their arms to salute."

"Yeah..."

Things were out of phase between them. Maybe it was because they didn't have Clayton to kick around anymore.

"Say, how's the ensign?" Poulos asked, trying to rescue their lagging conversation.

Scotty pulled himself up in his chair. "Bonnie? She's always around. But too much togetherness kills passion, you know?"

Poulos didn't know. "I'd like to try that sometime."

"Passion?"

"Togetherness."

Scotty looked at his buddy as if thinking, you've got a long way to go. "You missed the boat on that Greek nurse. She had the hots for you."

"Greek women are not known for unbridled emotion."

Scottie shrugged that it wasn't his problem. "Bonnie told me you made her cry when you didn't show up for your date."

Poulos wanted to dry up and blow away. "I guess I'll never live that down."

"It's not as if you really gave a shit."

"What do you mean?"

"You let a live one get away."

"I couldn't help it!" Alex shot back defensively.

Scotty shifted in his seat from one cheek to the other. "Well, don't lose any sleep over her. There's a lot of cunt in the world that's better looking."

"Damnit, Scotty, watch what you say!"

"Hey, you're the one who keeps bad-mouthing Greek girls, not me."

"Ok, ok."

"I didn't know you felt that strong about her. I'll have Bonnie get her home address and you can write her a love letter in Greek."

"Why would she want to hear from me?"

Scotty stared up at the ceiling. "You got me, pal."

An uncomfortable silence prevailed. It was obvious the visit had come to a dead end. Poulos wished now he had not visited Scotty. Their remembrance of each other would have been fonder if they had never seen each other again.

Scotty limped Poulos to the front entrance.

"Take care of yourself, old buddy."

There was a fleeting moment when they would have hugged but self-consciousness intruded and they simply stood awkwardly facing each other in the doorway.

"At least you should let me do what that fucking admiral did," Scotty said.

"What's that?"

"Shake your hand."

It was getting dark and the wind had picked up. Alex wandered about the hospital grounds, feeling wistful and sad and filled with longing for Jenny. There was such an odd mixture of emotions coursing through him he didn't know how to isolate his feelings so he could deal with them one at a time. Nothing he did fit the occasion, somehow, and it bewildered him. He really wanted Jenny's address so he could write to her but he wouldn't admit it to himself. And when he parted from Scotty, the person with whom he had closely shared his life for the past year, he did so more as an acquaintance than a buddy. If only he had come here with Browning and Witter, he would have felt more at ease. The four of them would have wisecracked and slapped one another on the back in that offhand manner that disguises true affection.

His meanderings took him to MNP-13, the building where Clayton spent his last month of life on shore. It was no accident Poulos turned up here, even though initially he tried to hide it from himself. His reason for going on liberty was less to bid Scotty farewell than to see Steiner, the doctor who had treated Clayton. And that's really why he begged off coming ashore with his buddies--he didn't want Witter to think he was finally following his advice to see a psychiatrist. But that still didn't stop him from wishing Witter had been around to help take the edge off his awkward visit with Scotty.

"Christ," he said out loud, "am I a bundle of contradictions, or what?"

He walked into the building. The receptionist was sitting behind her PBX. She had the current issue of All Hands open in front of her. The magazine was turned to the center section featuring the news of the week. She looked up at him. Recognition flickered in her eyes. "Say, aren't you the sailor who got the Silver Star at that big ceremony? How do you like being in the limelight?"

"It's too bright," he said, working the rim of his hat around with his fingers.

"Enjoy it while you can." She folded the magazine and looked at him expectantly, waiting for him to tell her why he was here.

"I wonder," he said, still fidgeting with his hat, "if it might be possible to see the doctor who treated RB Clayton?"

"Dr. Steiner?" She gave him a confidential smile. "I'm sure he'd like to see you."

"I wouldn't know about that."

"You tried to save his patient, didn't you?" She pulled a jack out of the hole it sat in and plugged it into the switchboard. "Dr. Steiner?" she said into her mouthpiece. "That sailor who got the Silver Star for trying to save RB Clayton is here." She stared at Poulos as she spoke.

He shifted his feet, hoping she wasn't going to do something silly like ask him for his autograph.

When she disconnected she said, "Can I have your autograph?"

He smiled as he bent over and wrote his name across the magazine cover.

"Isn't that interesting," she said, "you're left-handed."

Poulos found Dr. Steiner sitting at a cluttered navy-issue, gray-metal desk. Behind him was a stamped-metal shelf on which were family pictures and layers of books lying flat instead of upright. A Picasso print from the artist's classical period hung on the wall. The doctor was typing on an Underwood bolted to a rolling stand. He pushed it out of his way when Poulos walked in.

"Al Steiner," he said.

They shook hands across the desk.

Dr. Steiner was small and wiry. He looked as if he always needed a shave. His hair was black and full. He was wearing khakis without insignia or tie. His eyes were playful and he had a ready smile. Poulos guessed he was in his forties.

"Normally I don't see walk-ins but I always make time for heroes." He spoke with a distinct New York accent. "Sit down."

There was a couch and a chair. Alex sat in the chair.

Steiner stared openly at him. Poulos twitched.

"Is the chair ok?"

"I beg your pardon?"

"Every time someone sits down in my office they seem uncomfortable. Do you think it's the furniture?"

"No, sir."

"Please don't call me sir."

"Doctor."

"You know, I don't even like doctor. In fact, I don't like any labels on people. It inhibits conversation. Would you feel better calling me Al?"

"I don't think so."

"Of course not. Too much conditioning. How about Doc? Still too tough for you?"

"No, I can handle that."

"Where are you from? Wait, let me guess. Midwest. Wisconsin."

"Minnesota."

"Close. I'm from New York."

"I never would have guessed."

Steiner smiled. "You Greek?"

Alex nodded.

"I'm Jewish. My parents came from Russia. I grew up on the Lower East Side."

"When my father came to America in 1910 he worked on Delancey Street."

Steiner slapped the desk. "My old neighborhood!"

Poulos had the feeling Steiner would have said that whether he grew up there or not. "He lived over an ice cream parlor."

"Was it called Meshugennah's by any chance?"

"I doubt it. The ice cream parlor was owned by a Greek. My dad worked for him, his first job in America."

"What's Greek for crazy?"`

Alex had to think a moment. "Trellos."

"I like Meshugennah's better. You know something? If I had my life to live over I'd live over an ice cream parlor just like your father."

Poulos wondered if Steiner kidded like this with everybody. He couldn't imagine him kidding with Clayton, however. Maybe Steiner was doing it for his benefit to get him to relax. It seemed to be working. "I don't think you would. My father made ice cream sixteen hours a day. He told me that one summer he made enough ice cream for the entire population of New York."

Poulos expected a laugh from Steiner but it was evident he wanted to do him one better. "My father worked in a cigar factory rolling cigars. Guess who sat next to him on the bench?"

"Who?"

"Moss Hart's father."

"The playwright?"

Steiner nodded. "His father said to my father, 'I roll cigars so my son can write comedies for people to roll in the aisles.'"

Alex thought the joke was a bit strained but he nodded appreciatively. "Not bad."

"You don't have to say that unless you mean it."

"Did you ever meet Moss Hart?"

"We had lunch together!" Steiner slapped his knee. "Seriously, though, we did live in the same tenement. Hart's first play, Once in a Lifetime, a collaboration with George S. Kaufman, opened in 1930."

"The year I was born," Poulos said.

"I was twelve. The play was so successful the Harts moved to a better neighborhood. The Steiners were no longer good enough for them. Moss got a swelled head."

"He should have seen a psychiatrist."

Steiner smiled appreciatively. "You're pretty quick."

"I never thought so."

"Is that why you came to see me?"

"No," Poulos answered, trying to appear offhand. "I came to see you about Clayton."

"What about Clayton?"

"Well, what did he tell you?"

"While he was on my couch?"

Poulos looked at it. "Is that where he sat?"

"Not sat, lying down, but from either position, I can't tell you what he said. That's privileged information."

"Like a confession?" he asked, thinking of Mary Lou.

"More or less. Why are you so interested in what Clayton told me?"

Poulos twisted his hat.

"Why don't you lay that thing down before you tear it to shreds?" Steiner pushed aside a file folder and placed his elbows on the desk. "To put your mind at ease, I can tell you that Clayton said a lot of things that would bore you silly."

"But why did you have to give him shock treatments?"

"It's the most effective cure for intractable depression, which is what Clayton suffered from. ECT was developed at Columbia in '39 when I was a student there. A chemical is getting attention now...lithium, and it's supposed to be a highly effective psychotropic, antipsychotic, anti-anxiety and anti-depressant drug. But for now ECT is still the best for what ailed Clayton. When he left here he was feeling a lot better and, as far as I was concerned, he could stay in the navy. But not everyone agreed with me, especially that Captain of yours, what's his name, Bullshit?"

Poulos covered a grin. "Blessing."

"He's trying to get me reprimanded for sending Clayton back to the Sprague. He claims I compromised the ship's morale and safety by returning a psychotic sailor to active duty instead of giving him a medical discharge. Clayton was here for a month and I got to know him pretty well. He was an interesting kid, far brighter than I took him for when he arrived, and I grew to like him. My first responsibility is to my patient, not some asshole captain worried about promotion. Clayton needed to prove to himself that he was ok, that he could make a comeback. I gave him the chance. But I might have been wrong."

"You weren't."

"He's dead, isn't he?"

"You are not to blame."

Steiner leaned casually back in his chair. "Then who is?"

Poulos knew he had been manipulated. He ran his fingers along the edge of Steiner's desk.

The doctor smiled. "Shall I put you out of your misery?"

"I don't know what you mean."

"You know damn well what I mean. Clayton talked about you a lot. In fact, you were his number one subject. And you are dying, if I may use an inappropriate expression, to find out what shit he dumped on you. Am I right?"

Steiner had such a fixed, piercing gaze that Poulos had to stop looking into his eyes.

"Let's make a deal. I'll waive doctor-client privilege. Clayton is dead anyhow so it won't make any difference to him. Tell me about his last day on earth and I'll tell you what he said about you. Fair enough?"

Poulos thought back about how defensive he was when Jenny suggested he see Steiner. And now, willy-nilly, here he was, sitting in his office. He wondered how she would react if she knew he finally followed her advice. But, he quickly corrected himself, he came here not to find out about himself but to find out about Clayton. "Didn't you read the report on his death?"

"You ought to know the navy by now. Nothing is allowed to rock the boat except water. Clayton deserves the truth."

"That's what Voltaire said," Poulos interjected. "The dead deserve the truth."

"You read Voltaire. You are rather sophisticated for the regular navy."

"I'm a reservist."

"So am I. Peculiar isn't it that regular guys like you and me are not in the regular navy."

Poulos laughed. Steiner was certainly disarming. He was going to great lengths to create a bond. Maybe they had something to share after all: a nagging guilt over Clayton's death. He was feeling more at ease. "So what do you want to know?" he asked.

"Start at the beginning."

For Poulos, the beginning was the day he jumped ship to see Jenny, but he found himself backing up at the gentle urging of the doctor, backing and backing until he told Steiner about his first altercation with Clayton.

"And you dumped the dirty bag all over him?"

Poulos nodded sheepishly. "Did he tell you about that?"

"Not right away."

"I wish I hadn't done it."

"We all have wishes like that."

Poulos looked at Steiner. "I suppose you think I'm a pretty rotten person."

"More immature than rotten."

For some reason, that label stung Poulos more than if Steiner had simply told him he was rotten.

"You know," Steiner continued, "there was nothing so bad between you and Clayton that couldn't have been resolved with a little professional help."

"Clayton should have seen you sooner?"

"You should have seen me sooner."

"Wait a minute, Doc, I didn't come here to..."

"Yes, you did."

"You don't even let me finish my sentences."

"I don't have to. I can read your mind." Steiner seemed to be enjoying himself at Poulos's expense. "Let's return to your tale of woe. You alluded to a nurse you were willing to go AWOL for."

Poulos nodded.

"What's her name?"

"Jenny Betheras."

"Sounds Greek to me."

"It is...was."

"Was?"

"Her tour is over. She returned to the states."

"Is that why you were jumping ship--because you wanted to see her before she left?"

"Yes."

"Where was she billeted?"

"Physio-therapy."

Steiner nodded.

"Did you know her?"

"No."

"She knew you."

He appeared pleased, as though he had been paid a compliment. "Maybe my reputation has outgrown these hallowed walls."

"She spoke highly of you. She..." Poulos stopped in mid-sentence.

Steiner leaned forward, his posture forcing Poulos to continue. "She thought I should see you."

Steiner's eyes twinkled as he settled back. "That is one sharp nurse. Tell me about her."

"What's to tell?"

"Is she smart?"

"Really smart."

"Good looking?"

"In a dark sort of way."

"What does that mean?"

Poulos shrugged. "She's Greek."

"Why do you have a problem with Greek women?"

He felt his pulse quicken. "I thought we were talking about Clayton."

"We never stopped. He was as confused and angry as you are."

"You had a whole month with him."

"That's why I'm talking fast. Mind if I dig a little deeper? Do Greek women remind you of your mother?" When Poulos didn't respond, he continued: "It's not uncommon for conflicted men to have issues with their mothers. So don't feel as though I'm singling you out."

Despite the provocations, Poulos was spellbound, like watching a cobra unwind from a basket.

"If you had to pick one word to describe your mother, what would it be?"

Poulos didn't have to stop and think. "Psychotic."

Steiner raised an eyebrow. "I haven't heard anyone describe his mother in quite that way before, or as emphatically. You would make an interesting paper. What is it about her that makes you say that? Give me an example."

"Well..." Poulos said, and then described the time he took her to the University Hospital. "When she saw the Neurology and Psychiatry sign in the lobby, she ran out of the building and I had to chase after her."

"What else?"

Poulos hesitated before answering. "She called a...a close friend who isn't Greek a poutana, a whore."

"Was your mother afraid you'd marry her?"

Poulos winced.

Steiner noticed. "You can walk out of here any time you want. I may not be able help you feel better but I can help you understand, and from that you may feel better."

"I'm fine."

"Did you ever consider that your mother's dislike of non-Greek women may mirror your dislike of Greek women?"

Poulos had never thought of it quite like that before. "Like a quid pro quo?"

"I take it your mother was born in Greece."

"Yes."

"Typical clash of culture with the first generation, but what you've told me is not enough to make me think your mother isn't like thousands of others who emigrated to America."

"Maybe I'm overreacting."

"What you're saying comes from the kishkes--gut to you."

Poulos questioned whether he should tell the doctor the things Jenny said about his mother, not that different from what Steiner was touching on. But he did not want the doctor to think that Jenny had been playing armchair psychiatrist with his emotions.

Steiner was staring intently at Poulos. "Something is bothering you."

"I don't think I should talk about it."

"Let me throw out a hypothesis. Your feelings toward Clayton are tied up with your feelings toward your mother. Do you think that's too far-fetched?"

"Of course it is."

Steiner rested back in his chair. "So do I."

Poulos was confused. "Then why..."

"I want you to prove me wrong. Tell me what it is you don't want to talk about, what's bothering you."

Poulos was afraid of opening a Pandora's box, afraid of finding out more than he wanted to know. He looked down at his scarred hand and realized he had it balled into a fist. He worked his fingers open. The damaged tissue was whiter than usual because he had squeezed the blood out of his palm. An unexpected wave of deja vu washed over him. Fearful memories began to crowd out the present. "Jenny..." he began.

"What about Jenny?" Steiner leaned forward again. "Is it something she did?"

"Said..."

Poulos opened up his left hand.

Steiner partially rose from his chair, leaned across his desk and stared at it. "Are you left-handed?"

"Yes."

He sat back down. "Looks like a third degree burn."

"I was told I burned myself accidentally, but now I'm not sure." Poulos felt as though he was betraying a confidence. Not Jenny's, his mother's.

"Why aren't you sure?"

"Jenny suggested it might not have been an accident."

"Do you agree with her?"

"I don't want to."

"Why not?"

"If it wasn't an accident, how did it happen?"

Steiner had a sympathetic look on his face. "Are you capable of answering that question yourself?"

Poulos's eyes began to water. "When I was little I grabbed the flame on the kitchen stove. That's what I grew up hearing."

"From whom?"

Poulos shrugged. "My mother, my father. My uncle. When I asked about it, they told me I was fascinated by the fire and wanted to touch it."

"What did Jenny tell you?"

Alex shifted in his chair. "She said that if I had touched the flame on my own, the burn would have covered my whole hand, instead of a small area which more likely would have been caused by a single flame, like a pilot light."

"So the first time you heard that there may be another explanation was when Jenny offered it?"

"Yes."

"How did that make you feel?"

"I got pretty upset."

Steiner kept burrowing. "At Jenny or your mother?"

The question startled him. "I got upset at Jenny for suggesting that I see a psychiatrist. That's how your name came up."

"Good for her."

"The night ended on a sour note. She sent me an apology and I made a date to see her on her last night in Japan. I got in trouble with my division officer who put me on report. I was so desperate I jumped ship. Clayton tried to stop me. The rest you know."

"And for your efforts you got the Silver Star."

"That's the navy for you."

Steiner nodded in agreement.

"Why did you ask me if I'm mad at my mother?"

"Because you should be."

Poulos laughed nervously. "What are you trying to tell me?"

"Maybe you should tell me."

He began to shake uncontrollably.

"Was your mother alone with you when you burned your hand?"

"Dad was at the store. He was always at the store."

The truth slowly began to sink in, but he was still in too fragile a condition to reflect on it rationally. Perspiration broke out on his hairline. Was it hot in here or was it just him?

"Are you saying my mother did this to me?" He looked down at his hand as if it didn't belong to him. "I was just a baby. How could she do a thing like that?" He felt as numb and as nerveless as the dead tissue of his scar.

Yet he still found room in his anguish to laugh at the absurdity of believing he had burned himself rather than accept the notion that his mother had done it to him. And now, finally understanding this, he felt wave upon wave of unacknowledged anger pouring out of him, an overwhelming flood of anger at his mother for inflicting this unspeakable pain on her son.

Steiner was silent, watching Poulos carefully. Finally he spoke. "Try to understand your mother's state of mind, and maybe you can grow to accept what happened. I'm not saying it's going to be easy."

He straightened in his chair. "From what I gather, your mother had a pathological fear of lefthandedness. That's not as uncommon as you might think, especially among uneducated immigrants who come from cultures where custom and superstition govern their lives. For her, being left-handed was the mark of the Devil. You know where the word sinister comes from?"

Poulos shook his head.

"It comes from Latin and means from the left." Steiner paused, watching Poulos's reaction. "Perhaps now you can understand why she was afraid to see her child favoring his left hand. Her beliefs convinced her that you were possessed by the devil. She had to use a form of exorcism to burn him out of you. Can you accept that explanation?"

Poulos wanted to shout to the world that the devil wasn't in him, it was in his mother. But he said nothing. He was too shaken by the knowledge that in one painful, irrevocable moment she had destroyed not only his left hand but also his security, his trust, his very childhood.

The one person with total dominion over him had conditioned him ever after to be wary of everyone in authority, presumed or otherwise--not only his mother but also Lt. Radinger, Father Bassagni, even RB Clayton. The revelation gave brutal logic to his painful shyness--his persistent anxiety that if he said something wrong he would suffer not only teasing and ridicule but, far worse, punishment. Metaphorically speaking, in addition to his physical scar, he carried an emotional scar as well--a subconscious fear of getting burned again.

"Try giving your mother the benefit of the doubt," Steiner said, as if he were seeing into Poulos's mind. "This burning incident may have been the final, desperate measure in a series of measures to get you to change to your right hand. Like switching your spoon or the toys you played with. From there she might have gone to spanking your hand, hitting it hard enough to hurt. When none of this worked, she held your hand to the pilot light. I'm sure she did not intend to burn you badly, just enough to teach you a lesson. But it doesn't take much to inflict damage to tender, young skin."

Poulos shuddered at the image of his palm turning red and blistering. "Sometimes I dream about a smooth membrane that starts wrinkling at the edges, like vellum catching fire. It wakes me up. I'm full of goose bumps and sweating all over."

"I doubt if you'll have that dream anymore. That was your subconscious acting out the event."

Poulos wondered what might have been. "Would I be a different person if she hadn't done that to me?"

"In certain ways, I suppose. All of your life you've been carrying around a shitload of unresolved guilt, unconciously wondering what you did that was so unutterably awful that she had to burn your hand to punish you for it. If your mother had the courage to tell you what really happened, I think you would have accepted it and that would have been that. But not knowing the truth took a heavy toll. Guilt, insecurity, suspicion of authority. It got in the way of building healthy relationships with people like Clayton."

"But why Clayton?"

"It has to do with transference. Something about him set you off. His manner, his physical appearance, his attitude...any of those things. You began acting out deep-seated resentments really aimed at your mother. Our psyches work in subtle ways their wonders to perform. Clayton had displaced your mother and you took out your aggressions on him."

"But I didn't want him to die."

"Of course you didn't." Steiner's eyes lost their playfulness. "Neither did I."

The wind was scraping tree branches on the roof and spattering rain against the window panes of Steiner's office. He swiveled in his chair and looked out. "Storm. Hadn't noticed."

Poulos checked his watch. He couldn't believe how much time had passed. "I better be getting back."

"Your last night in Japan. Not a pleasant way to spend it. I hope I wasn't too hard on you. Normally, what you accomplished tonight takes weeks, months. Sometimes never." Steiner eyed him closely. "One last question. Did your mother succeed in making you righthanded?"

"No," Poulos replied defiantly, "I'm lefthanded and I'll stay that way to my dying day."

"Good for you. That means you didn't knuckle under, if I may use another inappropriate metaphor. If you had, you would never have got this far in understanding yourself."

"How much do I owe you?" Poulos asked kiddingly

"In civilian life you couldn't have afforded me." Steiner smiled. "Let me give you my card." He foraged through the narrow drawer above the desk's kneehole. "I have them somewhere." He found one and handed it to Poulos. "Write me a year from now and tell me how you're doing."

Poulos slipped the card into his jumper pocket.

"How are you getting to the landing?"

"Taxi, bus. Whatever comes first."

"Either way you'll get soaked. Tell you what. I'll get a jeep out of the motor pool and give you a ride."

"You don't have to do that."

"You're a hero, remember?" Steiner grabbed an olive-drab slicker from his closet and slipped it over his shoulders. Alex waited at the entrance as Steiner ran across the yard and down the street to the motor pool. He was back in a few minutes with a jeep, rain beating on its canvas roof; headlights on bright. It was really coming down. Poulos ran the short distance to the parked jeep. He jumped in and fastened the side curtain to keep the rain out.

"Work the wiper for me." Steiner said above the rain drumming on the canvas roof.

Poulos took over the manual operation of the windshield wiper and Steiner drove to the boat landing, a small ticket booth with benches and a dock supported on oil drums. The dock was heaving up and down as waves crashed over it, flooding the shiny wood before receding, only to do it all over again. An outdoor light hung from a metal pole that waved in the wind, casting eerily moving shadows. Normally the landing would be crowded with sailors lined up at the booth to buy fares back to their ships.

A handwritten sign was taped to the inside of the window. "What does it say?" Steiner asked. "My eyes are too old to read that far."

Poulos cleared the windshield and squinted. "No boats. Go to Harbormaster Pier." He leaned back against the hard cushion. "Shit, the storm cancelled rides. I have to go to the Harbormaster Pier. Can you take me there?"

"I know this base like I know the Lower East Side." Steiner backed up and turned around. Poulos continued to move the wiper back and forth. He was mighty lucky to have Steiner driving him. A few minutes later they pulled onto a wide pier that had a troop ship tied alongside. Next to it was a long one-story wood building.

Steiner stopped at an entrance with a protective overhang and put the gears in neutral, idling the engine. "You'll have to spend the night and catch a ride to your ship in the morning."

Poulos looked out the windshield at the riveted steel of the ship's hull glistening from the rain. "Isn't this the ship where Clayton stayed after he was released?"

Steiner nodded. "He needed a transition between the hospital and the Sprague, so I had him bivouac here until he felt he was ready."

Poulos slumped in his seat. The downpour washing the windshield blurred his vision. Or was it tears blurring his vision?

"You going to be all right?"

"What if this is a ghost ship."

"Clayton is not a ghost."

Poulos pulled himself erect. "I appreciate what you did for me."

"I did it for myself as much as for you. I was responsible for

Clayton. When word came back that he died, I took it pretty hard. In my business you want success, not failure."

"What will I be?"

"It's up to you. Put this crap behind you and get on with your life."

"I hope I can do it."

"Trust your instincts."

They shook hands. Poulos unsnapped the jeep's side curtain and jumped out. He stood beneath the overhang and watched Steiner turn the jeep around and drive away, its deeply grooved tires spraying standing water.

THE FINGER

Poulos waited till he no longer could see Steiner's taillights. For a brief moment, he wanted to chase after the jeep--feeling like the person who had thought of the perfect comeback after it was too late. But the pelting rain, tossed horizontally by wind gusts, drove him inside the building. He took off his hat and swiped at the droplets that had collected on his blues. His shoes got the worst of it, but there was nothing he could do about that except hope they would dry without curling.

He went into a waiting room that resembled a small-town train depot, with rows of wood benches and banks of fluorescent light fixtures hanging from metal rods. Half of the tubes were either burned out or failing. On the seaward wall, a big sign hung above a set of double doors:

Through These Portals Pass The Best Damned Coxswains In The World

At the front was a high counter with a second class quartermaster sitting behind it reading a paperback. Poulos went up to him.

"No boats tonight," the quartermaster said without looking up.

"My ship is leaving for the states in the morning."

"What time?"

"0700."

He dog-eared the page he was reading and closed his book. "Depending on the weather, we'll try sending a T out at dawn. What ship you on?"

"Robert B. Sprague, DD884."

The sailor scanned a typewritten list. He flipped to page two; then to page three. "Sprague, Sprague," he muttered. "Oh, yeah, Berth 178." He consulted a shiny, oilcloth map of Tokyo Bay hanging on the wall. It was dotted with colored pushpins to mark ship locations--red for battle wagons, blue for carriers, and assorted other colors for cruisers, tincans, tenders and oilers.

"Shit, man, you are practically in the Pacific Ocean." He pointed to a position on the far right of the map, at the edge of the map's border. "Pretty tough getting a T way out there. You might have to report to base headquarters in the morning."

"What for?"

"Reassignment."

"Reassignment?" To Poulos that had all the appeal of a hog bladder. "What about my stuff?"

"Supply will requisition you some new clothes. But it'll cost you a couple months pay."

"Why?"

"You're responsible if you miss your ship."

He did not want to miss his ship, and he was not going to if he could help it. For all of her drawbacks the Sprague was where he belonged. Not only that, she was heading home in the morning and he didn't want to get stuck in the Far East.

He looked around the empty waiting room. "I can't be the only one caught by the storm."

"There are a couple of dozen guys crapped out on the Stanton. You're welcome to join them. Reveille is at 0600."

"Got anything to eat?"

"There's a mess downstairs. Help yourself."

The stairway was lighted by a bare bulb. Poulos walked down. At the the bottom he heard water sloshing beyond a wide metal door. Must be the boat landing. Opposite was another door that opened into a lounge of sorts with a beat-up sofa, a pair of metal chairs, a well-used ping pong table, a Kelvinator gas refrigerator, and a makeshift gedunk stand with a coffee urn and a stack of mugs sitting on top. He smelled rancid coffee. He opened the refrigerator. There were half a quart of milk, a loaf of stale bread, and butter. In the storage shelves under the stand was a box of sugar. Better than nothing.

He buttered two slices of bread and cut the heavy acidity of the coffee with milk and sugar. He belched his way up the stairs to the waiting room.

Across the pier was the Stanton and a dry rack but Poulos couldn't shake the specter of Clayton hovering somewhere in the dark. This waiting room, at least, was well-lighted if not clean.

"Mind if I sleep on a bench?"

"Suit yourself."

He laid down on a back bench, using his hat for a pillow. It was unmercifully hard. After a few minutes he changed his mind, Clayton's spirit be damned. He dashed across the pier in the driving rain and sprinted up a gangway that led to the second deck of the towering troop ship. Close by was a hatch. He opened it and stepped into a cavernous sleeping compartment. Red globes cast an eerie glow on bunks that were stacked eight high. Three hundred men could sleep in here. Bodies stirred as he dogged the door shut. He found a rack and sniffed the fartsack for body odor. Could be worse.

He took off his shoes and socks, and draped the socks over a rung. He undid his neckerchief and pulled off his jumper, folding them neatly. He laid on his back, put his hands behind his head and stared into the gloom thinking about what Steiner told him. Subconsciously Poulos had rediscovered his mother in Clayton's tightly wrapped, disapproving personna. He had become the new bane of Poulos's existence, a continuation of what Poulos had tried to run away from. It was a weird oxymoron. Two personalities--unknown to one another and of opposite genders, thousands of miles apart, and of vastly different ages--merged in his disturbed state of mind.

Life is full of contradictions so why should his be an exception? It reminded him of James Thurber's description of a building as pretty ugly and a little big. He allowed himself a grudging smile when he thought of Thurber's humorous juxtapositions. Could be Poulos's problems were no different--pretty ugly and a little big--but on further reflection, he decided that they were not little nor pretty--just big and ugly.

"Are you out there, Clayton?" Poulos whispered into the shadows, more to comfort himself than to communicate with the dead. "I learned a lot from Steiner. I learned that I carried you and my mom around like a matched set of luggage--heavy baggage I should have dumped sooner. If only I had followed Jenny's advice, you'd be alive now."

He stared hard, unblinking, as if trying to materialize Clayton. "I'm sorry," he said out loud.

"So am I," a drunken voice replied in the dark.

Poulos fell into a deep and seamless slumber, not stirring until the noise of metal banging on metal woke him up. He rolled over, upset that anyone could be so fucking inconsiderate. He forced his lids to separate. A bos'n was standing in the open doorway, the early morning light outlining his burly frame. "Drop your cocks and grab your socks!" he yelled.

Bitching and scratching echoed throughout the compartment. Rubbing sleep from his eyes, Poulos drew himself to a sitting position and pulled his socks off the rack. He yawned as he slipped them on his feet and then put on his shoes. He unfolded his jumper and drew it over his head, and slipped his neckerchief under his talleywacker. He didn't have a comb so he made a claw of his left hand--easy for him to do--and drew his fingers through his hair. He put on his hat and rubbed his scratchy jaw. He looked around in the morning light. Everyone was in the same condition--unkempt, uncomfortable, unshaven.

He stepped out on the deck and shivered in the dank air. The overcast sky and dishwater sea met at a barely discernible horizon. The rain had stopped but the wind was still blowing hard, and the whitecaps had a we-dare-you meanness to them. Somewhere out there, in that gray vastness of Tokyo Bay, the Sprague was preparing to weigh anchor--her deckhands going about their established routines of readiness.

"Shit," Poulos swore aloud, and walked down the gangway, across the pier, and into the waiting room where he joined a scraggy lot of sailors standing around or sitting on the benches--most of them smoking cigarettes, all with concern on their faces. Technically they were AWOL, like Poulos, and it was up to each skipper to decide what, if any, disciplinary action would be taken against a sailor who should have kept track of the weather and got his ass back before the boat warning was issued. Poulos could easily guess what Radinger was saying in the wardroom right now: "It will serve the bastard right if he misses a ride home."

Presently the Harbormaster, a chief petty officer with an armful of hashmarks on his sleeve, picked up a mike and clicked on the PA system. His voice crackled out of two speakers mounted in the corners of the room. "Attention, all hands," he said. "The seas are still rough but with daylight and no rain we're going to try getting you on board your ships. We're sending out a pair of Ts, numbers 316 and 317. I'll call out the name of your ship. Pay attention, I'm only saying this once. Three-sixteen goes to the Kearsarge, Soley, Prairie and Craig. Three-seventeen goes to the Gwin, Forest Royal, Wadsworth, Farragut and Oriskany. Proceed to the lower level."

No mention of his destroyer. He went to the counter. "Excuse me, you didn't call out the Sprague."

"The what?"

"The Sprague, Berth 178."

The Chief checked his clipboard. "Sorry, Mack, too far out. Looks like you report to headquarters."

Poulos was in a state of shock. They couldn't do this to him!

Sailors began to queue at the doorway over which the sign about the Best Damned Coxswains in the World hung. As Poulos watched them proceed down the stairway, pangs of loneliness coursed through him. He was now totally friendless, at the mercy of an unfeeling, uncaring naval bureaucracy. A man without a ship was a man without a country--belonging to no one, part of nothing, adrift and rootless. Until yesterday the Sprague was the ship he couldn't wait to say Sayonara to. But now he longed to be on her. He would miss his cramped and smelly compartment, the mustard and ketchup stains on his rack, the heaving seas and the heaving stomachs. He would miss all of these because they were not only familiar, they were also his: his compartment, his rack, his shipmates.

He began to think about the guys he would never see again. Dave Witter, the tall, handsome guy with the lopsided face; A. John Browning with his owlish horn-rimmed glasses and nonpareil record collection, Ernie Klein who didn't know the meaning of shampoo, Lt. Gildenhall and his lost trust, Ensign Porteous and his puerile humor--hell, even Ltjg Radinger and his birthmark was beginning to look good. In a flash of insight, Poulos understood that he had taken his life for granted; had never bothered to consider what it would be like to lose everything. More than a year ago, in a grandiose gesture of self-pity, he ran away from Minneapolis to let the world know how hurt he was--not unlike someone attempting suicide just to get attention. Alone now in the Harbormaster transit room, he was reliving the same agonies--not by his own hand, but by the fickle hand of a system he could not influence. Before, he didn't appreciate what he had--friends at sea, a family at home--but now he was willing to take classes in humility if only he could get a ride back to the Sprague.

He heard electric starters grind and the muffled roar of big-time marine engines come to life. Without further reflection, he passed through the same portals used by the best damned coxswains in the world, and ran down the stairs to the boat dock. The first landing craft was already pulling away, churling white foam from under its stern as it bobbed into the waves. The second T was getting ready to shove off. A deck hand was loosening the lines and tossing them into the boat. The coxswain began to throttle his engines.

"Wait for me!" Poulos shouted and jumped over the gunwale onto the craft's narrow main deck. The coxswain sat high up in an open turret, braving the winds in a foul weather jacket and a knit cap pulled low over his eyes. He was startled by Poulos's sudden appearance

"Get down inside, goddamnit, before you're washed overboard!"

Poulos jumped into the flat hull with a dozen sailors who were leaning their backs against the bulkhead to maintain balance. They were in for a rough ride. The craft was nothing more than a steel box with a flat bottom and a bow door that once dropped down to form a ramp for invading tanks and troops but was now welded shut. There were no seats; nothing to hang on to.

The coxswain put his dual marines on full throttle, and the T hit waves that felt like brick walls. The bow door reverberated from the pounding water. The sailors bounced and caromed about in their enclosure; it was easy to get bruised. Salt spray filled the air and within minutes everyone was soaked and shivering.

Ahead loomed an aircraft carrier. It was a harrowing transfer. Two sailors climbed onto the narrow upper deck and crouched, clinging to the gunwale as the coxswain maneuvered alongside the accommodations ladder, angled like a stairway. Heavy seas made contact difficult but the coxswain used a combination of throttle and rudder to maintain proximity to the ladder so the two sailors could jump off safely. They waved their thanks as the landing craft drew away and headed for another ship.

The coxswain made four additional touch-and-go maneuvers until he was left with Poulos. He idled his engines to cut down on noise. "What's your ship?" He scowled down, wondering why Poulos hadn't got off yet.

"The Sprague!"

"The what?"

"Robert B. Sprague, DD884." He pointed in the general direction of the harbor's entrance. "Berth 178."

"Fuck! That's not on my list."

"We're this far, what's a mile or two more?"

"A mile or two?" The coxswain surveyed the harbor as the T pitched and yawed. "Shit, man, that's gotta be five. You're nuts if you think I'm going to drive clear across the bay for you!"

"I thought you were the best damned coxswain in the world."

"What?"

"Isn't that what the sign says?"

"Fuckin' A!" he shouted proudly.

"Well, then, why are you afraid to try for my ship?"

That did it. "All right, you bastard, I'll show you who's afraid!" he yelled above the noise of the roaring engines and the thudding waves. The coxswain lunged his landing craft into motion, spun it around, and headed toward the gaping maw that was the entrance to the bay. The T banged and lurched. Maybe it was his imagination, but Poulos suspected the coxswain was seeking out especially high breakers to give him the ride of his life. It seemed to go on forever but eventually he let up on his throttle and the landing craft slowed. "We're coming up on the Sprague!"

he shouted down at Poulos. "I'll make one pass at her. If you don't get off, that's your tough shit!"

Poulos hoisted himself up to the narrow upper deck and gripped his fingers around a hawsehole. His eyes stung from salt spray as he looked out. Dead ahead lay the Sprague, her white bow numbers the only contrast in a blending sea and sky of gray. Lazy smoke curled out of her stacks indicating activity in the engine room. The decks were dotted with sailors in life jackets and white hats whose brims were folded down to keep them from blowing away. They were pointing at the T. Poulos thought he saw the Captain up on the bridge looking through his binoculars.

The coxswain made as if he wanted to ram the Sprague. Startled deck hands jumped back. At the last possible moment, the coxswain reversed his engines and swung the boat hard to starboard so that he could edge up to the Sprague. It was nip and tuck. In a quiet sea, the T's upper deck where Poulos crouched would be at the same level as the Sprague's after deck. But the deep troughs made the landing craft go up and down like a broken elevator. One second Poulos was eye-to-eye with the waterline; and the next he was staring into the startled faces of seamen waiting to grab him. The coxswain's timing was immaculate. He bumped his T against the Sprague's hull just as the two decks came even. This was it: one pass or tough shit.

Poulos reached out with both hands. If he missed he would be tossed into the water and either crushed between metal plates or slip under the waves and become mincemeat in the T's screws, neither of which had much to recommend it except a quick death. But strong arms grabbed Poulos's elbows and shoulders and yanked him over the rail just as the T dipped down again. The coxswain gave his engines full throttle. As he pulled away he shot a middle finger in the air.

"Friend of yours?" one of the deckhands asked.

With Poulos safely on the fantail, whoops of delight went up from sailors who won their bets that he would make it in time before the Sprague set course for the US. At reveille the odds were five to one he wouldn't turn up, but when the watch on the bridge spotted the T pounding toward them, the odds fell like an anchor. Nevertheless there were doubters who kept the betting going. They studied the size of the waves and decided only a dumbass would try leaping off a pendulating landing craft. But for the majority, Poulos's unexpected appearance on the high seas had the weight of mythology. He had already gained awed respect when he thumbed his nose at authority and still got the Silver Star. So when the crew saw the windblown, soaked figure hanging on for dear life, Poulos was elevated to legendary status. He had disappeared during one of the meanest storms in the Far East since the typhoon of '44, and appeared again like an apparition out of the overcast on a commandeered T. They were true believers now. Here was a sailor who could do anything, hold the seas or part them--whatever it took to get back aboard the Sprague. He was met with applause, back-slapping and cheering, except for Lt. Rauenzhan, the Exec, who met him in the midship's passageway.

"Where the fuck have you been?" he thundered. "All of WESPAC has been on full alert trying to chase you down."

Poulos placed his hand over his racing heart. The heady mix of surviving a harrowing journey plus receiving a wild ovation was making it hard to talk. Between breaths, he said, "Me, sir?"

"Who do you suppose? Everyone else is on board and accounted for. The Captain was afraid you had fallen into the drink like Clayton. How do you think that would have looked in the press? They'd start calling us the drowning ship. I haven't seen the old man this worried since we ran aground."

"Sorry, Lieutenant."

"If it wasn't for that fucking Silver Star you'd get a court-martial, you know that? We should have weighed anchor a half hour ago."

Poulos stood on the deck shivering.

"What's the matter?"

"Is it all right to change into some dry clothes, sir?"

Rauenzahn finally looked at how soggy Poulos was. "Get the fuck below and clean up."

The duty bos'n piped sea detail, and the Sprague's new screws vibrated the aft deck plates. Poulos walked forward, grabbing braces and pipes and hatch wheels as the Sprague pitched and rolled her way out of the bay and into open water. Radinger was waiting in the midship's passageway; his chubby legs spread to maintain balance. He had an expression on his face that was difficult to read.

"I've witnessed a lot of things in this man's navy but this is the first time I've seen a ship kept waiting for a fucking seaman."

"It was nice of the Captain."

"Nice?" Radinger snapped. "He thought you drowned, which would have suited me fine, but I know where you were."

"You do?" Poulos asked in all innocence.

"Don't toy with me, Poulos. You were screwing that nurse. She must have been something special to risk missing a ride home."

"I wasn't with her, Lieutenant. I told you, she went back to the states."

"Oh, yeah? And if you weren't screwing her, who then? Some horizontal Jap pussy?"

Poulos decided the time had come to turn over a new leaf with his division officer and try sincerity. "To be completely honest with you, Lieutenant, I wasn't screwing anybody. I was seeing the psychiatrist who treated Clayton."

Radinger stared in wonder, as if he were watching a magician and thinking, how the fuck did he do that?

"Sure," the lieutenant replied, "and what was his name, Sigmund Freud?"

The Sprague took a southerly route out of storm range, to where the trade winds were gentle and the seas flat. The sun shone every day, warming the decks and turning the Pacific into a dazzling blue. Off-duty sailors removed their shirts and sunned themselves. Memories of the Far East dimmed inversely to the anticipation of going home. Two days after leaving port, the ship crossed the International Dateline at the 180th meridian, where ships usually set their clocks back 24 hours. Because the Sprague crossed the line on Sunday, sailors expected an extra day off, but the Captain waited to set the clocks till the ship docked at Midway Island a day later, on Monday.

Poulos complained to Browning. "Did you expect the navy to give us two days off in a row?"

"It doesn't matter anyway. Ernie and I still have to type up 237 certificates for crossing the Dateline." It was a tedious job even if it was good for crew morale. The certificates were printed on heavy paper suitable for framing and were difficult to roll around the platen. Poulos filled his waste basket with frequent mistakes typing in names above an illustration of Neptune riding a dolphin and brandishing a trident with arrow-shaped tips.

While the Sprague reprovisioned, the sailors went ashore on the tiny island and chased earth-bound goony birds that bobbed and weaved like inmates in an insane asylum. And why not? Anyone would have to be crazy living on this Godforsaken piece of barren real estate, including the small marine garrison stationed there. Midway was but a minor interruption. The Sprague was back at sea in a matter of hours and set a course for the Hawaiian Islands, a much more hospitable environment. In the early morning hours of the fifth day out, a cluster of blue-green volcanic rises capped by crowns of cumulus clouds appeared on the horizon. As the Sprague plied closer, Poulos followed other sailors to the bow for an unobstructed view. Azure blue water whooshed by as the ship cut the sea in two. Awed by the tropical paradise, he wondered what went through the minds of Captain James Cook and his men when they first set eyes on these islands in 1778. Better yet, what went through the minds of the Polynesians when they first laid eyes on white men? One thing was certain, Hawaii was never the same after that.

The Sprague entered the narrow channel of Pearl Harbor in early afternoon, moving slowly, respectfully, past the the sunken Arizona, its rusted remains a ghostly presence felt by everyone on the destroyer. The Sprague docked alongside a pier in the South Loch under a brilliant sun. Officers wore khaki, enlisted men whites. Liberty was assigned by division; sailors lined up on the main deck and waited impatiently for the Sprague to tie up so they could be the first off. Alex stood in the doorway of the Ship's Office and watched the sailors crowd the gangway so they could run to the PX and buy cigarettes; then check out the American dames. The liberty-depleted ship was pleasantly quiet. Poulos sat down and put his feet on the desk.

Gildenhall came by and stuck his head in. "Going ashore?" he asked.

After Poulos was awarded the Silver Star, their positions had curiously reversed. Poulos was now a person of influence, while Gildenhall was still on Radinger's shitlist. The lieutenant was deferential, even awed, in front of the enlisted man.

"Later," Poulos replied. "I'm meeting Witter and Browning at the Royal Hawaiian. What about you?"

"I have the duty." He put his elbows on the door counter. "That was quite a jump you made. You could have fallen in and got cut up by the screws."

"I didn't have time to think about it."

"How come you missed the high-water warnings?"

"I was engrossed in a conversation with Clayton's psychiatrist." Poulos debated whether he should tell the officer about how profound it was, but decided that he no longer had that kind of intimacy with him.

"That's not what Radinger is saying about your last night in the Far East."

"Is he spreading crap about me?"

Gildenhall smiled. "Crap about a 14-year-old Japanese girl who was willing to do anything to satisfy you."

"He knows that's not true. Why is he doing this to me?"

"Maybe he wants some of your glamor to rub off on him."

"Tell him to rub up against Clark Gable."

"You're not reading this right. Everybody wants his hero to be a virile lover."

"Hero?" Poulos scoffed. "I spent the night on a transit ship with a bunch of drunks."

"Anyone watching you dangle from that LST will never buy that, even if it is true. They won't believe you risked your life for anything but a nubile piece of ass. The irony is that the more you deny it, the more convincing Radinger's shack-up story becomes. You should be flattered."

"How can I be flattered by a lie?"

"Sometimes it's better to ignore a lie than try to correct it. What you have created is a legend. And a legend is nothing more than an exaggeration of the truth. Where's the harm in that?"

Poulos showered and changed into his whites. He went ashore and took a green and blue taxi to the Royal Hawaiian, ruminating over his conversation with Gildenhall. He sat with the window rolled down and took in the smells as well as the sights of the palm-lined avenues; the luxuriant shrubs and the flowers growing in colorful profusion everywhere he looked. Back home these were delicate house plants carefully tended in small pots and placed in windows with a southern exposure; here they were as ordinary as weeds. The thoughts going through his head were like that too--weedy and in need of cultivation. After his session with Steiner, Poulos felt obliged to keep Clayton's memory alive, but it was no longer fashionable to talk about him. According to Gildenhall, Poulos was now a hero and heroes did not express self-doubt.

The taxi turned off Kalakaua Avenue onto the curved drive of the pink-colored Royal Hawaiian. A Polynesian doorman in a gray uniform and white gloves opened the door and greeted Poulos with a cheery "Aloha!" He walked through the airy lobby to the wide expanse of terrace that opened out on the white sands of Waikiki beach and the blue waters of Mamala Bay. It was a gorgeous afternoon and Poulos walked along the beach to get a better view of Diamond Head. He could feel the heat of the sand through his shoes. Here and there sunbathers were lying on towels but Waikiki was not crowded. He walked by an elderly woman in a canvas recliner.

"Yoohoo," she called out to Poulos. "I always ask sailors where they're from."

"Minnesota."

"So am I!"

Small world Poulos thought to himself. "Are you on vacation?"

"Oh no, I live here."

"How long?"

"Twenty-seven years next March."

Poulos smiled. So much for small world. He waved goodby and

continued his stroll, but closer to the water. The gentle surf caressed the beach before falling back, leaving a smooth coat of firm wet sand to walk on. When he reached the Moana Hotel he crossed over to Kalakaua Avenue and followed the sidewalk back to the Royal Hawaiian. A trolley passed him. It was a quiet street.

He sat on a leather chair in the lobby, crossed one leg over the other, rested his hat on his knee, and waited for Witter and Browning to show up. They were late, having taken in the sights of Oahu on a tour bus including a visit to the Dole pineapple plantation up the valley.

Before dinner they drank fruit-filled cocktails on the terrace overlooking the beach. It was the most spectacular setting they had ever experienced. Poulos wondered what it would be like to live here permanently, like that old woman from Minnesota. He wondered if, after 27 years, she was bored by the unrelenting beauty, and that's why she spent her time looking for sailors from Minnesota.

They took a taxi into Honolulu and found a movie theater featuring the film everyone was talking about, From Here to Eternity. The beach scene where Deborah Kerr told Burt Lancaster that she had never been kissed like this before was so goddamn passionate they squirmed in their seats.

"I wonder what beach that was filmed at?" Browning asked afterward.

"Somewhere near the blowhole," Witter said. "Remember we stopped there?"

"Oh yeah. I'd like to pay my respects to the sand that she was lying on."

"Maybe they'll put up a shrine to mark the spot," Witter said.

"What did you think of Sinatra?"

"Not bad for a crooner. Maybe he'll get an Oscar."

"No, that skinny guy should get one," Browning said.

"Montgomery Clift? Very intense."

"I liked Burt Lancaster," Poulos said to Witter. "You look like him."

"Me?" Witter said, definitely flattered.

"Except for the teeth. But you're the same build, and your hair waves like his."

"Wasn't that something the way he took that fifty-caliber machine gun and shot down the Jap Zero from the roof of Schofield Barracks?" Browning said.

"That was a BAR," Witter replied. "Nobody can fire a fifty caliber machine gun from the hip, not even Burt Lancaster."

They had overnight passes and rented a cabin at the Comstock Hotel

Apartments across from the Royal Hawaiian. There were no windows, only openings in the wall protected by wide overhangs and shutters, and a roof of palm fronds, but they liked the rattan furniture and grass mats. Before turning in, they went down the block to the Merry-Go-Round Bar for a beer and ran into Carter, a career petty officer from the Sprague. Petty officers didn't mix much with enlisted men unless they felt like it. Carter had the smooth-faced vacuity of a California beach bum. His identical twin brother dated Ann Blythe, and he liked to brag about the time the diminutive actress ran up to him in the lobby of the Roosevelt hotel and kissed him before realizing he was the other twin.

Browning let it slip where they were staying. Half an hour after returning to the Comstock, there was a pounding on the door and Carter walked in carrying a shiny pastel-pink shopping bag with a rolled-paper handle and the Royal Hawaiian logo printed on the side.

"I just made it to the gift shop before they closed." He reached in the bag and removed a frosted green bottle of Remy Martin Cognac and four snifter glasses wrapped in white tissue paper.

"What's all that for?" Browning asked.

"I came to celebrate."

Poulos found it hard to hide his disapproval. It was late and he wanted to sleep. "Celebrate what?"

Carter unwrapped the glasses and handed them out. "Your safe return to the Sprague that won me two-hundred bucks."

Browning was impressed. "That's nearly three month's pay!"

"For you maybe." Carter smiled broadly. "I placed my bet that Poulos would make it back when the odds were still five to one."

"What's in your breast pocket?" Browning asked.

"Havanas," Carter replied. "I couldn't afford a whole box, so I got four." He passed these around and opened the bottle. He poured an inch into the bottoms of the belled glasses. "Nectar of the gods," he said and swished his Cognac before sipping it. A film of oil clung to the sides.

They lit their cigars and in a few minutes the room was thick with smoke.

"Those fucking Cubans really know how to make cigars." Carter leaned back in his chair and blew smoke toward the thatched ceiling.

Browning studied the bottle on the coffee table. "Ree-mee Martin?"

Chambers corrected him, using French pronunciation.

Browning tilted his head to show how impressed he was. "What does VSOP stand for?"

"Very Superior Old Pale."

"No shit."

Carter lifted his glass to Poulos. "A votre sante!"

"Isn't it kind of late for boozing?"

Carter's feelings were hurt. "Cognac is not booze."

"I'd like to turn in."

Carter looked around as if he couldn't believe his ears. "So the hero wants to turn in. Tell me, Browning, and you too, Witter, did either one of you turn in the night Poulos was screwing that Jap virgin?"

"Now she's a virgin?"

"While you were in the sack with her I was in CIC monitoring WESPAC traffic."

"I was reading signal lights on the bridge," Witter said.

"And I was verifying ship positions in the whole fucking bay," Browning said.

There followed a silence of heightened expectation as they waited for Poulos to describe the terrific screw that caused them to stay up all night.

"Well?"

"Well what?"

"Was she worth it?"

The very same question asked by Scotty on the rickshaw ride back from Mamma Naffi's echoed in Poulos's head. "Yeah," he said again, "she was worth it."

The sailors returned from liberty wearing leis and the compartments were quickly overpowered by the sweet smell of gardenias draped over racks. Some even reported for duty wearing the leis until the Captain got on the PA system and ordered them tossed overboard before "the entire crew gets sick from this stinking smell." There were groans and bitching and tears of sad farewell as the Sprague's wake became a trail of fading blossoms. A few wags imitated the twanging of ukeleles by pinching their noses and exhaling the Hawaiian love song through their nostrils.

The sun sank slowly in the west and, by nightfall, the pleasant memories of Hawaii were replaced by the still more pleasant thoughts of home. Three days later the flat horizon of the vast Pacific took on a subtle bumpiness in the east. California lay ahead. The Sprague went to quarter speed as she approached coastal waters, and spent the last night out in a holding pattern between Santa Catalina and San Clemente Island so that she could enter San Diego Bay at midmorning.

A big homecoming was planned. The Sprague would dock at the foot of West Broadway so that wives, children and girlfriends could greet their loved ones. The decks were already shipshape because of the cleanup for the award ceremony in the Yokosuka drydock, and only a little touch-up painting and brass polishing were needed. The sailors got out their blues and waxed their shoes to yet another high shine. Those who could be spared stood in neat rows on the main and O1 decks. An aerial photographer in a Piper Cub followed the Sprague through the channel and took pictures that would later be on sale in the wardroom.

The day was slightly overcast but mild; the channel waters as smooth as glass. The Sprague moved at three knots, just enough to maintain headway. Closing in was the San Diego skyline and the tree-lined boulevard of West Broadway. Poulos was on the bridge. The Captain had ordered him to stand by with his Silver Star in case a local photographer wanted shots.

The lines went out and the Sprague gently bumped the pier. A clot of greeters standing behind a chain link fence waved and shouted names of sailors who stood on the maindeck waved and shouted in return. The gangway went out and there was a surge that brought the two groups together in a crush of joyful reunion. Poulos guessed that the women who got hugged were wives, and those who were lifted off the ground and spun around were girlfriends.

Blessing met a tall, handsome woman and two impish boys who pulled on their dad's trouser leg while he kissed his wife. Porteous ran his palms up and down the ass of a girl who looked to be still in her teens. Radinger was carefully embracing a reedy woman who was perfectly turned out in a white hat and gloves, and a dress appropriately of navy blue.

He studied them with sustained curiosity, the fat lieutenant handling his skinny wife as he would a limited-edition porcelain figurine. Guess who steers the helm in that family.

Witter joined Poulos on the bridge. "Look," he said, pointing to Browning who was surrounded by his parents and a younger brother. They had driven down from Boring, Oregon, to meet the ship.

Browning was moving his fingers rapidly and for a moment Poulos thought he was drumming to an imaginary riff but he was actually using sign language.

"Did you know A. John had a deaf brother?" Witter said.

"I didn't even know he had a brother," Poulos replied.

Browning noticed Poulos and Witter watching and gave them the thumbs up.

"Tough, isn't it?" Witter said.

"What's tough?"

"Not having someone meet you. I have to go all the way to Toledo."

"It's nice to see Browning close to his family." Maybe that's what was bothering Poulos. He wasn't close to his parents the way Browning was. In fact, he wasn't close to anybody. It was hard to admit, but he could not think of a single soul who would care about him enough to meet his ship the way Browning's family did.

He climbed onto the flagbag and thought about his mother and father, his uncle, and his wife whom he abandoned. This was his family, well, not exactly that, more a collection of non-sequitors. A family is what Browning had, parents shedding tears of happiness to see their son again, and an obviously proud younger brother.

Who did Poulos have? Uncle Gus: the last person on earth he wanted to see. Mary Lou: the last person on earth who wanted to see him. His mother: a baby burner. His father: keeper of his mother's dark secret. As much as he wanted to avoid facing the inevitable, the moment the Sprague touched American soil he knew he couldn't avoid the day of reckoning any longer. Minneapolis was three days away on a Greyhound bus--across the mountains rising from the valley of San Diego, through the desert and the great plains, and up the Mississippi River.

The Orient he had escaped to was but an interlude, a hiatus of hiding from a past that was finally catching up to him, as he knew it would, and he had to face it like the proverbial traveling salesman: nose to nose and belly to belly.

He wondered how it would all shake out.

THE CAR

The Greyhound bus turned into the depot on First Avenue North and drew alongside an angled platform at 6:30 a.m., right on time. The driver killed his Cummins Diesel and opened the door. Escaping air hissed out of the bus's compressors and Alex thought to himself, my sentiments exactly. He was stiff from sitting up for three days and two nights. He stood and pulled at his crotch. His uniform did not leave enough room where it counted most. After the long overnight ride from Kansas City he had to piss real bad. He got into the aisle and followed his fellow passengers--old people mostly--onto the platform.

Cold air greeted him. On the concrete wall above the platform, a big circular thermometer registered 18 degrees. When he left San Diego three days ago, it was in the seventies.

He shivered waiting for the driver to open the baggage compartment in the bus's underbelly. The driver slid suitcases onto the platform for passengers to help themselves. Alex's seabag came out last, of course. He threw it over his shoulder and went into the waiting room. Passengers dispersed through the main doors into the street, some alone, others with family or friends. He checked his seabag in a locker, went to the men's room, relieved himself at long last in a stained toilet, and washed his hands and face, looking in the mirror at the stubble on his cheeks. Then he went into the Depot Coffee Shop. He sat at the counter and ordered eggs, buttered toast, and coffee.

"Coffee right away, please," he asked the bone-thin waitress. She poured steaming coffee into a cup and brought it to him. She studied his ribbons, including his battle star. "Home on leave?"

"Just got in."

"How long you been gone?"

"Fourteen months."

After breakfast he retrieved his seabag and got out his peacoat. He turned it to face him, placed his arms into the armholes and flipped it over his head--a trick he learned to keep his talleywacker from getting tangled in the collar. That extra piece of drapery had long outlived its usefulness; in fact Alex wasn't even sure of its original purpose, unless it was to protect uniforms from oily braids sailors wore two hundred years ago. On windy days it flew up and smacked you on the back of the head.

He buttoned up, pulled his dress blue flat hat over his forehead and walked outside into the nippy air. He could see his breath. He was home all right. He went to the taxi stand and waited, his seabag at his side. Inside his bellbottoms, cold air crawled up all the way to his balls.

A yellow taxi finally pulled alongside. The cabby cracked his window. "You want that in the trunk?"

"It can ride with me." He slid his seabag along the back seat and climbed in.

"Where to?"

"3941 Xenwood, St. Louis Park."

"First or second alphabet?"

"First."

The cabbie drove up Hennepin Avenue, the same route Alex took home on the streetcar from the university. He turned right on West Lake Street and Alex looked for the Hasty Tasty Restaurant where he and Mary Lou had breakfast more than a year ago, their last meal together. He was surprised to see that the restaurant was not there, just a vacant lot.

"What happened to the Hasty Tasty?"

"Burned down last New Year's Eve. Big fire. You should have seen it."

Alex stared out the rear window as the taxi drove on, wondering if everything he came in contact with was somehow doomed for destruction.

His heart grew heavier as he passed other familiar sights--Lake Calhoun completely frozen over, Minikhada golf course, its fairways and greens dotted with dirty snow, the uneven assortment of stores and houses on Excelsior Boulevard and, finally, Lilac Lanes Shopping Center where his dad's candy store was located. As the taxi slowed for the intersection with Highway 100 Alex looked at the store front, its narrow windows decorated for Christmas. There was a little fake tree with ornaments and lots of red ribbon. That was new. Alex briefly wondered where his old man got that.

"Turn right at the next corner," he said to the driver. His pulse quickened as they came down Xenwood. Was there ever a time it did not.

The driver pulled up and Alex reached in his jumper pocket for some bills.

"Good luck, sailor," the driver said and drove away.

I'll need it, Alex thought. He stood on the sidewalk and looked at the house that held so many unpleasant memories. He noticed that the storms had been puttied and painted--one of those jobs he never quite got around to doing. His old man must have hired someone. Alex lugged his seabag by its handle to the back door and peered in the window. The kitchen light was on. His father was at the stove in his slippers and bathrobe. Alex tapped on the glass. His father came to the door and opened it.

Alex hauled his seabag into the kitchen. The linoleum was sticky.

"Don't let the cold air in," his father said.

He propped his seabag against the dining room wall, next to the door leading up to his attic room, and laid his peacoat and hat over it. He noticed that the carpet needed vacuuming and the glass on the coffee table was covered with finger prints and fly-swat stains. He went to the kitchen table and sat down. The butter in the butter dish was soft and bits of crumbs were stuck to it. He couldn't understand why everything was so messy. His mother was always neat as a pin.

"You got my telegram?"

His father picked up a buff-colored half-sheet from the counter. "Came yesterday." He looked at his son as if finally acknowledging that he had been gone.

"You're thinner."

"Must be the uniform."

His father turned off the Calrod on the stove and poured steaming water into the drip coffee maker. He put white bread into the toaster and carved slices of kefalo tiri on a plate.

"You want breakfast?"

"I ate at the depot."

His father poured coffee and dosed it with cream and sugar. The toast popped up and he slathered it with butter. He began slurping and chewing. Even if Alex was hungry he would have lost his appetite by now.

"Food better there?"

"Where?"

"The depot."

Already, a put down. “So,” Alex said, changing the conversation away from him, “how are things at the candy store?"

"I decide to sell it."

"Sell it?" Alex was surprised. "How come?"

"Too much work at my age."

At any age, Alex thought. He couldn't imagine anyone with an ounce of brains buying that business. "It's going to be tough finding a buyer."

"You think so?"

"It's a small, one-man operation, Pop. You don't even have up-to-date equipment."

"I got good will. I sell that."

Alex didn't want to get in an argument so soon after getting home.

"Ok, Pop."

"So you think I can't sell it?"

"I didn't say that. I just think it will be hard."

"It's a good thing you weren't around to give me your expert advice. I have a buyer."

Alex was surprised. "Anyone I know?"

His father poured more coffee. "Sure, you know him. Tony Pappathos."

Alex could not believe what he just heard. It was a joke surely. He had to laugh.

"What so funny?"

"I know more about making candy than he does."

"You buy the store, then."

"Me? What would I do with it?"

"What you say Tony can't do."

Alex couldn't help but feel a twinge of jealousy. "When is he taking over?"

"He work at the store now. I teach him the business and then he buy it on a contract for deed."

"Who's idea was that Christmas tree in the window, Tony's?"

His father nodded, pleased. "You see it? He's a clever boy, that Tony. He even fix the storm windows."

"Tony is just trying to show me up. Can't you see through him, Pop? He doesn't have a life of his own so he takes over mine."

"You don't want it, so why shouldn't he?"

Alex worked to calm himself. His father was right. He left a vacuum and Tony filled it. Simple as that. "Where's mom? Isn't she up yet?"

"You take a long time to bring up your mother."

"That was a bombshell about the store you just dropped."

"I drop another one."

"What now?"

"Your mother is in a nursing home."

Alex stared at his father.

"Why you act so surprise? You forgot the night you tell us you leave for the navy? You forgot how bad she cry, how hard she shake?"

No wonder the house was in such a mess. No one to clean it. "Why didn't you write and tell me?"

"What you do?"

"I could have applied for a hardship discharge."

"Hardship?" his father snapped. "You even know what that mean?"

Alex rubbed his forehead. He was getting a headache. "How is she?"

"She has to have 24-hour care."

"How can you afford that?"

"Uncle Gus help." His father looked down at his coffee. It was shameful that he could not afford to take care of his own wife.

"Can I see her?"

"You have to ask to see your mother?"

"Just tell me where she is."

"Brook View. Down the block on thirty-nine street after you cross Alabama."

"I don't remember a nursing home that close by."

"Who sees anything until they need it?"

"Can I have the car keys?"

"What for?"

"To see mom!"

"The navy not make you tough enough to walk?"

Alex went for his hat and coat. He wasn't with his father a half hour and already he had to get out of the house.

Hoping to prove his father wrong, hoping the nursing home wasn't where he said it was, unwilling to admit that he was shivering not from the cold but from the apprehension of seeing his mother again, with his hands thrust deep in his pockets, he trudged past snug bungalows on frozen lawns, crossing Yosemite, Zarthan, and Alabama--the first street of the second alphabet--where 39th dead ended at the bottom of a downgrade. At the end of the street, hidden behind a row of houses, was a plain one-story, cinder-block building with a flat roof. Sure enough, a sign above the entrance read Brook View Nursing Home. His old man was right after all.

Alex stood in front, looking at the windows frosted over from too much indoor humidity, at the metal flashing with peeling paint, at the chain link fence separating an asphalt parking lot from the private lawn next door. Calling it Brook View was the height of ostentation--forget that the nursing home borrowed its name from Minnehaha Creek which meandered in frozen stillness through a field of prairie grass on the other side of the dead end.

The cold forced him, finally, to walk up the narrow sidewalk to the front door and push it open. If anything, the interior was more unwelcoming than the exterior. He was in a lounge of sorts with a sorry collection of potted plants and motel-style furniture. Ahead was a long, poorly lit hallway with an uneven linoleum floor. He followed it, peeking into each room that he passed--spartan spaces with two beds and a curtain between, filled with personal mementos but not patients. Where the hell was everybody?

At the end of the hallway he found an eating area--you couldn't grace it by calling it a dining room--and there they were: a bunch of old, stooped people having breakfast at small square tables. The scene gave Alex a start. White-haired men and women with bibs tied around their necks were gumming scrambled eggs and porridge from plastic dishes on plastic trays. There wasn't a sound except masticating.

Suddenly, a sharp, high-pitched voice cried out, "Is it free, nursie? Is it free?"

A supervisor who was cutting up eggs for a patient eyed Alex curiously. She was heavy-set. Her nurse's cap was pinned on crooked. "No visitors till after breakfast."

"I came to see my mother."

"What's her name?"

"Chrysoula Poulos."

"Chrissie?" she asked, surprised. "She told me her son was dead."

Alex tried to smile. The final rejection, telling everybody my son is dead. All he could say was, "She's a great kidder, my mother."

Confusion marked the supervisor's features. "Well, she's over there." She pointed to an emaciated figure whom Alex would not have recognized. She was tied with a padded belt around the waist to a wheelchair, and bent over so far her face was nearly into her breakfast tray.

"Why is she sitting alone?"

The supervisor lowered her voice. "The other residents don't like to eat with her."

"Residents?"

"We don't call them patients."

"How about inmates?" He walked over to her table and sat next to her.

"Feed her while you're at it," the supervisor ordered. If Chrissie had a son, after all, let him help out. "We usually don't get around to Chrissie till the others have finished."

"Can't she feed herself?"

"Look at her."

Alex was engulfed with sadness. "Her food must be getting cold."

"We do the best we can."

Her hair was pulled into a tight ponytail by a rubber band, and the bridge of her glasses was taped to her nose to keep them from slipping down. Her arms lay across her lap like sticks of kindling. She was staring unblinking at a breakfast of orange juice, stiff scrambled eggs, oatmeal congealed in milk, and black coffee.

"Ma," he said gently.

She cocked her head sideways the way a robin listens for worms. She looked at him suspiciously as she would a stranger.

"It's me...Alex."

The synapses in her brain sorted through data until she realized who it was.

"Eisai arga." She wanted to know why he was late.

"Ma, I've been gone more than a year."

She lifted her head up as far as it would go, which wasn't much, and scrutinized his uniform out of the corners of her eyes. "It's Monday?" she asked.

"Monday?"

"You go to navy training."

"Yes," he said, resignedly, "it's Monday. Here, drink your juice." He directed a bendable plastic straw to her lips. She opened her mouth and bit down, clenching it firmly in her teeth.

He tried to pull it free. "Let go, ma."

The supervisor came over. "Chrissie does that all the time. Now you see why the others don't want to eat with her." The nurse bent down and spoke into his mother's face. "We know that isn't right, don't we, Chrissie?"

"Does she understand?"

"She understands, all right." The supervisor started yanking on the straw. "Stop biting, Chrissie!"

"Maybe if you didn't call her Chrissie."

The supervisor straightened. "What would you prefer, Her Majesty?" She walked away.

"That supervisor is a real stinker, isn't she?" he whispered to his mother.

Relieved that someone was finally taking her side, she relaxed her hold on the straw and began sipping. As he cut up her eggs, he thought, if I ever get like this, kill me.

After breakfast, he wheeled his mother to her room, number five. Her bed was next to a drafty window looking out on the parking lot. Personal items in the room were those of his mother's roommate, Ellie, according to the name inked on a wide piece of white medical tape stuck to the headboard of Bed 1. There were framed family pictures on the dresser, a sampler on the wall that read "God Bless Our Home", and a yellow afghan folded over the back of a chair.

All that he recognized of his mother's was her eikonostasi with its small rendering of Jesus and a votive candle. It sat on the floor in a corner. Why didn't someone hang it for her?

Alex leaned on the window ledge and studied her sagging against the foam rubber restraint around her middle. She had to tilt her head at an awkward angle in order to look at him. As if it was getting too heavy to hold up, she rested her head on her shoulder. Alex wondered what, if anything, was going on inside that pressed-down cranium of hers.

He wanted to unload his secret, let her know that he knew she burned his hand, but it was like beating a dead horse. She was nothing now, not an adversary, not someone he wanted to get even with, not even a human being. What sat there, helpless and hapless, was withered tissue and brittle bone, a mummy not yet mummified.

He left the nursing home when his father showed up. He walked back to the house, unpacked, showered and shaved, and put on civvies from his closet. He was pleased to see that his old clothes hung loosely on him. He was in better shape now than when he went in the navy. The car keys were in the kitchen drawer where his father always left them. He went outside wearing his peacoat and opened the garage. His father didn't use the station wagon much in winter and so he was relieved that the engine caught after the third try. The car needed gas and air. He stopped at a service station and then drove to the Nicollet Apartments. He circled the block and parked in the back lot where he had helped Mary Lou unload her mattress. He got out, went to the rear entrance and rang the intercom to the caretaker's apartment.

"I'm looking for Mary Lou Stachich," he said to the disembodied voice.

"She moved out months ago."

"How many?"

"Six, maybe eight."

"Did she leave a forwarding address?"

"Not with me."

Alex got in the car and drove to Patty's house in Richfield, passing slowly, trying to see into the big picture window. It didn't look as if anyone was home. He despised its cookie-cutter architecture, not bothering to consider whether his attitude had anything to do with the fact that he never felt welcome there. He made a U-turn at the intersection and drove past the house one more time, "Sayonara," he said waving it a final goodby.

He stopped at a Sinclair station on West Lake Street to use the pay phone. He had called the newspaper so many times he knew the number by heart. An unfamiliar woman's voice said, "Mr. Rand's office."

"Mary Lou Stachich, please."

"She doesn't work here anymore."

"Do you know how I can reach her?"

"May I ask who is inquiring?" The voice was guarded.

"A friend, Alex Poulos."

The voice became friendly "I remember you."

"Who is this?"

"Donna Redpath. You came by the office once and Mary Lou introduced us."

Alex struggled with his memory. He began to recall a stringy blonde with a mouthy smile who couldn't take her eyes off him. "Aren't you tall and blonde?"

"You remember," she said, obviously pleased.

"I never forget a pretty face." He figured a little blandishment couldn't hurt.

"Did you two split up?" There was a sense of expectancy in her question.

"I went in the navy and we lost track of each other."

"Gee, that's too bad."

"Do you know where I can find her?"

"She talked about going to school to get a degree. She said she wanted to better herself."

"Where?"

"I don't know, but Mr. Rand wrote a letter of reference for her."

"Can you tell me who it was written to?"

There was a moment's hesitation. "Gee, I don't think I can."

"May I talk to him?"

"He's in New York for an ANPA conference."

Damn! he thought, I'm so close. "Donna, I have to go back to my ship in a few days. This is the only chance I'll have to find Mary Lou. Can't you help me?"

"I really shouldn't..."

"Please?"

Alex waited, holding his breath.

Donna came back on the line. "The letter was addressed to the Chancellor of Bemidji State Teachers College."

He couldn't thank her enough.

He drove home and put the car away before his father returned. He walked to the Citizens State Bank across Excelsior Boulevard from the strip mall where the candy store was located.

"I want to close out my savings account," he told the receptionist.

She directed him to a loan officer at a desk behind a low-railed partition. He was portly with the demeanor of a mortician. "You'll forfeit your interest for six months," he warned.

"How much?"

He punched the keys on his adding machine. "Sixteen dollars and twenty-two cents."

"I need the money to buy a car."

The officer looked at the balance sheet in Alex's folder. "You were saving $50 a month out of your navy pay. With two-and-a-half per cent compound interest your account is now worth..." the machine clicked out a total. "$731.27."

"Fine."

"May I recommend retaining the $31.27 to keep the account open? You may want to start saving again."

"Not in Minneapolis."

The officer showed disappointment as he cancelled the account. "Shall I make out a bank draft?"

"Cash."

"That's a lot of money to carry around," he cautioned.

"It won't be in my pocket very long." Alex was given a form to sign and directed to a teller who counted out fourteen fifty-dollar bills, three tens, a one, and change. He had never seen so much cash before. He folded the paper money inside his wallet and dropped the coins into his pocket. He left the bank and walked to a bus stop, suspecting everyone who passed him of being a robber. He waited in the cold twenty-five minutes, shifting his feet and crunching his chin into his jacket. The sun was setting when he got off the bus at 16th and Hennepin, in front of Hansord Pontiac.

"I want to buy a car," he said to the first sales person who bothered to look at him, a man as old as his father with slicked-down, dishpan-gray hair.

He pumped Alex's hand. "Joe Fugle's the tag and selling cars is my bag." He pointed to a showroom full of glistening sheet metal and chrome.

"I can't afford a new car."

"Let me get my overcoat."

They went out to the lot where Alex spotted a late-model pastel-pink Chieftain convertible with a light gray top and a hood ornament of an Indian chief whose chrome headdress swept all the way back to the windshield wipers.

Fugle followed his gaze. "Leather chairs. Driven by the boss's wife. Only 8,000 loving miles."

Now that he had made the decision to buy a car, Alex was thinking beyond Bemidji. Instead of taking a Greyhound, he now could drive to Mills Gap and then cross-country back to San Diego where he would sell it. A ragtop would be easy to peddle in Southern California. "How much?"

"Yours for only nine-ninety-five."

Alex whewed.

Fugle smiled confidently. "We have the best financing in town."

"I'm home on leave from the navy."

Fugle finally took note of Alex's peacoat. "Have a relative co-sign the note, your father maybe."

Sure, Alex thought, in a minute. "What have you got that's cheaper?"

Overhead display lights suddenly came on and reflected off the shiny hoods lined up in neat rows. They walked up and down, turning the night air steamy white as they exhaled.

"Just what are you looking for?"

"A reliable battery, an engine that doesn't burn oil, good tires, a radio, and a style that doesn't look like a preacher drove it."

Fugle pointed to a tan, forty-six Pontiac coupe. "There she is. One of our post-war models. Just 33,000 miles, good rubber and battery, seat covers and mats, and a Philco pushbutton that locks in six stations."

"How much?"

"Six-ninety-five."

Fugle started up the engine and Alex drove the car around the block until the heater warmed his ankles. He liked the way it ran. He also like the way Fugle referred to the car as a she, just like the Sprague. Alex could talk to her on the long journey that lay ahead.

They went inside to see the sales manager. Alex peeled off twelve fifties and smacked them on the manager's desk.

"Take it or leave it."

The manager took it.

Alex drove out of the lot pleased with the deal but when he reached

Lake Street he began having doubts. Should he have plunked down five hundred and negotiated from there? He asked his new possession, his tan Pontiac coupe with seat covers and floormats, Philco radio and antenna on the fender, and she purred back at him that he did just fine.

He drove past the empty lot where the Hasty Tasty once stood and he didn't even notice. He spotted a Standard Station with a sign that advertised 5 Gallons for $1 and had the tank filled. Alex asked the uniformed attendant for a map of Minnesota.

Then he drove back to his father's house.

THE SEARCH

While waiting for the car to warm up in his father's driveway, Alex unfolded his road map and studied the route he would take to Bemidji, a two-hundred-fifty mile trip. It was 8:30 a.m. He could be there by early afternoon if he didn't dawdle. He figured he needed only one stop for food and gas and decided to make that Sauk Centre, the birthplace of Sinclair Lewis. He'd never been there before and thought it would be novel, he pardoned the expression, to drive up Main Street. He wasn't sure but he thought he spotted his father looking out of the living room window as he drove away.

His father was subdued the night before when Alex showed off his new car--not new in the literal sense but new in what it symbolized, independence and a clarity of purpose. There should have been congratulations to a son who walked right out of the house and bought a car. Isn't that what his old man always nagged him about--taking control of his life?

One by one the small towns fell behind him: Buffalo, Annandale, Paynesville. He decelerated to twenty-five miles an hour as he drove down main streets with the obligatory farm implement store, drug store, feed store, cafe, beer tavern, grain elevator and railroad depot; and speeded up to fifty again when the rolling farmland plowed for winter reappeared. Alex reached Sauk Centre at ten-thirty. He gassed up kaddy-corner from the Palmer House Hotel and asked the attendant where Sinclair Lewis once lived.

He followed the attendant's directions up Third Street to a small, turn-of-the-century prairie house in the shape of an L. A porch protected the front entrance, its posts decorated with lace brackets. There was no street number, and he wondered how mail was addressed to the people who lived here now--simply the Sinclair Lewis House?

A metal door on the foundation wall was black from coal dust. In his novel, Lewis vividly described his father banking the furnace fires at night, just the way Alex's father did when they lived in Waseca. No doubt the two basements were of the same vintage, dominated by a cast-iron furnace whose round, paper-wrapped ducts coursed across the ceiling like outsized octopus tentacles. Alex could still hear the clanking of the heavy grilled door when his father latched it shut and feel the heat of glowing embers pouring out of the furnace's belly. The mess made by coal dust and ashes must have driven his mother wild. He drove back to Main Street and headed north on 71 through Long Prairie, Wadena, and Park Rapids, the topography gradually altering from open farmland to thick stands of pine growing almost to the edge of the two-lane highway.

Alex pulled into town at two-thirty in the afternoon. Fish houses dotted Lake Bemidji's smoothly frozen surface. It had not yet snowed here, a dry winter so far. He crossed railroad tracks and drove past the concrete statues of Paul Bunyan and Babe the Blue Ox for which Bemidji was widely known, prime examples of naive art found in many rural American towns, crude and artless yet honest and straightforward. Paul had a barrel chest and broad shoulders but small, almost dainty, hands and feet. His red-and-black plaid shirt was garishly painted. On his head was a black cap that looked like something a French Legionnaire would wear. He sported a wide handlebar mustache and sideburns, and a two-bladed axe was at his side. Babe was painted in his traditional baby blue. He had long horns growing out of his head and a solid black nose. His contented gaze was more like that of a cow than an ox. The figures were huge; Paul was a good twenty feet tall. Alex had to admit that he liked them.

A block further was an arrowed road sign pointing to Bemidji State Teachers College. He turned on Birchmont Drive, a two-lane road that ran parallel to the lake's wooded shoreline. He parked along the curb, got out and stretched. Maybe he was imagining it, but he could feel Mary Lou's presence. He found the Bursar and Records office in the Manfred W. Deputy Hall and got in a line of students requesting copies of transcripts.

It was a slow process waiting for photostats to be made. Finally he was next.

"Name?" the clerk asked.

"I'm not a student here, but I'm looking for someone who is. Her name is Mary Lou Stachich." He had decided before entering the building that Mary Lou would continue using her maiden name. Not very likely, he reasoned, that she would use Poulos after what happened to her in the Greek church.

The clerk looked over Alex's shoulder at those who were in line behind him. "Would you move aside, please?" She consulted a woman sitting at a desk marked Registrar. A pencil was stuck in her hair.

She came over. "Whom are you looking for?"

"Mary Lou Stachich"

She pulled her pencil out and began writing on a pad. "Mary Lou..."

"S-t-a-c-h-i-c-h."`

"And who are you?"

"My name is Alex Poulos."

"What is your relationship to Miss..." she looked down at her pad "...Stachich?"

He wasn't sure how far to get into this. "We were good friends...once."

She gave him a frank look. "It's not our policy to give out information on students."

He leaned forward, hoping to evoke her sympathy. "We lost contact with each other when I went into the service."

She looked at his peacoat. "Navy?"

"Yes, ma'am."

"I lost a cousin in Korea," she said. "Marine. Inchon invasion."

She went to a stand-up file and opened the S drawer. She flicked through several 3x5 index cards. "No Stachich here."

"Maybe she's not registered this semester."

"She'd be here if she had gone to school at all this year."

Well, he thought, maybe she is using her married name. "How about looking up Poulos?"

"Poulos? Isn't that your name?"

Alex smiled apologetically. "We got married before I went into the service."

The registrar probably assumed it was one of those whirlwind weddings before shipping over. Close enough. She pulled open the P drawer and began sorting through the cards. "P-o-u-l-o-s?"

He nodded.

"Nothing under Poulos either."

He was confused. Donna Redpath sounded so convincing on the telephone. "Are you sure?"

"I am sure." The woman's patience was wearing thin, Korean veteran or no.

He thanked her and went outside. He was so certain he'd find Mary Lou he did not consider that his mission might end in failure. All the way to Bemidji he was carried along by the fantasy of watching her run to him just like the women who greeted their sailors when the Sprague docked in San Diego. Disconsolately, he buttoned his peacoat and walked down to the lakeshore. The sun was casting Surreal shadows of tree trunks and bare branches on the smooth ice. He sat on a park bench until he was chilled to the bone. He had to keep moving or freeze to death. He walked back to the campus, determined to check out every female until he was satisfied that Mary Lou was not among them. He stared hard at each girl he passed. On more than one occasion, a coed hurried her step, alarmed by the man with hunched shoulders and glaring eyes. He went from building to building, circling the campus until he felt his blood congealing. He was ready to go back to the car when, incredibly, he thought he saw her across the quadrangle, wearing an army surplus poncho, her face obscured by a fur-trimmed hood, running up the steps of Charles K. Sattgast Hall with books under her arm.

He raced across the frozen grass to catch up. As he pulled open the heavy metal door, he saw her go down a hallway and enter a classroom. A bell rang and the classroom door closed. Alex stood in front of the door resisting the urge to go in and check to see if in fact it was Mary Lou.

And if she was, what then? He had no idea how she would react upon seeing him, especially in front of a roomful of students. Better wait.

He unbuttoned his coat and paced up and down the hall like a zoo animal. It seemed an eternity when the bell finally rang fifty minutes later. He stood to one side as students filed out of the classroom, zipping or buttoning their coats and jackets for the plunge back into the icy cold. The room emptied and Mary Lou did not come out. He peeked inside, and there she was--talking to her professor, a middle-aged man wearing a cardigan, bow tie and pleated slacks. He was packing a briar pipe with tobacco from a black leather pouch.

Mary Lou was different. No wonder he wasn't sure he recognized her. Her flowing amber curls were cut short and her freckles were no longer hidden under layers of face powder. Also missing were rouge and mascara, not even lipstick. She wasn't plucking her eyebrows either. And where were the buttons and bows she loved to wear? Everything on her was army surplus--pants, boots, a formless khaki cable-knit sweater. Even so, the familiar ache in his groin came back. Mary Lou could cover herself with an awning and still arouse him. And, because the interplay with the professor was obviously deeper than a discussion of next week's term paper, he felt a pang of jealousy as well.

As he stood in the doorway staring, she felt his alien presence and turned. She stopped talking in mid-sentence. Shock froze her mouth open. The air was suddenly filled with anxiety and apprehension.

The professor studied Alex with pedagogic thoroughness. He exchanged a meaningful glance with Mary Lou and she nodded. She must have told him about Alex.

The professor slipped his briar into his sweater pocket and stepped protectively close to her. "Keep your distance or I'll call the campus police."

Alex was in no mood for phony heroics. "Don't you have a class to teach?"

Mary Lou grabbed the professor's arm before an aggressive move could be made. "He has a hard time being serious."

"Why are you referring to me in the third person? I'm standing right here aren't I?"

"See what I mean?" Her eyes were unforgiving. "How did you find me?"

"Donna Redpath. She looked up the letter of recommendation Mr. Rand wrote for you. Can I come in?" There was no reply and so he took that as a conditional yes. He stepped into the classroom.

"Are you alone?"

He glanced behind him. "Nobody, not even the campus police. Look in the hall if you don't trust me." When he said that, he realized there was no earthly reason why she should trust him.

"You show up out of nowhere and expect me to trust you? Where have you been for god's sake?"

"In the Navy.

"To see the world?" Her voice dripped with sarcasm.

"To run away," he said as truthfully as he knew how.

"You didn't run far enough."

"Is Korea far enough?"

That seemed to temper her a little but she was still reacting to a year of pent-up fury. "Not if you were able to find me."

"Now that I have, can we go somewhere and talk, a coffee shop maybe?"

The professor finally asserted himself. "Whatever you have to say, you can say in front of me."

"It's all right, Clark."

So his name was Clark.

"You said yourself that you can't trust him."

"I did once," Mary Lou said plaintively.

The professor gathered his notes from the lectern and stuffed them into his briefcase. "I'll be in my office if you need me," he said, obviously hoping he would be.

Alex stepped aside to let him pass and felt the animus flowing from his pores. After he left the room, trailing his irritation behind him, Alex asked, "Clark what?"

"Chambers. He teaches educational psychology."

"Known him long?"

"Long enough."

Alex could guess what that meant. He began walking down the center aisle between rows of student chairs.

Mary Lou's cold stare stopped him halfway. "Don't think you can get friendly just because we're alone."

"I thought it might be easier if I didn't have to shout across the room."

"You exaggerate, as usual."

"You told me a million times not to exaggerate." He hoped for a smile but all he got was stony silence. "You've changed."

"You noticed?"

"How could I not notice? You're dressed like an anarchist."

She spread her arms as though doing a fashion shoot. "This is campus de riguer."

"Not the Mary Lou I remember."

"The Mary Lou you remember died in the Greek church, or has your convenient memory helped you forget what I went through that Sunday, the curse your mother laid on me, the scratch she put on my face..."

It was then that Alex noticed the fine white line cutting through the freckles on her cheek.

"Why didn't you leave with me that Sunday when I asked you, begged you, to come with me, escape from that madhouse of a church? The last memory I have of you is holding your mother's nose."

It was a painful memory but he promised himself that he would face up to everything. "Nothing that I say can ever change what I did but I want you to know that I am no longer that person."

"Why should that even matter? It's too late."

"I know, but I want to tell you that after you ran out of the church, I looked for your wedding ring."

She sighed. "I threw it away because it no longer meant anything to me."

"It meant something to me."

"Did you find it?"

"Under the altar. I lifted the linen. It was like looking under a woman's skirt."

Mary Lou managed a sardonic parting of the lips. "I'll bet that priest had a fit."

"He had a fit, all right." Alex took an exploratory step forward. This time he was not rebuffed.

"Where did you go?" he asked. "I got in the van and drove all over looking for you. I stopped at your apartment and sat on the stoop, watching the streetcars go by, hoping you'd get off the next one."

"You expected me to take a streetcar with a bloody face and eyes nearly swollen shut from crying? A policeman picked me up. He thought I had been attacked. He was right about that. He wanted to take me to the hospital but I asked him to take me to St. Cecilia's."

"So that's where you went."

"Even Charlie Chan's number one son could have figured that out."

"I wasn't thinking clearly that day."

"Nobody was."

"Why didn't you go to Patty's?"

"How could I face my sister? She warned me about marrying you and she was right. The nuns in the convent took care of me. Without them I wouldn't be here today. I'd be in a mental institution or, worse, buried in a public cemetery."

"A public cemetery?"

"In case you didn't know, that's where Catholics go when they commit suicide."

"Mary Lou..."

"You think I'm joking? I wanted to die. I wouldn't eat. All I did was stare at the wall. The nuns held my hand to help me sleep because I was having terrible nightmares. A week passed before I even knew what day it was." Mary Lou gripped her arms as if warding off a chill. "If you had found me walking the streets before the officer did, what would you have done?"

"I don't know."

"It's just as well, then."

Alex wasn't sure if Mary Lou wanted to hear his side, but he had to get it off his chest. "After you didn't show up at your apartment, I drove around till I ran out of gas. I pulled off the road and sat in the van till it got dark. Then I began seeing my reflection on the windshield every time a car went by and, I thought, who the hell is this person anyway? My mind had gone blank. I didn't know who I was anymore. My brain had erased all of its memory like a tape, and it scared the hell out of me. I sat in the van for hours before I could remember who I was and what I was doing there. I finally understood that I had to do something with my life or, like you felt, end it. So that Monday night at my naval reserve meeting I went to the office and signed up for active duty." Alex paused to laugh at the recollection. "The duty yeoman thought I was crazy because I had a student deferment, but the Base Commander signed my orders right away. He didn't want to let a live one slip away. Friday morning at five o'clock I was on a train to Pier 91 in Seattle."

"How did your mother deal with that?"

"It broke her health. She's in a nursing home."

Mary Lou was unphased. "I can't feel anything for her."

"I understand."

"No, Alex," she contradicted, "I don't think you do, not yet anyway. Not until I tell you what happened to me after I left the convent. I thought long and hard about staying there. I couldn't go back to work, I couldn't even face Patty. Mr. Rand was unbelievably patient. He made sure my salary was paid while I was in the convent, waiting for me to decide what I wanted to do. At first I believed I could lead a life of service by becoming a lay nun but the better I got, the more I realized I did not have the commitment. Not just my face was scarred, Alex, my soul was, too. I didn't realize how much I had changed. I was so naive and trusting before..." Mary Lou became lost in the memory of the way it was. Her eyes warmed but then they hardened again as she continued her story. "So, as I said, I went back to the old life, returned to my job a sadder and wiser woman, or so I thought."

"What happened?"

Mary Lou waved her hand in the air like someone not wanting to be interrupted. "One day a process server turned up at work--out of the blue. He handed me a subpoena as if I were a common criminal. I had to appear in civil court and tell the judge why my marriage to you should not be ended. Can you imagine? I had to come to your defense as if I were the one who wanted to preserve our marriage. The lawyer made it appear as if the responsibility was on my shoulders, probably to make sure I wouldn't have a financial hold over you. The marriage was dissolved just like that!" She snapped her fingers.

Alex was totally confused. "Aren't we still married?"

She stared at him. "Haven't you talked to your uncle?"

"I haven't been in touch with him at all. Uncle Gus was behind this?"

"Except that he paid other people to do his dirty work." She began crying. "I was all alone, Alex, how could I fight him without you? He had everything, I had nothing. He won, I lost."

"We both lost."

"You don't know the half of it. What frightened me when you turned up was that if you could find me so can your uncle."

"You're not even registered."

"Yes I am."

"I checked at the Records Office. No Stachich, not even Poulos."

"It's Wolinski, my mother's maiden name. I had it legally changed when I moved here."

"Why did you do that?"

Mary Lou set her jaw defiantly. "To get away from your uncle! You've never been stalked, Alex. You've never had to look out your front door and see a man sitting in a car. When you go to work he follows you and parks outside your office. And when you go home at night, he follows you back."

"Who was he?"

"A private detective. Some chain-smoking meathead your uncle hired."

"What did he want?"

"Not what. Who."

It took a while to sink in, like something trapped in quicksand. "Oh lord..."

"Your uncle wasn't satisfied enough that he annulled our marriage. He also wanted to take my baby from me."

Now Alex understood undeniably that he had abandoned Mary Lou, left her vulnerable and alone. "I tried to write you...ask you.... I started a letter a dozen times but I could never finish it."

"The story of your life."

His lips trembled fighting back tears. "Was it a boy or a girl?"

"A boy."

The news filled him with wonder.

"Seven pounds eleven ounces."

Questions flooded his brain. What does he look like? Who's taking care of him? "Can I see him? I know I have no right to ask, but even from a distance."

"You can't see him, Alex. I gave him up for adoption."

The tears were unstoppable now. "Did you hate me so much you didn't want to be reminded of me?"

"Don't talk like that. The hardest thing I ever did was giving him up, knowing I'd never see him again, but it was better than having your uncle take him from me. I cried my heart dry. There isn't anything left inside me but emptiness."

Alex thought about his own childhood, stolen when his mother burned his hand. And now another childhood was stolen from him, the son he would never know, never play with, never see grow up. "I wish you would have written me, given me another chance."

"You had your chance."

The blunt and brutal truth of her statement would have felled him in another time, but now he was able to absorb it and go on. "What about Stanley Muller? You said he would marry you."

"Your uncle scared him off."

"Uncle Gus didn't know Stanley even existed."

"That private detective saw me with him, and found out who he was. Stanley got a certified letter from the lawyer threatening to name him as a co-respondent. Clark told me there wasn't any legal merit, just scare tactics, but it worked. Stanley stopped calling. And that isn't all. Your uncle sent me a letter, too. He didn't have the guts to write it himself. He instructed his lawyer to pay me two thousand dollars if I gave up my baby to him. He claimed it was his flesh and blood. Can you imagine anything so cruel? I gave my baby to Catholic Social Services. I can feel good about one thing at least. Your uncle didn't get his hands on him."

Alex turned and looked out the window at the frozen landscape, as bleak as his soul. "I'm sorry."

"Being sorry isn't enough, Alex. It will never be enough. I had to give up my baby. It broke my heart to say goodby."

The tears burned his eyes. His lost fatherhood hurt as much as her lost motherhood, mutual pain they would share the rest of their lives.

"He was a gift from God. Dark hair and a perfect body."

"When was he born?"

"May ninth."

What was I doing when my son was born, Alex tried to remember. The routine of navy life did not differentiate from day to day, unless there is a battle, or the ship runs aground...or the woman you love has a baby.

"Every May ninth I will mourn him," Mary Lou said.

"He didn't die."

"To me he did."

Alex wiped the tears from his face. "How long did you have him?"

"Less than an hour."

My son, Alex thought. "Did you give him a name?"

"The doctor wrote Baby John Doe on his birth certificate. If I had kept him I would have given him a name that wasn't Greek, like Joshua."

"Old Testament."

"Better than Alex Junior."

Was Mary Lou's humor bittersweet or just bitter? "You can have more children."

"I'm over thirty. You think my chances of getting married are any better now?"

"What about Clark? You two seem pretty close."

"Clark is divorced and he's got a son my age. He's not about to start over with me."

"Are you living together?"

"He has a house on Drexel. It's an arrangement of convenience."

"He's old."

"Old men are more dependable."

"But not very exciting."

Alex was able to nudge a small smile out of her. "I've had enough excitement for one life."

"What are you going to do after you graduate?"

"Get a job teaching. I'd like to work at the Red Lake Indian reservation. Those kids need a lot of help."

Alex was discovering how much more interesting Mary Lou had become. It was ironic that the experiences that drove her from him had made her more appealing.

She was watching him, reading his mind. "I suppose you're thinking to yourself that this doesn't sound like me. Well, life is full of surprises. We think we know where we're going, but we really don't."

Alex unbuttoned the top of his shirt and pulled out his dog tag chain. Mary Lou's gold wedding band dangled between the two tags. "I've carried this with me ever since I rescued it." He pulled the chain over his head and opened the clasp. He removed the ring and held it out to her.

Her eyes began to shine. "Why do you want to give it to me? I threw it away, remember?"

"I thought you might like to have it as a keepsake."

"For what?"

"For what might have been."

She let her tears fall freely. It didn't matter because there was no mascara to streak. "I loved you, Alex. There was never anyone else."

"I wish we had met now instead of two years ago."

"Sad, isn't it?"

THE FUNERAL

Alex was surprised to find it dark when he returned to his car, forgetting for the moment that the sun sets a lot sooner this far north. The engine was stiff but it finally caught. As he waited for the temperature needle to move, he tuned on the local radio station, KBUN, and wondered if the call letters stood for Bemidji Up North. The announcer, Steve Cannon, was a good story teller. "My old man was listening to a Gopher-Illinois basketball game on K-Bun," Cannon said. "I asked him what the score was. 'Thirty-nine to thirty,' my dad said. 'Who's ahead?' I asked. He said, 'Thirty-nine.'"

Alex laughed. He could use some levity. Cannon gave the weather forecast and Alex returned to his somber mood: "Eleven degrees below tonight; high tomorrow, if we're lucky, zero. These temperatures were brought to you by Green Giant Frozen Vegetables."

Even though the car heater was going full blast the power of suggestion worked its will and Alex shivered. As he drove around Bemidji, he half-listened to the stories, the commercials, and the occasional music coming out of the speaker on the metal dash. His car lights illuminated small hand-painted wood signs next to single-lane roads announcing Bart's Cabins or Live Bait or Boat Rentals or Harry and Emma's Lakeshore Lodge. But these were signs of summer. Where do Bart and Harry and Emma spend the winter months? Florida?

Ahead was a professionally painted billboard with its own light source: Madden's Lodge, Open All Year, Low Winter Rates. Alex was tempted. Driving two hundred fifty miles back to Minneapolis on a sub-zero night gave him pause. But spending it in a cabin, whose profound stillness would be broken only by wind off the barren lake, was even less appealing. How could he contain his churning emotions knowing Mary Lou was sharing Clark's bed only a mile away? If he drove home, the risk of breaking down on a lonely road and freezing to death in a matter of minutes at least gave him something different to think about.

He saw a roadhouse restaurant advertising Fish Fry All You Can Eat and decided to fill up his stomach as well as his gas tank before leaving town. He pulled into a parking lot nearly empty of cars. He opened the door and the smell of frying fat and stale beer almost made him go outside again. But it was a warm, well-lighted place, and so he sat in a booth and ordered the walleye and a bottle of Grain Belt. After his third helping Alex was stuffed. He asked the young waiter, evidently a college student, what the record was for fish consumption in one sitting.

"Nine fillets."

"That guy must have been huge."

"No," the waiter said, "he was as thin as a crappie."

Alex drove back to town and, on an impulse, began looking for Drexel, the street where Mary Lou lived. He came upon it without warning and nearly drove through the intersection. He braked, turned left and headed down the residential street in low gear, looking at the frosted windows of neat, modest, single-story bungalows with smoke curling out of their chimneys in the vain hope of catching a glimpse of her--a last if not lasting memory of how she looked.

He suddenly felt ashamed. "You damned fool," he said out loud, "you're nothing more than a peeping Tom."

These were not the instincts Steiner told him to trust. Disappear from her life as she disappeared from yours. He returned to the main drag and stopped at a Standard station where he had the tank filled and the oil and anti-freeze checked. The attendant told him he could shorten his trip a half hour by taking 64 through Motley. The name appealed to Alex. Motley was an apt description of his state of mind. On his way out of Bemidji, he waved to Paul Bunyan. He had the funny notion that Paul's eyes were following him as he crossed the tracks and began his lonely trip back to Minneapolis. Thank heaven Steve Cannon was still on the air with his nutty humor. He listened till Cannon's voice faded and finally disappeared.

It was two-fifteen when Alex pulled into his father's driveway. He let himself in, used the bathroom and climbed the narrow stairs to his chilly attic room. He undressed and crawled into his bunk bed, huddling under an extra blanket. As tired as he was, he drifted in and out of slumber second guessing himself. If only he had left the Greek church with Mary Lou. If only he had gone to St. Cecilia's to find her. If only he had not volunteered for active duty. If only he did not get married in the first place. If only he had gone to Greece with Uncle Gus...if, if, if!

He woke up late and vaguely nauseated. He had eaten too much deep-fried fish. He went downstairs to find that his father had gone to the store, probably dipping turtles while Tony separated pecans and caramel, something Alex used to do. No doubt they made a better team--Tony who had lost his father and Theodore who had lost his son. They filled one another's emptinesses.

Alex padded around the still house, finally realizing there was nothing left for him to do in Minneapolis. He might as well pack up and leave. He ate cereal and went to the Triple-A office.

"How much is a membership?" he asked the young woman behind the counter.

"Fifteen dollars."

She gathered maps of the states he would drive through--quite a pile as it turned out.

"Are you sure you can do this in...how much leave did you say you have left?"

"Twelve days."

She traced his journey to Mills Gap and back to San Diego on half a dozen regional maps with a red marking pen, making a giant u-turn across the U.S., but she had trouble finding Mills Gap. "Are you sure there is such a town?"

"There has to be. West Virginia."

She finally found it tucked in a valley not far from the North Carolina border. "The roads don't looked paved. Are you sure you can get there?"

Alex grabbed his bundle of maps and got out of there before she could utter one more "Are you sure?" and he lost confidence that this long trip, somewhere in the neighborhood of 4000 miles, was doable. If he hit bad weather anywhere he would be late from leave, AWOL again. This time he would not escape Radinger's wrath.

He returned to pack his seabag, and bade the house goodby as he drove off. He couldn't leave town before bidding his father goodby as well but before that, though, a final trip to Brook View, the nursing home Alex was once convinced did not exist. As he pulled into the small lot and surveyed the scene before him, he wished it did not. Dry leaves blown against the fence resembled charred bodies trapped next to a locked exit in a ballroom fire. Bare branches of a scraggy poplar scratched the overcast sky. Everywhere he looked, the deadness of winter reminded him of his mother.

He went inside and found her alone in her room lying on her side, her boney hip poking the sheet like a knife point. She was staring into the gray light coming through the window, her eyes glinting through lids crusted with matter. She smelled of stale urine. He opened the window a fraction to let in some air. He drew the chair up to her bed and sat down. There was no dignity in what he saw, just flaking skin and raw bedsores. Who cared about her enough to come and visit? Where were the cards and the flowers and the family pictures?

"I'm leaving, ma. I came to say goodby."

A tremor shook the sheet, all that was left of a lifetime of compulsive drudge work--scrubbing and scouring and flushing as though some diabolical voice was telling her that floors were never shiny enough, shirt collars never white enough, windows never clean enough, intestines never empty enough, a left hand never right enough...

He knew he would never see her again. The time to tell her was now, tell her that he had finally figured out, with the help of the good Doctor Steiner, that she was the one who burned his hand.

"There's a movie that keeps running in my head," he said to her, "of a little boy on the kitchen floor of an old house. His mother is at the stove getting dinner ready. The little boy is playing with blocks at her feet. Using his left hand he lays out the blocks to follow the geometric pattern of the linoleum because he understands she likes things neat and orderly. She yells, Thexia! thexia! He doesn't know what that means but it scares him and he is even more careful lining up the blocks with his left hand, thinking that if he makes the line perfectly straight she will stop yelling at him. Suddenly she reaches down, messes up the blocks, take his right hand and forces him to rearrange the blocks. He keeps trying to use his left hand because this is the only way he can make the blocks line up perfectly, his right hand just doesn't work. His mother gets angrier and all of a sudden she picks up the little boy..."

Alex leaned back in the chair. "That's it, ma. The screen goes blank. Can you tell me how the movie ends?" Guilt spread over him like a shroud as he stared at her, thinking that he had taken unfair advantage of a helpless creature. He should just have let it go. Hadn't she suffered enough? Isn't her Parkinsonism sufficient retribution?

Her eyelids fluttered. A tear slowly built up, eventually spilling over the bridge of her nose and falling to the pillow case. After a while a sound so soft fell from her mouth that Alex almost missed it. She was trying to speak.

He leaned forward again. "What, ma?"

"Toh aikana na sou proseho."

"Protect me from what?"

"O Thiavolos eitan mesa sou."

Alex shook his head remorsefully. "No, ma, the Devil wasn't inside me. He was inside you." He did not realize it immediately but these were the last words he spoke to her and the last words she would ever hear.

He bent down to kiss her papier mache cheek, an expression not of love but of farewell. She emitted a long sigh and the tremor stopped.

Her eyes now stared without seeing. Alex called down the hall for the supervisor who came into the room as though she had been interrupted from something more important than the death of a patient, which for her was no doubt routine. She checked his mother's lifeless pulse and said, "She's expired."

Expired? Alex thought. Like a driver's license? "At least she isn't shaking anymore."

His father took the news stoically. Alex could not tell over the phone if there were any tears. Except for a quick intake of breath there was no other expression of emotion.

"We have to make funeral arrangements," Alex told him.

"Tony take care of everything. He know what to do." his father spoke without emotion.

"Dad, listen. The doctor has to sign the death certificate before the nursing home can release the body. Because she is a welfare patient, she will be sent to the county morgue unless we arrange for a funeral home to pick her up first. I can take care of it here, while I wait for the doctor."

By the time Alex got to the house two hours later, Tony had it all cleaned, an impressive feat given how far his dad had let the house go to seed.

"Nice job," Alex said.

Tony smiled, pleased to be complimented. "I also took the opportunity to call the Priest and the Ladies Philoptohos Society telling them about your mother."

This was something Alex would never have thought about. He begrudged the fact, but Tony did know what to do.

The Ladies arrived an hour later laden with food. They set up a buffet on the now spotless dining room table. Little by little the house began to fill, cousin Coula and her mother, other more distant relatives, friends of the family, everyone solicitous and friendly. No hard feelings, Alex's mother was dead, the misadventure with Mary Lou forgotten.

Even Tony's mother was friendly. The hanky in her hand was already wet when she arrived and she gave Alex a forgiving pat on the cheek.

Father Karfatsis came to bless the serving dishes of salads, meats, breads and desserts spread across the table. He stood over the food and crossed it three times, mumbling boilerplate Greek much of which Alex did not understand or bother to listen to. The priest was formal and cool to Chrisoula's son, probably still unable to forgive Alex's defilement of his church. Maybe he needed more nudging from God. In any case, Alex was grateful that he did not remain long.

Uncle Gus finally showed up at six. When Alex saw the big Packard turn into the driveway, he retreated to the kitchen. He did not want to be part of the greeting committee, the adoring collection of Greeks who treated him like royalty just because he was rich.

Gus came into the kitchen looking for Alex. "Ah, here you are." He extended his arms for an embrace, but Alex found it impossible to reciprocate. Gus dropped his arms, puzzled. "Why aren't you with the guests?"

"I thought I'd wash some dishes."

"Let the women do that," he said dismissively. "Be grateful you saw your mother before she slipped away. When my mother died, the news took over a month to get here. The time to mourn had passed. I did not cry. In fact, to this day, I have not cried over her death."

"Join the club."

Gus gave Alex a sharp glance. "I know this is a difficult time, but you should be grateful you were not cheated as I was, out of a chance to grieve at the appropriate moment...with loved ones to support you."

"I don't need the support of loved ones." He stressed the last two words cynically.

Gus walked over and shut the door, closing them off from the guests, and motioned Alex to sit at the kitchen table. "Your mother just died. At least have consideration for her." He made a small grunt as he sat across from Alex.

"Consideration is the last thing on my mind."

Gus shook his head in dismay. "Why are you acting like a stranger?"

"I feel like one." Alex held out his left hand to show his scar. "See this? It was mom who burned me. I didn't do it to myself."

"She told you that?"

"No, but she didn't deny it either."

Gus shifted his bulk and the screws holding the seat squeaked from the torque. "Forgive her, Alexandros. Forgive her ignorance and her superstition. She was being driven mad by untold demons."

"That sounds familiar. She said she had to burn the devil out of me, like exorcism, because he was forcing me to use my left hand." As Alex stared at Gus's round nose, his round glasses, his round chin, a sudden insight gripped him. Everything had come full circle. "You knew she did this to me, didn't you?"

He looked down at his polished nails. His Masonic ring reflected the ceiling light. "Yes," he said.

"Why didn't you tell me?"

Gus forced himself to look at Alex. "You want to reawaken old hurts, old regrets?"

"Yours or mine?" he said. "You have to tell me everything you know, every detail. You owe that to me."

"All right, my boy, if you insist. I can only tell you what I observed after I got to Waseca. Your father had called to tell me something bad had happened but he didn't elaborate. When I got there, I found your mother next to your crib, rocking it back and forth. Your hand was wrapped in a bandage and a little wood brace like a paint stirring stick was taped to your arm to keep you from bending it." Gus hesitated, fighting back emotion. "The doctor had given you something to make you sleep but the expression on your face..." Gus stopped, sighed deeply and then continued. "Your eyes were squinted shut as if the medicine could not keep out the pain."

Who was this child fighting pain? Alex asked himself. A stranger.

"I spoke privately to the doctor. He knew what happened but it wasn't something you talked about in those days, so we agreed to call it an accident."

"An accident," Alex asked, "my mother burned my hand and you called it an accident?"

"My boy, things were different then. You lived in a small town, people would gossip, your father had a restaurant, a reputation to protect. This would have hurt his business."

"Did you talk to mom?"

"She was in an extremely fragile state." He sighed heavily. "It would have served no purpose to fan the flames..." Gus bit his tongue. "That was unfortunate. I apologize."

"It doesn't matter. The damage was done when you kept it a secret, even from me."

He looked pleadingly at Alex. "But everything has turned out all right, hasn't it? Look at you...tall, handsome, a smart young man any father would be proud of."

I ran away, Alex thought bitterly. I abandoned my wife and my child. Who could be proud of that?

"I'll do whatever I can to make things right for you. Order the finest casket, the most expensive flowers."

"You think you can buy anything including a guilt-free conscience? Well, it's going to stop right now. I'll take care of Mom's funeral."

"On a sailor's income?" Gus almost sounded patronizing.

"I'll get a bank loan using my car as collateral."

"So that Pontiac parked in front is yours. I thought I knew all the cars the Greeks drive. If you needed a car you could have used mine."

Sure, Alex smiled to himself, use Gus's big Packard to find Mary Lou. "Thanks for the offer but I needed a car to drive to Bemidji yesterday. Dad's isn't dependable."

"Bemidji?" Gus asked with mild curiosity and then, as he thought about it, his features changed from casual interest to sharp focus. "Who did you visit up there?" he asked guardedly.

"It wasn't a visit so much as a search."

"Well, my boy, this has been a busy time hasn't it? I don't know which has affected you more on this sad evening, your mother or..." Gus stopped.

Alex smiled, but it was a bitter victory. "You still aren't able to mention her name, are you? Shall I say it for you?"

"Please don't be cynical, my boy. So you found her."

"I did."

"You accomplished something in a day that I could not over several months." Gus checked to make sure a quarter-inch of shirt cuff was showing as if the news was nothing important. "Did she say anything about me?"

"Don't ask her to join your fan club."

"I would not have expected her to invite me."

"All the money you spent on lawyers and private detectives was wasted."

Gus straightened. "What are you driving at?"

"She had a son."

Gus looked down as though a heavy weight were pressing on his head. "Is she raising him?"

"She gave him up for adoption. You lost, Uncle Gus," Alex added, not because he enjoyed saying it, but because he owed it to Mary Lou. He owed her more than he could ever pay back.

"You lost as well, my boy," Gus said, sighing heavily. "If you had faced up to your responsibilities instead of running away from them you would now have a son."

"He's better off with a family that will take care of him."

"And you don't think you could take care of him better than some stranger?" His voice became vehement.

"You wanted to take him away from his own mother!"

"But he would have had advantages she could not possibly give him, the best private teachers, travel to Greece, learning the classics.

Think of it, Alex, he could have become what I always wanted to be, a priest."

Alex felt his stomach roil. "Why didn't you get married and have a son of your own rather than trying to buy Mary Lou's to justify your own missed life?"

Gus sighed deeply. "Let's not argue like this, Alex, not until you've heard the whole story. Then maybe you will have more sympathy."

"Sympathy for whom?

"For all of us, my boy, for all of us." Gus withdrew his silver cigar case from his inside coat pocket and selected a panatella. "Mind if I smoke? I have more to tell you and it helps soothe the nerves." He went through the ritual of snipping off the tip of his cigar and lighting it, puffing clouds of smoke into the air. He studied the glow, as red as a warning light. "May I ask you a personal question."

"What is it?"

"Do you still have respect for me?"

"What I feel now is nothing."

"No feeling at all? How sad. It would be better if you hated me. At least that is an emotion." Gus twisted the cigar between his fingers. The tobacco leaves crinkled. "You may be right, Alex. Perhaps I am compensating for the family I never had."

"A rich man like you had the pick of every Greek girl in town."

He patted his ample stomach. "When I was thinner you mean? I didn't have time for women. As a young immigrant I became obsessed with getting rich. I set a personal goal to be worth fifty thousand dollars when I was forty. I made it by the time I was thirty-six. Now I'm worth several times that."

"What does all that wealth buy, Uncle?"

He sighed. "Clearly not the one thing I wanted." He stared out the window as if trying to penetrate the cold darkness beyond the pane. "I thought money would buy me affection but all it buys is attention. Will anyone mourn me when I die?"

Alex thought that an odd question, but he sensed that his uncle was heading into uncharted territory. "Are you concerned no one will?"

"Greeks are very good at expressing grief, but none of their tears will make up for yours." He reached for the ash tray by the telephone that Alex's father used and broke cigar ash into it with with his little finger. "I haven't told you this before but you are the chief beneficiary in my will."

The news did not surprise Alex. He recalled, during the depression, Gus's visits to Waseca when he would secretly place a fifty dollar bill--a munificent sum in those days--into his left hand, pressing it against his scar. Alex gave the bill to his mother after Gus had left. Gus must have known Alex would turn over the money to his mother. He just didn't want to give it to her directly, as though she was a charity case.

Alex didn't want to have anything to do with Gus's money. "Why don't you give it to Mary Lou. She deserves it more than I do."

Gus's smile was ironic. "I'll take that as a comment from a young man who is not yet over a love affair. But you will get over it. Time dissolves yearning. Fading memory does the rest."

"How do you know, Uncle Gus? Have you ever been in love?" Alex was tempted to add, with someone other than yourself, but he held his tongue.

Gus looked at Alex a long time before answering. "Let me assure you, Alex, the world did not begin the day you were born. If we could climb into Jules Verne's time machine you would see me as a young man fighting the same emotions you are fighting."

Alex was getting intrigued. "She must have been someone special."

"Indeed she was."

"Was there anyone trying to break the two of you up?"

"I made my own mistakes."

"Maybe you should have let me make mine, too."

"My intentions were sincere, my boy. I didn't want you to repeat those I made, hoping to save you the pain I had to live through. But I forgot the lesson I learned years ago: one learns by making errors, not being protected from them." He looked again at the darkness beyond the window. Frost was starting to form on the glass from their body heat. "Strange isn't it how we think we can take our secrets to the grave."

He turned and faced Alex again. "I am going to tell you something that I have managed to relegate to the dustbin of my personal life, an incident of the thousands that make up one's life, and I thought I would never have to tell you about it. But you changed the rules when you insisted on making the past relevant." Gus reached inside his jacket for his wallet. He removed an old Kodak snapshot with a scalloped white border. The picture showed a dapper young man in a straw hat and a smiling, beautifully stylish woman dressed like Daisy in the Great Gatsby. They were standing next to a touring car with fat white-wall tires, the man with his foot on the running board. "I was thirty when this was taken."

Alex pointed to the woman. "Who's that?"

"Don't you recognize her?"

He looked again, taking his time. Finally he asked in surprise, "Is that mom?"

"We had just returned from a day trip to Minneapolis to buy her trousseau at Young-Quinlan, my wedding present."

The only photograph of his mother as a young woman that Alex was aware of was the oval wedding portrait in the living room. She was stone-faced in her lace crown and brocaded dress. Alex always believed that the bouquet of lilies in her hand was shaking when the photo was taken. It made him think of Mary Lou's flowers shaking in her arms.

"She and dad were married in 1928." he said.

"In October. The photo was taken two months before that." He put the snapshot away. "The man wearing the straw is now in failing health whose doctors at Mayo have told him to lose weight and quit cigars, neither of which by the way he plans to do. So what I am about to tell you may not seem real in your eyes unless you see me as I once was--as you are now."

Gus hesitated, either waiting for Alex to reply or to build expectancy. For Alex it was the latter.

Finally Gus spoke: "I was in love with your mother."

Alex snorted. It was the most preposterous thing he had ever heard.

"I know this is not easy for you to accept. I know for a fact it is not easy for me to tell you, and now that I have, you deserve to know the whole story." When Alex opened his mouth to say something, his uncle put a finger to his lips. "I know you want to protest but I'd rather you did not say anything until I'm done."

Gus sighed deeply. "Your mother and I grew up in Niata. We were second cousins, her aunt was my father's niece. Even at a young age I was attracted to her. She was pretty and long-legged, with a mischievous sense of humor. She liked to hide behind a wall and jump out and surprise you. Then she would laugh and run away. (Ma never laughed) When I was fifteen I sailed to America and first settled in Minneapolis. Your mother followed six years later. She had grown into a tall, handsome woman. I was totally smitten and could not keep my eyes off her. But I was not the only one. All the young Greek bachelors were looking for wives including your father. Since your mother and I were cousins I could only stand and watch. I moved to Worthington to put distance between us. But my loneliness only served to make me yearn for her even more. The news came that your father proposed to her. He asked me to be his coumbaro. As your mother's cousin I could not refuse. The coumbaro's responsibility includes being godfather to the firstborn child, which is what I became for you.

"The wedding day was a joyous occasion for everyone but me. Standing next to your father during the ceremony made my heart ache. The bride I wanted for myself I had given away to your father. The reception was at the Masonic Temple a block from the river. We dined, drank and danced. I was second after your father to dance with the new bride." Gus paused to soak in the memory. "She was so graceful." (Ma was not graceful at anything) "Late into the night I stepped outside for some fresh air. I walked to the Lake Street bridge over the Mississippi, a block away, and leaned over the cement balustrade and watched my tears fall into the water below. I thought briefly about joining those tears but I came to my senses and pledged, on the night of your mother's wedding, that if I couldn't have the woman I loved, I would have everything else that money could buy.

"In those days, we settled in different towns so as not to be in competition with one another. Your father opened the Crystal in Waseca, Doc Villas opened the Chicken Shack in Medford, George Boosalis the Olympia in Faribault. I had the Sweet Shoppe in Worthington. Once a month we got together at one another's homes to play penny-ante poker, smoke cigars, tell jokes and talk business. When we met at your home I could sense that not all was well. Your father did not appreciate what he had, a lovely wife who was a wonderful cook. She kept a tidy house and spent long hours in the restaurant. I felt pity for her. When it was time to leave I went upstairs to the bedroom for my overcoat. Your mother followed me. Suddenly we were in each other's arms. It was over in an instant, both of us filled with embarrassment and guilt. I left so quickly I did not even bid your father goodby.

"The following spring, your father drove to Chicago to visit a nephew newly arrived from Greece. While he was gone your mother came to see me, taking the doodlebug train. This was not unseemly, after all we were cousins. I fixed dinner and we sat in the parlor visiting into the night. I was ready to drive her to the Prairie House Hotel for the night but instead, making the excuse that it was too late to go out, I suggested that she use the spare bedroom. Rightly or wrongly, it was the gravest decision of my life. One night, just that one night, changed everything forever." Gus's cigar had gone out.

He stared at the dead tip of ash for a moment. "We made love. The result was a child. He was born February 1, 1930."

Alex's scalp prickled with the sensation of a million tiny insects. "That's my birthday." As he looked at his uncle's face, at the painful truthfulness in his eyes, the firm I-am-telling-you-the-truth set of his mouth, the thrust of a determined chin to clear the air once and for all, when Alex took all this in, he suddenly went weak. If there were anything for him to grab, like a branch on a cliff, he would have clung to it for dear life. Opening below him was a chasm so deep, so dark, so nether-worldly that if he fell into it he could not be saved.

Gus always stayed at the house when visiting the Poulos family but this night he chose instead to go to the Howard Johnson on Normandale. He excused himself, explaining that Alex and his father needed their privacy in a time of grief. Besides, he needed to go to bed early. The hasty drive from Worthington had all but tired him out. He did look tired at that. Gus's departure was a signal for the others to make their goodbys, and the wake collapsed on itself. By the time the last guest left, Alex had developed an enormous, pulsating headache. His eyes began to go out of focus as he searched through the medicine cabinet and the drawers in the bathroom and the kitchen looking for the aspirin his mother kept around the house, like an alcoholic squirreling bourbon.

"Where's the aspirin?" he asked through the bolts of lightning hitting his brain.

"I take them to the nursing home for your mother," his father said from the bedroom. He was putting on his pajamas, getting ready for bed.

"Every bottle? Every pill?"

"Why? You got a headache?"

Alex stared at the framed icon of Saint Mary propped against his mother's casket, wishing her stern countenance could ease the barrenness of his soul. Saint Mary's Byzantine stare gave nothing away, certainly not redemption. Even if he were a religious person, nothing in the Christian doctrine of forgiveness could prepare him for the revelation that the man sitting on his left, the one called father, was a pretender to the throne, while the one on his right, the man called uncle, the man of a thousand vanities, was his real father; while inside the polished oak coffin lay the bane of their existence--his mother, the woman of a thousand secrets, who departed this mortal coil without so much as an apology.

Bands of color from the sun shining through the stained glass windows crawled across her coffin like ghostly serpents.The funeral was mercifully short. Father Karfatsis conducted the ceremony with such speed even the native Greeks had trouble following him. No doubt he was still smarting from the humiliation he suffered the last time the Poulos family had gathered in his church.

Following the interment at Lakewood Cemetery, the Ladies Philoptohos Society served a luncheon in the church hall. There were so few people, they set up only two round tables. The hall felt cavernous.

The drive home was unmarred by conversation. Instead of coming in, Gus dropped them off at the curb. Alex stood next to his father and watched the Packard pull away. They went inside. His father sat on the sofa and picked up his Greek newspaper. He'd already read every line.

Alex climbed the narrow stairway to his attic room. He sat in his bunk bed till the afternoon sun slipped behind the roofs of the houses and left a residue of gold on the western horizon. Then he got up and turned on the ceiling light. He opened the small access door leading to the attic behind the wall of his room. Cobwebs and cold air greeted him. He dragged a dust-laden cardboard box with a Dayton's logo into the light and began searching through mementos of his past in order to justify his presence. He sifted through photographs, envelopes of baby hair, baptism announcement cards, letters, a one-piece jumper suit. He sat cross-legged on the floor and went through a shoebox of snapshots and found only images of him as an infant, nothing later. He found a baptism picture. Gus, his nouno, was holding Alex up to the camera. His father stood to one side. A step or two behind them was his mother, her hands folded behind her back smiling self-consciously.

Alex pushed the photos aside and opened a box tied in a ribbon. Under layers of tissue he found his mother's wedding dress--white silk faded to ecru. Under more tissue was her wedding veil. It fell apart in his fingers, the crumbled lace a symbol of her disintegrated life. If she and Gus had not let their simmering passion boil over Alex would not have been born. He would not be anything, not even dust. He pushed the box aside, got to his feet and lay down on his bunk. Tears fell from the corners of his eyes.

THE DRUGGIST

Alex crossed over the frigid, slow-moving waters of the Mississippi River and entered Wisconsin, a landscape of rolling hills and spruce-topped granite cliffs lending visual variety to an otherwise boring drive. He had planned to leave Saturday, the day after the funeral, but his father asked him to stay through the weekend out of respect for his mother. Alex agreed but in his heart he was already gone. He had put his own family behind him. Now he was thinking about the family Clayton had left behind.

The extra day eliminated any excuse for not paying a visit to the candy store. It didn't make any difference, though. He no longer felt threatened by Tony's pre-emptive involvement in the Poulos family. In fact he was grateful that Tony was taking care of his father for whom Alex, since the thunderbolt hurled by "Uncle" Gus, now felt a strange detachment.

When he pushed open the door and came in, he had to admire the improvements Tony had made to the place. The walls were painted a fresh cream color. The candy case wood trim shone with fresh varnish. There was new linoleum on the floor. The wrapping table behind the partition had been replaced with a Bakelite counter. Downstairs, the basement was even more impressive. The masonite paneling behind the stove had been covered by a sheet of stainless steel, easy to wipe clean. In the corner where the dipping table used to be was a wire-mesh conveyor powered by an electric motor and a trough with a heating element underneath. Tony was operating it.

"What's that?" Alex asked.

"A dipping machine," his father said proudly.

Alex watched rows of cream centers getting covered by a steady flow of chocolate, and coming out the other side with perfect rivulets across their tops. When the candy cooled, Alex helped Tony cup the chocolates and put them in stock boxes. Then he packed two-pound assortments printed with Christmas wreaths. For the first time in his life he enjoyed working in the store, and the morning passed quickly. When the time came to leave, Tony and Alex shook hands.

"Tony is doing a good job," Alex told his father as they went outside to his car. He climbed in and sat in the driver's seat with the door open.

"You ever come back?"

"There isn't anything for me here."

"You sure?"

"Pop, remember when you told me you left home when you were fifteen? Well, I'm twenty-four. It's about time."

"You plan to find a better life somewhere else?"

"I don't know if it will be better but it will be a life. I didn't have one before."

Tears formed in his father's eyes. "Maybe you write."

"I'll write." Alex started the engine and closed the door. His father stepped out of the way as he backed out. Driving up Excelsior Boulevard, he saw his old man through the rearview mirror still standing there, alone and in the cold.

Alex drove through Janesville and crossed the border at Rockford in late afternoon. The sun set behind him as he skirted Chicago on the expressway. He drove through Gary, Indiana, his car bouncing over rough roads. To the dusky north, steel mills belched acrid, dark smoke out of their giant stacks, dirtying rooftops for miles around.

He stopped overnight in South Bend, staying at a Howard Johnson near the home of the Fighting Irish. If he were in Pennsylvania, he wondered, trying to amuse himself, would the football team be called the Fighting Amish? The next day he sped nonstop through Ohio on the Turnpike. By nightfall he reached Wheeling whose landscape was an unremitting collection of treeless hills pierced by mine entrances and grimy valleys crisscrossed with railroad tracks. He stayed in a small ma and pa motel called the Appalachian Spring and ate a home-cooked dinner of roast pork, collard greens and apple pie.

In the morning he had grits with his eggs before commencing what he expected to be the final leg of his trip. Mills Gap was almost due south of Wheeling, from one corner of West Virginia to the other, but the switchback mountain roads forced a measured pace. The Appalachians undulated like the swells of a green ocean. Thin pines climbed gentle slopes, and picturesque towns nestled in glens with burbling creeks running through them. The natural beauty was leavened by the poorness of the state. Houses, especially those of Negroes, went unpainted and unrepaired. Alex would have found the South a strange and forbidding place were it not for W.J. Cash's book safely tucked in his seabag along with Clayton's hat and the Silver Star. He thought he could make Mills Gap by nightfall but he had only covered 250 miles at dinnertime. He stopped for the night in a town called Hominy Falls.

Early afternoon of the fourth day Alex entered Mills Gap, population 1827. He drove down Main Street, a three-block cluster of brick buildings with carved capstones which dated to the 19th century. At an intersection, he spotted a stream flowing behind the buildings. On its banks was a dilapidated wood-frame building with a large paddle wheel, the mill after which the town was named no doubt. Since Mills Gap was nestled in a narrow valley, that would explain Gap.

He stopped in front of a Rexall drugstore to use the phone. Seeing the sign reminded him of Jimmy Durante on his radio show singing, ”Rexall, Dat’s all, How do you do?” He opened the door and a bell jangled over his head. He found himself transported back half a century. Hand-carved display cases were packed with balms, analgesics, laxatives, antacids, cough syrups and stimulants. A soda fountain ran along one side with a black marble counter and twisted-wire stools. Above the wood-framed mirror was a molded cardboard sign which read: Drink Dr. Pepper at 10, 2 and 4.

In back, behind a glass partition, the druggist was wrapping a prescription for an elderly woman. "Help ya?" he asked in a hillbilly drawl after the woman walked out. He leaned on an antique crank cash register of cast iron. He was middle-aged with thinning hair and wore a white jacket.

"I'd like to use your phone."

"You're not from around here. Up north some-ers."

"Minneapolis."

"Where they have them car races?"

"That's Indianapolis."

It didn't seem to matter, to him the north was vast and foreign. "Who you want to call?"

"The Claytons."

He straightened, putting a little distance between himself and Alex. "Why you want to talk to the Claytons?"

"I knew their son, RB."

The druggist’s eyes narrowed with suspicion. "You from the goverment?"

"If you call the navy the government."

"If you're in the navy," he asked, "why ain't you got your uniform on?"

"It's more comfortable traveling in civilian clothes."

The druggist didn't seem to be buying that. "You here to see CR?"

"CR?"

"CR is RB's daddy."

Initials appeared to run in the family. "Yes, I am."

"Your comin have anything to do with RB's gettin his?"

"Getting what?"

"He got done-in, drowned in Japan, or maybe you didn‘t know that."

“I knew that.”

“But did you know it was the commies that done him in?"

"The commies?" Alex said in disbelief.

"He was workin for em, and he done somethin he shouldn'ta, so they had to get rid of him." The druggist lowered his voice. "RB was what you would call a quiet boy. Didn't mix none. Kept to his room readin books he ordered from that commie-front organization, the Book of the Month Club."

"What books?"

"Books by Ruskies."

"Tolstoy? Dostoevsky?"

"An another one name of Check-Off."

Alex was amazed at the extent of this man's lunacy. "RB liked to read great literature. What's wrong with that? Besides, he worked in the Ship’s Office. He was a typist."

"Says it all, don't it?" the druggist said. "He wasn't no steamfitter or machinist. He knew how to send coded messages disguised as regular writin."

Alex had to keep himself from laughing. The druggist was dead serious.

"CR says that his boy drowned in a accident. Nobody believes that...he's secretive, jus like his boy." The druggist pointed a finger of warning at Alex. "They's a lot of commies in this country posin as ordinary folks like RB. And then he up an join the navy." The druggist snapped his fingers "Jus like that, one day he's here an the next he's gone."

That reminded Alex of his own hasty exit from civilian life. "That hardly makes him a communist."

The druggist lifted his chin in a show of not buying for a second Alex's argument. "What about the payoff money his daddy got from the navy to keep his mouth shut?"

"The ten thousand?"

"See! You even know how much it was!"

"Every family gets the same amount. It's the survivors' insurance benefit."

"Well it benefited CR all right. He got hisself a new car."

Alex sighed inwardly. There was no sense arguing with him. Apparently his mind was conditioned by a pathological fear of communism that was spreading through the country. Also, Alex figured, by turning RB into a mysterious figure, the druggist could add some spice to his otherwise predictable and boring life.

The druggist came out from behind the partition and motioned Alex to sit at the counter. "Don't get visitors very often, so I'll treat you to a Coke." He went behind the soda fountain and dispensed Coca-Cola into a bell-shaped glass, adding a splash of cherry syrup in a final flourish. He stuck a straw into the glass and set it in front of Alex. He then walked to the front of the store and removed a candlestick telephone from an alcove in the wall. He pressed the cradle several times in rapid succession, making a clicking sound like an old man working his dentures. He kept a watchful eye on Alex as he waited for the operator.

"Martha, this here is Harvey Wells. Connec me to the Claytons. I got a visitor in the store wants to talk to him." He lowered his voice. "Says he's a navy man but he ain't wearin a uniform."

Alex sipped his Coke at the soda fountain, wondering if he hadn't stirred up a hornet's nest of intrigue. He was a yankee coming into town unannounced and asking to see the family of a suspected communist agent. If Harvey Wells was suspicious before, he was paranoid now.

The druggist talked into the telephone, "Hello, Missie? This here is Harvey Wells at the drugstore. Let me talk to your daddy...well get him into the house...this is important...be a good girl an get him on the line." Harvey put his fingers over the mouthpiece.

"RB's little sister, Missie," he said to Alex.

The druggist fidgeted as he waited. "CR," he said suddenly, "there's a sailor here askin' about you...knew your boy...sittin at my counter right now drinkin a Coke compliments of the store. You want me to put him on?" He motioned to Alex. "He wants to talk to you."

Alex came over and stood next to a glass case filled with ointments. He picked up the phone. "Mr. Clayton?"

"That's reverend Clayton," the druggist corrected.

Alex covered the mouthpiece. "How's that?"

"He's a preacher."

The news unnerved Alex. He never had any luck with the clergy.

"Excuse me...reverend."

"Who is this?"

"My name is Alex Poulos."

There was a short intake of breath. "So God has answered our prayers."

"Pardon?"

"My apologies for expressing my thankfulness out loud. Our son wrote us a great deal about you."

Alex felt his face redden. "He did?"

"Finish that Coke. I'll be right over."

Alex watched through the front window of the store, his heart fluttering as though missing a beat. He was off to an inauspicious start. First, the goofy druggist spilled out conspiracy theories about RB, second, he learned that RB's father was a preacher, and third, most disturbing of all, was the news that RB wrote “a great deal” according to his father, about Alex. What did RB say about him? As he stood at the window, almost twitching with nervousness, he saw a maroon car pull up next to his--a new De Soto sedan. A large man got out. The bell over the door jangled as he came in.

Reverend Clayton was thick-boned and heavy-jointed. He wore a baseball cap set far back on his broad head to reveal a shock of unruly, rust-colored hair. He had on coveralls over a white dress shirt. His face was flushed from excitement or high blood pressure, perhaps both. His gray-green eyes were giving the sailor an unabashedly frank appraisal.

Alex felt his cheeks flush from the attention but the Reverend smiled warmly to put him at ease.

"I was raking the church yard when you called," he said, shaking Alex's hand. His grasp was as firm as a Rotarian's. He stepped back to fit all of Alex into his field of vision. "I thought the final chapter in my son's life had been written when I received a letter from your Captain."

Alex almost winced recalling the hypocrisy he was forced to write. "I wanted to write my own letter,” he said, “but I couldn't adequately express what was on my mind. That's why I came, to talk to you in person."

The druggist, who was listening intently to the conversation, slitted his eyes perceptively because he knew a secret agent would never risk putting anything on paper.

Reverend Clayton and Alex waved goodby to Harvey Wells and went outside. Through the window they could see him already on the phone, spreading the news no doubt of a potential takeover of Mills Gap by a communist party cell. Reverend Clayton smiled as he opened the door to his car. "Harvey has a vivid imagination, but he's harmless."

"Glad to hear it."

"Follow me home; it's not far. By the way," he added, as if he had decided to voice an inner thought, "my wife, Bess, was hit pretty hard. We all were, of course, but she is having a difficult time dealing with it."

"I don't want to distress Mrs. Clayton. Maybe it would be better if you and I go somewhere and talk. I saw a park where the old mill is located. We can go there and sit on a bench."

"No, no, I just need to warn you that Bess may not have all of her Southern hospitality back yet."

"How do you feel?"

Reverend Clayton stared fixedly at Alex. "You wouldn't have come if you didn't think it was important."

Alex got in his car and followed the De Soto down tidy streets. Homes were modest and every yard had a garden. The neighborhoods were not dirt poor like the ones he drove through in Wheeling, just poor. Strangely, he did not see any black-skinned people. Reverend Clayton slowed as he passed a white clapboard church with a sign on the front lawn. A tiny shingled roof covered the church name:

The Evangelical Assembly
Of Our Savior
The Lord Jesus Christ
Welcomes You

Under the sign were movable letters that announced Sunday Service and School 10:30 a.m., and a Prayer Meeting Thursday 7:30 p.m. Today was Thursday.

Reverend Clayton turned into the driveway of a parsonage next to the church, a white, two-and-a-half story frame house with a front gable. Alex parked at the curb and got out. The house he was looking at was centered on a spacious lot with mature graceful trees whose leaves were falling. The church next door was a larger copy of the house except that it had a steeple on the right hand corner and Gothic-shaped windows. Behind the church was a country graveyard bordered by a fence of iron pickets. Many of the markers were leaning and weather-beaten.

A woman who looked a little weather-beaten herself was standing on the porch. She was thin and her lips were thin-set. Her dishwater blonde hair was parted down the middle and tied in back. In her plain one-piece Sears Roebuck dress, she looked like a Dorothea Lange photograph from the thirties. She squinted suspiciously even though she was standing in the shade. Alex was so interested in her that he didn't immediately notice a teen-age girl looking at him through the screen door, a girl with a round, cheeky face and an open expression. Her body was in transition from girl to woman. She shifted self-consciously on gawky legs. Reverend Clayton walked up the sidewalk ahead of Alex, and pulled the woman forward to meet him. The girl stood quietly inside the house, trained no doubt to stay in the background until acknowledged.

"This is my wife, Bess," the Reverend said.

Alex extended his hand and she reluctantly accepted it. The palm of her hand was rough. "Pleased to meet you."

She was not pleased to meet him.

"And this is our Missie," Reverend Clayton said, pointing to the girl framed in the doorway. "Come and shake Mr. Poulos's hand."

Missie came out on the porch. "I thought you were a sailor," she said.

"I am."

"Then why haven't you got your uniform on?"

Mrs. Clayton gave her daughter a tug. "Watch your manners."

"That's ok," Alex said. "My uniform is in the car."

"Will you wear it while you're here?"

"Let's go inside," the Reverend interrupted.

The Clayton house was filled with antique rockers and straight-back chairs, and columnar metal floor lamps with fringed shades. Embroidered antimacassars not unlike his mother's were pinned to the arms and backs of the upholstered pieces. A wood stove of black iron warmed the parlor. The black stovepipe went through a hole in the high ceiling. The doors had side trim and lintels of dark oak, and high baseboards ran around the walls. The strip oak flooring was covered with oval braided rugs. To the right, opposite the front door, a stairway led to the dark void of the second story.

The Reverend pointed to a mission rocker upholstered in horsehide.

Alex went over to it.

"That was RB's favorite chair," the Reverend announced.

Alex reacted as if he were disturbing the dead.

"Please, sit down. RB would have wanted you to."

Alex forced a smile and settled back. He tried rocking. Mrs. Clayton kept a watchful eye on his reaction--too much comfort must be sinful he figured--and so he gripped the armrests as if his hands were nailed to them, hoping this would convey the proper impression.

Meanwhile, RB's family stood in a line like people waiting for a table at a restaurant. What are they waiting for, why don't they join him?

"Can I get you something?" Reverend Clayton asked as if remembering his manners.

"The Coke at the drugstore was enough."

There was a pause. "You must be tired from your trip. We'll put you up in RB's room."

"No need to go to all that trouble," Alex said quickly. "I'm not staying long."

"You have to spend the night somewhere."

"I'll go to a motel."

Missie snickered.

Alex looked at her. "Did I say something wrong?"

"We don't have motels in Mills Gap," the Reverend said. "We open our homes to travelers."

"You're generous."

"We're Christian," the Reverend replied as if that explained everything. "Tell me, are you a man of faith?"

Alex hesitated. What did he believe in after all? He had denied his Greek orthodoxy for so long he felt uncomfortable talking about it. "I was baptized in the Greek Church."

This appeared to be the opening the Reverend was looking for. "We have a prayer meeting tonight."

Alex stopped rocking. "A prayer meeting," he said, recalling the sign.

"Right after dinner. Perhaps you would care to join us."

"What is the program?"

"God is the program." The Reverend looked at Alex with hope in his eyes. "Maybe He will encourage you to be His witness."

Alex swallowed hard. "I don't think I'd be good at it."

"Don't worry. God will show you how."

Alex lugged his seabag into the house with Missie holding the door. She led the way up the narrow staircase to a rear bedroom, its corner window overlooking the cemetery across the yard. Alex dropped his bag on the bed and the springs under the mattress creaked.

"No one has slept in RB's room since he died," Missie said.

Alex realized now that fate had pushed him here. He looked out the window. "Is he buried in that cemetery?"

Missie stood next to him and pointed to a new, gray-marble headstone that stood straight and unstreaked. "He didn't get very far--from this room to that grave. But in between he did."

"In between is where we met," Alex said, regret coloring his words. He studied the room, the quilted bed cover, the bed stand and bed lamp, the dresser. He expected to see photographs of RB but there weren't any, just a framed print of Jesus, the very same one Alex received for participating in a Sunday school Christmas pageant when he was a child. The print had to be the all-purpose reproduction of Jesus used by churches everywhere, depicting a bearded, long-haired caucasian, a far cry from the real man, a ragged rabbi wandering the streets of Jerusalem.

Missie saw him staring at the picture. "You're not very religious are you?"

He knew he could be honest with her. "Not much."

"Neither was RB."

Alex was surprised. "Really?"

"That's why he got out of the valley. Pa wanted him to be a preacher but RB wanted something different. He was a dreamer, looking farther than the town limits. His face was always in a book. The closet is full of them."

Alex wanted to apologize for so misunderstanding RB.

Missie could read it in his eyes. "Did you come here to make yourself feel better about my brother?"

"Is that what you think?"

"That's the only reason I can think why you came all this way."

"How do your mother and father feel?"

"Pa's glad you came. Ma isn't."

"I don't want to hurt her."

"She already is. My brother came home in a box."

Mrs. Clayton prepared meat loaf, mashed potatoes, and okra. "We weren't expecting company," she said apologetically.

"It looks delicious." Alex started to sit down, but the others stood behind their chairs with heads bowed.

"Excuse me," he said and hopped back on his feet just as the Reverend began the blessing.

"Dear Lord," he prayed, "today You brought us Alex. You placed Your hand on his and guided him here. We accept him in our presence as You have accepted him in Yours, and we welcome Alex in our home. We are in humble gratitude for Your providence."

Alex glanced at Mrs. Clayton as they intoned their amens. A tear appeared in a corner of her eye only to be wiped away by a quick movement of her hand. They pulled back their chairs and sat down. Dinner plates were stacked in front of the Reverend and he served up the food from steaming serving dishes.

Alex hated okra--it was too slimy--but he forced himself to eat it.

Conversation was polite and centered on where Alex came from, a state as foreign and cold as Siberia. When asked about his parents, he told them that his father was living but that his mother was not. "She died of Parkinson's disease while I was home."

The image of a person trapped by such a debilitating illness brought on a prayerful silence.

Reverend Clayton slid another slice of meatloaf onto Alex's plate. "More okra?"

"No thanks."

He gave Alex a paternal smile. "I had to force RB to eat his vegetables. He was a beanpole." He laughed gently at his little play on words.

Mrs. Clayton went to the kitchen and made a pot of coffee. She brought a plate of brownies to the table. "I didn't have a chance to make dessert," she said. "These are from yesterday."

"Makes them chewier," Alex said, discovering that his offhand attempt at humor was tried on the wrong audience. "I mean I like them that way."

"I have to get ready for the prayer meeting," Reverend Clayton said as he munched down a brownie. He stood and slid his chair under the table. "Finish your dessert, Alex," and to Missie he said, "Come along and get dressed."

"Ok, pa." She followed her dad out of the dining room and turned, peeking around the corner at Alex. She cocked her head. "You'll wear your uniform won't you?"

Mrs. Clayton stacked the dirty dishes to carry them into the kitchen.

"Can I help?" Alex asked.

"This is woman's work." Exactly what Gus had told him only five days ago in his parents' kitchen

"At least I can carry the glasses." He picked them up and followed her into the kitchen. She put everything into a large metal sink bolted to the wall. The water pipes and trap were visible from underneath. There was a coil refrigerator in the corner and next to it a dated stove standing on iron legs with a baking oven, cast-iron gas burners and porcelain control knobs, the same vintage as the stove he remembered from his childhood. He stared fixedly at it.

"I suppose where you come from you never seen an old-fashioned stove." Her tone suggested that Alex was too good for them.

He stood in front of it, studying the little blue glow of the pilot light as if he were examining its properties. Presently he passed his left hand over the flame. The heat moved across his palm like a thermal Doppler effect. He thought it would frighten him but it didn't. He turned and looked at Mrs. Clayton. "We had a stove like this in the house where I grew up."

Her face was drawn. Her unfashionable dress hung shapelessly on her frame. She was small-chested. Her knuckles were bony. She reminded him of his mother. "Where was that?" she asked

"A town in southern Minnesota not much bigger than Mills Gap."

That seemed to please her. He was a small-town boy like her son, and the town's "southern" location didn't hurt either.

"Did you grow up in Mills Gap?" he asked.

"Born and raised. Furthest I ever got was Charleston, to get married."

"South Carolina?"

"West Virginia. The capitol."

"Sorry."

"That's all right. I don't know anything about where you're from either." She poked a rubber stopper into the sink drain and turned on the hot water faucet, then reached for a box of Fels Naptha in the lower cabinet, and poured some powder into the water. Yellow suds billowed around the dishes. "I'll just let them soak for now."

"My mother never did that."

"Did what?"

"Leave the dishes in the sink. She had to wash them right away."

Mrs. Clayton blushed. "I usually do that but I got to get ready for the meeting."

"Maybe I shouldn't go."

"Why not?"

"I'm not sure you want me to."

"You feel that from me?"

"I think it bothers you that I came."

For a moment she questioned Alex with her eyes, then asked, "Why did you come?"

"To set things straight."

"What's to set straight? RB is dead isn't he?"

Alex stared down at the linoleum. Its floral pattern was all but worn away.

"I could understand better why you came if you and RB got along. But you didn't. When he was in..." she hesitated, finding it difficult to say the word..."in that ward, he wrote long letters home, letters the doctor told him to write because it would make him feel better getting things off his chest. He was always trying to figure out why you hated him."

Alex felt blood tingle his cheeks. "I hated myself more," was all he could think of to say.

She fought back tears. "That's small comfort when you're here and he isn't."

Mrs. Clayton's reproach followed him like a dog he couldn't shoo away. He went upstairs and closed the door to RB's room, isolating himself from the rest of the house, and removed his dark blues from his seabag. Tucked inside his hat was the little velvet box containing the Silver Star. He set it on the dresser next to the print of Jesus and commenced dressing, buttoning the thirteen buttons across his groin and pulling on his jumper, as tight as a straight-jacket. As he tied his neckerchief in front of the dresser mirror he noticed that Jesus's eyes were following him no matter where he stood. It disconcerted him even though he knew, rationally, that this was nothing more than a painter's artifice, having the subject look directly at the viewer, but these were the eyes of Jesus, who was not blaming or admonishing or criticizing, just looking at him.

Alex dared to look directly at the image. "Ok, Jesus," he said, as though having a conversation with the Almighty. "Here I am in RB's bedroom, looking at the same portrait of you I remember from Sunday school. Is this a coincidence or did you have a grand plan that brought me from there to here? And if you have one, what the fuck is it?"

He allowed himself to free-associate the way Surrealists did to activate the subconscious. Curiously what surfaced was not a flash of inspiration but the faint echo of Reverend Clayton telling him that if he found it within his heart, God would show him how to bear witness.

Hmm, Alex thought, and an idea began to percolate in his head. He removed the Silver Star from its velvet shrine, tucked it into his jumper pocket, and waved goodby to Jesus.

Downstairs Mrs. Clayton and Missie were waiting for him at the front door. Mrs. Clayton wore a gabardine coat and a felt hat with a feather Robin Hood would have admired. Missie had changed into a frilly thing with a rose-colored satin sash.

She oohed when she saw Alex coming down the stairs. "You know," she said, "I never saw my brother in a uniform except in snapshots."

They walked outside into the night air. It had grown cool but they were only steps away from the church. They took a shortcut across the lawn and townspeople walking up the sidewalk stepped aside to let them go first.

The door to the church was held open by a tall, skinny man in a rumpled suit and string tie. "Deacon Jasper Brown," he said and admitted them with the sweeping gesture of a lanky arm.

Alex entered The Evangelical Assembly of Our Savior the Lord

Jesus Christ, filled with scrubbed faces and clean collars. Heads turned with the precision of a marching band as Alex walked down the center aisle. At the rate the pews were filling Deacon Brown would have to set up folding chairs. Evidently Harvey Wells got the word out. Alex looked for him in the sea of faces and eventually spotted him, grinning conspiratorially.

The interior of the church was severely simple. The walls and vaulted ceiling were painted white. There were no icons, no altar, not even candles to suggest that this was a house of worship. In front on a one-step platform stood Reverend Clayton behind a lectern of light-stained oak. Sitting in a row of chairs behind him were the church elders, seven in all, whose features were so chiseled they looked like carvings.

In his dark business suit Reverend Clayton appeared as if he were going to conduct a sales meeting. In a way he was, selling Jesus to Alex. Mrs. Clayton led them to the front pew where they sat.

There was an incredible air of expectation as Reverend Clayton held up his hands for silence and announced in a practiced baritone, "Friends, this is the finest turnout we've ever had for a prayer meeting. I know that many of you came out of curiosity, but whatever method the good Lord uses to bring His flock together is all right with me."

"Amen!" someone shouted.

"The young sailor in the front row with my wife and daughter is Alex Poulos, on leave from his ship in San Diego. Alex knew our son RB and he came to pay his respects. I like to think that Jesus guided Alex to our midst."

"Praise the Lord!" another person shouted.

Reverend Clayton bowed his head revealing the full expanse of his carrot-colored hair, which he had combed down with water. His grasp on the sides of the pulpit began to tighten, turning his knuckles white. Everyone became still. Not even a stomach gurgled. Suddenly the Reverend shouted “Jesus!” as if he had been punched in the solar plexus.

Alex heard a woman moan. He wondered if she was having an orgasm.

"Lord Jesus!" Reverend Clayton shouted again, looking out at his congregation. There was fire in his eyes. "Do You hear my voice?"

If He didn't, Alex thought, He needed a hearing aid.

Several people joined in. "Are You with us, Lord?"

"Give us a sign," the Reverend pleaded. "Let us know You are in our midst!"

A woman shrieked "Sister Mattie! Has the Lord arrived?"

"He's here!"

Sister Mattie reached for the sky and swayed. One by one, people began swaying and reaching just like Mattie, crying out that they were being touched by the Lord Himself.

Watching this power of mass persuasion in full flower, Alex realized how easily one can get caught up in a wave of religious hysteria, even a rationalist like him.

A man a few rows back stood. "They ain't a soul among us so pure he ain't above confessin." He proceeded to admit that he had overcharged on a propane gas delivery and promised to make good on it.

"God forgives you, Clifford!"

A man confessed that he chopped firewood on land belonging to someone else.

"God forgives you, Bobbie Lee!"

A man admitted to having evil thoughts but he did not elaborate. There was a general nodding as if this were familiar territory. There was probably a lot of sexual repression in this constricted congregation. Another man stood with tears running down his cheeks. He spoke so softly that people had to strain to hear him confess to purchasing a pack of naked lady playing cards on a trip to Norfolk, "at a sailor store near the navy base." Alex felt the hackles on his neck rise, wondering if the man were singling him out as an abettor. When the sinner announced the seal was not yet broken and he was going to burn them like the trash they were, there was an audible sigh of relief, probably from the man's wife.

After a while the meeting began to die down like a fire that needed stoking. Reverend Clayton looked at Alex. "Let God give you the courage to stand and bear witness to His presence and succumb to His powers of forgiveness."

The elders sat like a panel of judges.

When Alex didn't move, Missie leaned around her mother and whispered, "It's your turn."

He felt his scalp tighten. Is this the reason he drove twelve hundred miles into the lap of Appalachia, to stand up before a churchful of evangelists and admit his failings and his weaknesses, and then ask some transcendent and ineffable presence he didn't believe in to forgive him?

He got to his feet and a hush fell over the people. Reverend Clayton motioned Alex to join him. Other confessors simply stood at their places; why did Alex have to get up and stand in front of everybody?

"Come forward, come forward," Reverend Clayton directed.

Alex resignedly stepped on the platform and faced the parishioners of The Evangelical Assembly of the Lord Our Savior Jesus Christ, or was it the Evangelical Assembly of Our Lord Jesus the Savior, or the Savior of our Evangelical Lord...

"God is waiting," the preacher said.

Was God really waiting? Believers thought He was. Wide-eyed expressions attested to that; faces of plain folk, open and forthright, unmarked by doubt. What should he confess in front of these people? That his irresponsible actions drowned Clayton? That he came to Mills Gap to appease his ghost?

Clayton deserved more than that and so did they. That's what Jesus's eyes were telling him, you are looking for redemption in the wrong place. He felt the Silver Star in his pocket. Voltaire was wrong, the dead don't deserve the truth, they deserve fiction, a glorious piece of fiction to justify God's forgiveness. And everyone will believe his words because he is bearing witness. He told Mrs. Clayton that he came to Mills Gap to set the record straight, and he will, but not in the way she expected, not with contrition, regret and tears but by countering the wild accusations Harvey Wells was spreading about her son. Alex will deliver to these believers the stuff of legend, and turn RB Clayton into their town hero. They might even erect a statue of him.

He gripped the lectern. "Jesus!" he shouted, the first time he used the word when he was not swearing. "Can You hear me?"

As if on cue, Sister Mattie raised her arms. "He hears you, Brother Alex!"

Brother Alex? Ok if she says so. Alex shouted back, "And I hear You, too, Jesus!"

Reverend Clayton stared in confusion. God didn't talk directly to laity. "You actually hear Jesus?"

Alex thought hard, realizing he had got carried away. If I were in Jesus's shoes, or were they sandals, what would I say? His mind was awhirl until he remembered the advice Dr. Steiner had given him, quite appropriate since Alex thought of Steiner as a savior.

"Not literally," he said, "but listening to Clifford and Bobbie Lee, to say nothing of the man who bought the naked lady playing cards, I knew I lacked the courage to bear witness as they did, so I asked Jesus what to do, and a voice in my head which I took to be that of Jesus said to me, Alex, trust your instincts."

Relieved, the Reverend looked out on his flock. "Praise the Lord!"

Everyone praised back.

On firmer ground now, Alex continued. "I had been under orders not to reveal the circumstances surrounding the death of RB Clayton. However, after talking to Harvey Wells, I realized I had to put a stop to the unfortunate lies being spread about him."

Harvey nearly lifted himself off his seat.

"If these lies go unchecked, we will be playing right into the hands of the Communists, who would like nothing better than to tarnish the proud heritage of the United States Navy for which RB so proudly served. This is the way Communism, a Godless system by the way, likes to work: spoil one apple and pretty soon the whole barrel is rotten."

Alex had their attention riveted like the plates on the Sprague's hull, before she ran aground, that is. He glanced quickly at the Reverend next to him and Mrs. Clayton and Missie in the front row. They all wore the same expression: one of perplexity but he also detected patience. They were waiting to see where the hell he was going with this story.

Alex took a deep breath and waded in. "I am not at liberty to be any more specific than to tell you that RB Clayton played a crucial role in naval intelligence and for that service he received a coveted award during a special ceremony that included admirals." At least that part was true. Alex reached into his pocket and pulled out the medal. He held it by its ribbon for all to see. "Here it is, the Silver Star awarded to RB Clayton."

There were murmurs of awe and admiration, even scattered applause. Alex felt confident that he had managed to pull it off when Harvey Wells stood up and said, "That there star don't look real. Why it ain't even shiny."

Alex studied the medal that had been stored for months in its little velvet box. "All it needs is a little polish."

"Well, you better polish your story too cause if RB were doin spy work he were doin it for the Commies and not for the Navy."

The murmurs of admiration turned into wiggles of discomfort, as Harvey had managed to sow doubt in Alex's field of make-believe. His mind went into high gear. He had to think fast or he would totally lose the congregation. He could see the Reverend in his peripheral vision, whose look of deep concern was mixed with a fervent gaze heavenward.

Alex gulped air. "Mr. Wells, weren't you the one who told me that RB read Russian literature?"

Alex waited for Harvey's nod to build suspense.

"You were right, but for the wrong reason. Naval Intelligence had assigned these books to RB so he could prepare himself for undercover work against the North Koreans. As you may know, the North Koreans have Russian advisors. What better way to get into the mind of a Rusky than to read the same books he reads? Doesn't that make sense?"

A few heads nodded. Alex was making some progress.

Harvey remained standing in a defensive posture. "I'd just like to know how come you pult that so-called coveted award outa your pocket like it was sittin there. How come Reverend Clayton don't have it? He got RB's insurance money didn't he? Why not that medal?"

Several parishioners nodded in support.

"Harvey Wells, are you witnessin or speakin outa turn?" Someone said from behind Alex. One of the elders was speaking.

"Just makin a comment, Andrew. Anythin wrong with that?"

"Why, you ain't even current on your tithin."

"That sign out front, don't it just say welcome?" Wells shot back, "Or welcome only if you're caught up on your tithin?"

Alex was relieved that attention was drawn away from him, at least for the moment, so he could collect his thoughts. He wasn't out of the woods yet, not by a long shot.

Reverend Clayton added a few more precious seconds when he raised his hands and said, "Gentlemen, this is a house of worship, not a court of law."

But Harvey Wells was not to be deterred. It was as if Alex had become the druggist's public enemy number one. "None of what he says jibes, Reverend. This here stranger comes into town and into your home and right away he has all the answers. I say again, how come he shows up a year after RB drowns with that Silver Star convenient in his pocket? If he can answer me that, I will catch up on my tithin." Harvey held up his check book and waved it for all to see.

Stirrings of discontent grew in volume. The same mob psychology that had everyone talking to Jesus a few moments ago was now drowning out this alien presence, this sailor who may be, for all they knew, an emissary of Satan. Alex grew desperate and his mind went blank. Try as he might he could not think of anything to say.

Reverend Clayton came over and placed his arm around Alex's shoulder. "Alex is too modest to talk about himself but his Captain wrote to me that he jumped into the water and risked his life trying to save my boy. Now, I ask you, does that sound like someone you can't depend on?"

A new rescue plan flirted in Alex's brain, courtesy of the Reverend. "Mr. Wells," he said, feeling as if he were coming out of the other side of a hurricane, "the Silver Star I am holding is the one given to me at the same ceremony that RB posthumously received his Silver Star. I just wanted to show it to you so you can see what RB's looks like."

"Well, then, show us t'other one," Harvey said, rocking confidently on the balls of his feet.

"T'other one?" Alex asked.

"You know, the Silver Star that RB got."

Alex leaned close to the Reverend and whispered in his ear, "Does the miracle of loaves and fishes include metallic objects?"

The Reverend shook his head regretfully. There was only one Silver Star and everyone knew it. Alex nestled the medal back into his pocket.

The charade was over. There remained only for him to admit that everything he had said was a fabrication. He will be heading back to San Diego in the morning, but the Reverend will have to remain behind to deal with the fallout created by this yankee who, rather than bear witness, was bearing false witness. How can Reverend Clayton go on preaching to the faithful? Who will believe him now?

Alex could not let down this red-headed preacher who had befriended him. He had to do something. Think, think. Or was it pray, pray? Then, as if the miracle he had hoped for was manifesting itself in another way, he saw again the eyes of Jesus following him out of RB's room and into the church. The penetrable eyes flashed like emergency flares and illuminated the dark recesses of his mind, clearing away the confusion that had been dogging him ever since he stood up to bear witness.

What is bearing witness anyway? Can you find God only in visions, or can you find Him in temporal accomplishments? To a bricklayer why can't God be a straight wall, to a baker a risen loaf, to a pilot-a three point landing? Maybe that's the answer: God is where you find him. And right now Alex found God clearing a path in his brain so he could think again. He felt an aura surround his body which made him tingle.

"Mr. Wells," he said, "I will answer your question, but first let me elaborate on my mission here. Naval Intelligence believes that NK agents infiltrated the naval base where our ship was in drydock and threw RB into the bay to drown him. An investigation was ordered at the highest levels of the navy's command structure, COMCRUDESPAC, WESPAC and CINCPACFLT, to determine how RB's cover was blown. I was ordered to come to Mills Gap to find the source of rumors that may have inadverdently compromised RB's clandestine operations."

The news electrified the congregation.

"I am not saying these rumors were intentional, but I am saying that they brought unneeded attention to RB for whom secrecy was a matter of life and death. Remember the World War II posters about loose lips sinking ships? That's what happened to RB, he was sunk, or rather drowned, by a loose lip."

Disapproval began to bubble around Harvey Wells like water coming to a boil. He wiped his forehead with the back of his hand.

"Gettin hot in here, Harvey?" the elder behind Alex asked.

Harvey sat down. He might have to sell the drugstore and move out of town.

"And now Mr. Wells," Alex said, "I will answer your question about the Silver Star. There is only one, but as God is my witness, its permanent home will be RB's bedroom, draped over a picture of Jesus."

He held out his arms and shouted, "Hallelujah!"

A woman shouted "Hallelujah!" in return. He looked for the source. It was Mrs. Clayton, her face beaming up at him.

The meeting adjourned after a resounding closing prayer by Reverend Clayton. It was such a stem-winder, the entire congregation stood except Harvey Wells who remained seated in the pew making out a check to The Evangelical Assembly of Our Savior The Lord Jesus Christ. He had to use two lines.

The first thing Alex did when he returned to RB's room was to drape the Silver Star with its ribbon over the picture of Jesus. After he got in bed, he left the lamp on so he could look at it. From this angle and in this light, one could imagine Jesus Himself wearing it. Alex settled back on the pillow, his arms behind his head. It had been quite a night. He had succeeded in shutting up Harvey Wells and preserving RB's reputation. So what if he did stretch the truth. The end was what counted. Who would gainsay that the medal was not where it belonged? The townspeople were free to visit the Clayton house and see for themselves.

He turned off the light, fluffed the pillow and closed his eyes. There was a tap on the door. He sat up and switched the light back on.

"Yes?" he said.

The door opened. Reverend Clayton looked in. "It's late. I hope I didn't wake you."

"No. It was a big night."

"I'll say it was." Reverend Clayton entered. He was wearing an old, brown terrycloth bathrobe with lots of snags in it, and brown leather slippers. "I hope you are comfortable in RB's bed."

Alex patted the mattress. "Fine."

Reverend Clayton went to the dresser. He touched the Silver Star. "Except for this, RB's room is just the way he left it." He looked at Alex. "What made you think of the picture of Jesus?"

"I had one just like it."

"Perhaps it was more than coincidence." He smiled. "We owe you a great debt of gratitude."

"It was my way of asking RB's forgiveness."

"His soul is at peace now."

"Mine, too."

"Bess commented on how nice it was to have a young man in the house again. To hear sounds coming from RB's bedroom. Drawers opening and closing, bedsprings creaking."

"Even snoring?"

Reverend Clayton laughed. "Even that. This room was beginning to feel like a mausoleum. No one wanted to go in it. Now there is life again."

"But I leave tomorrow."

"You'll be back."

Alex nodded. Their lives had become intertwined. After the meeting people had filed by and shook Alex's hand. Some hugged him. Many gripped his shoulder. When he and the Claytons returned to the house, walking across the dewy grass, they joined hands.

Alex realized that a spiritual intertwining had also occurred. In the short period of an afternoon and evening, a bond had developed between them. He belonged to RB's family. They were kind and gentle, plain and simple. No artifice. No masquerading. Just ordinary people.

"May I?" Reverend Clayton asked, wishing to sit down.

Alex pushed himself back against the headboard to make room for the big-boned preacher. He sat at the foot of the bed and the mattress sagged. "From the day RB was born," he said, "I wanted him to follow in my footsteps. He could have; he had the right credentials. Son of a preacher. God-fearing. Knew the Bible backwards and forwards, learned to read by it. But he was shy; it paralyzed him to stand before a group of people. He would stutter and shake." Reverend Clayton sighed regretfully. "Maybe I pushed him too hard. When he turned eighteen he took the Greyhound bus to Norfolk and enlisted."

"He had to find himself," Alex said, speaking from his own experience.

"I see that now. But at first I was hurt and disappointed. I prayed every day that he would give up the navy and come home, help me run the church and eventually take over. But RB died instead. As a result I stopped praying. I lost touch with God. He abandoned me the way RB did. There was bitterness in my soul. I lost interest. My brothers and sisters sensed it. My indifference helped spread the rumors about RB. I was lying in bed just now thinking about it, and suddenly it came to me. The answer to my prayers. Not directly, mind you. God is not imperative in the sense that He gives us clear orders to march by. He tests us constantly. He makes us question our faith. He makes us think. In our prayers we tend to ask for easy solutions. But God is too busy and also too subtle for our temporal minds. Jesus was a teacher after all. He demands that we learn not to take our religion for granted but to respect it and nourish it."

Alex was transfixed. He was listening to the best damn sermon he ever heard. He had sat through endless Greek remonstrations by Father Karfatsis, as well as a Catholic drone by Father Bassagni, yet it was at the foot of the Appalachians in a tiny town that he heard an evangelical preacher make better sense than the other two combined.

He kept wanting to interject a "hallelujah" here and there, but it wasn't appropriate. He really wasn't listening to a sermon. He was listening to a man baring his soul.

"So I asked myself," Reverend Clayton continued, "why did God bring you here? As I listened to you tonight, weaving your imaginative tapestry that borrowed truth here and fable there, watching you hold the Assembly in the palm of your hand, I thought to myself, if only RB could have been like you."

Alex felt his face redden.

"See how symmetrical God's work is? The person RB wanted most to be like is right here, in his room, sleeping in his bed."

"I can't replace RB."

"I know that. But I still hoped you would fulfill destiny the way I had once prayed RB would. But this is not how God answers prayers. It is as unrealistic as asking God to bring RB back." Reverend Clayton sighed.

"I had to get beyond self-pity. That was my problem: I was so involved in my own grief I wasn't paying attention to what God was really telling me. This is how he answered my prayers: he was telling me to bring myself back, back to Him. And that's what you did for me tonight. You were God's messenger and His message was, get on with your life, CR Clayton."

Alex knew perfectly well where Reverend Clayton was coming from. God's message to the preacher was the same to Alex: stop feeling sorry for yourself and get on with your life. Alex understood that now. "May I ask you a question?"

"Of course."

"Does CR stand for something?"

Reverend Clayton smiled. "Just as RB might stand for something? No one outside the family has ever learned the meaning of our initials."

"I'm not prying, Reverend Clayton."

"You deserve to know. The practice started with my father who was also a preacher. When I was born he opened the Good Book and put his finger on a page. It landed on a reference to Christ Redeemer, hence CR. When RB was born, I did the same thing. My finger landed on John, Chapter 18, line 40." Reverend Clayton looked at Alex. "RB wrote that you know the Bible."

Alex nodded. "In John 18: 40, Pilate asks the people to decide who should be freed, Jesus or Barabbas. They shouted, Release Barabbas."

"That's how RB got his name."

Alex woke up to the smell of bacon frying. The first thing he saw when he opened his eyes was the Silver Star draped over the image of Jesus. It was comforting. He stretched and got out of bed. He was happy to greet the new day. He washed up and dressed and came downstairs. He walked into the kitchen. Mrs. Clayton was at the stove. She was humming.

"Oh, you're up," she said, looking over her shoulder after hearing his footsteps. "Sleep well?"

"Best in a long time," Alex said.

"Hope you like grits."

"Love them."

"How do you like your eggs?"

"Sunnyside."

The back screen door slammed and Reverend Clayton walked in with Missie. "We were out raking."

"Back home we have to get that done by October."

"You're in the South now."

Breakfast was a groaning board of bacon and eggs, grits, toast, pancakes, orange juice and coffee. They ate heartily.

"I'll be heading out pretty soon," Alex said after the dishes were cleared.

"Wish you didn't have to leave right away." Missie was crestfallen.

"Got a long drive ahead of me. My leave is just about over."

"Will you come back?"

"You can bet on it."

"Will you be my pen pal?"

"Of course I will."

Alex went upstairs to pack his seabag. He remembered The Mind of the South and dug for it. He came down again with his seabag over his shoulder. It rubbed against the sloping ceiling of the stairwell. The Claytons were standing in the front hall.

"I almost forgot to give you this." He handed The Mind of the South to Reverend Clayton.

"I thought the Navy sent all of RB's belongings back to us."

"I borrowed it to read. I hope you don't mind."

"Mind? I'm overjoyed." Reverend Clayton returned it to Alex. "RB would want you to have it."

"This book meant a lot to him. He wrote in it. You should have it."

Reverend Clayton was hesitant.

"It belongs here with the Silver Star."

That convinced him. "I'll build a bookcase in RB's room and put all of his Russian books in it as well as this one. I don't care what Harvey

Wells says."

They laughed knowing Harvey had nothing left to say, and walked out to Alex's car. Alex stored his seabag in the trunk and opened the driver's side door.

"Alex," Missie asked, "do you have a sister?"

"No."

"I don't have a brother. I had one but I don’t have one now."

They stared at one other for a moment and then Missie ran to his arms and Alex lifted her off the ground.

"Now you have a new one," he said in her ear.

THE SOUTH

Alex was low on fuel and pulled into an isolated filling station on Route 219. On the cement island was an old-fashioned pump topped by a glass globe reinforced with woven wire, something Alex had not seen since he was a kid in Waseca. A green vintage John Deere tractor was parked over an open-air grease pit. The tractor's differential case was off. Tools were lying all over the place.

A man with dirty hands and coveralls climbed out of the pit, set his socket wrench on the tractor's metal seat and came out to the island. He wore an Army fatigue hat fingerprinted with motor oil.

"Minnesota," he said, examining Alex's license plate as he wiped his hands on a rag. He worked a long pump handle back and forth, filling the glass globe with frothy ethyl the color of rosé wine. He unscrewed the gas cap and inserted the nozzle. Gravity pushed gas into the tank.

As the tank filled, the mechanic cleaned the windshield and said in a twangy accent, "A buddy in my company was from Minnesota." He spat saliva the color of chewing tobacco on the ground. "Fourth Infantry Division, Utah Beach to the Rhine."

"What part of Minnesota?" Alex asked.

"Town called New Ulm. Used to kid him that he come all the way from New Ulm to capture Old Ulm." He laughed, revealing his stained teeth.

"Funny how close you get to someone fightin a war and, when it's over, you go home and that's the end of that."

"Have you ever tried to reach him?"

"What for? Everything that happened was in the war." The glass jug emptied. "Check your oil?"

"Good idea."

The mechanic raised the heavy hood. The long cast-iron engine looked like it belonged in a P47 Thunderbolt. "Them straight-eights are big hunkers, ain't they?" He pulled out the dipstick, wiped it clean, replaced it, and pulled it out again. He showed the dipstick to Alex. The oil was black below the ADD mark. "When you change this last?"

Alex shrugged. "I thought the dealer did it."

The mechanic looked at Alex as if he had failed the course in basic car maintenance.

"Lucky you made it this far."

“She has to take me all the way to San Diego.”

“Sailor?”

Alex nodded. “On leave.”

“If you’re goin that far then, you also need a lube job, and I better check them front wheel bearings, too."

“You’re the doctor.” Alex helped push the John Deere out of the way to make room for the Pontiac. He sat on the stool in the little office and watched as his car was being serviced.

The mechanic was right about wartime relationships. As close as he was to to Witter and Browning they'd fade from memory once he was out of the navy. Ironically the sailor Alex was the least close to was the one he would most remember, RB Clayton, and he was dead. He probably had more raw brain power than Alex and, instead of being proud of it, he hid it from everyone and consequently spent his short unhappy life being misunderstood. Finger pointing was nothing new to RB; it began when his father picked his initials out of the Bible. Imagine having your name associated with Barabbas--not just any convict but the convict who was spared over Jesus. If he hadn't been, Jesus might have survived--no crucifixion, no resurrection. Christianity would have been a backwater religion, even a minor cult. RB might have taken comfort in that--the common criminal for whom he was named saved Christianity.

The mechanic backed the Pontiac out, and Alex helped him push the tractor back over the grease pit. After he paid his bill, he reached through the window and opened the glove box for his AAA travel maps. He unfolded the one that said Southeast. "What's the best way out of here?"

The mechanic bent in close and ran a grease-encrusted fingernail across the border of West Virginia. "Stay on 219 till you get to Union...see that?...then get on 10 and jog off at 71...see that?... and then you pick up 103 at Bramwell..."

Alex wasn't out of West Virginia and already he was confused. "How about driving to Roanoke? From there it looks like a reasonably straight shot to Memphis on 221."

"You could do that."

Alex started to refold his map and stopped. He opened it again and studied it some more. "How far is Columbia?"

"South Carolina? Not more'n half a day's drive from Roanoke, I speck."

Alex refolded his map and tapped it on the roof, looking south. Jenny Betheras was two hundred miles away. It seemed inconceivable that he had driven all this way to meet RB's family and it never occurred to him that he was almost within shouting distance of Jenny's home town. Not shouting, maybe, but hollering. Isn't that what they call it in Dixie?

Should he chance it? Two hundred miles and another day--make that five to San Diego. He could still do it, especially if he were flying on the wings of seeing Jenny again. He felt so good about himself he was willing to try. If it worked out, fine, if it didn't, fine, too. Well, not fine, but bearable. Would she even see him? After all, he didn't show up for their date, didn't call, didn't write, didn't even give her an explanation. At the very least he owed her that, an explanation.

Yesterday he would have told himself: forget it. But this morning he woke up a different person. He had grown significantly, he could sense the change in him: it flowed in his veins, sang in his heart, shone in his eyes, and being so close to Columbia without giving it a shot...

"I think I'll head for Columbia," he told the mechanic.

"If you do that, pick up 311 at Paint Bank...cross into Virginia and follow Peters Mountain to New Castle. Then you cross Brush Mountain to Catawba...after that it's pretty straight to Roanoke." He looked at Alex. "Got that?"

Sort of.

Alex spent the next three hours navigating hilly country lanes, county roads and state highways, getting lost four times in the process. He crossed the North Carolina border at a village called Price. On his way to Charlotte, he drove through a town that advertised itself as the home of Dr. Grabow Pipes. He reached South Carolina in late afternoon. A border sign said he was entering the Palmetto State. He tuned his radio till he found a clear signal, WIS Columbia, and picked up the Slim Jim Hour which was sponsored by Black Draught, a tonic guaranteed to rejuvenate the system. Slim Jim had a barely understandable drawl but he made it clear that Black Draught was spelled the "Old English way, which is why some people call it Black Drought."

Alex entered the outskirts of Columbia at dinnertime and drove down Assembly Street, a wide thoroughfare that ended at the State

House--South Carolina's pre-bellum capitol illuminated by ground lights now that the sun had set, with a Greek portico of columns and pediment, and a Renaissance-shaped dome topped by a cupola where three flags fluttered from a pole above: US, State and Confederate. He put his car in low gear, driving slowly to take in the passing buildings--Belk's Dry Goods, Tapp's Department Store, and the Columbia Theater featuring a twin bill: Roman Holiday with Gregory Peck and Audrey Hepburn, and Shadow in the Sky with Ralph Meeker and Nancy Davis.

Alex was hungry and spotted a short-order eatery called the Sports Center. He found a diagonal parking space in front of an open-air shoeshine parlor where white-haired black men polished the shoes of dark-haired white men. He got out and stretched. A passerby noticed his Minnesota license and stared at it as if it had landed from Mars. He went next door to the Sports Center which got its name, apparently, from four pool tables in back, all of which were in use. The sound of clicking balls provided backdrop to a meal of a chili dog, which was remarkably tasty, and a bottle of Naragansett Ale. He burped back his dinner and decided to walk around and settle his stomach before calling Jenny. The air was mild. Back home this time of year he would be bundled up like an Eskimo but here he was comfortable in a sweater. He studied the people who walked by; white, middle-class, prosperous. Now and then a negro gave Alex a wide berth as if the white guy owned the sidewalk, a depressing thought. He also passed soldiers. There must be an army camp nearby. He crossed Gervais Street to the landscaped capitol grounds and saw a pair of water fountains on the corner with wood signs he had never seen before: White Only and Colored Only.

Appropriately nearby was a standard with an engraved sign that gave the hours of the Confederate Museum in the rotunda. He followed the sidewalk around the west wing and noticed several large bronze stars attached to the facade. They were placed randomly with no architectural pattern and it puzzled Alex until he realized that the stars marked gouges in the granite, the size Paul Bunyan would make had he taken his axe and pounded at the wall. But these were Civil War battle scars from Sherman's cannons no doubt, a graphic reminder, along with the Confederate Flag, that the South hadn't buried its ghosts. Maybe it never would.

He returned to Gervais Street. A block down was the Wade Hampton Hotel, an elegant-looking structure that bespoke Southern grace and hospitality. Alex felt like splurging, not a roadside inn but something in the grand style, and so he walked to the hotel. A negro doorman dressed like Lord Nelson ushered Alex into a hushed lobby that reminded him of a private men's club. The pillars and walls were encased in dark wood and the chairs in maroon leather. He went to the desk. An officious clerk glanced up from his copy of the Columbia Record and examined Alex's misshapen slacks whose creases had disappeared somewhere north of the Mason Dixon line.

The clerk slid a leatherette writing pad toward him. "Please fill out the registration."

Alex wrote down his Minnesota address and license number on the card.

"Are you attached to Fort Jackson?"

"Fort Jackson?"

"The army camp outside of town."

"I'm a sailor on leave passing through on my way to San Diego."

"That will be $14.75."

Alex handed the clerk a ten and a five.

He gave Alex a quarter from a cash drawer and a key to room seven-twelve.

He leaned over the counter. "Luggage?"

"My car is parked on Assembly Street. I'll bring it around later."

The clerk made a face as if he were not believing that dodge. A northerner without luggage driving across the country had all the markings of a one-night stand.

"I'd like to use your phone," Alex said. The clerk folded his newspaper and frowned, confirming his suspicion that Alex was contacting a woman, which was true, of course.

"Against the wall."

There were three desk telephones on a counter, one a house phone and the other two dial phones. Underneath was a shelf with telephone books for Columbia, Charleston, Spartanburg, Florence, and Sumter. Alex opened the Columbia book to the Bs and ran his finger down the names. He found two Betherases, John and Chris.

Which one shall I try first? He picked up the phone. His finger trembled as he dialed, giving proof of his inner misgivings. What if Jenny hangs up on him when she hears his voice? What if she isn't home? What if...

A man answered. "Hello?"

"Is this the Betheras residence?" Alex's voice was shaky.

"Who you want?" Except for the southern accent, he sounded just like Alex's dad.

"Jenny."

"You got the wrong Betheras. Jenny is my niece. You want to call Chris." He hung up just like that.

Alex kept his finger on the plunger. Having packed so much

expectation into this call he was suddenly drained, and the prospect of dialing a second time was as challenging as scaling a cliff. It took several seconds to build up his nerve again.

Meanwhile the desk clerk was keeping a watchful eye on him, gauging his nervousness as evidence of connivery. Might be time to call the house dick.

Alex smiled at him to display the confidence he lacked, released the plunger and dialed Jenny's number, but slowly, holding each digit on the finger stop, all the time coming up with excuses for not completing the call: he should move his car to the hotel lot and haul in his seabag to prove to the clerk he was a respectable traveler, go to his room and call Jenny from there, get a good night's sleep and call in the morning when he was rested.

As he delayed releasing the final number he pulled back his sleeve to check his watch--it might be too late now anyway--and his finger slipped from the hole it was guarding. He listened in a semi-paralyzed state as his call was being connected. There was a click of finality.

"Bah-they-russ raisy-dance," a female voice answered.

Alex could barely understand her drawl. She had to be a servant, likely a black servant. This was the South after all.

"May I speak to Jenny?" he quavered

"Jes a minute."

Alex waited with the finality of someone staring at a grenade whose pin had been pulled.

"Hello?"

Even though he knew it was coming, her voice startled him into the kind of frightful bashfulness he experienced as a child.

"Who is this?"

"Alex Poulos."

"Who?"

He was ready to die. His voice was so weak it didn't sound like him at all. He took a deep breath and said, too loudly this time and without punctuation, "AlexPouloswemetinYokosukaremember?"

"Alex?" she asked, surprised, shocked even. "Where are you calling from?"

He looked around. The clerk was watching. "The Wade Hampton Hotel."

Astonishment braided her words. "Alex, is this some kind of joke?"

"I really am in Columbia. Wait a minute..." He looked out the window. "The Wade Hampton is on the corner of Gervais and...I can't see the other street sign from here, but across Gervais is the capitol and off to the left about a block away, is what looks like a college campus."

"That's the University of South Carolina."

"Now do you believe me?"

"Did you get transferred or something?"

Oh God, he thought, where to begin? "I'm on leave. I have a car and I'm heading back to San Diego. I decided only today to come see you."

"Do you make a practice of deciding things at the last minute, or is it just with me?"

"I was near enough to take the chance of finding you again."

"Where?"

"Mills Gap, a town in West Virginia."

"What were you doing there?"

"Visiting the family of a sailor on my ship who died. He was the reason why I didn't show up for our date."

This made no sense at all to Jenny and he imagined her rolling her eyes. "And now you show up months later?"

"If I hadn't visited his family, I never would have thought of driving to Columbia to see you."

"You haven't seen me yet."

"But when you understand the geometry..."

"Geometry?"

"Don't you see?" he said, even though he knew she didn't. "It was a mathematical certainty that we would intersect again, like the Pythagorean theorem proving that the square of the hypotenuse is equal to the squares of the opposite two sides."

"Alex, you're not talking geometry, you're talking sophistry."

"Please, listen. The sailor who died, is at the very core of everything that's happened to me since I last saw you, including Dr. Steiner." Alex figured this would grab her attention, and it did.

"Steiner?" Jenny asked,

"We talked for an hour."

"Did you see him because of me?"

He exhaled pent-up breath. "Because of you, because of RB, because of a lot of things."

"You may have been a headache, Alex, but you never were a bore."

"Is that supposed to be a compliment?"

"For some reason my head stores song lyrics, and that line is from Thanks for the Memory."

"I'm sure your memory of me is enough to give anyone a headache."

They both laughed, the tension lessening.

"I'd like to make up for the date we missed," he ventured.

"How long are you going to be in town?"

"I have to get to San Diego by Friday."

"That doesn't give you much time."

"What about tonight?"

"Right now?"

"It's the shank of the evening."

"It may be for you. I'm not dressed to go out..."

"It doesn't matter."

"If you're at the Wade Hampton it matters."

"I'll meet you anywhere you say."

"I could see you at home--that is, if you don't mind coming over here."

"Will your parents mind?"

"You're Greek aren't you?" She gave him directions.

Alex got a city map from the desk clerk who helped him trace his route to 4150 Claremont Drive. He was cordial now that he knew Alex was going to visit someone living in a respectable neighborhood. Alex went to his car and followed Gervais east to Harden. He turned right and drove past a negro neighborhood of shanties with weatherbeaten wood stairs leading up to porches that leaned.

The clerk had told him to look for the Five Points Theater and turn left on Divine Street. Alex went up a hill and entered a residential area of perfectly landscaped homes, leaving abject poverty for wealth and privilege. He drove by a new, cream-bricked building and squinted at the name above the entrance: Dreher High School. Three blocks later he turned on Kilbourne, a winding, pine-lined avenue, and followed it to Claremont Drive, the street where Jenny lived. He slowed so he could read the numbers on street-mounted mailboxes until he found hers. He parked and looked out the car window at a large house perched on an elevated lot. A light was on over the front door as if company were expected. That's me, he said to himself. He got out and climbed a winding stone stairway, shivering as he went--less from the cool air than from excitement.

The two-and-a-half story house was sited on wooded grounds that seemed to go on forever. The entry porch was supported by twin columns that ran all the way to the roofline. He stood under the light feeling self-conscious. His slacks needed pressing, his sweater was pilling, and he should have put on a fresh shirt. He ran his fingers along his jawline. Stubble. No wonder the clerk was suspicious of him. Why didn't he take the time to freshen up at the hotel? Isn't that one of the reasons why he spent nearly $15 to stay there? As he pushed the doorbell, the only thought in his head was crafting an excuse for his appearance. Behind the door he heard a soft bing-bong, a sound made by a hammer hitting pipes of different lengths. A lot fancier than the jangling ring of his father's doorbell. He was busy smoothing his pants when the door opened and there was Jenny. They stared at each other, caught up in a moment of mutual appraisal as though they were meeting for the first time. This was not necessarily stretching the truth. They had seen each other only once before on a truncated date in a faraway place.

Jenny wore a pleated skirt and a loose pullover that hid her figure. Alex still couldn't tell what kind of body she had. One thing he could tell, however, was that she was heavier. Either navy fare didn't appeal to her or her mother's Greek cooking did. And he remembered Jenny as being taller. She was letting her hair grow out. It was nearly to her shoulders and made her face appear fuller. What had not changed were her dark brown eyes, dominant, intelligent and mysterious.

He thought to himself, funny how you romanticize someone in your mind and when you see that person again, you feel...what? Disappointment? Not that, exactly. Disenchantment. It was unavoidable. The woman who opened the door was not the Jenny of his dreams, not the Jenny he had idealized beyond all reality. Memory plays tricks; expectations don't measure up.

Was she feeling the same way about him?

She stepped aside. "Come in."

Alex entered a broad front hall with a plantation staircase curving up to the second floor. Alex could imagine Scarlett dressed in the gown she had made from window-drapes using that staircase to make a grand entrance. To the left, through an arch wide enough for a car, a living room ran the length of the house. To the right, half as long, was the dining room. The furnishings were French provincial. Somewhere in back a television set was on.

"I hope your evening wasn't too badly interrupted."

"We were finishing dinner when you called."

Alex expected dishes still on the dining table but the expanse of shiny Philippine mahogany was bare except for a centerpiece of waxed apples and peaches.

Jenny followed his gaze. "Nell has everything cleaned up."

"Nell?"

"The maid."

"She answered the phone when I called?"

Jenny nodded.

"How many servants do you have?" He almost said slaves.

"Besides Nell, there's Sadie, the cook, and a gardener."

Alex's mother hoed the small vegetable garden behind the garage, scrubbed clothes on a washboard, ironed everything including sheets and underwear, not to mention baking pies at the restaurant. She was her own maid, cook and gardener. He looked at his watch. It was nearly eight o'clock. Back home dinner was over when his father quit belching, usually around six. "Is it a custom in the South to eat this late?"

"Mother and I wait for dad so we can eat together."

"You told me he has a produce company."

"He works from dawn to dusk. It's a demanding business. Rotting lettuce doesn't sell."

Rotting or not, lettuce had provided the Betheras family very well.

They were still standing in the front hall, working to get over the feeling of strangeness that constrained them.

"So," Jenny asked, "what did you think of Dr. Steiner?"

"Amazing."

"Let's talk about it." She led him into the living room where they sat on a pastel green davenport with an arched back. A full cushion separated them."The last time I saw you you were wearing your uniform."

"It's in the trunk."

"Did you rent a car?"

"I bought one with money I saved from my navy pay. When I get back to San Diego I'll sell it."

"You look different in civilian clothes. I don't think you felt comfortable in dark blues."

"Enlisted men are not usually comfortable in the company of officers."

"Even so, you were stiffer then. You're more relaxed now."

Alex smiled, feeling good about what she said. It made him venture further. "Remember what I said about uniforms, particularly the ones officers wear?"

"How could I forget."

"I was pretty critical."

"I got even."

"As a matter of fact you did."

She folded her hands in her lap and crossed her ankles. "I said some unfortunate things. I'm relieved you saw Dr. Steiner."

"I walked into his office one person and left another." He proceeded to tell her about his session with the psychiatrist. "At the end he asked me if I was more angry at my mother or at you."

Jenny played with the pleats on her skirt. "What was your answer?"

"I told him I was angry at both of you."

"Are you still angry?"

"Not at you."

"But at your mother?"

The question brought back in a rush the vision of his mother lying on her side, shrunken and twisted, death granting her wish. “She died when I was home.”

Jenny stared fixedly at Alex. "I am so sorry. Please accept my sympathy.”

He closed his fingers over his scar as though he were closing a chapter of his life. The rippled tissue no longer held any mystery. He knew everything there was to know about the mark on his hand, and how it explained the ripple effect on his relationships with RB Clayton, Uncle Gus, Mary Lou, even his lost son. Why waste energy grinding over a past that had no pertinence with the present. Let it die with his mother. He wanted to convey this to Jenny as well. "She was very sick. She had Parkinson's and it was just a matter of time. She suffered enough with the guilt of burning my hand."

“Have you forgiven her?”

He smiled. “I’m working on it.”

“Good. I have the feeling that in time you will.” She slid across the cushion and tucked her legs under her, her knee almost touching his thigh. “I never expected to see you again."

"Me either. What was going through your mind when I didn't turn up at the hospital?"

She was calm but her eyes radiated emotion. "I was hurt. When my plane took off over Tokyo Bay the next morning, I looked down at the ships moored there, wondering which one was yours. I said goodby and good riddance so loud the person sitting next to me turned and stared."

Alex felt like Jenny had shot him out of a circus cannon. Desperately he sought a net. "I'll make it up to you."

"How?"

He looked around as if seeking inspiration. "I'll give you the moon, take you to a star..."

"You've seen too many Bette Davis movies. What's wrong with just saying you're sorry?"

He felt his cheeks flush. Why did he find it so hard to show contrition? "Nothing," was all he could come up with.

Jenny brushed her hair back with an irritated flick of her fingers.

It was an opportunity to alter the conversation. "You used to have a cowlick."

"It's gone now that I'm letting my hair grow. I'm getting rid of my military cut. It makes me look less a woman."

"You're a woman no matter how short your hair is."

She blushed. "I didn't think you noticed."

"Are you going with anyone?" he said, sticking his neck out.

"Going with anyone?"

"You know...steady. With a Greek guy, I mean."

"What if I said yes?"

"I would call him lucky."

"Is this from the sailor who stood me up on my last night in the Far East?"

"I couldn't get off the ship, Jenny. I got put on report."

She shook her head.

"I know what you're thinking: I can't get along with brass. Well, you're right. My division officer caught me reading a book during muster." He went on to explain how this otherwise minor infraction escalated out of control.

"I hope the book was worth it."

"It was, The Catcher in the Rye."

"It's a great book. I have it upstairs in my bedroom."

To Alex, nothing was better than sharing the same taste in literature. "Don't tell me how it ends."

"You can borrow it."

He was delighted. The novel that had strained his friendship with Gildenhall was cementing his with Jenny. "This time no one will take it away from me." Feeling more at ease now, he continued explaining the seemingly inexplicable, going from Salinger's book to the Silver Star. "RB deserved the medal more than I did so I gave it to his parents. That's the reason I came to West Virginia. When RB was in the psychiatric unit, you probably can guess who treated him."

Jenny's eyes widened. "Dr. Steiner."

Alex nodded. "By treating RB, Steiner got to know me better than I knew myself. The last thing the doctor said to me was, follow your instincts."

"Did you follow them here?"

He nodded. "It took a while but I guess I finally got my date."

Jenny invited Alex to meet her parents. She led him down a long hall to a ceramic-tiled porch overlooking an illuminated garden of rocks and paths and flower beds. The furniture was white-painted wrought iron. The cushions had bright floral patterns. A space heater in the corner hummed warm air.

Mr. and Mrs. Betheras were sitting together on a settee watching television. They were not physically large but nevertheless substantial-looking, as if life had treated them well. Mr. Betheras was much older than his wife, typical of Greek marriages. He was in his shirtsleeves with the cuffs rolled up. She wore a dark dress with white piping, trim and proper.

"Mom and Dad, I want you to meet Alex Poulos."

Alex came forward and shook the hand of Jenny's father. He was sharp-eyed, reflecting a sharp mind, and portly, the symbol of prosperity for men of his age. "Sit there," he commanded, motioning to the chair on his right.

As Alex sat he caught his reflection in the glass top of the wrought iron coffee table, as serious as a man in a witness chair.

"Jenny," he told his daughter, "shut off the television."

She turned off the set and sat in a matching chair opposite Alex. The quartet made a half-circle of stiff postures waiting for someone to speak. In one of those unpredictable moments, they all began talking at once and just as suddenly they all stopped.

Jenny's father said, "Everyone has so much to say, we all talk at the same time."

"We'll get done quicker that way," Alex said.

Jenny's father laughed. "You know Greek?"

"Not as well as Jenny, I'm sure."

"She speak perfect Greek," he said proudly.

"I grew up in a small town. We were the only Greeks. I learned listening to my parents."

"Where you from?"

"Minneapolis."

"Not where you from in America, where you from in Greece."

"Oh. My father is from Haraka and my mother from Niata, in Laconias."

"I know where that is. We come from Roumeli, my wife and me."

Roumeli was in northern Greece where the soil was richer, the climate wetter, and the people better educated.

Where Alex's parents came from the ground was hard, the climate arid, and school went to the fourth grade.

"What your father do?"

"He's a candy maker." Alex was still embarrassed to admit that his father, in comparison to Mr. Betheras, was a working stiff.

"You have a momma?" Mrs. Betheras asked,

Jenny leaned forward ready to intervene on Alex's behalf.

"She died while I was home on leave," Alex said.

"Too bad." Mrs. Betheras said politely. She had a small voice and her accent, like that of her husband, was a mix of Greek and Southern. There was something about her that Alex was trying to find words for and they finally came to him: she was a sweet little lady.

"Alex's mother had Parkinson's disease, Mom," Jenny added. "It's the kind of illness where you shake all the time."

Mrs. Betheras nodded sympathetically. "Your papa? He's ok?"

"He misses my mother."

"You should be with him," Mr. Betheras said imperatively.

"I have to go back to the navy."

"What you do after you get out like Jenny did?" Betheras asked.

"I haven't decided."

"How old are you?"

"Twenty-four."

"Twenty-four and you don't know what you going to do?"

"I have to finish school first."

"What you study?"

"Humanities."

Betheras looked to his daughter for help.

"It's the combined study of art, literature and philosophy, dad."

"What's the matter with law?"

"Law?"

"You can be a judge."

"I don't think I'd be very good at that."

"So what you good at?"

"Writing." It came out sounding apologetic.

"You can make a living with writing?"

"Some people do." Alex was getting the third degree and Betheras's generation was nothing if not direct--especially to a northerner who came to see his remaining single daughter. These immigrants did not dance around the bush; it wasn't in their nature. Betheras and his brethren came to America at a time when the country was awakening as the giant it grew to be. And to succeed in a competitive, raw, environment they had to be competitive, raw and ambitious themselves. Mr. Betheras was a hard-nosed businessman just like Uncle Gus. But not like Alex's father, who might have been if he hadn't been pounded down by forces beyond his ability to control.

"I got two daughters. The other one is married so now it's ok for Jenny, the youngest, to get married, but she has to marry someone who will take good care of her."

"Dad," Jenny interrupted, "you're talking very personally to someone you hardly know."

Mr. Betheras acted surprised. "Sure I know him. You talk about him all the time."

Jenny's cheeks reddened.

"Christo," Mrs. Betheras clucked-clucked at her husband, "me tous stenohoristes." Don't embarrass them.

Alex laughed. He was beginning to like Jenny's dad. "I'm not embarrassed," he said, speaking for himself.

Mr. Betheras nodded affirmation that it is all right to speak your mind as long as it doesn't embarrass another man. It's not so important that a woman might be. "This Alex seems like a nice Greek boy, Jenny. What more you want?"

"Time, Dad," Jenny said, a bit firmer than she probably talked to her father. "We've only spent a couple of hours together."

"I didn't meet your mother until a month before I marry her."

Mrs. Betheras gave her husband a long look. "That was the old days."

"It was ok then it should be ok now."

"You never ask if it was ok for me," Mrs. Betheras said, her eyes teasing.

"Your papa say it for you."

"I think people should be allowed to make their own decisions," Alex said.

"You think that works better?"

"Yes, sir."

Mr. Betheras leaned over and embraced his wife. "You sorry you marry me?"

Her answer was a playful squeeze of his arm.

Mr. Betheras got back to the business at hand. "So," he said to Alex, "you interested in my daughter?"

Alex glanced at Jenny for her reaction but she looked down at her lap and her dark hair, longer now, hid her face. She pressed her hands between her legs, pulling her skirt tight--at least now he was able to see the outline of her thighs. Again, even as he tried to drive this from his mind, he began making comparisons with Mary Lou. And as soon as he thought of Mary Lou he recalled how her mere presence excited him. Jenny didn't excite him that way, but two brief encounters are not a fair test. The night they danced in the nurse's party room, he liked holding her close, but he was not stirred the way Mary Lou stirred him. Still, Jenny had a Cracker Jack mind. He enjoyed talking with her, sharing books and ideas. She was well-versed in everything Alex was familiar with, and more that he wasn't. Mary Lou was passionate but you can't build a lengthy relationship, like the rest of your life, on that alone. But then, as Alex discovered on his visit to Bemidji, Mary Lou was not the empty head he once took her for. The student who wore army surplus and short-clipped hair was very different from the Catholic he eloped with and who bore his child. Jesus, but life is full of contradictions.

"You take plenty of time to answer," Betheras said.

"I'm sorry, Mr. Betheras, I was thinking over what you said." It sounded as if Alex were hedging his bet, which made Jenny lift her head and brush her hair back, her wide-spread eyes telling him that she didn't give a damn what he thought. She was proud of her Greek heritage, proud of an orthodox religion he found oppressive, proud of a culture he found wanting, proud of Mediterranean attributes he found unsatisfactory.

Under her unwavering stare, Alex re-examined Jenny's Greekness--her strong nose and high forehead, her olive complexion and ebony hair--features he had considered second to the Heidis of the world. His ideal had always been the Varga Girl with pearly skin, flaxen hair and sculpted breasts. White was the common youthful preference as in "I'm going out with a white girl tonight" with no regard to the ugly import of that comment. A white girl as opposed to what? A Greek so dark she could pass for black like Nell in the kitchen? Alex found himself feeling uncomfortable. Here he was in the deep South where he should know that such comparisons are callous and insensitive. Jenny was not the problem, he was. She was not unattractive, it was his perception of her, of any Greek girl for that matter, that was unattractive.

What's more, and he can thank Uncle Gus for this, he was no longer married. The annulment freed him so he could be serious about another woman without suffering pangs of guilt. Finally, something positive in his heretofore mixed up world to be happy about.

"Mr. Betheras," Alex said, "I wouldn't have driven this far if I wasn't interested in Jenny." He looked at her as he spoke so as not to miss her reaction. Her dark eyes gave nothing away.

Mrs. Betheras called Nell into the family room. She had a wide-open expression like Butterfly McQueen.

"You like coffee or tea?" Mr. Betheras asked Alex and just as he was about to say yes to coffee, Betheras added, "this late at night, we drink tea."

"Oh," Alex said, "tea is fine."

The maid left and returned inside of a minute with a silver service and a plate of kourabiedes, coated white with powdered sugar. Evidently this was a regular routine.

After tea and small talk, Mr. and Mrs. Betheras announced they were going upstairs to get ready for bed. Alex assumed it was a ploy to leave the two young people alone together.

Everyone stood. Alex shook hands with Mr. Betheras. Mrs. Betheras turned her cheek up for Alex to kiss. "Kalo taxithi," she said in her small voice, Greek for bon voyage.

Alex watched them walk through the hall and disappear up the stairs.

Nell came in. "Anythin' else, Mizz Jenny?"

"You can go home now, Nell."

The maid disappeared into the kitchen. In another minute the back door opened and Alex saw her through the window. She had her coat and hat on.

"How does she get home?"

"Bus."

"I could give her a ride."

"It would embarrass her. She wouldn't want to appear uppity to her family being chauffered home by a white man. Besides your Minnesota license plates would attract unwanted attention, especially with a black woman in your car."

Alex had a lot to learn about the South, none of which he found particularly appealing. "That's a pretty garden out there."

"There's not much to see right now but in the spring, it's stunning. We have lots of azalea and rose bushes, and magnolias and dogwood. Did you know that Jesus was supposed to have been crucified on a cross made from a dogwood tree? After He was nailed through His hands and feet, so the story goes, dogwood blossoms showed small stains on their tips like blood."

"There's a lot about the South that's new to me, including dogwood."

They sat back down, this time sharing the settee Jenny's parents had vacated.

"Don't take dad too literally," Jenny said. "He thinks all Greek women should be married."

"To a Greek man of course."

"That goes without saying. He does like you, though. But regardless of what he said, my father is not speaking for me. I'm not interested in getting married. I've gone back to school."

"School?" Alex asked in surprise.

"I'm in the pediatrics program at the University of South Carolina."

Alex was impressed and, if he had to admit it, a little intimidated. "Your father must be proud."

"You know how he feels. He'd rather see me taking care of my own children rather than someone else's."

"You can do both. Doctors get married."

"It will take eight years to go through medical school and finish interning. By then I'll be too old to be a mother."

Alex didn't want to hear the same words he had heard from Mary Lou, even if they were expressed for different reasons. "You don't have to wait until you finish school to get married."

"Greek men aren't known for helping in the kitchen or changing diapers."

Alex wanted to say, try me, but only nodded.

"What does your mother think about this?"

"She's already a grandmother if that's what you mean. But seriously she told me to do what I want."

Alex marveled at having a mother like that. "Med school is tough."

"I've never done anything tougher except seeing a sailor die on the operating table."

Alex felt a twinge of jealousy--not because there was another man in Jenny's life but because of the commitment she had made to becoming a doctor. He was on the losing end of that one. "I'm keeping you from your books."

"I'm used to staying up late. I average four hours sleep a night."

"We can write to each other once in a while."

"I would like that. Give me your address."

Jenny rose and Alex followed her back into the living room. She sat at an elegant secretary with a carved crest and finial with an inlaid polished-leather desk pad. She withdrew a sheet of note paper from a pigeonhole and dipped a pen into an inkwell. "Robert B. Sprague, right?"

"DD 884, FPO, San Francisco."

Alex watched her write. She held the pen with firm fingers and wrote with a confident motion. "I don't see how you'll ever become a doctor," he said.

She turned her head and looked up at him sharply. "Why not?"

"Your handwriting is too neat."

She laughed and pushed her shoulder playfully against his hip. It was the first time they touched casually since the night they danced together in Yokosuka. But that time belonged to another life, not this one.

Jenny came out on the front steps to say goodby. "You're leaving in the morning?"

"Maybe we could meet for breakfast at the Wade Hampton. You're right next door."

Jenny shook her head. "I have classes all day."

"Will you even have time to write?"

"I'll make time." She snapped her fingers. "Oh, I almost forgot." She opened the door to go inside. "Wait here." She returned in a moment with Salinger's novel. "Mail it back when you're finished."

"Can it wait till I get out of the navy? I'd rather deliver it instead of the postman." The thought of not seeing Jenny for another year made him wish he could spend more time with her now, even if only for a few minutes between classes. He was just barely breaking the surface of getting to know her.

She had her arms crossed to ward off the chill. "Have a safe trip," she said.

He took a step forward and put his arms around her. Jenny undid her own arms and wrapped them under his, gripping the back of his shoulders as they hugged. Alex pulled away so that he could kiss her, but she freed herself and placed her fingers on his lips as though gently hushing him.

"Not yet," she murmured.

He did the same on her lips, brushing them lightly with his fingers, feeling the warm air of her breath. He ached to put his mouth on hers, but they kissed only with their fingers.

THE END

Alex drove down West Broadway to the San Diego YMCA and parked in back. He got his seabag out of the trunk and went inside. The lobby smelled of chlorine from the pool downstairs. He took a room for the day to shower and change into his dark blues. Then, following directions from the reservations clerk, he drove to an art supply store on E Street where he bought illustration board, a broad-nibbed pen, and a bottle of India ink. He paid the clerk $2.85. His car was parked in front and, using the hood as his drawing board, he penned a sign:

FOR SALE
GOING OVERSEAS
MUST SELL
$650
Leave Message Broadway Pier
A. Poulos YNT3
USS Sprague DD884

The nib was angled the opposite way he wrote and where the letters should be thick they came out thin and vice versa. Why don't they make pens for left-handers? he asked himself as he wedged the sign into the passenger side window well.

As Alex climbed out of the car, the store clerk joined him on the sidewalk. He wore elastic bands on his arms to keep his shirt cuffs pulled up. "So that's why you bought the art materials." He looked the car over. "Forty-eight, forty-nine?"

"Forty-nine."

"How many miles?"

"Forty-three thousand, almost all highway."

"Runs good?"

"Like a top."

"Six-fifty?" The man walked to the front and looked at the Minnesota license plate. He shook his head doubtfully. "Bad weather up there. Hard on cars."

"Look," Alex pounded a fender with his fist, "no rust."

"My son is going to college up in Compton, and I was thinking he could use something to get back and forth in."

Alex patted the hood. "Couldn't find a better runner."

They settled on five-seventy-five, shook hands to seal the deal and walked to the man's bank on Broadway, California First Trust, to make the transaction. A loan officer made out the papers and Poulos signed the title over to the buyer, Clarence Tomes.

"How do you want the bills?" the banker asked, presuming Alex, being a sailor, wanted cash.

"I'd like to open a savings account."

"An excellent decision," the loan officer replied with a warm smile, happy to see the money staying with the bank.

Tomes gave Alex a lift to the Fifth Avenue landing. It was strange riding in a car that he himself had driven nearly four thousand miles. He hoisted his seabag over his shoulder and shook hands through the window. "So long, car," he said as Clarence turned the Pontiac around and drove off. It was like bidding farewell to an old friend.

He checked the location map in the landing office for the Sprague's berth. She was in a nest alongside the USS Grand Canyon, AD-28. He sat on a wood bench in the sun to wait for the water taxi to pick him up. He leaned against the seat back and thought about his long road trip. He'd never seen so much highway and he didn't think he'd ever care to again. Their numbers swam in his head: Route 78, Route 82, Route 66. And the varied landscapes of America: the foothills of the Ozarks, the dry flat land of west Texas, the deserts of Nevada, the snowy peaks of the Rockies. Four days and four motels. He lost count of filling stations and rest stops and public toilets and lunch counters. Thank heaven he had Jenny's image and The Catcher in the Rye to keep him company.

His mental meanderings returned him to his one night in Columbia. After he left her house he drove the softly quiet streets back to the Wade Hampton, and took the elevator to his room, the negro operator standing silently by his controls as the car lifted them to the seventh floor. From his window Alex recalled standing in the dark and looking out on the city. Behind the capitol, its dome illuminated in the dark, was the campus of the University of South Carolina where Jenny took her classes.

He got in bed and slept fitfully. Rational thoughts mixed with irrational dreams, erupting like heat bumps on an otherwise smooth road. A black man and white woman walked into the lobby of the Wade Hampton. Poulos recognized them as the couple who got married in Mason City. When they asked for a room, the clerk called the house detective who arrested them for miscenegation. "It's against the law in South Carolina," the detective said to the woman, "you nigger lover." The scene shifted to a medical classroom filled with students in white coats sitting in an amphitheater. They were listening to Professor Chambers giving a lecture on anatomy. Mary Lou was on a stand stark naked and Chambers touched her genitals and the tips of her breasts as he droned on about her sexual attributes. Among the students was Jenny, rapidly taking notes with the same pen she had used to write down his navy address. His mother made a brief appearance trying to get into the amphitheater but Alex kept pushing the door against her. The last thing he remembered before falling into untrammeled sleep was the abstract image of burning skin that had once haunted him but now was merely a curious vestige of a troubled past.

The sound of a marine engine brought him back to the present. A water taxi pulled alongside the pier and Poulos climbed aboard with a few other sailors who had straggled in. The ride on the protected waters of San Diego bay was the diametric opposite of a month ago when the Harbormaster LST had unceremoniously dumped him off in the threatening seas of Tokyo Bay.

The placid waters coupled with his sanguine nature caused him to break into song. Initially surprised, then delighted, the other sailors joined in, as well as the coxswain, providing a chorus of male voices, if not in perfect harmony, at least in full throat:

The coffee in the navy they say is mighty fine.
It's good for cuts and bruises and tastes like iodine.
Oh, I don't want no more of navy life.
Gee, mom, but I wanna go home.

Poulos managed another verse before the taxi pulled alongside the nest, which was just as well because that was the only other one he knew:

The biscuits in the navy they say are mighty fine.
One rolled off the table and killed a pal of mine.
Oh, I don't want no more of navy life.

Gee, mom, but I wanna go home...

The Sprague was the outside ship in the nest of four destroyers and the coxswain held his boat against her accommodations ladder at the fantail until all the sailors had disembarked. Poulos went last since the others belonged to the sister ships tied next to her athwartships. He tossed his seabag over the railing and climbed aboard. The hum of generators caught his ear.

He looked forward, up the length of the ship. The US flag fluttered on the yardarm. The whaleboat hung in its davits. The five-inch cannons wore their canvas. The portholes were lugged open. Everything was familiar, even the rust spots. He was home.

His seabag over his shoulder, he walked forward to the quarterdeck and checked in. Ensign Kuder, the OOD, was absorbed in a shit kicker and hardly looked at him. Poulos dropped his seabag by the door to the Ship's Office.

Ernie was inside typing. "You're back."

Poulos entered the cramped space. "What's new?"

"Mail." Ernie picked up a stack of envelopes in the wire basket. "These are yours." He handed them over.

Poulos sorted through them, a windfall of correspondence. Letters from his dad, Gus, Mary Lou, Missie Clayton, Reverend Clayton, Mrs. Clayton, and, he whooped for joy, Jenny.

Ernie said, "I can't remember you ever getting a single letter. And now you got, how many, seven? And they all came in the last few days."

"My fan club."

"Something."

Poulos hauled his seabag into the office. "I'll stow it later," he said amidst Ernie's objections that there wasn't room for it. On his way to the chart house to show Witter and Browning his stash of mail, he ran into Ltjg Radinger in the fore and aft passageway. Poulos stood to one side, pressing himself against the bulkhead, and snapped a salute as the officer walked by.

"Drop your fucking arm. You're not making points with me."

"Just following regulations, sir."

"You? Follow regulations?" the lieutenant snorted in mock humor. "Don't make me laugh."

"I'm serious, sir. The Manual on Military Conduct, Chapter Two, Article VI, states that a smart salute is a sign of discipline."

Radinger pushed his hat to one side and scratched his head. "You been chewing peyote?"

"No sir. I just got back from leave."

"Too bad. It's been nice and quiet."

"I've changed, Lieutenant."

Radinger eyed him up and down. "You still look like the same dickhead to me."

"No sir, I've become a model of discipline."

"Just can the shit, Poulos." Radinger's birthmark was starting to heat up.

"I'll prove it to you, sir. Did you know that the word discipline comes from the latin to teach? From here on I will be a student of discipline so I can learn how to improve my self-control and efficiency. I will be a model sailor that you can be proud of. One thing I've learned already, lieutenant, is that discipline is a character builder, not a destroyer of individuality."

Radinger stared as if in shock. "Shut the fuck up, will you? You're driving me crazy!" He turned and stalked down the passageway.

Poulos smiled to himself. He finally figured out how to handle Lieutenant Radinger.

Browning and Witter were playing cribbage on the chart table. "Fifteen-two, fifteen-four, four hearts are eight, and knobs is nine."

When Poulos came in, Browning said, "Where have you been?"

"You know where I've been. Home on leave."

Witter shuffled and dealt, acting as if Poulos hadn't gone anywhere. "Want to play?"

Poulos fanned out his envelopes. "I'll play these."

"Shuffle them."

"Can't you see, they're letters." He handed the bundle to Browning. "Seven," Poulos said proudly. "And you said I never get mail."

Browning went through the envelopes one at a time. "Where the fuck is Bemidji?"

"Northern Minnesota."

"Who's Wolinski?"

"A girl I know."

"You know a girl?"

"Two of them."

"Who's the other one?"

"Don't you remember? Jenny Betheras."

Browning and Witter exchanged surprised stares. "The nurse?"

"I got a letter from her, too."

"I thought you blew it with her." Browning pulled Jenny's envelope free and held it up to the light. "What does she say?"

"Hey," he protested, "that's personal."

"We know her, too, don't we?" Browning made as if to open the envelope.

Poulos grabbed it from him. "I see you guys haven't changed a goddamned bit."

"And you have?"

He climbed the ladder to the flying bridge and settled down on the flagbag. He was alone. There was no one up here now that the Division was in port. On the starboard side, the Yarnall, Sumner and Orleck were lined up in perfect rows--destroyers identical in every detail except for their bow numbers. The collection of pilot houses, smoke stacks, masts and gun mounts gave Poulos the sense that he was in a hall of mirrors. He sorted through his letters, debating in what order to read them. One thing he had decided upon before reaching the bridge: he was going to save Jenny's letter for last.

The first letter he opened was from his father. The address was written in an unfamiliar hand. Tony's no doubt. His dad probably didn't trust his own handwriting to do a clear job addressing the envelope. Poulos expected to see the letter in Tony's hand as well, but he was wrong. The letter was in his dad's handwriting, an awkward blend of Greek characters adapted to English. Poulos could only guess how long it took his father to write these words. Dear son, he began:

I worry about the long drive you make. You write me as soon as you get this so I know you are fine. Everything is sad when you went away. The house is quiet. I miss Mother. But God took her. It was for the best.

Hard to find words. Easier for me to write Greek but not easy for you to understand. I hope this is clear what I write.

I always want to be a good father. You were a good boy growing up. You minded your mother and me. But instead of seeing you as a man I only see you as a child. I never talk to you as a man. I was afraid if I tell you what was in my heart you would leave. Well, it happen anyway. You are gone.

So what does it matter now? I was very sad you marry that girl but even sadder when you left for the navy. Better to stick it out with her then run away. I see that now. It’s not a problem who you marry as long as you love her and stay by her. I did not do so well with your mother and with you. These are my regrets and I always have them now.

Uncle Gus invite me to go to Greece with him for Pascha. I say all right. He pay my way. First time I visit my village in forty five years. I write my sister that I come. I will see her children first time. They all grow up too. Tony, he take care of the house and store while I go. He is a nice boy but he never be what you are to me.

You are a grown man and you will live your own life. I am proud of you, remember that and I love you very much.

Father

Poulos looked up from the letter. Tears blurred his vision. Will he ever visit home again? What would be the purpose? He thought of Jenny. She would be the purpose. If something serious developed between them, she'd come to meet his family as he met hers. He smiled thinking of bringing her to Minnesota, the Southern Belle of his short story, not Fitzgerald's, a summer visit, not a winter one. And if she became part of his life could he share with her his buried past, exhume it, and let her examine it as a pathologist would a corpse? Well, Dr. Betheras, would you accept me as the person who married and abandoned another woman, became the father of a son he never knew? Maybe it was too much to ask but she would have to know. Then and only then could he dump the load of deceit that had weighed him down and compromised his relationships with everyone he came in contact with.

Almost resignedly, he folded the letter into his pocket and opened the one from Gus. Unlike his father's, Gus's syntax was smooth and effortless, in the formal style of an educated man.

My Dear Alexandros:

All the way back to Worthington I saw only you in the windshield. Not the highway, nor the farms nor the telephone poles nor the towns. Your face never left me.

I apologize with all my heart for the difficulty and pain which I know I inflicted upon you. I should have moved far away to another state when you were born and got out of your life altogether, but my love for your mother and for you was overwhelming. I could not stay away. That is why I came so often to visit.

I tried to watch you grow up from a respectful distance. But I look back on my role as a doting and interfering uncle with some regret. And now that I revealed who I am, I pray I have not compromised your relationship with your father. He is your father. I have no right to make any prior claim on you.

My love for your mother could not save her from herself. If anyone deserved to suffer it was I, not she. I hope there is forgiveness in your heart.

I know now it was wrong to interfere in your marriage to Mary Lou. It was reckless of me to drive her into hiding and force her to give up her son. He was your son, too, and he would have had the Poulos name had I not interfered. I was blind to everything but my own selfish need to possess my grandchild, and now I have lost him forever.

You are still in my will and shall remain so regardless of what you said in the kitchen which, upon further reflection on your part, I feel confident you will remember as words expressed out of anger. You are a young man of principle and fairness. I know you will do what is right.

I asked your father to accompany me to Greece for Easter and he agreed. Once I hoped you would be the one to travel with me. I still look forward to that possibility.

Your "Uncle" Gus

The letter was surprising in its candor and forgiveness. He read it twice more. Everything Gus wrote was the opposite of what Poulos expected. He was prepared to denounce Gus, blame him for everything, but now he found himself feeling compassion. Well, if his uncle-read-father can express it, so can Poulos. He put the letter aside and picked up the one from Mary Lou. This one surprised him the most. He never expected to hear from her again. He ran his thumb along the mucilage of the flap and unfolded a typewritten sheet of Bemidji University stationery, no doubt from the desk of Professor Chambers. Apparently they were still living together. So what? he asked himself, she's no longer anything to me.

Dear Alex:

I still can't believe you found me. I was so careful. When I wake up in the morning I still look out on Bixby expecting to see a parked car with a detective in it. If that ever happens again, Clark said he would call the police but there is no reason to worry any longer, is there, if you told your uncle that I gave up Joshua.

Clark wishes we could move somewhere else, as far away from Minnesota as possible. But, you know, Clark can't just up and go. He has tenure here. He's 51 and wants to stick it out till retirement. Isn't that weird? Of the two men in my life, one hasn't found a job and the other is thinking about retirement.

I decided not to tell Clark I'm writing you. He knows it's over between you and me, so that isn't the reason. The fact is he doesn't trust you and thinks you will tell your uncle where I am. I know you won't but I don't want to upset him. You are probably asking yourself, why am I writing you? If you hadn't found me I wouldn't have. But when you suddenly showed up again, you awakened memories I thought I had buried forever. I suppose it was naive of me to believe I could get over losing Joshua. Still, I was making progress until I saw you that cold afternoon. It's even colder now. After you left I couldn't get out of my mind all the things we once meant to each other. I still can't. This is probably why I am writing you. I want to hold on to those good memories. If we concentrate on those, maybe we can be friends.

I'm studying hard and getting good grades. I'll bet you never expected that of me. I've been doing some practice teaching at an elementary school on the reservation, and I'm discovering that teaching is fun. The Indian kids are precious and they need so much help. Maybe that's what God decided for me: to help the disadvantaged. I'll be content doing that.

Love, Mary Lou

PS. I bought a gold chain and put my wedding ring on it. I wear it around my neck just the way you did.

PPS. If you decide to write me, send your letter to PO box 32, so Clark won't see it. Like I said, it's better that way. Good luck, Alex, and be careful over there.

Poulos reread the letter half a dozen times and each time he was unsure just exactly what Mary Lou's intentions were. She was getting her life back together, but was she also putting him back into it? He had to admire her grit. She was tough, resilient. He thought he was over her, and yet her words rekindled his emotions. He lay back on the flagbag and looked up as if heaven were in the cloudless California sky. Nope, just a wide expanse of blue so brilliant it stung his eyes. He sat up again and took Jenny's letter from the bottom of his little stack. He tapped the corner on his knee. Maybe the solution was in here. Maybe Jenny wrote things that could help him forget Mary Lou. He wanted to rip it open and compare it to Mary Lou's letter but he resisted the impulse. The best for last, he repeated to himself, and opened Missie's letter. Her handwriting had matured since the letter to her brother Poulos had found in RB's locker. When was that? It seemed a lifetime ago.

Dear Bro (this pleased him):

I told all my friends in school that you are my new brother. They keep asking me if you are going to take Dad's place when he retires. Mom has started singing in the choir again during Sunday worship and you should hear Dad's sermons.

You better write because if you don't I'll really get mad. Tell me about every thing you do and about any battles you fight. But be careful. I don't want to lose another brother.

Love and Kisses, Missie

Poulos put the letter down with enormous good feeling. If he had accomplished anything positive in his lifetime, his relationship to Missie was the greatest. He opened the one from her father.

Alex, Dear Friend in God:

Bess polished the Silver Star and it shines as brightly as the Star of Bethlehem. Each night we pray in front of it for the joy that has come into our hearts since your visit. Our prayers also include you and your safe return to our midst.

As I told you that night in RB's room, after my son's death I questioned my faith; even lost it for a time but it was simply mislaid. You helped me find it. You have a calling, Alex. Keep that in mind as you look to your future.

Yours in Christ, CR

Poulos smiled to himself. Even the Reverend's handwriting looked Ecclesiastical. He opened the letter from Mrs. Clayton. It was a note, really, written on a plain card. She had a cautious, somewhat cramped, handwriting, but her message was not.

My Dear Alex:

I am writing this as you leave Mills Gap. I want to put my feelings down right away so I won't lose the precious moment your presence gave us. Thank you for bringing RB back. Oh, I know he is dead--I can write that now without shivering--but his spirit is not. I pray for your safe return.

Bess

It was time for Jenny's letter. Now that he was ready to read it his heart began racing. He held the envelope in his hand as though he was weighing it for postage but in truth he was fighting back uncertainty because, now that he had come to her letter, the last one, he feared the worst, not untypical of him, that she might be writing him a Dear John, a kiss-off, a sayonara. Despite the fact that, as Greeks, they shared familiar ground culturally, they lived worlds apart physically. South Carolina was as different as any state could be from Minnesota. He hoped Witter would climb up the ladder for conversation, to give him a reason for delay. But no one came. He remained alone with his growing doubt. For a brief unsettling moment he even entertained the notion that he should send the letter back to her unopened, dump her before she could dump him. He berated himself silently as a fucking asshole for committing an act that was not only pointless--what if it wasn't a Dear John?--but also inherently cruel. He dismissed it as a panicky reaction of the person he once was, a momentary atavistic throwback to his pre-Steiner days. Angry at his silliness he tore off the end of the envelope, blew it wide and withdrew several lined sheets from a spiral notebook, sheets that would otherwise have been filled with notes from a pre-med course on Fundamental Laboratory Techniques in Chemistry, or something like that.

The tiny holes on the left-hand margin had been ripped apart. He could hear her tearing each sheet from its spiral with rapid, minute bursts like the sound of lady fingers going off. His own fingers were not exploding but they were certainly trembling.

Dear Alex:

I work on this letter whenever I find a moment, which isn't often. Notice that I am no longer using the lower case in referring to the first person singular? I realize now that it was a silly affectation, a reverse kind of snobbery. You might say that I've been humbled by the incredible load of courses and studying required of me. I breezed through nurse's training but this is the Big Time. As I look around the medical library I see only one other woman, the librarian.

Tuesday ten p.m. at home. You made a positive impression on my father. He thought you were bright and nice-looking, in a Greek sort of way. He is a real traditionalist. I suppose your own parents are too, or were in your mother's case. You know what that means. My father loves grandchildren. So far he has only one, my sister Maria's little girl, Anna. He wants a grandson, too, especially one I might produce. I'm the youngest and the daughter he dotes on the most. He has never pushed me but I know what is on his mind.

Wednesday two-fifty pm. Waiting for Introduction to Hematology to start. In a very real way we just met. I discount our evening in Yokosuka because it had an exotic quality to it, two people so far away from home. It didn't seem real to me, somehow. How did you feel? We know so little about each other. At least you've met my parents and seen how I live. I can't help but think of that short story Fitzgerald wrote, the one you told me about: the Minnesota soldier and the Southern belle. I read it when I got home. I feel a little like that girl, with a magnolia blossom pinned in my hair, and I suppose you feel like that soldier, with ice crusted on your eyelids.

Wednesday 11 pm. Dog tired but I just wanted to write some more. You know what we both need? We need to find the center of our beings.

The point where we start burning white hot like an acetylene torch. But how do we know for certain where our center is? I read someplace that whatever you do that makes you forget time is where your center is. Maybe mine is in medicine. When I read and study, I do lose track of time. Maybe yours is in writing. We also need mentors. Who are those persons who can reassure us, when we're too tired to think straight, that we're on the right course? Can you be my mentor and I yours? I don't know. And can there be more than one center in someone's life? Can there be a common center between two people? I don't know the answer to that either. Going to bed.

Thursday 7:15 am. Breakfast. Didn't get enough sleep. I'm going to mail this letter today even if I pass out trying. Alex, I think writing to you is good for me. It may be a tonic, another concentration to take me away temporarily from the terrible demands of studying. I may fail at what I'm doing but it won't be for lack of Herculean effort. (Can I refer to Hercules, a Greek god, even if I am a mere mortal Greek female?) Bear with me. I write goofy things because I'm too tired to do otherwise and I may write something I may regret. Such as make a promise I'm not ready to keep. I can't be any clearer than that.

As for you, my Greek Friend, remember what the good Dr. Steiner said: follow your instincts.

As Ever,
Jenny

He folded the letter as if handling a rare manuscript and laid it next to Mary Lou's. Two women, neither of whom knew of the other's existence. Ah, the dilemmas facing him. He was not anxious; he was fascinated. He returned to the Ship's Office for his seabag and dragged it through the midship's passageway, bumped it down the ladder to the galley, dragged it across the mess hall and bumped it down another ladder to his compartment. He opened his locker, changed into his work clothes--chambray shirt and dungarees--and put away his dark blues. He tucked the letters in and closed the locker.

Already in his mind he was playing around with responses. He would call Missie "Sis." He would write Reverend Clayton that no one could walk in his footsteps, and Bess that he was flattered by her attention to him. He would write Gus that it was better to look ahead than look back, and tell his dad that he loved him. And Mary Lou...what would he write her? He'd have to think about that. And to Jenny he would write that he would definitely trust his instincts.

He laid the book she had lent him on his fartsack. Interesting, he thought, I left with The Mind of the South and returned with The Catcher in the Rye.

He went looking for Lt Gildenhall but did not find him anywhere on deck, and so he ventured into officer's country, down the narrow passageway to the door with Gildenhall's name on it. He knocked lightly with one knuckle.

"What is it?"

"Yeoman Poulos, sir."

The door opened. Gildenhall was in his stockinged feet, his hair slightly mussed. He had been resting on his bunk.

They looked at each other across the open doorway, sharing the discomfort of being seen alone together, especially by the officer's stateroom.

"I finally finished it," Poulos said, holding up The Catcher in the Rye. He wished he could discuss Holden Caulfield's search for truth in a phony world with the lieutenant, but it wasn't to be.

"How was your leave?" Gildenhall politely asked.

"I met Clayton's family."

Gildenhall's blue eyes grew a shade darker. "How did that go?"

"Not bad."

"Not exactly a ringing endorsement."

"Actually it went very well."

"I have this sense of you being different. Something happened along the way."

"A lot happened," Poulos said without going further.

Gildenhall asked, "Any news about the nurse?"

"She's not a nurse anymore. She's a pre-med student at the University of South Carolina."

"Good for her."

"That's what I said."

Gildenhall looked at him for a moment. "So, where does that leave you?"

"Patient, I guess."

Poulos returned to the Ship's Office and sat down at the Underwood. Knock off ship's work had been piped and he had the place to himself. The sun shone through the open porthole, placing a round bright spot on the filing cabinet over his shoulder. As the sun was setting below Imperial Beach, Poulos reflected on his days in the navy. He was among its severest critics, known in the vernacular as a habitual bitcher, but maybe he had found a home after all. Life on board the Sprague was not all that bad. Bed and board, good friends, Browning's jazz records, gedunk and coffee, exotic places to visit.

Hell, he had a whole year to think about re-upping. He got out a sheet of onion skin and wound it into the typewriter. He looked at the blank paper for a few seconds, thinking about Mary Lou, about Jenny, about the future and the past. His fingers began tapping across the keys.

About the author

Peter Georgas grew up in Waseca, a small town in southern Minnesota where his father owned the Crystal Café and Candy Kitchen. He earned a BA in Journalism from the University of Minnesota. After graduating, he went on active duty for two years as an enlisted man aboard a destroyer. His experiences during the Korean War served as inspiration for this book. Following a decade in advertising, he joined the staff of Walker Art Center in Minneapolis as the museum's first full time publicist. Later, along with his family, he moved to Austria, where he was Director of the Salzburg Seminar. He and his wife now live in the Linden Hills neighborhood of Minneapolis.

67790845R00231

Made in the USA
Lexington, KY
22 September 2017